"I can't stop, Bronte," he whispered, even though he suspected that she already knew.

He spread his fingers wide, cupping her cheek, his thumb brushing over her lips, once, twice.

"I keep telling myself that you're married—"

"I'm not married. The divorce was official months ago. The marriage . . . a long, long time ago. And the last of the papers was mailed earlier tonight." The words were whispered—and he sensed that something had happened in the last couple of days to make her believe them. There was no hesitancy in her tone, as there had been the last time she'd spoken of her relationship with her children's father.

"Tell me if you want me to quit," Jace murmured, even as he bent down and prayed that she wouldn't.

"I don't want you to . . . quit."

She smiled and he was lost—lost in her smile, lost in the sweet scent of her hair and the velvety texture of her skin. Then his lips touched hers.

RENEGADE

LISA BINGHAM

BERKLEY SENSATION, NEW YORK

BERKLEY
SENSATION

An imprint of Penguin Random House LLC
375 Hudson Street, New York, New York 10014

RENEGADE

A Berkley Sensation Book / published by arrangement with the author

ISBN: 978-0-425-27853-6

PUBLISHING HISTORY
Berkley Sensation mass-market edition / January 2016

PRINTED IN THE UNITED STATES OF AMERICA

10 9 8 7 6 5 4 3 2

Cover art by Danny O'Leary.
Cover design by Lesley Worrell.
Interior text design by Kelly Lipovich.

Penguin
Random
House

To Helen and Syd.
Thanks for being such wonderful friends.

ACKNOWLEDGMENTS

I'd like to thank Leis Pederson and her team at Berkley for all their hard work, my wonderful agents at Browne and Miller for their support, and all the hired hands on the family farm for volunteering appropriate jargon for the Taggart Ranch.

FLIGHT

What creatures these,
Broken and reformed
In nests hanging
By a thread,
Hidden in rusty leaves
Away from predators' eyes?

Do they know
When spinning silken coffins
That fear of the unknown
And the agony of recreation
Must pay the price
Of precious freedom?

—B.C.

ONE

WATERBOARDING.
    Caning.
The Rack.

Bronte Cupacek tightened her fingers around the steering wheel and swore to heaven that when the government of the United States outlawed cruel and unusual punishment, there should have been special provisions made for mothers locked in minivans for the duration of a cross-country trip. Especially if said minivan contained two adolescent siblings who'd been at each other's throats twenty minutes into the journey.

What had she been thinking?

But then, she hadn't been thinking at all, had she? On that first, chilly April morning, she'd been so consumed with guilt, panic—and yes, a healthy dose of fear—that she hadn't bothered to consider the ramifications of her actions. With the haste of a thief leaving the scene of a crime, Bronte had awakened her two daughters at the crack of dawn, helped them cram their belongings into all the suitcases they possessed, and then stuffed everything into the "Mom Mobile." Less than forty minutes after their frantic preparations had begun, she maneuvered away from the brownstone she'd shared with her husband for sixteen years, and began the long drive west.

Bronte hadn't even looked back as Boston was swallowed up in her rearview mirror. She drove in a daze, the black highway an endless ebony ribbon stitched down the middle with yellow thread. For the sake of her girls, she pretended that she'd been planning this spontaneous adventure for months. They visited Gettysburg, Mt. Rushmore, and highway markers commemorating countless historical sites—all much to Kari's dismay. At fifteen-going-on-thirty, she considered history of any kind "lame" and Bronte's choices in entertainment "lamer." Lily was less inclined to complain, which worried Bronte even more. With each tick of the odometer, she retreated into mute, self-imposed exile—to the point where Bronte would have suffered any personal indignity for just a hint of a smile.

By the time they'd reached the Great Divide, Bronte had given up telling her girls they were "on vacation." Clearly, she'd been no better at hiding the need to flee than she'd been at disguising the bruise on her cheekbone. Day by day, it faded from an alarming shade of plum to the sickly yellow of an overripe banana. She'd tried to conceal the injury with layers of foundation, but at bedtime when she rubbed the makeup away, she would catch her daughters surreptitiously studying the telltale mark. But they didn't ask what had happened. Somehow, they must have known that to acknowledge something was wrong would pry the lid off Bronte's tenuous emotional control.

She supposed it was that need—that *obsession*—to finally put this journey behind her that caused her to pull off the road and stare blankly at the sign proclaiming:

BLISS, UTAH—POPULATION 9672
(Sign donated by Bryson Willis—Eagle Scout Project 2014)

The world still had Boy Scouts?
"Why are you stopping?" Kari demanded. She glowered

at Bronte from the passenger seat, radiating the pent-up vitriol of a teenager who'd been forced to leave her friends two months before the end of the school year. "Let's just get to Grandma Great's house. The sooner we get there, the sooner we can go home."

Bronte had heard that same demand at least once an hour for the last *bazillion* miles, and it took every ounce of will she possessed to bite back her own caustic reply. Her daughter didn't know it yet, but Bronte had serious doubts about ever returning to their "life" in Boston.

Phillip had seen to that.

There was a stirring from the rear of the van. Like a groundhog cautiously emerging from its burrow, Lily raised her head over the edge of the seat and blinked in confusion.

"Is this Great-Grammy's?"

Kari rounded on her sister before Lily had the time to rub the sleep from her eyes.

"What do you think, genius? That Grandma Great lives on the side of the road?"

"Enough," Bronte barked automatically. The fact that Kari rarely got along with her younger sister had only been exacerbated by hours of travel. The teenager was like a chicken, pick, pick, picking at her more sensitive sibling until both Lily and Bronte were raw.

"If you can't be nice, keep your opinions to yourself, Kari."

How many times had Bronte said *that* in the last hour . . . week . . . lifetime?

Kari rolled her eyes and huffed theatrically. She was barely fifteen and already filled with rage and defiance. Bronte had to get a grip on their relationship before Kari discovered the truth about her father or . . .

Don't think about that now. Not yet. Later. Once you're at Annie's, you can take all the time you want to decide what to do. Away from Phillip's influence.

She nearly laughed aloud. Yes, she was away from her husband's influence—thousands of miles away. But he could have been sitting in the seat beside Bronte for her inability to forget him. His ghost had accompanied her every step of the way—and her phone was filled with unread messages, texts, and emails that she should have erased the instant they appeared.

Should have erased.

But hadn't.

Because there'd been a time when she had loved him so much that a handful of kind words from him had felt as intimate as a caress.

But that had been a long time ago.

A million years and two thousand miles ago.

Ultimately, the state of her marriage had become a case of fight or flight. This time, she'd chosen flight. And after coming so far, she didn't have the strength to confront her own actions, let alone those of her daughter. But soon. They were almost at her grandmother's farmhouse. Once there, she could burrow into the peaceful solitude of this tiny western town and begin to piece together the torn remnants of her lifelong dreams.

"Are you going to drive anytime soon?" Kari inquired, her tone dripping with sarcasm. "Or are you waiting for a sign from God?"

Closing her eyes, Bronte counted to ten before responding.

"I haven't been here since I was seventeen, Kari. I need a minute to get my bearings."

Kari huffed again, fiddling with the button to the automatic window, making it go up, down, up, down. The noise of the motor approximated an impatient whine.

"I thought that's why we bought a map at the last gas station," she grumbled under her breath. "If you'd get a GPS like everyone else . . ."

Please let me get through the next few miles without resorting to violence, Bronte thought to herself as she put the car in gear, waited for a rattletrap farm truck laden with bags of seed to pass, then eased into the narrow lane.

As they drove through Bliss proper, Bronte grew uneasy. Over the years, she'd imagined the area would remain like a time capsule, unchanged and completely familiar. Either

her memories were faulty, or urban sprawl had begun to encroach on this rural community. To her dismay, she could see that some of the mom-and-pop establishments had given way to newer, sleeker buildings bearing franchise names and automated signs.

For the first time, Bronte felt a twinge of uneasiness. She'd tried to contact Annie, without success. What if they'd come for nothing? What if Annie couldn't offer Bronte the haven she hoped to find?

Instantly, Bronte rejected that thought. Grandma was the one constant in the world. A beacon of love that made no demands. That's why, when Bronte felt as if she'd drown in her own silent anguish, she'd gravitated instinctively to the spot where she'd been happiest. A place where she wouldn't have to present a chipper façade to the world to hide the fact that everything she'd once held dear had long since crumbled to dust.

"Well?"

Bronte had stopped at a red light—probably the only one in town. In her efforts to orient herself, she'd missed the change to green. There wasn't another soul in sight, but trust Kari to pound home her irritation at the minute delay.

"It's this way," she murmured—more to reassure herself than her children.

Turning right, she prayed that she'd chosen the correct side road. Victorian farmhouses and bungalows from the thirties were crowded by newer, turreted McMansions that looked alien in such a rural setting. But as she wound her way along the old highway, she began to pick out landmarks that were familiar to her: the train trestle that spanned the creek; the box-like outline of pine trees surrounding the pioneer cemetery; the old mill which had apparently been converted into a bed and breakfast.

"It's not far now," she reassured her children.

"I hope so," Lily admitted, her eyes wide as she studied the passing scenery.

Ashamed, Bronte realized that she shouldn't have let so much time elapse before coming to Utah. But Phillip had insisted that any place without a Starbucks or a subway wasn't worth visiting. So, Bronte had kept the peace and arranged for Grandma Annie to visit them every year. But her children had been denied so much because of Bronte's cowardice. They'd never ridden a horse or hiked up a mountainside to drink from an icy artesian spring. But this summer, they would have a chance.

"I have to go to the bathroom," Lily whispered. "Will Grandma Great let me use her bathroom?"

"No, she'll make you pee in a bush, stupid."

"Kari!"

Raindrops splattered against the windshield. Leaning forward, Bronte eyed the flickers of lightning with concern. They were almost there. They should be able to outrun the storm.

Lily stirred restlessly in her seat. "How much farther?"

"Less than a mile."

Intermittent drops continued to strike the glass, leaving perfect circles in the dust, but Bronte hesitated to turn on the wipers. The blades—much like her tires—should have been replaced months ago. If she turned them on now, the rain and dirt collected on her car would muddle together in a streaky mess, and she needed to see the towering willow tree that marked the end of the lane . . .

There!

For the first time in years, Bronte felt a flutter of joy and hope. They were here. They were finally here!

Slowing the car, she turned into a narrow gravel road. The tires crunched over the weathered ruts, the noise bringing a sense of excitement that edged out the weariness and pain.

A strip of winter-matted grass grew up the middle of the track, and puddles gathered in the potholes. On either side of the lane, fence posts had been linked together with strands of barbed wire. The fields beyond were as she'd remembered, loamy carpets of brown sprigged with chartreuse shoots of sprouting grain. As they drew closer to the house, the fences gave way to dozens of lilac bushes, which had grown so closely together that they formed an impenetrable hedge. To Bronte's delight, she saw that the first bud-like leaves were beginning to appear. Sometime in May, they would explode into a fragrant wall of purple and pink and the air would grow rich with the scent of the blossoms and the drone of bees.

"Look!" she exclaimed to her children. "It's only the second week in April, but Annie's lilacs are starting to get their leaves." She cracked the window, allowing the heady fragrance of rain and soil to fill the car.

Lily eagerly pressed her face against the glass, but Kari remained stony and silent. Nevertheless, Bronte sensed an expectancy in her daughter's posture that hadn't been there before.

"Where's the house?" Lily breathed.

"Past the next bend."

As Bronte eased around the corner, a part of her was a child again. She expected to see Annie waiting on the stoop wearing a cotton dress cinched tight by an all-encompassing apron. Bronte could almost smell the yeastiness of freshly baked bread that clung to the house and taste the moist carrot cookies that were pulled from the oven as soon as she and her siblings arrived. As soon as Bronte ran up the front steps, she would be enveloped in her grandmother's warm, bosomy embrace. She would breathe deeply of Annie's unique scent—face powder, lilies of the valley, and Nilla Wafers, which Annie stowed in her apron pockets for when she needed a boost.

Bronte was so enveloped in the memories that it took Kari's sharp inhalation and Lily's plaintive "oh" to pierce the fantasy.

Easing to a stop, Bronte peered more closely through the rain-streaked windshield. As her eyes focused on the weathered farmhouse, a mewl of disappointment escaped her lips.

If not for the porch light and a dim glow emitted from the garret window, Bronte would have thought the house had been abandoned. Weeds choked the once beautiful flowerbeds and the lawn was burned and nearly nonexistent. The sagging wrap-around porch was missing half a dozen balusters and the front steps were rickety and threatening to collapse.

The outbuildings had suffered a similar fate. Bronte remembered the chicken coop, barn, and garden being painted a pristine white. When she'd seen them last, they'd been perched on an immaculate lawn edged by tufts of peonies and irises. But if any of those perennials had survived, they would have to fight their way through thigh-high weeds and thistles.

"I thought you said this place was *nice*."

Kari's tone made it clear that she thought Bronte teetered on the verge of senility.

Bronte didn't bother to comment. What could she say? Her memories weren't so gilded by age and distance that she could have mistaken this . . . this . . . *mess* for the idyll she'd enjoyed each summer.

Reluctantly, she eased the car closer to the main house. Rain began to fall in earnest now, but even the moisture collecting on her windshield couldn't hide the utter neglect.

"Are you sure Great-Grandma lives here?" Lily whispered.

"Of course she lives here," Kari snapped. "But Mom didn't bother to tell us what a *dump* it is."

Rain pattered against the roof of the car, the rhythm growing frantic as the downpour increased. Conceding to the inevitable, Bronte switched on the wipers, waiting vainly for the streaks of grime to be swept away—as if by cleaning the windshield, she might find the condition of Annie's house had been a trick of light and shadow.

If anything, the view was more depressing.

A part of her wanted to throw the car in gear and leave. Bronte didn't want to consider that her fondest memories could be tarnished by this current reality. But she honestly couldn't go any farther. She'd pinned her hopes and her endurance on reaching Annie's house. Now that she was here, she didn't have energy left to alter her plans.

Needing to validate her decision, Bronte turned off the car. For several seconds, the drumming on the roof and the ticking of the cooling engine underscored the silence.

Then she said, "Stay here."

There were no arguments as Bronte grasped the map from the dashboard. Holding it over her head, she threw open the driver's door and darted into the rain. Avoiding the damaged step, she hurried to the relative shelter of the porch and pressed the doorbell.

As she waited for her grandmother to appear, Bronte could feel her children's gazes lock in her direction. Once again, she realized that she should have waited until she'd been able to reach her grandmother. If Grandma Annie had known they were coming . . .

What?

What would she have done?

Weeded the flowerbeds? Thrown a coat of paint onto the house?

Why hadn't it occurred to Bronte that she and Grandma Annie had aged at the same rate? In her mind's eye, Annie had remained the same vivacious woman she'd been when Bronte had seen her last. She must have slowed down in the past few years. Obviously, the maintenance of the property had become too much for her.

What if she wasn't up to an impromptu visit?

Bronte's gut crawled with new worries. *Damn, damn, damn.* She'd been desperate to get her children away from the trouble brewing at home. Bronte had thought that if she had time alone with her girls, she could mend the brittleness that had invaded their relationships. Then, when the opportunity arose, she could explain that the move from Boston was permanent.

As well as the separation from their father.

"Ring it again!" Kari shouted from inside the car.

Forgoing the doorbell, Bronte opened the screen and pounded with the knocker. Annie could have grown hard of hearing. She had to be . . . what? Eighty-five? Eighty-six?

Why hadn't Bronte kept in touch more? Why hadn't she pushed aside Phillip's overwhelming demands and reached out to her grandmother? Instead, Bronte had grown so ashamed of her situation and her inability to make it better, that she'd limited her contact to cheery phone calls and the "too, too perfect" letters tucked into family Christmas cards.

The grumble of a distant engine drew her attention. Allowing the screen to close with a resounding bang, she wiped the moisture from her face as a pair of headlights sliced through the gathering gloom.

For a moment, she was exposed in the beams as a pickup rolled from behind the barn and headed toward the lane. At the last minute, the driver must have seen her, because the path of the truck altered, veering toward Bronte and her children.

A growl of thunder vied with the sound of the engine as the vehicle jounced to a stop. It was a big truck, purely utilitarian, with a stretch cab and jacked-up wheels with shiny rims unlike anything Bronte had ever seen in Boston. The window to the passenger side slid down and a man leaned closer so that she could see his shape like an indigo cutout against the pouring rain. Much like the truck, he was built for hard work, with broad shoulders and powerful arms.

"Do you need some help?"

His voice was deep enough to carry over the drumming of the rain and something about its timber caused her to shiver.

Using the map as her makeshift umbrella, Bronte ran closer. "Yes, I'm looking for Annie Ellis. I can't get an answer at the door. Do you know if she's expected back anytime soon?"

The stranger in the truck removed a battered straw cowboy hat, revealing coffee-colored hair tousled by rain and sweat and eyes that were a pale blue-gray. A faint line dissected his forehead—whiter above, a deep bronzed tan below, conveying that he spent most of his time in the sun. He had features that could have been carved with an ax, too sharp and square to be considered handsome, but intriguing, nonetheless.

"Exactly who are you?" he asked bluntly.

Normally, she would have bristled at such a tone, but she was tired—emotionally and physically. All she wanted was a hot cup of tea and sleep. Deep, uninterrupted sleep.

"My name is Bronte Cupacek. Annie is my grandmother."

The man's gaze flicked to the van, the Massachusetts license plates, and the children who were pressed up against the windows watching them intently.

"Ah. The Boston contingent."

Something about his flat tone rankled, but before Bronte could decipher his mood, he delivered the final blow to an otherwise devastating few months.

"Your grandmother fell down the stairs yesterday afternoon. She's in a local hospital."

TWO

———◆———

JACE Taggart watched as the woman's face fell in disappointment. Then her eyes widened and she blinked at him with a Bambi-in-the-headlights stare rimmed in ridiculously dark lashes. Even wet and bedraggled, she was pretty in that Bostony, high-maintenance sort of way.

But the look of horror that crossed her features couldn't be feigned.

"Is she all right?"

Jace hesitated before responding. The woman's posture had grown so brittle that he wondered if any more bad news would cause her to shatter.

"She's . . . not doing too well," he said reluctantly. "She'll be in the hospital for a while."

She grew even paler.

"Th-the hospital . . . it's still . . . uh . . ." She pressed a finger between her brows and closed her eyes, as if doing so would help her retrieve the memory. "Is it still on the main road beyond the middle school?"

Jace shook his head. "No, a new one was built about ten years ago, but Annie was taken by Life Flight to the medical center in Logan." He pointed to the lane that led back to the highway. "Go back where you came and turn left onto the old highway. You'll head north about three miles, turn right, and then follow the road over the mountain. Once you're in Logan, you'll see signs showing the way."

"O-okay."

Inexplicably, Jace couldn't tear himself away. There was something about her that begged for his help, but Jace pushed the sensation aside. All his life, his family had accused him of collecting strays—cats and dogs when he was young, then troubled friends, and finally lonely women. Lord help him, after his last relationship, he couldn't handle another needy female. With spring planting to be done, wet weather making many fields inaccessible, Bodey raising hell, and Barry retreating socially . . .

Jace had too damned much to worry about. There were days when he felt like the weight of the world was crushing down on him to the point where he couldn't breathe. The last thing he needed was one more "project" sucking up what scant emotional and physical energy he had left.

Nevertheless, he couldn't ignore the twinge of guilt he felt at abandoning Annie's granddaughter—especially when he sensed that this woman was closer to her breaking point than he was. But even as his gaze flicked to the dark bruise marring her cheek, she stepped away.

"Thank you."

There was no escaping the "I don't know who the hell you are, so keep your distance" tone or the wariness that stiffened her spine. Her gaze flicked to the minivan, then back to him again as she analyzed how quickly she could get to her children if Jace posed a threat.

Much as he would with a startled colt, Jace eased back, lifting his hands in a silent calming gesture. He kept his voice low and soothing as he said, "Glad I could help."

Then, since her posture continued to radiate her unease, he replaced his hat, touched a finger to the brim, and forced himself to turn away, rolling up the window again. But it took more effort than he would have imagined putting the truck in gear.

He drove with unaccustomed slowness, watching Bronte Cupacek grow smaller in his rearview mirror. She was tall and slim—too slim if the sharp jut of her collarbones and wrists were any indication. The way she'd wrapped her arms around her waist seemed self-protective. In the sheeting rain she looked vulnerable and fragile. Defeated.

No, not quite defeated. Despite the haunted look in her eyes, there was still a defiant tilt to her chin.

One that might only be for show.

The minute she disappeared behind a hedge of lilac bushes, Jace swore, bringing the truck to a halt. For several long minutes he sat there with the rain pummeling the roof, thinking of all the things he *should* be doing. He had four hired men to orchestrate despite the rain and wet fields. Bodey had just bought a new mare at a recent auction, and Elam needed his signatures on a land lease. Barry, Jace's youngest brother, would be arriving home from an outing with his Scout group in the next ten minutes.

That thought caused a frown. Although Barry had suffered brain damage from an automobile accident years ago, he was generally very social. Jace usually had to threaten to hogtie him to a chair to keep him from running down the lane to wait for his Scoutmaster. But lately, Jace couldn't get him to go with the other boys his own age—and Jace was damned if he knew why.

Shit.

But even as he moved to put the truck back into gear, something tugged at his conscience, urging him to check on Annie's family. One more time.

Growling at his unaccustomed indecisiveness, Jace slipped his cell phone from his pocket and quickly dialed his elder brother, Elam.

The phone was answered on the first ring. "Hey, Jace."

"Are you still on the ranch?"

"I'm finishing up. I left the leases on your desk."

"Thanks. I'll sign them as soon as I get in." Jace paused, then asked, "Are you in a hurry to get home?"

Since Elam and Prairie Dawn Raines had become a

couple the previous summer, Jace had seen a real change in his brother. Where once he'd been stony and wracked with grief after the death of his first wife, now he was more relaxed and easygoing, quick to smile and even quicker to lend a hand at the ranch. Often as not, when he was finished with his work breaking colts, he would join P.D. at her restaurant in town or head to his newly built cabin on the hillside.

"Nah," Elam said. He must have been on his way into the Big House because Jace heard the squeak of the front screen. "P.D.'s meeting with a supplier until seven or eight, so I'll probably hang around here and use the weights or something. What do you need?"

"Could you pick up Barry and hang on to him for a while?"

"Sure. What's up?"

Jace sighed. "I don't know. I was driving past Annie's and some of her relatives were there."

"They must have heard about the accident."

"Not exactly. It came as a shock."

Elam sighed. "That's a hell of a welcome."

"Yeah. I think I'll make sure they get to the hospital. Annie's granddaughter wasn't real clear on how to find it." As if the words gave Jace the permission he'd been seeking, he began turning the ranch truck around.

"Don't worry about Barry. After her meeting, P.D. is taking the rest of the night off, so she'll enjoy spoiling him. She was bringing flatbread pizza from Vern's, so I'll go with Barry and get some sodas at the Corner. Then, since it's the weekend, we'll keep him Friday and Saturday night. He was asking when he could have another sleepover at the cabin. I'll have to bring him with me to the ranch tomorrow morning. I've got buyer appointments throughout the day, but as soon as I've finished, I'll take him with me to Vern's. The band will be playing, and he loves that."

"Thanks, Elam."

"We'd enjoy having him even more. Maybe you should take some time off."

And wasn't that the truth. Sometimes Jace felt like crawling out of his skin with the need for a few hours of blissful solitude. Although Elam didn't know it yet, Jace had already begun thinking that once the harvest was in and the winter wheat planted, he might go somewhere. Alone. Somewhere other than Taggart Hollow.

But it was too soon to mention it to his brothers—it wasn't even something that he allowed himself to think of all that often. It was a half-formed idea that had begun to take root in his brain, growing stronger with each day, until he would find himself toying with the idea of seeing Austria in winter this time, or a tour of Italy. Or England. It'd be cold as hell in January—

"Jace?"

Realizing that his brain had wandered down a trail that might never come to fruition, Jace quickly yanked his thoughts back to the matters at hand.

Elam.

Barry.

Check.

Now he could make sure Annie's granddaughter had everything she needed.

Jace ended the call and carefully drove back down the rutted access lane toward Annie's house, wondering why his pulse had begun to beat faster.

THE prospect of another journey—even one of only a few miles—proved to be too much for Bronte's twelve-year-old van. After she had received directions from the unknown neighbor on how to find the medical facility, she'd returned to her car. Ignoring Kari's complaints and Lily's questions, she'd turned the key.

Click.

Then . . . nothing.

She couldn't even get the radio or the windshield wipers to turn on.

That final defection—even one directed at her by an in-animate object—was more than she could bear. Dropping her head to the steering wheel, she fiercely bit the inside of her cheek and held her breath to control the sobs that battered at her heart.

I will not cry. I will not cry. Not in front of my children.

A knock on the glass brought her upright. Unable to roll down the automatic windows, she cracked the door open.

"Car trouble?"

It was the man from the truck. He hunched protectively over the door, shielding her from the rain with his body—and that instinctive kindness was nearly her undoing. Too late, she felt a drop of moisture plunge down her cheek. Praying he would think it was from the rain, she savagely swiped it away.

"I-I don't know what's wrong. Sometimes it takes a minute or two to get the motor to turn over, but it's never gone dead before."

He seemed to consider things, and then gestured to his truck. "Climb in. I'll take you to see Annie."

His offer merely heightened her mortification. From birth, independence had been drummed into her so strongly that she felt uncomfortable accepting favors from anyone—even family. Accepting such a gesture of kindness from a stranger . . . this was too much.

But when she tried to protest, he rolled open the side door and smiled at Lily. "Hey, there. Would you like to see your great-grandma?"

Lily's eyes grew huge, and she perched on the edge of her seat as if ready to bolt.

"My name's Jace," the man said. "I'm an EMT, so I was the one to ride with your great-grandma in the ambulance to our local hospital, then help her get onto the helicopter. I know where to find her. And since I'm an EMT, I have to promise to never, ever hurt anyone." He gave her a wink. "You'll be safe with me, especially with your mom along."

Lily continued to hesitate, but Jace seemed more than willing to give her time to make up her own mind. Finally, she nodded.

"Climb into the truck, then. We'll be there in no time."

Lily looked to Bronte for permission.

Bronte knew that she would have to swallow her pride and accept his offer of help. There would be no rest for any of them until they'd seen Annie. To enter her grandmother's house and climb into her beds would be unthinkable without assuring that her needs were being seen to first. So she nodded to Lily in the rearview mirror. The girl scampered through the rain, clambering into the back of the stretch cab.

Kari, on the other hand, shot Bronte a WTF glare, but before she could openly complain, Bronte warned, "Not a word." Huffing, Kari opened her own door and stomped through the puddles.

Bronte followed more slowly, gathering her purse and phone before joining her children. By that time, their unsuspecting Samaritan had revved the engine and turned the defroster to high so that the lukewarm air blew against her hot cheeks.

"Are you sure you want to do this, Mr. . . .?"

He held out a hand—the hand of a workingman, with long fingers, scuffed nails, and calluses that rasped against her palm. Here in the land of Boy Scouts, there were men who worked hard for a living—and the sensation of his rough skin against hers caused a strange frisson to race up her arm.

She wanted to snatch her hand back, to sever a connection that was more charged than it should have been. But somehow, she managed to keep her cool—even as her heart hammered against her chest. In that seemingly innocent gesture, someone other than her husband or children had touched her. Until now, she hadn't known how much she'd hungered for such simple human contact.

"Jace Taggart." After a brief, firm shake, he released her to throw the truck into gear, then gestured to the fields on either side of the lane. "My brothers and I lease most of your grandmother's ground. We've been neighbors for years." He pointed to a distant sparkle of lights. "That's our place over there."

Bronte remembered the ranch in the distance, although she'd never met the Taggarts herself. She and her siblings used to sneak close to the pasture fences to catch a glimpse of the horses and their foals. Occasionally, they would see one of the boys who lived there, but not nearly enough to satisfy their curiosity. For some reason, to be sitting next to one of the kids she and her sister Carroll had once ogled—a boy all grown up into an even more powerful male—was disconcerting.

They lapsed into silence—and she was grateful. Manufacturing small talk would have taxed what few brain cells were still functioning at this point. Her sister, Carroll, a graduate of West Point, would have called this whole experience a "clusterfuck of gigantic proportions." Instead of fleeing to a familiar sanctuary where she could lick her wounds, Bronte had compounded them.

God had a horrible sense of irony.

"What happened?"

She wasn't aware that she'd spoken the words aloud until they broke through the muffled drumbeat of the rain and the faint country-western song playing on the radio.

Jace glanced at her, the light from the dashboard painting the angles of his face in blue. He had sharp features—a prominent brow, deep-set eyes, a narrow nose, and a square jaw with a slight cleft. The striking angles reminded Bronte of the rough-hewn, half-finished statues by Michelangelo that she'd once seen in Italy. As if the artist had walked away in mid-sculpt before he could soften the edges.

"Annie fell down the stairs of her house. She broke three ribs, her leg, and her wrist." He frowned, turning onto a larger highway before continuing. "Unfortunately, it was nearly twenty-four hours before she was found. The wrist and leg needed surgery to repair and she had a reaction to the anesthesia, so she's in ICU."

Good heavens. Her grandmother had undergone surgery and no one in the family had known?

"Will she be all right?"

Jace glanced at her again, obviously not wanting to paint a rosy picture when there was still cause for concern. So he answered instead, "Annie is tough. If she has her way, she'll pull through."

Yes, despite her grandmother's affectionate nature, she'd always had a will of iron. She wouldn't let a fall keep her down for long.

That thought resurfaced when they arrived at the hospital and dodged out of the rain into the lobby. The facility was one she'd never been to before, and when they stepped inside to the smell of new carpet and paint, she realized it must be a recent addition to the older section.

Shepherding her children ahead of her, she followed Jace to the bank of elevators at the end of the lobby.

Lily's hand stole into hers. "Mommy?"

"Yes, sweetheart?"

"When are we going back to Gramma Great's?"

She squeezed her fingers. "I don't know. Not for a while, I guess. We need to make sure that Gramma Great is okay."

As they stepped into the waiting elevator, Lily seemed about to say something more, but as soon as the doors closed, she cast a nervous glance at Jace, and shrank into the corner.

Her daughter had always been shy around strangers, especially men, and Jace Taggart was no exception. He cut an imposing figure in his cowboy hat, bulky Carhartt jacket, and faded jeans. A tall woman herself, he towered over her by several inches—enough so that if he drew her toward him, she would fit under the jut of his chin. Phillip, on the other hand, was a scant inch shorter than Bronte.

Inwardly, she slammed on the brakes. Where had that thought come from? She had enough problems without mooning over the first local male who crossed her path.

Thankfully, the doors slid open before she had time to examine her own thought processes. They hurried down the hall, Lily lagging behind Bronte, so she had to tug on her daughter's hand to help her keep up.

Once at the nurses' station, Bronte released her, leaning forward. "Is it possible to see Annie Ellis?" she asked the nurse who stood behind the counter making a note in a three-ring binder. "I'm her granddaughter."

"Mommy?" Lily tugged at her shirttails.

She touched the top of Lily's head, smoothing the hair that had escaped from her braids. "One minute, sweetheart."

The nurse checked a bank of monitors, then smiled. "She's in ICU, which means only one visitor at a time, fifteen minutes every hour."

"Mommy?"

She touched Lily's shoulder in reassurance. "Don't worry. I'll be right back." She pointed to the corner where the hospital had planned for such situations. "Why don't you go wait over there? They've got books, toys, and a television set. I bet you could find some cartoons." She smiled, then gestured to Kari.

For once, Kari didn't argue—thank God. Maybe it was the promise of a television set or the FREE WI-FI ZONE placard on the wall. In any event, she took Lily's hand, pulling her toward a plastic table and chairs in colors that seemed too garish for the subdued waiting room.

At the last minute, Bronte remembered Jace. Her brain scrambled to remember if she had enough money in her wallet to hire a car or a taxi so he wouldn't be inconvenienced any more. But he'd already folded his lanky frame into one of the chairs and picked up a copy of *People*. She had a brief flash of the absurdity of this thoroughly western male holding up a periodical with a picture of Lady Gaga on its cover before the nurse held her badge up to a security lock, then waved her into the ICU.

JACE waited until the door bounced shut, then tossed the magazine back on the table. Under the brim of his hat, he watched Bronte's daughters. The older girl was all gangly limbs and braces, a combination of child and adolescent. He could see some of Bronte's features reflected in her, but where her mother was calm and collected, Kari was quicker to anger and emotional outbursts—which he supposed was typical of most teenagers her age.

Lily, on the other hand, was small and quiet with dark *Little House on the Prairie* braids. Even now, she huddled next to the window, one finger idly tracing raindrops that streaked down the glass. She seemed intent on disappearing into the corner unnoticed.

Jace wasn't sure why, but the sight tugged at his heart.

Pushing himself to his feet, he spoke to the older girl. "I'm going to make a few calls, then I'll be back."

She barely glanced at him, her thumbs moving wildly over the tiny keyboard of her iPod. "Sure. Whatever."

Jace had a feeling that as soon as he left the room, the teenager would forget he'd ever spoken to her, so he'd better be quick.

As soon as he'd punched the button for the elevator, he dialed his phone. Bodey, who was three years his junior, was slower to answer than Elam, his voice husky. "Yo."

"Where are you?" Jace asked bluntly.

"I'm . . . occupied."

Jace fought the urge to roll his eyes. Knowing Bodey, he was probably with a lady. Bodey went through women like a soap star through Kleenex. The hell of the matter was that he usually came out of the brief flings as the woman's best friend.

"How close to the ranch are you?"

" 'Bout ten minutes. Why?"

"I need you to head to Annie's," Jace said as he stepped into the empty car and punched the button for the lobby. "Turn up the heat, then get your tools and repair the front stoop. You've got about an hour, maybe an hour and a half."

Jace heard a female murmur something in the background. Bodey must have covered the phone because his response was muffled. Then, "Why the hell am I going to Annie's? I thought she was going to be in the hospital for at least a week?"

"Annie's granddaughter and her kids have shown up in town. They're at the hospital now, but they'll be staying in Bliss. Near as I can tell, they came cross-country without knowing she'd been injured."

"Shit. That's got to be a shock."

"Looks like they're dead on their feet, especially the granddaughter. I'd hate to have them sleep in a chilly house or trip on those loose boards."

"I've got about an hour before I have to meet with one of my cow-cutting sponsors, so I'll do what I can. We'd be better off tearing the whole stoop down and building her a new one before she gets back. But I'll see it holds together for a day or two."

"Thanks, Bode."

As soon as he'd terminated the call, Jace punched in the number of one of his hired hands. The door to the elevator opened and he stepped into the hall just as the boy answered.

"Jace! What's up?"

"Hey, Tyson. I know you worked with a mechanic for a couple of years. Do you have any experience with minivans? It's a Buick or a Chrysler, I think."

"A bit."

"Before you hit the fields tomorrow, drop by Annie's and have a look at the van parked out front. Annie has visitors and their vehicle died at the door."

"I'm in the area. I'll take a look at it right now and call you back."

"I appreciate it."

"No problem."

Now that the most important details had been seen to, Jace strode in the direction of the cafeteria. He wasn't sure when Bronte and her kids had last eaten, but he could grab them something to drink and a snack. Sodas and coffee. No, tea. Bronte Cupacek looked like the sort who would drink tea. An herbal tea. Especially this late at night. Maybe after a visit with her grandmother and a sip or two of something warm and soothing, some of the tension would ease from her frame.

Jace didn't bother to examine why it was so important to him to provide that tiny gesture of comfort—or why he found himself so affected by the shadows in her eyes.

He was being neighborly, that was all.

THREE

———•∎•———

BRONTE had never liked hospitals—probably due to an emergency appendectomy when she was six. The scents of antiseptic and misery seemed to hang over her like the thunderclouds outside, but she pushed the sensation away. This wasn't about her. It was about Grandma Annie being hurt and alone without any of her family even knowing what had occurred.

Why hadn't Annie arranged to call one of them after her fall?

But then, Bronte realized Annie had probably been frightened and in pain, unable to notify anyone. Even if she'd been coherent enough, that wasn't Grandma Annie's style. She was fiercely independent; any show of weakness was a cardinal sin. Only once had Bronte's father suggested to Annie that she should move to a retirement home. Drawing herself up to full height, she'd demanded that James Ellis stay out of her affairs. She could take care of the farm herself, and if she couldn't . . . well, she could always "hire a boy to do it."

Bronte couldn't help smiling as Grandma's familiar

motto rang in her ear. But the smile faded when Bronte realized that Annie had found a "boy" to help her. Jace Taggart. And there was nothing "boyish" about him.

The nurse stopped in front of a striped curtain. Perhaps the designer had believed the muted shades of orange, gray, and beige would be soothing. To Bronte, they were simply a reflection of the storm outside and her own muddy fears.

"Remember, fifteen minutes at the most. She's being kept sedated, so she might not even realize that you're here."

Bronte nodded. Gripping her shoulder bag more tightly, she ducked through the curtain.

Once on the other side, she stutter-stepped to a halt, her eyes clinging to the tiny figure that barely managed to fill out the blankets.

Her grandmother was thin, so thin. It had been a good five years since Bronte had seen her last, and in that time, Annie seemed to have shrunk to a miniature version of the robust woman she'd once been. Her hair had turned white and wispy, so baby fine that the pink of her scalp showed through. An arm wrapped heavily in bandages was propped up on a pillow. The other lay across her chest, and fingers twisted with arthritis gripped the blankets with bird-like digits draped in wrinkled skin. An IV ran from that hand to the stand beside her bed, and Bronte winced at the pain it must have caused for a needle to be plunged into such fragile flesh.

Rounding the bed, Bronte reached for Annie's free hand, mindful of the tubes and lead wires that ran from her body. Stroking her grandmother's knuckles with her thumb, Bronte leaned forward, kissing Annie's forehead as if her grandmother were a child.

In that instant, emotions thick and strong rolled over her, and she was nearly overcome with the need to protect her grandmother, to lessen her pain, to let her know that she loved her and she'd been so wrong to wall herself off from Annie's obvious need.

"Grandma Annie? I'm here. You're not alone anymore."

If Annie heard, she gave no sign. Her breathing continued in soft puffs around the cannula, the rhythm irregular and shallow, as if the pain gripped her even through the medication. She'd turned her cheek slightly into the pillow, and the position had caused her ear to fold over on itself—and for some reason, that sight, more than the leads and the bandages and the garish bruises clutched at Bronte's heart.

Gently, Bronte smoothed Annie's ear back into place. As she did so, she was struck by the delicate softness of Annie's skin—like a newborn's, but stretched, lined, and spotted, as if each blemish bore testament to the fears, joys, and sorrows she'd endured.

Bronte thought Annie's eyes flickered. In that second she felt the same fierce surge of emotion that she'd experienced when her children were placed in her arms for the first time. This woman, who had done nothing but love Bronte unconditionally, needed her care in return. For the first time in weeks, months . . . *years,* Bronte felt as if she were being thrown an anchor in the midst of a stormy sea.

This was what she had instinctively longed to find when she'd fled Boston. This sense of rightness, of homecoming, of safety. Not that anything had been solved by coming to Bliss. But this sense of being *needed*—not simply to run errands, cook, and clean, or wrap her arms around her swiftly imploding marriage—eased the heartache that sat in her chest like a lump of lead.

"I love you, Grandma," she said, leaning close to brush her lips against her cheek. "We'll get through this somehow."

The rustle of the curtain was her cue to leave. Bronte waited until the nurse and she were well away from the other cubicles to whisper, "How is she?"

"As I said, she's stable right now. The doctor will give you more details when he makes his rounds in the morning, but her vitals are strong. She's a fighter." The nurse tipped her head, eyeing her with concern. "You're not from around here, are you?"

Bronte shook her head. "No, I live in—"

She stumbled. How could she finish the sentence? Like a petulant child, she'd run away from home, and she really couldn't envision going back anytime soon. She didn't belong anywhere.

No. That wasn't right. She belonged here. In Bliss.

Since the nurse still waited for an answer, she said, "I just arrived. From Boston."

The woman nodded. "If you don't mind my saying so, you look exhausted."

Which Bronte supposed was a nice way of telling her that she looked like hell. For the life of her, she didn't know the best way to respond to the nurse's comment. Her hand twitched with the need to shield the bruise from her gaze, even as her brain warned her that doing so would only call more attention to it.

But this woman didn't wait for her to defend her appearance. Instead, she offered her a small smile, her gaze flicking from her eyes to the bruise, then back again. "The meds are going to keep Annie out of things for a while. I know you want be here, but it might be better if you got some rest tonight. Then you could come back in the morning when you're feeling more like yourself."

More like herself? How could that be possible if she didn't know what that meant anymore?

Bronte wanted to argue, to insist that Annie had already been alone too long and that Bronte was more than willing to stay. But deep down, she knew this woman—*Steff!* according to her name tag—was right. She had more than herself to think of tonight. Kari and Lily had been pushed to their limits as well. They needed food and beds and freedom—more than a hotel room could offer. Tomorrow, they could sort out the rest: settling in, fixing her car, seeing to Annie. Maybe she was taking for granted the fact that Annie would open her home to them, but she didn't think so. Grandma Annie had always welcomed them with open arms, and Bronte doubted her modus operandi had changed. Besides, Annie would need someone to take care of her once she returned home.

Bronte didn't even allow herself to consider the prospect

that Annie might not return at all. Bronte refused to acknowledge the fragility of the figure she'd left in that bed in the ICU. Instead, she focused on her grandmother's iron will. Annie would be coming home. Soon.

BRONTE stepped back into the waiting area and stopped short, her mother's instinct warning her even before she'd completely crossed the threshold that something was wrong. In an instant, she noted that Jace was gone. Lily sat hunched in the corner, her face averted, her shoulders shaking in silent sobs. Kari, her hormone-laden, oblivious, teenage daughter, was plugged into her iPod, completely unaware of her sister's distress.

"What happened?" she asked, then swore beneath her breath and snatched one of the headphones out of her ear. "Kari, what happened to your sister?"

"How should I know?" Kari demanded, rife with the self-righteous indignation of puberty.

"I told you to keep an eye on her."

"No. You didn't," Kari said with the dreaded eye roll. Dear God in Heaven, every time she did that, Bronte's fingers twitched—and she'd been one of those anti-spanking proponents.

"Where's Jace?"

She shrugged. "He told me he was headed somewhere, but I forget."

Great. So Bronte had no idea if he was planning to take them home or if she should make her own arrangements.

But even as the thought flashed through Bronte's mind, a snuffling sob from the corner pushed her toward her younger daughter. She was a good yard away when the ammonia-like sting of urine assaulted her nostrils.

Oh, hell. Forget Mother of the Year. Bronte would be lucky if her children survived through adolescence.

"Come on, sweetie," she said, crouching down next to Lily. "Let's get you cleaned up."

When Lily lifted her chin, her eyes were big and wet,

like cornflowers dappled with rain. But rather than the re-crimination Bronte had expected to find, there was only misery and humiliation. "I tried to . . . to tell you . . ."

"I know, honey," Bronte said with a sigh, sweeping strands of wet hair from Lily's cheeks. "It's my fault. All my fault."

Taking Lily's hand, Bronte managed a whispered explanation to *Steff!* who directed them to a large handicapped restroom in the hall. Once there, Bronte helped her daughter strip off her wet clothes. Within seconds, there was a tap on the door, and *Steff!* handed Bronte a small bar of soap, a clean towel and washcloth, a bag for Lily's soiled clothes, and a child-sized hospital gown.

As Bronte soaped and rinsed her daughter's lithe form, memories of Lily as a toddler came crashing back—bubble baths and afternoons at the pool, bedtime and potty training. How many times had she run a washcloth over her daughter's body, wiping her clean of the day's adventures so that she could climb into bed smelling of soap and baby shampoo?

While Lily shivered in the cold hospital bathroom, mortified and miserable, Bronte felt a fleeting instant of peace in the familiar routine. For an instant, she remembered that what was truly important was the well-being of her children. As long as they were safe and warm and fed, she could withstand almost anything.

Bronte helped Lily slip into the hospital gown, wrapping it as tightly as she could around her. Then she drew her daughter close, hugging her, hoping that her trembling would ease as she absorbed the warmth of her body.

"No harm done," she whispered.

"But—"

"Shh." She stroked her hair, rocking her ever so slightly. "It was my fault. All my fault."

She should have remembered that Lily had said she needed to use the bathroom. She should have listened when Lily had tried to talk to her. Lily's shyness had grown almost paralyzing over the past year—to the point where she would rather die than talk to a stranger. And Kari . . .

Well, she couldn't blame Kari for inattentiveness when Bronte had cavalierly displayed it herself.

"Don't you worry about a thing, pumpkin. As soon as we get back home, we'll climb into bed. Come morning, everything will be better. It always is."

But the words sounded empty, even to Bronte.

"Is Gramma Great's our home now?" Lily asked, her voice barely a whisper—and Bronte instinctively knew that there were layers of meaning beneath Lily's question. As much as Bronte might have tried to shield her children and obscure the true motives for their flight beneath the guise of fun, her dear, sweet, darling Lily had sensed the under-currents of tension like a dowser finding water. With Kari, she might have prevaricated. But she sensed that Lily wanted—*needed*—the gift of truth.

"I don't know, sweetie. I think, at least for now, we'll stay here. Gramma Great will need our help once she gets out of the hospital—and I think you'll like it here."

She couldn't be sure, but she thought that the tense line of Lily's shoulders eased.

"Would that be okay?" Again, Bronte offered her daughter a choice, knowing that, like Bronte, Lily needed at least the illusion of control.

She was rewarded with an eager nod and a quick, gamin smile, and Bronte's heart flip-flopped in her chest like a grounded fish. If her children only knew how completely they held her heart in their palms, merely by being happy.

She gathered Lily's things, stuffing clothes and shoes into the bag. She was taking Lily's hand when there was another soft tap on the door.

"Is everything okay?"

Steff! was beginning to grow on Bronte. Especially when Bronte opened the door to find the nurse bearing a soft fleecy blanket. "Look what one of my friends found for you in pediatrics," the woman said, patting the furry fabric. "The minute she saw it, she knew it was meant to go to you."

"Why?" Lily asked in a barely audible whisper.

"Well, she heard your name was Lily. Is that right?"

Lily nodded.

"Then this is definitely yours." *Steff!* shook it open.

It was a simple blanket, probably one of hundreds made by a ladies' civics group or a local 4-H club. A single layer of fleece had been fringed at the edges and tied into decorative knots. But the bright blue fabric was covered with dozens of fat cartoon frogs basking on flowering lily pads.

"I think that a blanket covered in lily pads should belong to a girl named Lily, don't you?"

This time, there was nothing shy about her daughter's grin. She accepted the gift with a sigh of delight, rubbing the soft fabric against her cheek.

"Thank you."

"You're welcome, honey. But you know what this means, don't you?"

Lily shook her head.

"You should never accept a gift from a stranger, so we'd better not be strangers anymore." She held out her hand. "I'm Stephanie Sato, but everyone around here calls me Steff, so you be sure to do the same."

Lily shook the woman's hand and nodded, then Steff helped her wrap the blanket around Lily's body for warmth.

"All done here?" The deep voice interrupted the introductions.

Bronte wasn't sure how, but she'd all but forgotten about Jace Taggart. When he loomed beside her, tall and broad and male, she grew tongue-tied and self-conscious.

"Ready to go?" he asked.

"Yes. Thank you." She turned to Steff. "Will someone call? If there's a change?"

"Of course."

Bronte reached into her bag, digging around the flotsam of tissues, packets of moist towelettes, hand cream, sunblock, and fruit snacks that had slowly edged out the quaint bottles of perfume, embroidered handkerchiefs, designer lipsticks, and manicure supplies that had graced her pocketbook before she'd given birth. Toward the bottom, she found a scrap of paper—a receipt from a McDonald's in

Cheyenne—and a pen. She scribbled her contact information and handed it to Steff.

"That's my cell phone if you need it."

"I'll clip it to Mrs. Ellis's chart." She waved to Bronte's daughter. "Bye, Lily."

Motioning to Kari, Bronte trailed Jace into the hall. Lily ran ahead, pushing the button to the elevator while Kari followed, her eyes still glued to her iPod and her thumbs frantically moving across the screen, sending one final text before she lost the Wi-Fi signal.

As they waited for the doors to open, Bronte turned to Jace. "I really appreciate all you've done for us tonight."

"Glad to help," he said, unconsciously slapping his hat against his thigh. "Annie is a good friend."

The doors slid open with a soft *ping*. After they'd stepped inside, Jace leaned against the railing, idly watching the lights march toward the ground floor.

"While you were in the ICU unit, I stepped out to make a couple of calls," he said, his voice rumbling in the close confines. "One of my hired hands is a decent mechanic, so I had him drop by Annie's and check your van. He thinks the battery is to blame. You've been leaking acid. Tyson will pick up a new one at the auto parts store when it opens in the morning. He should be there after nine to install it. If that's your only problem, it will save you an expensive trip to the shop."

The elevator opened, but her feet were rooted to the floor. She was stunned that a man she'd barely met had taken her so completely under his wing. "I . . . Thank you."

The girls ran ahead of them to the revolving front entrance to the hospital. Lily shuffled Morticia-like against the tight stricture of her blanket, and too late, Bronte realized she was about to run outside barefoot.

Lily seemed to discover the same thing, because she came to a halt, stopping the revolving door in the process. Kari, who was trapped in one of the sections behind her, banged on the glass shouting, "Why did you stop, you little creep!"

Jace sidestepped the revolving door, using one of the side

exits. Swinging Lily into his arms, he said something to her that made Lily smile and released Kari from her momentary prison.

The rain had eased while they'd been inside, becoming a fine mist. Yards away from the truck, Jace touched a button on his key fob and the vehicle rumbled to life. By the time they climbed inside, the interior was warm and filled with a heavenly aroma. On the center console, there was a beverage holder with four cups and a stack of food containers.

"I hope you don't mind, but it's been a while since I've eaten, so I got enough for everyone. There's hot chocolate for the kids, coffee or chamomile tea for us. There's also steak fingers and gravy for a snack, if you're hungry."

Steak fingers and gravy?

Before Bronte could warn Jace about the dangers of having kids and gravy in the same vehicle, her girls reached for the containers.

Jace seemed to read her mind. "Don't worry. It's a ranch truck. They can't do anything to hurt it."

Bronte seriously doubted that statement. She turned to offer a warning to the backseat. But when she found her girls talking and giggling with one another as they dunked bite-sized pieces of chicken-fried steak into white gravy, she turned to Jace instead. "Thank you."

"My pleasure."

She reached for the container of tea, gravitating toward the familiar, soothing scent of chamomile. It didn't escape her that, despite his insistence that he'd bought the food to ease his own hunger, he didn't sample anything but the coffee. The fact that he'd given Bronte and her kids a way to save face in accepting the food was infinitely touching.

Bronte hadn't planned on eating anything herself, but when her children insisted that she try the steak fingers, she realized why her girls had wolfed them down. After miles and miles of traveling interspersed with fast-food hamburgers, pizzas, and sandwiches, the steak fingers and gravy offered a hint of a home-cooked meal.

More than ever, Bronte prayed their journey was over.

She and her children needed to stop living out of a suitcase. They needed fresh air and sunshine, regular meals, and a daily routine. They needed . . .

Peace.

As if sensing her tumultuous thoughts, Jace didn't bother to try to engage her in casual conversation. He lapsed into silence, his fingers tapping against the wheel in time to the country ballads easing from his radio. Yet, there was no tension to the silence. Instead, it wove around her, soothing her nerves, allowing her to sip her tea, breathe deeply, and let the knotted muscles in her shoulders unwind.

"Long day?" Jace murmured.

Bronte glanced at her children, but for once, they were getting along as they played a game on Kari's iPod.

"Yeah." The word held a wealth of meaning. Long day, long month, long year.

Her gaze skipped to the clock on the dashboard and she was amazed to find that it was only seven in the evening. She was sure it would have been closer to midnight. But then, she'd driven through several time zones.

"When did you leave Boston?"

She squinched her eyes shut, trying to count backward. "Uh . . . six days ago?"

He whistled softly. "You must have driven straight through."

She nodded, her eyes opening in time to see the concern in Jace's.

"That's a tough haul, especially without a relief driver."

Tears prickled at the backs of her eyes at the memory of the fear and desperation that had forced her to flee. As if sensing a portion of her emotions, Jace took her hand.

The gesture was so unexpected—so warm, so comforting—that Bronte caught her breath. When he squeezed slightly, as if offering her silent encouragement, the memories faded beneath something closer to wonder.

When was the last time anyone had taken her hand and offered her encouragement—all without being asked to do so? For so long, it had been Phillip who'd received all of the attention and well wishes of the few friends who hadn't abandoned them. Bronte couldn't really blame them, since most of them had known Phillip for much longer than they'd known her. But Bronte had been hurt when these "friends" had begun to treat her as if she were part of the problem, rather than the only person fighting for a solution to their marital woes.

Jace's thumb strayed to caress the back of her hand before he seemed aware of what he'd been doing. To his credit, he didn't immediately release her.

"You must be exhausted."

Her laughter was rueful. "You have no idea."

"Well, you're here now. So take it easy the first few days."

Take it easy. Bronte wasn't sure she knew what that meant any more. For years, she'd been working double jobs—one at a coffee shop and another transcribing hand-written research notes for a local professor and typing them on a computer. In order to make sure her girls didn't feel that they were being ignored, she tried to complete most of the transcribing after they'd gone to bed, working into the wee hours of the morning.

She wasn't quite sure how either of those occupations would help her find employment here in Bliss. Work was probably limited in such a small town. And even though there were only six weeks left of the school year, it was important that she get her kids enrolled as soon as possible so they could make friends before summer vacation. Then . . .

Jace squeezed her hand again.

"You look like your brain is going to explode."

A rueful laugh burst free. "It might. I thought that once I arrived at Annie's, I could take a few days to get accustomed to the area."

"You can still do that."

She opened her mouth to argue with him, then simply shook her head, realizing that she didn't want this man to know how desperate her situation was.

Jace glanced at her again, seeming to invite her to confide in him, but she offered him the same plastic smile she'd perfected over the years to hide her true feelings. She'd learned long ago that she was alone in her struggles. Although help might have been offered by Phillip's friends, they hadn't really wanted her to accept.

But she could tell that Jace saw through the subterfuge because the smile he threw her in return was openly amused. "Give it a try, okay?"

He released her then, subtly, when he made the left-hand turn back into Bliss. Immediately, her gaze fell to the long, slender fingers gripping the wheel, even as the warmth of his touch continued to soak into her skin like a phantom caress.

Again, she was struck by the way a man she'd known for only a few hours already knew more about her situation and her emotions than most of the people she interacted with at home.

No. Not "home." Boston wasn't "home" anymore.

"Thanks," she said softly. "I'll do that."

FOUR

———•———

BY the time they arrived at Annie's home, both of her
children were asleep. Without being asked—not that
Bronte would have the chutzpah to do so—Jace gathered
Lily in his arms and carried her into the house. Bronte was
startled when he walked right in, but then she remembered
that Annie never locked her doors. She probably wouldn't
know where to find a key after all these years.

It took several minutes for her to wake Kari enough for
the teenager to stumble into the house. Bronte tried to guide
her upstairs, but Kari veered into the living room and dropped
onto the couch, pulling a folded afghan around her body.
Bronte left her there and stumbled back into the entryway.

Jace's boots clattered on the steep treads. "I put Lily in
Annie's room," he said with a hitch of his thumb in that direction. "Do you need help bringing anything in from your van?"

She shook her head, slightly flustered. Here in the cramped
confines of the hall, she became even more aware of his
height, the width of his shoulders in his jacket, and the button-
down shirt that hinted at a hard, flat waist and well-defined
musculature. His shirt had been tucked into jeans that were

butter soft, and the narrowness of his hips was emphasized by a leather belt with an oval silver buckle.

For several long minutes, her gaze hung there, focusing on the gold-tinted figure of a horse and rider. Inexplicably, a fluttering began low in her belly—a tingling of awareness that she hadn't felt in a very, very long time. It spread through her body, branching out until it reached the tips of her fingers, so that they twitched with the need to—

What? Reach out and touch a stranger?

Her cheeks flamed and her gaze shot up to tangle with Jace's. Unable to look away, she watched a montage of emotions march across his face—curiosity, confusion, then a recognition of her need. But when she saw the first spark of interest flare up in his eyes, she took a step backward, folding her arms protectively across her chest.

But that was a mistake as well. Even though she refused to look at him, she could feel his regard shift to her breasts, and that fact alone—that for the first time in years, a man was staring at her chest—caused her nipples to immediately respond.

Damnit. He'd asked her a question. She should answer. Now. So that he didn't feel the need to stay any longer.

But for the life of her, she couldn't remember what he'd asked. Worse yet, she wasn't sure she wanted him to leave. Not yet. This man—this stranger—exuded warmth and strength and safety. In a single evening, he'd come to her aid, reassured her children, kept them warm and dry, and filled their stomachs, all without being asked.

"Thank you, Jace." The words emerged with a huskiness she hadn't intended but that she wouldn't have changed. Jace Taggart would never realize how close she'd come to the brink. She honestly didn't know what she would have done without his intervention—probably spent the evening worrying about her grandmother and cursing her own inadequacies. By shouldering some of the burden, however inadvertently, Jace had given her a chance to gather her dwindling strength and return to the fight.

His smile was slow and crooked and filled with hidden

undercurrents that hadn't been there before. Lordy, lordy, what it did to her knees.

"My pleasure." He gestured to the door. "Are you sure you don't want me to help with your luggage?"

Sheesh. That was the question he'd asked her earlier.

She quickly shook her head. "I'll go out in a few minutes and grab my overnight bag. Since the girls are already asleep, I'll have them get their gear in the morning."

He worried his hat in his hands for a minute, and then settled it on top of his head. "Well, I'll say good night to you then. I'll be back in the morning with Tyson so that he can see to your car. I'll stop on the way and get you a few of the necessities—milk and bread. It'll tide you over until you've visited Annie in the hospital again and can make a proper trip to the grocery store."

She opened her mouth, and then laughed softly. "Is everyone here in Bliss this nice to strangers?"

He shifted, clearly embarrassed, and then said, "Only if they're as pretty as you."

Then he settled his hat on his head and offered, "Good night, Bronte. Sleep well."

Before she could think of a response . . .

He was gone.

Bronte didn't know how long she stood there, staring into space, trying to corral the disjointed thoughts stampeding through her brain. Somehow, in the block of a few hours, everything had changed. She'd come looking for sanctuary, for a hole that she could crawl into and lick her wounds. She'd thought that if she ran far enough and fast enough, she could leave her troubles behind, not knowing that they'd accompanied her much like the baggage stowed in her van.

But then . . . even when she thought she would be completely crushed by her sorrow, the kindness, the consideration, and the hint of interest given to her by a stranger had offered her a pinprick of hope, one that threatened to flicker and disappear as his taillights disappeared into the darkness.

Sighing, Bronte forced herself to move. She staggered outside, swearing when she remembered, too late, that there was a loose board on the top step. But when she landed heavily, she discovered that the stoop had been repaired in the last few hours.

Another of Jace's miracles?

A serenade of crickets accompanied her as she waded through the damp grass to her car and retrieved her overnight bag. Then, too tired to think, she made quick work of washing her face and brushing her teeth.

In the stark bathroom lighting, the bruise on her cheek seemed even more garish. The injury was fading, true. But beneath the harsh fluorescent bulb, she was sure that she could see the outline of a pistol grip.

Whirling away from the image, she sat on the edge of the claw-foot tub, gulping air into her lungs. She'd told herself that once she arrived at Annie's she could cry and cry and cry until there were no more tears left to shed. But now, with so many people relying on her—Kari, Lily, and Annie—she knew she couldn't start. If she did, she'd never be able to stop.

Her gaze dropped to the bag open on the floor, to the thick envelope awaiting her response. All it would take was her signature on the legal documents inside. In the swipe of a pen, she could officially dissolve her marriage and relegate a relationship that had lasted half her adult life to the dustbin.

But she couldn't think about that now. Not when her heart was as battered and bruised as her face. Much as she wanted to move on, to find a new purpose, to dig herself out of this morass of misery, she was stuck in an unfamiliar limbo. She knew she couldn't—*shouldn't*—go back, but she also didn't know how to go on.

Which was why, in the end, she refused to make any decision at all. She simply flipped off the light and crawled into the high tester bed next to Lily, praying that the gods of sleep would be kind to her tonight.

THE Big House was dark and quiet when Jace let himself into the kitchen, closing the door behind him with a muffled *snick.*

Alone.

He couldn't remember the last time that he'd had the place to himself. Sometimes, he felt as if his life had become a tag team relay race. As soon as Barry had gone to Elam's or an activity, Bodey would need his help, or a hired man would need instructions, or a horse would turn up lame, or a cow would escape from a fence. It was as if the universe plotted against him, offering him barely enough time to think, let alone relax.

But now that he had a chance to do whatever he wanted, wherever he wanted . . .

He had no idea what he really wanted to do.

Out of habit, he opened the refrigerator door and stared inside. But there was nothing there that tempted him. The contents were a weird combination of bachelor fridge meets preschool with a selection of beers, half-empty condiments, juice boxes, an economy bag of carrots, and enough ranch dressing to drown a small horse. Jace could get Barry to eat just about anything as long as there was a puddle of ranch sauce on the side. True, sometimes there was more sauce than real food that went into his stomach, but Barry went through weird eating cycles—like this month's carrot fetish—where he would eat nothing but one specific item. So if Jace had to get creative to make sure his brother got some semblance of a balanced diet, he was willing to do it.

But tonight, nothing looked tempting enough to expend the energy to fix it.

Restless, Jace shut the door and threw his hat on the table. He supposed he could head to Vern's and get some dinner— maybe find some adult company. But even as the thought appeared, he dismissed it. Since Bodey had apparently hooked up with a new woman, he had the whole house to himself. All alone. Wasn't that what he'd been saying he needed?

Disgusted at his mood, Jace headed upstairs, intent on showering and changing into a pair of sweats. But even as he padded toward the master suite at the end of the hall, his steps slowed, and without thought, he veered toward the attic steps.

The flight of stairs was steep and narrow and covered with a fine layer of dust. Jace hired a local woman to come clean the house once a week, but there was no need for her to go up there. He supposed he should tell her to sweep off the treads, but this way . . .

He would know if anyone had been up here, prying into the person he'd once been.

Once at the top, Jace stopped, his hand closing around the knob to the upper door. There he paused, knowing full well that to open it would be the equivalent of poking a nearly healed wound with a pointed stick. He'd be better off heading to his study to get some book work done.

But even as he told himself to walk away, his fingers tightened around the worn brass.

Slam. Thump, thump, thump.

"Jace! Where are you? *Jace!*"

Jace released the latch as if it had caught on fire. Hurrying down the steps, he'd barely managed to reach the hall when Barry barreled toward him, all gangly arms and legs, his brow furrowed with intent. He held a brown paper sack in his hands, which he thrust toward Jace.

"P.D. told me to give you this." His face screwed up into a caricature of concentration as he tried to remember Prairie Dawn's exact words. "She said, 'Tell him not to bother with his own nasty cooking. And don't you dare spend a blessed . . .'" Barry paused to think. "'. . . a blessed minute of this ideal doing ranch burps or pest reports.'" Barry's eyes blinked in rapid succession, his lips twisting into a frown. "I don't know what that means. And who's Ed?"

It took a few seconds, but then, as if he could hear P.D. herself scolding him, Jace understood. *And don't you dare spend a blessed minute of your idyll doing ranch books or pesticide reports.*

Jace's lips twitched, but rather than answering Barry directly, he decided to have some fun and said, "I'm not sure who Ed is. Why don't you ask Elam?"

"Oh-*kay!*"

Without taking a breath, Barry whirled and thundered

back the way he'd come. But he must have gone only midway down the staircase before he turned around and came running back again. Jace barely had time to brace himself before Barry wrapped his arms around his waist and squeezed him with the unrestrained force of a sixteen-year-old boy who didn't know his own strength.

"Love you, Jace," Barry said. Then, he raced back down the stairs and out the front door, slamming the screen behind him.

Jace stood rooted to the spot, his chest seeming several sizes too small.

Shit, shit, shit.

In that display of uninhibited affection, his brother had once again wrapped Jace around his finger, and all the "coulda, woulda, shouldas" turned to ashes on his tongue.

Turning his back on the staircase to the attic and past choices that still haunted him, Jace followed Barry's path much more slowly. The scent of pizza and garlic wafted up from the sack—homey and comforting. Some borrowed affection.

That would have to be enough.

Jace had knowingly charted his current course when his brother had reached toward him from a hospital bed, his cheeks streaked with tears.

"Wait for me, Jace! Please wait for me!"

Jace had made his brother a promise all those years ago. Since then, he'd tried his best to keep it. So what if his future had veered away from the path he'd originally planned? He'd built a career and a life for himself that he could be proud of.

He was happy enough. He *had* to be happy enough.

Because there was no turning back now.

BRONTE woke to sunlight streaming through lacy Priscilla curtains, flowered wallpaper . . . and the smell of bacon.

Bacon.

She couldn't remember the last time she'd awakened to that heady scent. A year into her marriage, Phillip had grown rabid in his attempts to best his own marathon scores. He'd insisted on lean, center-cut bacon at first, then turkey bacon, then no bacon at all, merely a tofu bacon-flavored substitute with the consistency of overcooked liver.

She couldn't abide liver.

She couldn't abide tofu.

But that hadn't seemed to matter to Phillip. Just as, a few years later, the marathon scores would drop by the wayside as well.

"That man is here again."

Bronte started, twisting on the bed to find Kari looming over her like one of those vultures in a Snoopy cartoon. Her daughter must have retrieved her bag because Kari's hair was carefully arranged and her makeup firmly in place. She was wearing her favorite tight jeans and at least three layers of shirts. Obviously, she hadn't figured out yet that the chances of her meeting anyone she could impress with her efforts were slim.

"You look nice," Bronte said, her voice still thick with sleep.

If Kari heard the compliment, she gave no indication.

"Grandma doesn't have Wi-Fi," she said, disbelief coating every word.

"I wouldn't imagine that she would," Bronte mumbled in return. If Annie refused to buy presliced bread, Bronte doubted her grandmother had an iPad stashed away somewhere.

Kari stamped her foot in impatience. "How much longer before we head home? I don't like it here. There's nowhere to go and nothing to do." Her voice rose siren-like into a frustrated whine. "All my friends are going to school activities and their parents have promised to take them somewhere great this summer—and I'm stuck in the middle of nowhere in a creepy house that doesn't even have Wi-Fi! It's lame!"

"Get over it," Bronte mumbled in return, ignoring her daughter's petulance. Yawning, she settled deeper into her pillow. But her eyes had only been closed for a second when they popped open again. "What man is here?"

"Jack, Jess, Jethro . . ." She shrugged. "You know . . ."

she mumbled, distracted by whatever game was on her iPod ". . . that guy who took us to the hospital last night. He's downstairs making breakfast."

"There's a man doing *what* downstairs?"

"Making breakfast."

As soon as Kari's words sank into her consciousness, Bronte sprang out of bed as if she'd been touched with a cattle prod. "Do you mean Jace Taggart?" she asked frantically, searching for her overnight bag. "Jace is making breakfast? How long has he been here?"

Kari shrugged. "I dunno. Half hour maybe." She paused her game and grinned, meeting Bronte's gaze in a rare moment of eye contact. "But his hired hand is *hot* with a capital *H-O-T!*"

"Kari!"

"Just sayin'."

"Where's Lily?"

Kari shrugged, saying, "I dunno. It's not my job to keep track of her." Then, she wandered from the room with the same blind indolence that she'd begun using since Phillip had bought her that damned electronic device years ago. It was a wonder to Bronte that her daughter hadn't fallen down a manhole somewhere. Kari seemed to take it for granted that the universe would protect her while her mind roamed the infinite diversions to be found in a sixteen-gig hard drive.

As soon as Kari disappeared, Bronte scrambled to gather her clothes and rushed into the bathroom. With the smells of food permeating even the steam of her shower, she made the world land-speed record getting ready. Granted, she'd never make the finals in a beauty pageant. But she managed to tame her dark, wavy hair into a ponytail and throw on some makeup. Since they'd been on the road for days, her wardrobe selection was limited, but her jeans were clean and the white T-shirt wasn't too wrinkled.

She galloped down the stairs, slowing only on the last few treads so that she didn't run headlong into the kitchen.

When she crossed the threshold, Jace looked up from where he was frying eggs in a cast-iron skillet, and the intensity of his gaze had the ability to bring her to a stuttering halt.

Geez. The man had cut a powerful figure in the dark, but that was nothing compared to the way he looked in stark daylight. Jace Taggart was tall and lean with powerful shoulders and thickly muscled arms. His T-shirt was worn, clinging to him in a way that hinted at a chiseled chest and abdomen. Below the wrinkled hem, his long legs were lovingly sheathed in faded Wranglers.

Phillip wouldn't have been caught dead wearing Wranglers. He was more a proponent of designer jeans, which was a shame. But then again, Phillip wouldn't have looked nearly as good in the fitted denim. Jace Taggart had a tight ass and long, long legs and—

Stop it, stop it, stop it!

Tearing her gaze away, Bronte forced herself to concentrate on something else—the sunny yolks of the eggs in the skillet, the deftness of Jace's fingers as he handled the spatula. The long, slender fingers, and the—

Seriously?

"Feel free to start eating now, if you want."

Bronte bit the inside of her lip to keep her mind from leaping to an entirely inappropriate interpretation of Jace's remark. But she must have betrayed herself somehow, because Jace offered her a slow smile that caused her stomach to flip-flop like a landed fish.

She yanked her gaze away from Jace, only to discover that on the counter beside him was a platter heaped with bacon—*heaped!* Her mouth watered at the sight. Turning, she saw a table positioned beneath a large picture window. It was already laid out with paper plates, cups, and utensils. There was a carton of orange juice, a tower of toast, a bowl of crisp hash browns, and inexplicably, a plate of carrots with a small cup of ranch dressing.

"Sorry, my culinary skills are strictly from the frozen-foods section," Jace said as he scooped the eggs onto a dinner plate and carried it to the table. As he bent to set it down, Bronte was able to see that his jeans had begun to mold themselves to the shape of his butt and the bend of his knees. The man had a really great butt.

What was wrong with her this morning?

"I hope you don't mind the way I made myself at home," Jace was saying. "Annie and I have slipped into a habit of having breakfast together, and I figured you wouldn't have had much time to figure out where everything is."

Bronte quickly yanked her gaze away from Jace's backside. "No. I don't mind at all."

Mind? She couldn't remember the last time—if ever— that someone had taken the time to cook for her. Right now, staring down at a hot breakfast straight out of a *Waltons* rerun, she knew that if Phillip were here, he'd be complaining about the three "Deadly Cs," carbs, cholesterol, and calories. But she didn't care. Her stomach rumbled in anticipation of solid food rather than the coffee and diet soda that had been her mainstays during their hasty road trip.

Suddenly eager, Bronte leaned into the hall to call, "Kari, Lily! Breakfast!"

The side door squeaked open and a tall, gangly teenager stepped inside. He had a shock of brown-black hair that hung straight and thick into his eyes, pimpled cheeks, and a frame so long and lean he appeared more legs than body. He kept his gaze downcast as he moved toward Jace, all but hiding behind a paper bag bulging with groceries.

"You can put the sack on the counter, Barry."

As the boy moved forward, she could see that he used his whole body to propel the motion rather than merely his leg muscles.

"Do you want me to put the stuff away, Jace?"

Barry's voice was curiously monotone and measured, and Bronte immediately realized that the boy suffered from some sort of disability.

"No, you can leave it there." Jace gestured to me. "Say hi to Mrs. Cupacek. She's going to be staying with Annie for a while."

From behind his bangs, Barry directed his gaze to a point off Bronte's left shoulder.

"Hi."

She smiled, sensing that his stress levels had ratcheted up to infinity at being forced to talk to her.

"Hello, Barry. You can call me Bronte."

His gaze skipped to Jace. "Why is she named after a dinosaur, Jace?"

It took her a moment, but then she realized that he had linked her name to a brontosaurus.

"I'm actually named after an author. Charlotte Bronte."

Again, his face aimed in her direction, but his eyes remained a few feet off center.

"Why?"

She laughed. "I don't know. My parents were looking for trendy names for me and my siblings. Each of us is named after an author."

Clearly, Barry didn't see the logic in that. "I think you're named after a dinosaur."

Grinning, she shrugged. "Maybe you're right."

Jace touched his brother lightly on the shoulder. "Breakfast is ready. Why don't you go see if Tyson is finished with Bronte's car and tell him to come inside?"

Barry nodded, shuffling out the door. "I'm going to go get Tyson, Bronte."

When he moved out of earshot, Jace said, "Sorry about that. Barry has no edit button. He speaks his mind."

She watched the boy through the lacy curtains. "I like that in a person."

She felt, rather than saw, an air of tension ease from Jace's posture. His eyes, when they met hers, were clear and direct. Where last night, the color had been tinged with gray, in the morning light, they were a sparkling, lake blue.

"Barry nearly drowned in a car accident when he was ten years old. The resulting brain damage has left him . . . ten years old, for the most part. But he's a good kid."

A kid trapped in a body burgeoning on manhood.

"He lives with you?"

Jace turned to the refrigerator, gathering a family-sized bottle of ketchup and a mason jar filled with homemade salsa.

"Mostly, although he spends a good deal of time with Elam, my elder brother, and his girlfriend, P.D. My parents and little sister were killed in the same wreck. Elam was stationed out of the country at the time and my younger brother Bodey wasn't old enough to see to himself, let alone anyone else, so I took care of Barry."

Bronte was speechless. She'd thought that her problems seemed insurmountable at times, but she couldn't imagine negotiating such a devastating tragedy on her own. If her scrambled, mental estimations were even close to being true, Jace had probably been in his early twenties when he'd assumed the responsibility of both younger brothers.

She was saved from a response by Kari who clattered down the staircase and burst into the room. "Are we going to eat, or what?"

"Barry has nothing on my daughter's lack of an edit button," Bronte said under her breath, and Jace laughed.

FIVE

———•◦•———

AS if a silent dinner bell had been rung, Lily skipped down the stairs, and then came to a halt in the doorway. As soon as she saw Jace, her guard was up, even though she remembered him from the night before. She eased up to Bronte, wrapping her arm around Bronte's waist and shielding herself from full view behind her mother's body.

"Morning, pumpkin. Did you sleep well?"

Bronte felt Lily nod against her.

Barry burst in from outside, followed by another tall, gangly teenager with a shock of wavy blond hair and an infectious grin.

"Car's fixed," he announced, sliding into the chair beneath the window.

Jace gestured to his hired hand with a serving spoon. "Bronte, this is Tyson. Tyson, that's Bronte Cupacek and her daughters, Kari and Lily. They'll be living here for a while. Kari and Lily, this is Tyson and my brother Barry."

Bronte watched as Kari nearly dropped her iPod, giving Tyson—who had to be at least nineteen—one of those half-flirting, half-gobsmacked smiles of an adolescent who found herself right in the middle of a raging crush. Since Bronte had made it clear to Kari that there would be no dating, no boy-girl parties, no coed socializing of any kind until she was sixteen, she lacked the social skills to pretend to be casual. With barely a glance at Barry, she chose the seat next to Tyson, her iPod miraculously tucked into her pocket so that she could nervously fluff her hair.

Bronte fought to keep a straight face, finally turning to draw Lily toward the table. "Have a seat, pumpkin. We don't want things to get cold."

When Lily hesitated, Bronte sat next to Kari and pulled Lily down in the chair beside her. Too late, Bronte realized that she should have arranged for Lily to sit in the middle. Being forced to sit next to a stranger was tantamount to torture for Lily. But before Bronte could offer to change seats with her, Barry looked at Lily—really looked at her. Apparently, his shyness only extended to adults.

"Annie has a tree house out back," he blurted. "It's high. Really high. I can show you after we eat." He made the offer to include Kari as well.

Bronte cringed, anticipating a crushing reply from Kari, but she merely stared at Barry as if he'd lost his mind to suggest something so juvenile, so *plebeian,* as a tree house.

Lily, on the other hand, peeked at Barry in curiosity, clearly intrigued by the idea. Her gaze bounced to Bronte as if seeking permission and Bronte rushed to reassure her. "I think that's a great idea."

"We could go now, Emily," Barry said. "Do you want to go now?"

Bronte opened her mouth to correct Barry, to tell him her daughter's name was Lily. But in doing so, she caught the way Jace seemed to freeze, his eyes locking on Barry.

"Lily probably needs to eat first," she said slowly, wondering at the sudden undercurrents in the room.

"We can eat in the tree house, Emily." He turned to Jace. "Can we eat in the tree house, Jace?"

Jace cleared his throat before speaking. "I don't know if Bronte—"

Seeing her daughter's own eager expression, Bronte interrupted with, "Sure. I don't see why not."

As if they'd been friends for years, Barry and Lily jumped to their feet, each of them scooping a handful of bacon into their napkins, then heading for the door and slamming it behind them.

Silence seemed to flood into the vacuum of their absence. Then Tyson announced, "Jace, it appears the carrot curse has been broken. Now you'll be cooking bacon for a month."

Confused, Bronte looked at Jace in time to see him grimace. But before she could ask for a translation, Tyson continued, "Well, I'm starving. Someone pass the potatoes."

In an instant, the awkwardness was broken. As bowls were sent her way, Bronte filled her plate with more food than she'd probably eaten in a month. It was as if the sun streaming through the window and the old familiar smells of country cooking were reawakening a part of that teenage girl who'd once spent her summers here with Annie.

Tyson clearly had never encountered a stranger in his life, because he filled her in on the happenings in town. Jace and she finished their food and nursed the last few drops of orange juice while Tyson finished his second plate of food . . . his third . . . and his fourth—all of them liberally dosed with salsa. Through it all, Bronte noted that Kari watched him eat as if he were Zeus on Mount Olympus and she wanted to feed him grapes. Much to Kari's disappointment, seconds after he'd finally finished eating, Tyson abruptly grabbed an International Harvester's hat with FRIENDS DON'T LET FRIENDS DRIVE GREEN emblazoned on the front and stood.

What did that mean?

"Thanks for breakfast, Jace. I'll triple-K the angle field. She should be done by"—he looked at his watch—"ten?"

Jace nodded. "Brandon and Jess should be here by noon so that the three of you can start working on the ditches. Once Scottie gets out of school, we'll start drilling alfalfa down by the Rudds. It's probably the only field dry enough."

"Will do." Tyson touched his brim. "Nice to meet you, Mrs. Cupacek."

Kari looked miffed at not being included in Tyson's fare-wells, but her pride was saved when Tyson said at the door, "You and your sister should come to the ranch sometime and check things out."

"I will!"

Kari's response was much too eager, but Tyson was already halfway across the yard. She watched him climb into a dilapidated Toyota pickup and drive away in a spray of mud. Then she whisked her iPod out of her pocket. But seconds after turning it on, she squealed in frustration.

"There's no Wi-Fi!" She turned to Bronte in patent des-peration. "Can't I have a cell phone? Please, *please*," she whined. "All my friends have one."

"No."

"Then can I use your cell phone to text McKenzie?"

"Why don't you call her?" Bronte said wryly, pointing to the telephone bolted to the wall.

Pure horror crossed Kari's face. "I can't *call*. No one does *that* anymore."

"I do it all the time."

"Mother!"

Clearly, Bronte was asking the impossible—such as insisting Kari perform brain surgery with a rock.

"Fine," she relented. "But we're going to the hospital in a few minutes, so make sure you're ready to walk out the door."

She hadn't even finished her sentence before Kari was racing out of the room and tearing up the staircase—probably to update McKenzie on the ranch hand-slash-mechanic who was *H-O-T!*

"You may have a problem on your hands," she said to Jace, envisioning a summer when Kari trailed behind Tyson like a lovesick zombie intent on devouring his brain.

"Not as much as you're going to have," Jace said, his tone rife with amusement.

She laughed. "You're probably right."

Bronte wondered how on earth she'd come to this point—from utter misery . . . to laughter. No, her problems hadn't magically melted away—and the darkness was there, hovering at the edge, threatening to swallow her whole.

But right now, a little bit of sunlight had touched her soul.

As if sensing the serious veering of her thoughts, Jace leaned back in his seat, resting an ankle on his knee and laying his hand on his boot. "So you're going to see Annie?"

"As soon as I can clean up the breakfast things. It's the least I can do after you've spoiled us this morning."

He shrugged. "I didn't do anything but crack some eggs and tear open a bag of potatoes."

She wanted to tell him he'd done more, so much more. But to do so would require an explanation of how she'd come to be in Bliss, and she wasn't ready to bare her soul to anyone about that.

"I'll take charge tomorrow," she insisted. It wasn't until the words left her mouth that she realized she'd tacitly extended Annie's invitation to meet for breakfast every morning. What shocked her even more was that she wanted Jace to come.

And Barry, she quickly amended.

Jumping to her feet, she quickly began to gather the dirty dishes, wondering if she'd overstepped her bounds—or lost her mind. For all she knew, this man had a wife or other responsibilities waiting at his own home. He might have met with Annie only to discuss business matters concerning the ranch, and such obligations wouldn't extend to Bronte.

But before she could work herself into a dither, Jace said, "I'd like that. Sounds like Barry would as well."

From outside, there was the peal of laughter, Barry's a lower tenor and Lily's a staccato soprano.

"Barry must be showing Lily the tire swing," Jace said as he rose and peered out of the glass set into the door. "Yup. He's got her going pretty high, too."

Another high-pitched giggle shimmered through the air and Bronte couldn't account for the relief that swept through her body. Lily had been so somber and introverted lately. As much as Bronte had tried to keep the children unaware of the problems between Phillip and herself, Lily had somehow sensed the dark undercurrents. It was the only explanation Bronte had for the way her darling, chattering magpie had grown so serious and withdrawn.

It was her peal of laughter and the muted excitement of Lily's voice as she cried, "Higher! *Higher!*" that made Bronte realize that she'd done the right thing in coming to Bliss. It didn't matter that the proverbial shit would hit the fan, or that Phillip would be on the rampage as soon as he discovered what she'd done. If she could help her daughter to laugh again . . .

There wasn't anything Bronte wouldn't endure.

"So you'll be staying awhile?" Jace said, somehow providing an echo to her thoughts.

She nodded. "Yes. Yes, we will."

"I'll be sure to let the hospital know. I don't think there will be a problem, since you're family, but Annie gave me power of attorney in regards to medical issues a few years ago. Just in case."

Her brow creased. "She gave you power of attorney?"

Again, Bronte felt a wave of guilt. Her grandmother, her sweet, loving grandmother, had felt the need to make arrangements with a neighbor rather than her own family.

Jace's expression was kind. "I assumed she thought that having someone close was more practical."

Yes, if there was one constant in Grandma Annie's life, it was her practicality. But the fact that she couldn't trust one of her grandchildren to come to her aid stung nevertheless.

Jace threw the plates and cups into the garbage. "She'll probably need some long-term care once she's well enough to leave the hospital," he said, speaking the words with forced lightness as if he were walking through an emotional minefield. "If you'll let me know what you'd like to do, I'll be sure to tell—"

"She can come home," Bronte interrupted firmly. "She'll *want* to come home." Annie would hate going from one clinical setting to another. Like most folk her age, Grandma Annie fiercely fought to remain independent. That meant living in her own house. "If she needs a nurse to visit, that's fine, but I'd like to take care of the rest."

She saw a spark of approval in Jace's eyes. "I'll let them know."

As if realizing the enormity of what she'd volunteered to do, Bronte cast a keen eye over her surroundings. Although the kitchen was clean, it was cluttered—and she had no doubts the rest of the house would prove to be the same. There was no way Annie would be able to negotiate the stairs. That meant moving her bed to the first floor and ensuring the lower bathroom was adapted to her needs. She would need a ramp for a wheelchair, which meant the front stoop would have to be altered and the banisters repaired . . .

"You look as if your brain is galloping ahead at breakneck speed," Jace said with a grin.

Gripping her hands in front of her, Bronte surveyed the kitchen, making note of all the things that needed to be fixed in this room alone. "There's so much to do!"

Jace set the bottles of ketchup and salsa in the fridge, closed the door, and touched her arm. She couldn't account for the way that simple point of contact caused a warmth to spread through her body, easing away the icy chill that had been there for days.

"You came at a good time—if the weather holds, we'll have the corn in by the end of next week, and we've had a wet enough spring that the water won't be sent down the canals until mid-May. Barry, the hired hands, and I can help with the physical stuff. You concentrate on all that female ruffley stuff."

Bronte arched a brow. "'Female ruffley stuff'?"

His cheeks took on a hint of red. "Oh, wow. That came out sounding pure male chauvinist pig, didn't it?"

The fact that he'd recognized his error and so quickly corrected it immediately eased her pique. Phillip wasn't one to apologize. He said it made a person look weak.

"What I meant to say," Jace said, clearly choosing his words more carefully, "is that if you'd like some help with your plans, the boys and I would jump at the chance to do something nice for Annie. She's been a good friend."

Good save.

Since the offer put control back into her hands, Bronte found it easy to say, "I'd like that. But I'd like to do something to thank you for your help. Is there anything I can tempt you with?"

The innocent rejoinder hung in the air, rife with a layer of meaning that she hadn't intended. Clearly, the foot-in-mouth disease was contagious, because this time she'd been the one to speak too quickly.

Before she could correct herself, Jace grinned and seemed to consider his options. Her heart adopted a sluggish beat in her chest and she felt as flustered as her teenage daughter. His fingers tightened on her arm, and she thought she felt his thumb move in a phantom caress. He opened his mouth, closed it, then finally said, "A man can always be tempted by the promise of . . . bacon."

But even as she laughed, she knew full well that he'd given her the G-rated version of the answers that had popped into his head. Unaccountably, she wondered what the adult version would be.

Somehow, he must have sensed her thoughts because he dropped his hand and scooped a hat from the counter. Rather than the cowboy hat he'd had the night before, this one was a baseball-type cap with a logo for Western Seeds embroidered on the front. She'd thought that the simpler headgear would lessen the effect of his blunt bone structure. Instead, it gave him a boyishness that was at odds with the stark masculinity of his frame.

Lordy, lordy, how she loved the contrast.

"Well, I'd better get going," Jace said.

But he didn't move. Instead, he remained in the patch of sunlight streaming in from the door behind him. The buttery glow gilded the tips of the coffee-colored hair escaping below his hat. In the light of day, she was able to see that he was even younger than she'd first supposed—no more than his early thirties. Faint lines had only just begun to fan out from his eyes and bracket his mouth, but rather than detracting from his appearance, they made him seem that much more . . . real. Approachable.

But he was at least five or six years her junior.

Which was a shame.

Bronte's thoughts came to a screaming halt. What in the hell was she thinking? Didn't she have enough on her plate without adding a teenage-like crush? She wasn't the adolescent girl who'd sneaked through the grass with her sister to catch a look at the boys next door. She was a grown woman with children and an ailing grandparent to care for, not to mention a failed marriage at her back.

Failed marriage.

Again, she was reminded of the envelope waiting in her bag. It needed to be mailed. She would not be going back to Boston or to Phillip, and by hesitating in completing the formalities, she was merely delaying the inevitable.

But not today.

She couldn't bring herself to do it today.

Realizing that the silence had stretched out far too long, Bronte tried to remember the last thing Jace had said.

Leaving. He was leaving.

So why did she want him to stay?

She hurried to say, "Yes. Yes, I suppose you've got a lot to do."

The second the words left her mouth, she could have kicked herself. She didn't want to give him the impression that she was pushing him out the door. Quite the contrary. But she didn't want him to feel obligated to linger, either.

Damn. She suddenly felt as awkward and socially inept as Kari.

"If I get a chance, I'll drop by later tonight to make sure you've got everything you need."

Yes!

He gestured to the fridge. "I left my phone number under that magnet there. Don't hesitate to call if you need something."

"Thanks." Bronte unconsciously crossed her arms, and then uncrossed them again, when she saw the way his gaze dropped—for a second—to her breasts. Flustered, she shoved her hands into her pockets.

To her surprise, Jace grinned, clearly unabashed. Then, with a last wave, he disappeared out the door, calling for his brother.

A flurry of butterflies seemed to take up residence in Bronte's chest as she edged closer to the window and watched as Jace and Barry climbed into the truck. What had just happened here? She was tingly and nervous—and heaven only knew that she shouldn't be feeling this way. Not now. Not ever. She was a grown woman with two children who needed her undivided attention. She'd quit her job, left her husband, and moved cross-country to give herself some space from the male species. She'd be an idiot to allow herself to even think of . . .

Of what?

She couldn't bring herself to put these vague, tremulous . . . *heady* sensations into words.

"Mom!"

Bronte jumped away from the window as if she were a Peeping Tom seconds before Kari stormed into the room. "McKenzie says that I'm missing field day. Field day!"

Sighing, Bronte turned away from the sight of Jace's truck disappearing down the lane. Her role as referee, drill sergeant, and mother had officially begun for the day.

SEVERAL hours later, Jace found himself whistling as he let himself into the kitchen of the Big House. *Whistling.*

Wasn't that the damnedest thing?

Unfortunately, he wasn't alone. Bodey was slouched in one of the far chairs, frowning at his laptop. He glanced at Jace, looked away, then did a double take. As Jace hung his hat on the rack behind the door and shrugged out of his jacket, a slow grin slid across Bodey's lips.

"Who is she?" he asked bluntly.

Shit.

Jace scowled at his brother, pretending to misunderstand. "What the hell are you talking about?"

Bodey leaned back, crossing his arms and regarding Jace with narrowed eyes.

"The only time I hear you whistle is when you've met someone who piques your interest."

Jace opened the refrigerator door and pretended to search inside. "I don't know what the hell you're talking about."

Even though he wasn't all that hungry, he grabbed an apple from the crisper and straightened, busying himself with the drawer that held the knives.

"The fact that you won't look me in the eye is answer enough. Who is she?"

Inwardly cursing the fact that he'd come in the back door—and that his younger brother was a pain in the ass—Jace grabbed a paring knife and slammed the drawer shut again. Leaning a hip against the counter, he began to carefully remove the bright green peel. "Like I said: I don't know what the hell you're talking about. I spent some time helping Annie's relatives, then I spent five hours drilling angle field. Had to stop at the lower east corner because of the mud."

But Bodey wasn't listening. "Who's visiting Annie? A woman?"

Jace sighed, the apple peel beginning to form a spiral strip. He did his best to remain bored and pissy, but Bodey's prodding was having the opposite effect. Hell, if it weren't for the complications caused by her children, Bronte Cupacek would be Bodey's type—beautiful and sweet, and with legs up to her armpits.

"You're being an ass. Bronte is probably only here for the summer."

"Oooo. *Bron-tay,*" Bodey responded in a singsong voice. "So you're already on a first-name basis, huh?"

Jace might be approaching thirty-two, but there were times when Bodey could punch his buttons to the point where he felt thirteen and his instinctual response was to pound his younger brother into the ground. Growing up, Elam had been the calm one, the leader, the voice of authority among the boys. Bodey, on the other hand, liked to stir things up—and he generally hadn't been happy unless he'd started a fight. Since Elam would rarely take the bait, Jace was Bodey's favorite target.

But tonight, Jace refused to supply any further ammo. The last thing he wanted was for Bodey to head over to Annie's and find out for himself how perfectly Bronte fit into his dating criteria.

The rush of possessiveness that flooded through Jace was as surprising as it was inexplicable. If there was anyone on earth with an emotional NO TRESPASSING sign firmly in place, it was Bronte Cupacek.

"She's married," he said bluntly. That seemed to shut Bodey up for a few seconds, so he added, "And she has kids. One of 'em is a teenager."

Bam! The gleam in Bodey's eye disappeared. Bodey liked the ladies, there was no denying that. But he had enough sense to stick to women who were in a love-'em-and-leave-'em frame of mind. No single mothers, no emotional baggage.

"So how's Annie?"

And that quickly Bodey dropped his Super Asshole persona, and returned his attention to his laptop.

Jace couldn't account for the flood of relief he felt in knowing that Bodey wouldn't be rushing to Annie's house in the morning to check out the new visitors. The last thing Jace needed was for Bodey to be his usual charming, larger-than-life self.

Although why it should matter, he couldn't bring himself to say. Bronte *was* most likely married. And she *did* have children. So Jace had no right feeling anything at all for her other than mild curiosity. It was absolutely no business of his why she'd come to Utah. If he found himself wondering how early he could head over there in the morning, it was only because he wanted to make sure that her car was still working and her family was settling in—

"Jace!"

"Hmm?" He looked up from his apple to find Bodey staring at him.

"Annie?" his brother prompted.

Jace scrambled to remember what Bodey had been saying, but his brain seemed intent on reviewing the events of the morning—Bronte standing in the sunshine of Annie's kitchen, her acceptance of Barry, her tenderness toward her youngest daughter.

But when Bodey continued to eye him expectantly, he finally managed to say, "Annie's holding her own, but she's still in critical condition."

"That must be tough for the visiting relatives."

Jace tossed the ringlet-like peel onto the counter and cut a slice of apple. "You're not kidding. When I explained what had happened that first night, Bronte looked at me like I'd pushed Annie down the stairs myself." He slipped the apple into his mouth with the tip of the knife. "I think she was already at the end of her rope and the news threw her over another cliff."

Jace realized he should have kept his mouth shut, because the curious gleam reappeared in Bodey's gaze. But all he said was, "No wonder you're whistling."

Jace instantly bristled. "What the hell does that mean?"

"Sounds like a stray in the making," Bodey muttered.

Then, thank God, Bodey's phone rang, giving Jace the perfect excuse to walk away. Because, sure as shit, if he didn't leave the room right now, Jace *would* be pounding his brother into the ground.

SIX

———◆———

"LET'S go, Barry!"

It was a little after four that afternoon when Jace finally managed to break free from his ranch duties—all with the intent of making good on his promise to meet Bronte that evening.

He didn't allow himself to think too much on his reasons for making it a priority. Heaven only knew that after speaking with Bodey earlier that afternoon, the Fates had conspired against him. Equipment failures, muddy fields, and running short on seed had nearly upset his plans. But, uncharacteristically, he'd delegated the remaining problems to the hired men and had hurried back home.

Jace had barely turned the key to the truck when Barry came running out of the house, his hands filled with miniature ranch toys and plastic cows and horses.

"Do you think Emily will play ranch with me?" he asked excitedly as he juggled the tiny tractors, balers, and combines so that he could open the door and clamber inside.

Again, Jace felt a shock at Barry's use of their sister's name. Emily had been Barry's twin sister. She'd been killed, along with their parents, in a horrible winter accident oh so long ago. A lifetime ago, it sometimes seemed to Jace. For years, Barry had called out for her in his sleep and it worried Jace that Barry was using her name whenever he spoke about Lily.

"I don't know, Barry. Some girls aren't into playing with ranch machinery, you know. They like dolls and stuff like that."

Barry shook his head. "Emily likes to play with me."

Jace didn't bother to argue—didn't want to argue. He prayed that Barry was right and Lily wouldn't mind hanging out with a boy who towered above her and had already begun to show the beginnings of a beard. Jace had done his best to try to provide Barry with everything his brother needed. But friends couldn't be so easily supplied. The neighbor kids were loving and accepting, but they were interested in cars and jobs and girls. Barry still wanted to get down on his knees and till the carpet with his toy tractors.

"She sure liked that swing, didn't she?" Jace said, simply to see his brother beam.

"You ain't a-kidding, Jace. I got her goin' high, too!"

"But be careful, okay? You're almost a man and men have to watch over women and keep them safe."

"Even if they're still girls?"

"Especially if they're still girls."

"Okay, Jace. I'll take care of Emily."

"Lily. Her name's Lily."

Barry blinked at him with wide blue eyes. "I know that."

"Then why do you keep calling her Emily?"

" 'Cause it's the nickname I gave her. Friends gotta have a nickname. It's what makes 'em friends."

Jace opened his mouth to insist that Barry might want to choose a different nickname—one not associated with their late sister. But Barry was sorting his toys and it was clear that, to him, the subject was dropped.

Jace threw the truck into gear and eased onto the service road that would take him through Taggart Hollow to Annie's fields, then over the rise to her house. As he drove, Jace tried to convince himself that he was only helping out Annie. She was a good friend, after all.

But it was no good. He might be more than willing to drop by Annie's to help make some repairs, but he rarely took off from work several hours early so he could shower. Shave. Throw on cologne. Brush his hat.

Damn.

"What's-a-matter, Jace?"

Jace shook himself free from his thoughts. "What do you mean, Barry?"

"You look . . . funny."

"Funny how?"

Barry's brow creased in concentration. "Like you need to go to the bathroom or somethin'. Do you need to go to the bathroom, Jace?"

"No," Jace said firmly, knowing he needed to shut down this line of talk before they arrived at Annie's and Barry felt the need to audibly worry over it like a dog with a bone.

"Good. 'Cause you already took too much time in the bathroom getting ready."

In a single instant, Barry managed to bring Jace crashing back to earth. Heaven only knew that Barry was right. Jace was jittery and jumpy with anticipation—and there wasn't a reason in the world to be that way. The woman who had occupied his thoughts for the better part of the day had to be married. M-a-r-r-i-e-d. She had kids. She was loaded up to her eyeballs with palpable stress.

So why did Jace keep thinking he had more than one way to help her relieve some of that tension?

"You got that look again, Jace."

Hell.

"I was thinking, Barry."

" 'Bout what?"

"Whether or not Lily will want to play inside or outside with your equipment."

Barry nodded as if totally satisfied with the complexity of Jace's inner argument. But luckily, before he could comment, Annie's house came into view and Barry saw Lily on the rope swing beneath the tree house. As soon as she saw Barry, she waved and ran to meet him.

"Wait until the truck has rolled to a complete stop," Jace warned his brother.

Obediently, Barry edged closer to the end of his seat, one finger poised above the belt release. But as soon as Jace put the truck in park, he was leaping free, excitedly calling out to Lily, "Come on, Emily! Let's go play!"

The two children headed toward one of the barns and Jace watched until they settled in a spot in the old corral before he stepped out himself. As he did so, Bronte appeared at the side door.

"You have perfect timing," she called out. "I was taking some cinnamon rolls out of the oven when I heard your truck. Come have one while I show you the list I've been making. I need a second opinion."

Jace's boots rang hollowly on the side steps as he crossed into the house. Mentally, he added putting in a concrete stoop to his own collection of ideas. But as soon as he moved through the door, he was swamped by the rich scents of baking bread, cinnamon, rich brown sugar, and coffee. When Bronte turned her back to him and bent to pull a batch of rolls from the oven, his gaze zeroed in on her butt.

Bronte Cupacek had a great butt, rounded and firm and just the right size to cup with his hands.

Shit.

He obviously needed to get out more if this was how he acted in close proximity to a woman he'd barely met. A *married* woman.

She turned and he prayed she didn't see how far south his gaze had strayed. Thankfully, she seemed preoccupied with setting the hot pan on the stove, then grabbing plates from the cupboard overhead.

"I checked out the rooms on the ground floor, and I'm thinking that the office would probably make the best bedroom. It's close to the bathroom and the windows look out over the yard and the creek. I think Annie would like that."

She reached overhead again, lifting on tiptoes, and in

doing so, the hem of her shirt lifted, revealing a sliver of velvety flesh.

Jace knew he shouldn't look, but he couldn't help himself. Just as he couldn't help drinking in the nipped-in spot at her waist and the sweep of her spine as—

Bronte turned, catching him red-handed. He averted his eyes, but not before twin spots of color appeared on her cheekbones, chasing away some of the worry from her eyes.

"Sorry," Jace mumbled, knowing there was no sense denying that he'd been ogling her. "It's been a long time since someone as pretty as you has crossed my path."

His honesty heightened the color in her cheeks, but to her credit, she didn't chastise him. Instead, she seemed rather pleased by the offhanded comment.

"Maybe you need to get out more," was all she muttered as she turned away again, loaded cinnamon rolls onto two plates, then hooked two mugs through her finger.

"Coffee?" she asked.

He looked at the huge pastry on his plate. "I'd rather have milk, if you have it."

"Sure."

She took a gallon jug from the refrigerator and two glasses from the drainer near the sink, then snagged a small bowl of icing. After drizzling the almond-scented glaze on each roll, she took the chair diagonal from him.

"This is amazing," he said, looking down at the treat she'd laid out in front of him. The cinnamon roll was as big as the saucer, light and fluffy and golden brown. The filling swirled in dark counterpart to the golden dough, the rich cinnamon, and brown sugar studded with raisins and chunks of walnuts.

"Don't be too impressed. I can bake—bread, rolls, quick breads, cookies, cake—but that's about the only talent I have for cooking. Phillip, my . . . the children's father, mourned the fact that I could never figure out how to cook turkey tofu so that it was edible."

What the hell?

"Why, on earth, would you want to eat turkey tofu in the first place?"

His question seemed to please her, because she beamed.

Needing to shield himself from the power of that smile, Jace used a fork to cut off a bite of his roll. As the flavors rolled over his tongue, he was immediately inundated with memories of his mother. At the first snow of the season, she'd always made a cinnamon coffee cake, and this was just as good, if not better. There was a hint of another flavor, one he couldn't pinpoint. A spice that seemed to deepen the flavor of the spiral filling.

"What's in this? There's something besides cinnamon, something . . ."

"Cardamom. It's in the candied nuts."

"You'll have to let P.D. taste one of these." His voice emerged much too husky and he quickly cleared his throat. At Bronte's questioning look, he explained, "My older brother's girlfriend owns a restaurant in town. She's always looking for new recipes."

Again, Bronte's cheeks turned pink and Jace wondered how long it had been since someone had offered her a compliment. Not recently enough, apparently.

Unbidden, his gaze skipped to the hand circling her glass. She had beautiful, delicate hands with neatly trimmed nails painted in pale pink. But they weren't pampered hands. Nicks and faint scars testified that she was accustomed to hard work. Even more telling, there was a faint ribbon of paler skin around her ring finger rather than a wedding band.

She shifted beneath his gaze, drawing her hand into her lap. Then she changed her mind, setting her palm flat on the table.

"I'm not with my husband . . . my ex-husband . . ." She sighed. "My husband and I are divorced for the most part . . ."

Jace's brows rose. "For the most part?" he echoed. For some reason, his pulse had begun to drum in his ears. "Exactly how does that work?"

She sighed, beginning to trace the pattern of the table-cloth with her finger. "The formalities were all tied up months ago. All I have to do is sign a form acknowledging that I received the last set of papers."

"You don't want to sign them?" Jace asked gently, wondering why the answer was so important. It wasn't as if he planned to stake his claim on Bronte Cupacek—hell, they'd barely known each other twenty-four hours. Even if she were "all-the-way" divorced, getting himself tangled up with a newly single mother was a bad, bad idea. For both of them.

"No, I want to sign them," she said quickly. Then more slowly, "I *need* to sign them. I . . ." She took a deep breath, then glanced out the window. Kari had climbed into the doorway of the tree house and was madly tapping at her iPod, while Lily and Barry were still on their knees pushing Barry's toys through the dirt. "I'm worried how my children will react. But even more . . . I guess I've been afraid to sever that last tie to the woman I used to be."

The words throbbed with undercurrents, but Jace knew better than to ask for an explanation. Instead, he said, "You'll know when the time is right."

His remark seemed to surprise Bronte, and he supposed that she'd been bombarded with advice from well-meaning friends and family members. He'd bet all of them had urged her to sign the papers as quickly as she could and be done with it.

He knew what that could be like. When he'd first announced that he would be the one to assume Barry's care, there had been more than one person who'd told Jace that he simply wasn't equipped for the job. Whether he'd wanted their opinion or not, he'd received more than his share of unsolicited advice from people who honestly wanted to help—everything from putting Barry into a group home to experimental treatments, diets, and drugs. He'd even been told to have Barry's eyeballs read by a soothsayer living on the edge of town—which had been a raging WTF moment during those stressful days. Over and over, he'd been warned he could never completely fulfill the roles of his mother and father where Barry was concerned—and that much was true. But in time, he'd begun to see that Barry didn't need Jace to be his mother. He needed him to be his big brother. Yeah, Barry might be lacking in a few of the social graces that a female figure might have inspired. But in Jace's opinion, he'd grown into a pretty great kid.

Sensing that Bronte had shared more about her personal life than she'd ever thought she would, Jace changed the subject.

"How's Annie?" he asked, filling both of their glasses with milk.

Bronte looked relieved at the new topic. "According to the nurse, her vital signs are a little better. She woke up a couple of times while I was in the room, but I don't know if she knew I was there. I would have stayed longer, but my kids were getting restless."

"Why don't you head back after dinner? You can drop your girls off at my place."

"Oh, no," she said hurriedly. "I couldn't."

"Why not? I'll be there with Barry—and Bodey will probably be in and out. P.D. is coming down to the house to look through my mother's old recipe collection for ideas, so there will be a female presence there as well. We've got plenty of television sets, an Xbox, basketball hoop, and"— he paused dramatically—"Wi-Fi."

Bronte laughed, and he loved the way the brief expression of joy chased away the shadows in her eyes.

"Don't say that too loudly or Kari will want to live at your place full-time."

"Come on. What do you say?"

"You've already done so much—"

"I'm not doing anything I wouldn't have been doing anyway."

She bit her lip. Jace watched as it was trapped there for several long minutes as she thought things over. But she finally nodded, saying, "Thanks, Jace. I appreciate it."

Knowing that he might blow it if he allowed things to remain personal for too long, he gestured to the notebook in the center of the table. "So why don't we have a look at your list?"

IT was growing dark when Bronte stepped out of the ICU unit. Ignoring the bank of elevators, she took the stairs instead.

It had been nearly a week since Jace had first offered to watch her children while she went to the hospital. At first, she'd been reluctant to accept his help more than that one night. But it soon became apparent that her children were growing weary of the hospital waiting room. They much preferred the comforts of Jace's home—especially when he'd spent the last few evenings teaching them to ride by leading them around one of the corrals on a sleepy brown mare named Snowflake. They would run out to the car to meet her before she'd even brought the van to a halt, chattering about their rides. Unfortunately, that had left barely enough time for Bronte to do more than exchange a few pleasantries with Jace or wave to him from a distance, a fact that left her curiously . . . unsatisfied.

Thankfully, either Jace or Steff had managed to pull some strings, because once it had been established that Bronte was a close relative, she'd been allowed to stay in the ICU unit with Annie.

At first, Bronte hadn't known what to do. Annie had begun to experience problems with her breathing and she'd been placed on a respirator, which had helped to improve her color. The sight of more machinery hooked up to her grandmother's tiny body had been alarming at first. But after holding her hand and talking to her in a low voice, Bronte had felt the faintest pressure against her fingers. She couldn't be sure if it had been a spasm or if her grandmother had been trying to communicate with her, but she decided to believe it was the latter. So she began a one-sided conversation, telling Annie all about the children, the journey they'd had, the sights they'd seen. She'd abridged the events, focusing on the scenery and famous landmarks as well as some of the funny things her children had done and said.

To Bronte's surprise, the unburdening calmed her slightly. Maybe by relating the events of the trip, it became more . . . real. Boston was a long, long distance away, and she didn't have to go back. Ever. Now, all that remained was convincing herself of that fact.

When she ran out of things to say, Bronte took her tablet out of her purse and ordered an e-book by Agatha Christie, one of Annie's favorite writers. Unbelievably, as Miss Marple began to investigate, Annie's pulse seemed to grow more regular and her oxygen levels began to climb. By the time Bronte left, Annie seemed to be sleeping deeply with none of the restlessness she'd shown earlier in the day.

Stepping outside, Bronte inhaled the cool mountain air. Spring had arrived in Utah, bringing moist balmy breezes that would fade to dry desert winds once the weather grew warmer. She wasn't sure, but she thought she caught the deep loamy scents of the fields she'd passed on her way to Logan. The rich, dark earth had been tilled and furrowed and planted—no, *drilled* was the term she'd heard Jace use—with wheat, barley, and corn.

Spring had always been her favorite time of year. The dreariness of winter began to fade as the world awoke from its long hibernation. As Annie was fond of saying, "It's a time of new beginnings."

New beginnings.

Unconsciously, Bronte's steps began to slow, then halted. When she roused from her thoughts enough to become aware of her surroundings, she knew it wasn't a coincidence that a squat mailbox was right in front of her.

She hesitated—not in regret. No. The pause was more a way of saying good-bye to the life she'd once thought she would have. Then, she reached into her bag and pulled out the papers sent to her by her lawyer. After signing and initialing the spots indicated with fluorescent sticky notes, she slid everything into the prestamped envelope that had been provided, then dropped it down the chute.

As she turned and hurried to her car, Bronte thought that she would experience a wave of sadness. Instead, she felt as if a heavy weight had been lifted from her back. True, nothing had really changed. Her situation was no different than it had been ten minutes ago. She still had two children to raise, a job to find, an ailing grandmother to visit every day.

But she was going to do everything on her terms and in her way. For some reason, that brought a spring to her step.

TWENTY minutes later, Bronte pulled into the lane leading to Taggart Hollow. For the first time, she didn't see her children in the yard or the paddock. The only sign of life was Barry's miniature goat, Bitsy. Bronte had already learned that the animal, which was wider than it was high, had an obsession for junk food and would shamelessly beg for snacks.

She maneuvered her car into a spot next to a rattletrap pickup truck with a peeling bumper sticker proclaiming: SAVE A HORSE . . . RIDE A COWBOY! For some reason, the motto made Bronte's cheeks grow hot.

Truth be told, Bronte would have stayed longer at the hospital if her children had been with her, but she didn't want to impose anymore on Jace's hospitality—which was why she lingered in the car, suddenly nervous about knocking on the huge front door. Before she could psych herself into ignoring the nervous fluttering in her stomach, there was a sudden tap on her window, one that nearly sent her through the sunroof.

Jace stood on the other side.

"The kids have gone down to the barn with Elam, my older brother. We had a foal born last night, and they're helping him feed the mare and have a look. Why don't you come into the house and wait?"

The House. The Taggart Big House. How many times as a kid had she longed to see what it looked like on the inside? She knew all about the history of the place—as well as the smaller dwelling a hundred yards away, near the creek. The original Taggart ancestor who'd claimed the land had built a small cabin, the Little House, for his bride. But toward the end of the nineteenth century, another Taggart had made a fortune in cattle and built the Big House with all the ostentatious style of the nouveau riche.

It was an imposing structure. The foundation was made

of river rock and the façade of split logs. An ornate pine railing fashioned from slats of wood with cookie-cutter-like holes in the shape of pine trees marched around the entire structure. Supports made of thick, lacquered lodge poles gave the house a sturdy solidity that easily bore the weight of two more stories adorned with ornate gables and mullion windows. The house had a permanence to it, as if it had always been there, having somehow sprouted from the ground—a fact made even more evident by the towering pines and mature trees that surrounded it.

"Get out of here, Bitsy," Jace said good-naturedly before opening her door.

Bronte swung her legs out, then followed him up the front steps to the wide wrap-around porch.

"How's Annie?"

"The respirator seems to have helped. By the time I left, I was pretty sure that she knew I was there."

"That's a good sign."

He opened the screen door for her and, miracle of miracles, after all these years, Bronte stepped into the entryway of the "western mansion" she and her sister had ogled all those years ago.

Her shoes sank into a thick oriental carpet that ran down the length of the polished hardwood floors. Ahead of her, a massive staircase curled around to the upper floors, rimmed by a baluster carved with trees and foliage and running horses. Another ribbon of carpet ran up the center, held in place by gleaming brass rails. Here in the entry, a looming antique hall tree as large as her van flanked one side of the door, while the other had a solid-looking Victorian bench with lion heads carved into the armrests. The effect of the heavy pieces and polished wood might have been stuffy if it weren't for the pile of boots under the seat and scattered farm toys parked in random positions on the floor.

"Sorry for the mess. A bunch of men live here and we're hopeless."

She laughed. She couldn't remember the last time she'd had anything to laugh about.

"Barry uses the floor for his farming and ranching," Jace said, motioning to little tractors and pickups and other various pieces of machinery that were tiny replicas of the ones Bronte had seen working in the fields. "I've tried to teach him to park things in the 'shed,' which is an old cupboard in the family room. But as you can see, I'm not having much luck."

Jace motioned for her to follow him. On opposite walls, two doorways led away from the entry. To the right, she could see a formal parlor decorated with period antiques, a crystal chandelier, and an enormous fireplace. But to the left, she was led through a very modern family room with leather sofas, a huge television, and strategically placed side tables. A discarded pair of sneakers—probably Barry's—a news-paper, a plethora of remotes, and even more scattered ranch equipment and herds of plastic cows and horses proclaimed that this was a room for comfort rather than show. It was a guys' room, stripped of frills and focused on comfort.

"You're getting the benefit of a full deployment of Barry's machinery, I'm afraid. He had Lily helping him 'plant the south forty.'"

"I'll make sure she helps him pick them up."

"No need. Barry goes berserk if you move his stuff. Once a week, we have a lady come in, so he knows he has to drive everything into the barn so she can vacuum. Other than that, we tend to walk around it."

"That's sweet."

Jace grimaced. "It's not so sweet if you're walking through the room in your bare feet and land on a swather, but"—he shrugged—"he's come so far in the last few years, it's a foible I haven't bothered to corral."

He moved to the back of the room to a heavy swinging door with brass hand- and kickplates and held it open for her. As she passed through, she found herself in a kitchen that screamed "the seventies!" with oak cabinets, an avocado and harvest gold motif, and Formica cabinets with a set of mush-room shaped canisters that had probably been someone's ceramics project. If it weren't for the modern appliances, she could have believed she'd walked into a museum.

Although she'd tried to keep her expression neutral, Jace must have sensed her surprise. "I know. Horrible, isn't it? But everything works, so we've never bothered to update it."

"I'd be happy to give it an overhaul if you'd give me the go-ahead," a female voice wryly offered.

As the door swung back into place, Bronte could see a woman reaching to put a baking dish into one of the upper cupboards. She was tall and voluptuous—a fact made even more apparent by the tailored snap-front blouse she wore and her tight designer jeans. Her hair was long and loose, falling down her back in a riot of curls that Bronte wouldn't be able to re-create, even with a hot curling iron and a gallon of hairspray. When she turned to face them, Bronte was struck by her prettiness, but even more by the aura of happiness that seemed to surround her like an invisible glow.

Bronte immediately felt dowdy and flat-chested. Why, in all their encounters, had she assumed that Jace was single? Clearly, if he wasn't married already, he would be soon, because this woman had an easy familiarity with his kitchen—and with Jace—that Bronte absorbed even in the fleeting seconds they'd shared the same room.

"Bronte, this is P.D. Raines—"

"Short for Prairie Dawn," she inserted.

"I was getting to that," Jace groused good-naturedly.

"Sometimes, you forget." P.D. patted his cheek as she brushed by him to hold out her hand. "I'm Elam's girlfriend."

SEVEN

E LAM'S girlfriend.

Bronte feared that her smile was too bright—too telling—because P.D.'s eyes sparked with her own brand of humor.

"It's nice to meet you."

After a firm shake, P.D. tucked her fingers into her pockets. Jace leaned against a nearby counter. Now that introductions were made, it was easy to see that the familiarity Bronte had sensed was one of friendship rather than intimacy.

"It sounds like you've had a rough welcome to the area," P.D. said.

Bronte offered a rueful sound that was meant to be a laugh, but came out far more telling than it should have done. "I'm hoping Annie gets feeling better soon."

"Have you eaten?"

"Oh, I—"

"No. She hasn't," Jace offered before Bronte could think of a suitable noncommittal reply.

"I'll warm up some dinner."

"No, I—"

"She'd love that," Jace said, interrupting her again. Pushing away from the counter, he moved to pull out a chair for Bronte, leaning close to murmur, "Go with it. It's turkey night at Vern's."

Bronte didn't have a clue what that was supposed to mean, but with Jace standing so near, his lips next to her ear, the tiny hairs on her nape seemed to jangle in delight. She couldn't think of a response, so she sat down.

It didn't take long to see that—although this might be a bachelors' stronghold—P.D. knew her way around the kitchen. Within minutes, a steaming open-faced sandwich with ciabatta bread, smoked turkey, and roasted vegetables smothered in a rich cranberry chutney was placed in front of her.

"My deconstructed Thanksgiving-leftover sandwich."

Bronte had thought that she was too keyed up to eat anything, but the rich scents rising from her plate seemed to unlock her appetite. Instantly, the heady combination of hickory-smoked turkey and chewy bread, earthy sage and citrus-kissed cranberry brought her taste buds back to life.

"Oh, wow," she mumbled around the first bite, then quickly covered her mouth at the breach of manners.

P.D. laughed. "That's the kind of response I like." She made a shooing gesture toward Bronte's plate. "Don't stop. We've all eaten, so we can hold up our end of the conversation until you're done."

And they did. While Bronte slaked her raging hunger, P.D. used the time to regale them with funny stories about the restaurant and the "kittens" that Barry had coaxed out from under the cabin deck.

"Except they weren't kittens," Jace said. He slouched in his chair, his ankle resting on his knee, one elbow propped on the table. A slow smile spread over his lips and Bronte felt as if she were struck dumb. The expression was so genuine, so wistful, so . . . *kind* . . . as he thought of his little brother.

The food seemed to lurch in her stomach. What would she give if, just once, someone appeared even half that . . . *contented* as they thought of her? Even in the first few, passionate years of her marriage, she couldn't remember Phillip ever reacting that way. He'd been more possessive, his attitude more of a "look what I'm nailing on a regular basis" kind of smirk.

In time, she'd begun to hate that expression.

"He'd found a litter of skunks wedged into a hole under one of the supports," P.D. was saying, her hands gesturing as she spoke.

But Bronte was still watching Jace, seeing the way his eyes crinkled slightly at the corners.

"I nearly had a heart attack," P.D. said, a hand flattening over her chest, "because all of the windows were open and Barry was petting the baby skunk and scratching its ears. Apparently, he couldn't figure out why the stupid cat wouldn't purr when he was being so nice to it." P.D. took a quick breath. "As calmly as I could, I told him it was time for dinner and to leave the 'kitty' and come inside. Barry reasonably informed me that it wasn't even close to dinnertime—and since he's got us all trained to his schedule, I couldn't really argue with him. I had to come up with something quick."

This time, it was Jace who laughed, a low, quiet rumble that came from somewhere in the depths of his chest.

"Which is how we got Monthly Cake Dump Day."

Bronte must have looked confused because P.D. quickly explained, "The Cake Dump is a bakery here in town."

The explanation teased a memory from Bronte's brain. "The place with the doughnuts and hot rolls?"

"That's the one," P.D. affirmed exuberantly. "He put the 'kitty' carefully back in its hole, and we hightailed it out of there before mama could come home and catch us messing with her litter."

"Leaving the third day of every month as an official Cake Dump Day."

"It's a small price to pay not to have Elam's cabin covered in skunk spray."

P.D. and Jace laughed, and as she watched the bob of his Adam's apple, the unconscious way he rubbed the bridge of his nose, those damned lines at the corner of his eyes, she was inundated with a wave of hunger that took her completely by surprise.

Suddenly, she wanted to touch him. She wanted to reassure herself that he was real. She wanted to bracket his face in her hands and look deep into his eyes. But more than anything, she wanted to kiss him.

Whoa, girl. Just because she'd severed the last ties with her husband didn't mean she had the time or the energy to rush headlong into the arms of another. That would be a big mistake. *Big* mistake. The mere thought of how complicated things could get—juggling her present worries with the emotional seesawing of a relationship that could never be anything more than temporary . . .

Her brain threatened to implode from the mere thought of the risk. Not to mention the upheaval that would soon erupt with her children when they discovered the divorce was final.

Jace.

In the past week, she'd discovered that he had his own brand of worries. He was knee-deep in spring planting and running the business end of Taggart Enterprises. From what she'd heard so far, Barry was hell on wheels, but Jace had somehow managed to deal with his brother's special needs along with everything else.

Bronte joined in the laughter, but as her gaze flicked back to Jace, she realized how much he'd sacrificed over the last few years. He must have been in his wild twenties when the accident had occurred. To be that young and assume the responsibility of a sibling, especially one who'd suffered a brain injury?

It must have changed his entire life. Suddenly, he would have been confronted with rigid schedules, occupational therapy, doctors' visits, school challenges. Judging by the lack of feminine frippery in the house, it didn't look like he'd had a wife or girlfriend to help him. Even his brothers had been limited in their ability to lessen the load. If she remembered some of their earlier conversations correctly,

Elam had been out of the country and Bodey had been little more than a teenager himself.

Bronte wondered if his brothers were even aware of how difficult the shift in lifestyles must have been for Jace. Bronte fiercely loved her daughters. She would willingly step in front of a speeding bus if that's what she had to do to protect them. Until each squirming bundle had been placed in her arms, she hadn't understood how strong and all-consuming her desire to provide for them could be.

Yet, even with all that powerful emotion bonding them together, there were still days when she was severely tempted to send them both to military school. Kari could be petulant and obstinate and downright mean when she was in a snit. And Lily. Even her darling, shy Lily could whine and moan and pitch a fit worthy of a three-year-old. And the two of them together?

Lord, save her from the constant bickering and sniping.

So if Bronte had moments like that, even after having given birth to her daughters, how much more difficult must it have been for a twentysomething young man to step in and do the same?

What did that say about the man?

Jace looked up at her, and her expression must have grown serious, because his brows rose in a silent question. But Bronte wasn't about to confess her thoughts, so she merely smiled and looked away.

It wasn't long after that when Barry burst into the room.

"Jace! Elam sent me to get you. There's another baby horse about to get born-ded."

"Ah, hell," Jace muttered, pushing himself to his feet. He rounded to the back door, grabbing a hat and a thick jacket from the rack. "Which mare, Barry?"

"The one with a flower on her nose."

"It's called a blaze, Barry."

"Why? It looks like a daisy."

Jace seemed to think about that, then he nodded. "I guess you're right. The white patch on her nose does look like a daisy."

He seemed to become aware of P.D. and Bronte. "I'll, uh . . ."

"I'll rustle up a jacket for Bronte, then we'll come down to the barn."

Bronte was about to protest that she should probably take the girls home and get them out of the way. But when a slow pleasure slipped across Jace's features, dynamite couldn't have blasted her off the Taggarts' ranch.

"See you there."

He jammed his hat over his head and hurried after Barry into the darkness on the other side of the door.

P.D. was reaching for Bronte's empty plate, but she grabbed it herself and carried it to the sink. "I can rinse this off."

"Great. I'll get a jacket for you from one of the closets," P.D. said, crossing to the swinging door.

While she waited, Bronte quickly washed her plate and utensils and placed them in the draining board by the sink. By the time she'd finished, the woman had returned.

"Here you go."

It was another of the thick canvas jackets like the one she'd seen Jace wearing. But even as she slipped her arms into the sleeves, Bronte realized that it *was* Jace's jacket. She recognized the familiar spicy scent of his cologne.

"Ready?"

"Mmm hmm."

P.D. led her out the side door and slowly headed in the direction of the huge barn about a hundred yards away from the house.

"So . . . have you and Jace known each other long?" P.D. asked with utmost casualness.

"Oh, no," Bronte interrupted quickly. "We're not . . . he hasn't . . ."

Damn. Did P.D. think they'd had a long-distance relationship of some kind?

Bronte offered a too-casual shrug of her shoulders. "Jace has stepped in to help me the last couple of days."

P.D. looked patently unconvinced.

Bronte opened her mouth to explain that she was married, but stopped herself in time. Like a bolt of lightning, the truth hit her with sizzling certainty.

She wasn't married.

She hadn't been married for a very long time. Long before the divorce had been started, long before counselors and lawyers had become involved, her relationship with Phillip had stopped being a "marriage" in any sense of the word. Although there might be those who would argue that, since she'd failed to promptly send in the last of the paperwork, she might still be harboring doubts about her decision to leave Phillip, Bronte knew there were no Freudian interpretations to be made. A flimsy piece of paper couldn't negate what she already knew deep in her heart. She and the man she'd called husband for more than fifteen years were permanently and irrevocably split. What had once been a passionate romance had withered and died.

The process of their dissolution had begun so slowly and subtly that at first she'd been able to tell herself that Phillip's inattention was simply a phase, a result from the way he spent too many hours at the clinic. But he'd begun to change, becoming a dark stranger that she didn't recognize—that she'd begun to fear—until even the memories of the man he'd once been had begun to strangle.

Her fingers lifted to the bruise on her cheek that was nearly gone. Just as her skin was returning to normal, the quieter pace in Bliss was beginning to seep into her soul like a healing balm—one she was still having difficulty believing was real. But with each passing minute, her senses grew sharper and clearer, shifting from her inner pain to the possibilities that awaited.

P.D. looked contrite. "I hope I didn't offend you."

"No. Not at all." Bronte threw her a reassuring smile.

"I guess I jumped to conclusions with both feet. It seemed like there was some . . . *zing* between the two of you."

Zing?

Bronte shied away from admitting that there was anything more than friendship with Jace. Lord, wouldn't that be a horrible mess if she jumped from one man's control straight into the arms of another strong-willed male?

Or would it?

Stop it! Just stop. If there was anything that she had learned from her relationship with Phillip, it was the value of her independence. No one would ever take that away from her.

No one.

"If you're . . . interested . . . he's available."

When Bronte looked at her, both brows raising, P.D. clapped both hands over her mouth.

"Oh, crap. Forget I said that. I must be channeling my friend Helen. Once Elam and I agreed to team up for the Wild West Games, she couldn't resist pushing us together any chance she could, knowing that if we were given enough time alone, we would spontaneously combust."

The thought that she and Jace . . . that if they were together . . . *together* together . . .

A blazing heat seeped up her neck and into her face, raging so powerfully that she thought her hair might begin to smolder at the roots. But that was nothing compared to the warmth that pooled much lower . . .

No. *No.*

She couldn't allow herself to think about Jace that way. Not when her life was already more complicated than she could ever imagine. She had the immediate worries surrounding her grandmother's recovery and all of the challenges that went with it: getting the house ready, conferring with doctors and nurses, juggling the continual trips to the hospital. Then Monday, after putting off most of the details for a week, she needed to enroll her kids in school, set up a local bank account, and begin looking for a job. Once all that had been handled, she would tackle the more far-reaching concerns that would begin to appear once her daughters began asking the inevitable questions: Where's Daddy? When are we going back to Boston? Why did you divorce him?

Why?

She still didn't know how much she should tell them. Was it better to be completely honest?

Or preserve the illusion that she had manufactured for the past few years?

P.D. jerked Bronte from her thoughts with a hand on her arm.

"Are you all right?" P.D. asked, her fingers squeezing reassuringly through the thickness of Jace's jacket.

Bronte nodded, forcibly pulling her lips into a smile even as her eyes filled with tears.

No. Not now.

But P.D. didn't even wait for a response. Instead, she pulled Bronte into a hug that smelled of lemons and spices. "Shh. You don't have to tell me anything," P.D. whispered. "You've had a rough time of it, haven't you? That's why you came to Bliss. But what you'd hoped was a haven has probably been equally challenging."

P.D. drew back and Bronte opened her mouth, ready to deny that anything was wrong—just as she'd done a million times before. But when she met P.D.'s gaze, she saw that she was sharing this experience with a kindred spirit. Somehow, somewhere, P.D. had known pain, and the woman instinctively understood, even without an explanation.

Obviously sensing that Bronte wasn't ready to share, she wrapped Bronte's arm around the crook of her elbow.

"You've come to the right place, Bronte," she murmured. "Believe it or not, you're also mixed up with the right family."

"P.D.! Bronte!" Barry dodged into the doorway of the barn. In his wake, like a shadow, was Lily. She was jumping up and down excitedly—and the sheer joy on her face took Bronte's breath away.

"Mommy, hurry! The baby horse is coming!"

They picked up their pace, but Barry and Lily weren't satisfied. They met them halfway and grabbed their hands, pulling them into the barn and down a long center aisle that was lined on either side with individual stalls. They had almost reached the end of the enormous building when the children stopped and guided them to the gate where Kari stood leaning over the top rail, filming the events with her iPod.

Inside a large horse paced nervously in the straw while

Jace and another man—Elam, she supposed—waited on the fringes, ready to step in if their help was needed.

"Elam, this is Bronte Cupacek," P.D. said. "She's come to live with Annie."

Elam was slightly shorter than Jace, his coloring darker, his body lean and muscular. Bronte could see the similarity in their bone structure, but while Elam's features were all planes and angles, Jace's were even sharper, more defined.

The horse was breathing heavily, weaving softly as if to ease its pain. When it turned, Bronte could see that the hooves of the foal had already emerged.

"We've got a new mother," Elam said, "so she's nervous."

As if sensing that the time had come for her baby to be born, the mare lowered herself onto the straw. Jace and Elam took their positions to help. Thankfully, the horse had situated itself in such a way that Lily and Barry still had a view of the events, or Bronte was sure that the two of them would have climbed into the stall.

Bronte's attention was drawn away from the impending birth to the three youngsters who watched with rapt attention. As if sensing that Lily couldn't completely see, Barry boosted her up so that she could stand on one of the rungs of the gate. Then he placed a hand at her shoulder to steady her. On the other side, Kari stepped closer, giving her sister unconscious support.

Bronte was struck by the kindnesses being exchanged—and the simple sweetness nearly brought her to her knees. The truth hit her with the suddenness of a blow to her heart. She'd been trying to shield her children from the ugliness that had been brewing in Boston, but she could see now that her efforts had been in vain. As much as she'd tried to protect them from Phillip's transition from Jekyll to an unrecognizable Hyde, as much as she'd battled to keep their home life structured and safe, as much as she'd made excuses and tried to explain that "Daddy was sick . . ."

Her children had lived through every sordid, degrading, soul-sucking experience.

Dear sweet heaven, why had she waited so long to break away?

But even as the thought drummed into her head, she knew the answer. She'd stayed until she couldn't stay any longer. She'd stayed out of guilt, duty, and loyalty. She'd stayed under the misguided hope that he would change, that he'd wake up to what he was doing to himself and to them and he would return to the man he'd once been—even though she wasn't sure if such a thing was even possible.

She'd stayed until she hadn't dared to stay any longer.

As her children watched wide-eyed as life was being created in front of them—*life*—Bronte knew that she'd made the right decision in leaving. She'd made an even better choice by deciding to stay in Bliss. Kari and Lily were her only priorities now, and she would do everything she could to make up for the darkness that had surrounded them for so long.

"Look, Mommy, *look!*" Lily cried out.

Shaken from the morass of her thoughts, Bronte stepped forward to slide her arms around Lily's waist. In the stall, she saw Jace gently pulling at the long gangly legs of the foal, while Elam stood ready to aid the delivery of the head. Then, as if eager to greet the world, the tiny horse slipped free to its tail. Jace helped to ease the rest of the foal out while Elam helped the baby to break free of the placenta.

The animal shivered, bracing its legs in front of it as it seemed to absorb the weight of its own head. Wide-eyed, it blinked at the world around it. Sensing the hard work was done, the mare rolled to her feet, staggering slightly, then turned to sniff and nudge at the miniature version of herself.

While Elam and Jace tended to the afterbirth and tidying up the stall, mother and baby got to know one another. Soon, under the encouragement of the larger animal looming over it, the foal attempted to rise on wobbly legs. Elam and Jace remained on the fringes, not wanting to interfere with the bonding process taking place in front of their very eyes. Again and again, the tiny horse tried to stand, relying on its mother's gentle encouragement, until finally, it braced its

legs in a slightly comical, wide-spread stance that Bronte
wouldn't have thought would hold it upright. But it managed
to stay there. Then, with a shake of its tail, the foal seemed
to proclaim, *Ta-da!*

When Jace and Elam headed to the gate, Bronte lifted
Lily down so the men could slip back into the main aisle of
the barn.

"What is it, Jace?" Barry asked.

"A colt," Elam said as he and his brother moved to a
utility sink near the far wall and began to wash their hands.
"You'll have to start thinking of a name, Barry."

"What about Captain Kirk?"

Elam laughed, reaching for a paper towel from a dis-
penser hooked onto the wall. After drying his hands and
throwing the towel away in a nearby bin, he slapped his little
brother on the back. "We might need to think on that. He's
a thoroughbred quarter horse, remember? So we have to
register his name."

"We could register Captain Kirk."

Elam ruffled Barry's hair. "I think it's already been taken."

Barry looked disappointed, but not for long. "I'm cold.
Can we have some hot chocolate? With marshmallows?"

Bronte quickly inserted, "I think it's time I got the girls
out of your hair."

Barry's brow puckered. "No one but Elam's been touching my hair."

"She means that it's close to bedtime and Lily needs to
get her pajamas on," Jace said as he finished washing up
and they headed back toward the door. Elam and P.D.
remained behind, leaning against the gate, talking lowly.

"She could borrow some of mine."

As she stepped outside, Bronte glanced back in time to
find Elam and P.D. locked in a passionate embrace.

Bronte felt a surge of longing rush through her body.
Dimly, she remembered what it felt like to be held, to be
kissed, but it had been so long ago, and she'd been so young.
She'd barely been out of high school when she'd met
Phillip—and maybe she'd been too naïve to handle the

challenges to follow. Phillip had been nearly twelve years her senior. He was already established as a young, hotshot orthopedic surgeon. He had money, success, and drive.

But Bronte had since learned that there were more important qualities to be found in a companion.

"Please, Jace. I'll give Emily my Hulk pajamas. Let her stay for a sleepover."

Jace laughed, squeezing his brother's shoulder. "I don't think your clothes would fit her, Barry." He looked over the top of Barry's head to regard Bronte with warm, silver-blue eyes. "But if you asked nice, I bet Bronte would let Lily and Kari stay for a cup of cocoa. After all, we've got to watch the movie Kari was making and give her a chance to post it on Facebook before she leaves the Wi-Fi signal."

Bronte opened her mouth to refuse, but when she found both of her children regarding her with hopeful expressions, she immediately melted into a big puddle of mommy indulgence.

"I could use a cup of hot chocolate myself," she said.

The children whooped and ran toward the house.

EIGHT

———◆———

JACE glanced down at Bronte, finding a curious expression on her face.

"You okay?" he asked, wondering why, more than anything, he wanted to wipe away the crease of concern that marred her brow.

She appeared dazed—as if her thoughts had been a million miles away. Then, a soft smile began in her eyes, spreading out to lift her lips.

"Yeah. Yeah, I'm good."

Somehow, he sensed there was a wealth of meaning behind her statement that he didn't understand. But then, the crease disappeared altogether.

"Actually, I think I'm great," she said softly. "Thanks."

"For what?"

Her shoulders lifted, and damned if he didn't love the way she looked in his jacket, like a little girl.

No. Not a girl.

She might be slight and slim, but there was no disguising her very womanly shape—even when it was drowned in his Carhartt.

"That was . . . beautiful. I'm glad my children were able to see it."

Their steps slowed, then stopped altogether.

Jace felt a slow satisfaction settle through his body. "It never gets old. Each birth is an occasion."

"You're a lucky man."

Jace was pretty sure she was right because the cool breeze was teasing her hair and moonlight kissed her brow, the slender length of her nose, and those lips. She had great lips, full and kissable.

What the hell.

But even as he told himself to slam on the emotional brakes, he knew it was too late. Bronte Cupacek was like no woman he'd ever met—soft, tender, sweet. But there was more to his attraction than that. Yes, his brothers would probably accuse him of being drawn to her because of her vulnerability—and maybe that was true. But he sensed that her troubles had tested her to her very core, and she'd endured it all. Because there was a quiet strength to her manner. One that intrigued him.

Unbidden, he lifted a hand, pushing back one of the dark strands of hair that had escaped the ponytail at her nape. But even after the piece had been tucked behind her ear, he continued to touch her temple, her cheek, the slim column of her neck.

"I can't stop, Bronte," he whispered, even though he suspected that she already knew.

He spread his fingers wide, cupping her cheek, his thumb brushing over her lips, once, twice.

"I keep telling myself that you're married—"

"I'm not married. The divorce was official months ago. The marriage . . . a long, long time ago. And the last of the papers were mailed earlier tonight." The words were whispered—and he sensed that something had happened in the last couple of days to make her believe them. There was no hesitancy in her tone as there had been the last time she'd spoken of her relationship with her children's father.

"Tell me if you want me to quit," Jace murmured, even as he bent down and prayed that she wouldn't.

"I don't want you to . . . quit."

She smiled and he was lost—lost in her smile, lost in the sweet scent of her hair and the velvety texture of her skin. Then his lips touched hers.

She tasted of cranberries and sunshine, her mouth soft and full. But he didn't want to frighten her off. So he sipped and tested, reveling in the way that she leaned into him, one hand bracing on his chest—right at the spot where his heart had begun to knock at his sternum.

Still framing her face with one hand, he slid the other around her waist, noting that she was still so thin, almost fragile in his arms. Parting his legs slightly, he drew her against him, wanting to pull her into the safety of his arms, wanting to wash away her worries, if only for a few moments of pleasure.

When she seemed to melt against him, he couldn't help himself. His tongue bid entrance and was immediately received. Deepening the caress, he tasted her softness, her sweetness even as her own hands swept around his waist and she hooked her fingers into the belt loops of his jeans. Then, they were straining toward one another, hard to soft, male to female.

Instinctively knowing that he had to take things slow, Jace reluctantly drew back, resting his forehead against hers as they both gasped for breath. Somehow, he'd lost his hat. But even though he was manic about keeping it off the ground, he didn't even bother to look for it. Instead, he tried to think of something to say—knowing that Bodey would have a smooth line that would be appropriate for the situation. But since he couldn't think of anything, he remained silent, absorbing the warmth of her body, watching the tic of her pulse as it fluttered against her temple.

It could have been seconds, minutes, or hours when she finally took a step back. He let her go only because he feared that if he didn't, she would flee.

"I, uh . . . I . . ."

Obviously, she couldn't think of anything to say either, and for some reason, he found the fact incredibly endearing.

Nodding toward the house, he said, "Let's get you warmed up with some hot chocolate before you head home."

He didn't mention their kiss—even though it had been a great kiss as kisses went. A part of him wanted to crow from the rooftops that they'd finally succumbed to the temptation that had simmered between them for days, but he resisted the urge.

Instead, he took her hand and laced their fingers together. Then, spying his hat in the grass, he scooped it up and planted it on his head before escorting her into the warmth of the house.

FROM his vantage point on the service road, Bodey offered a low whistle.

"So that's the way the wind blows," he murmured.

His arm was draped over Ceci Kroener's shoulder, where it had been for the last hour while they'd talked and kissed beneath a row of towering poplars.

"I wouldn't jump to any conclusions yet," Ceci said. "From what I've heard, they've known each other for over six months, and Jace has been slow to do anything but watch her three children at night."

"I see the grapevine has been hard at work," Bodey said ruefully, instantly catching the inaccuracies in her statement. Ceci, who worked at one of the local beauty shops, had her pulse squarely on the town gossip, but as usual, the stories were exaggerated with each telling.

"Even so, I wouldn't trust what you've heard. Bronte has only been in town a little over a week, she and Jace did *not* know each other beforehand, and the woman has *two* children, not three. You can't blame the man for taking things slow." He leaned down to kiss her cheek. "Remember our first weeks?"

He loved the way her cheeks flushed with color. He knew what she was thinking. Unlike most of the girls he'd dated, Ceci had played hard to get at first. She'd said he was the kind of guy who couldn't maintain a relationship for more than a month, so why should she have anything to do with him? But, even though her estimation of his staying power was completely correct, Bodey had changed her mind about indulging in a quick, passionate fling within a couple of dates. After that, they'd hooked up anytime they could.

"That was different," Ceci argued.

"In what way?"

She grimaced, admitting, "I knew the first second I saw you that I'd have a hard time keeping my hands off you."

"I *was* irresistible," Bodey drawled.

Ceci elbowed him hard enough in the stomach that his breath escaped in a comical "*oof!*"

She shot him a pithy look. "Somehow, I doubt a woman who has traveled cross-country from Boston with everything she owns in her van is in an emotional place where she would tumble headlong into a romance. And there are children involved."

"Wow. On that point, the grapevine is being more accurate than usual. Her girls seem nice enough."

"I'm not just talking about the girls."

Bodey met her gaze, realizing that Ceci was also talking about Barry. "My brother isn't that big a deal. Elam has already made it clear to Jace that Barry can live with him. If Jace wanted, Barry and I could even move to the Little House and I could take care of him."

Ceci rolled her eyes. "You couldn't keep a hamster alive, Bodey. Besides, Barry is used to Jace being in the parental role. Your baby brother loves spending time with you—he'd love living with you. But I think he would soon begin to pine for Jace if he weren't around."

"Hell, the tongues must have been wagging like crazy at the Kut 'N Kurl."

But Bodey had to concede that she was right. Bodey was Barry's buddy and Elam's role was what it had always been—that of a big brother. But Jace . . . he straddled the line between brother and parent.

"I'm still rooting for them," Bodey said, his lips against

her ear. "Jace deserves someone special in his life." He tightened his arms even more. "Someone who will tempt him the way you tempt me."

He watched a wistful smile spread over her face. One that wasn't completely happy. Then Ceci sighed and met his gaze head-on.

"Come on, Bodey. Now you're trying too hard." She offered him a crooked grin. "We both know that, for the past week, we've been slipping into 'friend' mode."

Bodey opened his mouth to insist she was wrong, that he still counted the hours until he could be with her.

But staring down into a gaze that was a mixture of compassion and regret, he realized that Jace wasn't the only Taggart who'd been discussed at the shampoo sinks.

"Ah, hell," he muttered under his breath. In an instant, his posture sagged and the arm around Ceci's shoulders became that of a brother.

Ceci patted him on the thigh. "Don't worry about it, Bodey. We had a good run—longer than most girls you've dated."

Embarrassed, Bodey rubbed at the spot between his brows. "Look, I didn't start dating you with some kind of expiration date in mind."

"I know."

"Truth be told, I'd love to have someone steady in my life. Like Elam has P.D. But I can't seem to . . . sustain a relationship."

"I know." Ceci grinned. "Cheer up. Now you can play the field again."

Yeah. Whoop-ee.

Normally, Bodey didn't let his fickleness bother him. He was still young and sowing some wild oats. But seeing Jace and Bronte kissing in the darkness had brought out all sorts of feelings of inadequacy. Bodey loved women—he loved everything about them. He simply didn't seem to have the right genes to give him some sticking power. And after Elam and P.D.'s courtship had shown him how a real relationship should work . . .

He was beginning to think that something inside of him, some emotional means of bonding with a woman, was broken.

"I think you'd better take me home," Ceci said.

Bodey opened his mouth to argue, then shut it again. Ceci was right—and Bodey owed it to her not to try to draw things out when she was clearly ready to move on.

IF Jace had thought that the rest of the evening would match the magic of his first kiss with Bronte Cupacek, he was sadly mistaken. As soon as they walked through the door, Kari looked up from her mug, caught their linked hands, and scowled.

Suddenly, it was as if a bomb of chaos detonated. Kari jumped to her feet, shouting, "Is this why we came here from Boston? So you could cheat on Daddy?"

Lily, who'd been carrying her hot cocoa from the microwave to the table, lost her grip. The mug crashed to the floor, shattering, and splattering her legs with the scalding liquid. She began to sob, piteously, huge tears rolling down her cheeks. When Barry tried to move to comfort her, she screamed, "Get away from me. Get away from me! *Get away from me!*"

Jace watched the blood drain from Bronte's face. She staggered slightly, snatching her hand away from his, and rushed toward Lily. Grabbing a dishcloth from the counter, she tried to clean up the mess, but Lily dodged away from her, running outside.

"Now look what you've done," Kari said, her voice dripping with vitriol. "You've ruined everything! We never should have come here. Never!"

She ran out of the room behind her sister, slamming the door behind her. Barry tried to follow them, but Jace caught him around the waist. "No, Barry!"

"I have to go find Emily," he sobbed, huge tears running down his cheeks. "She's sad. She needs me."

"They need their mom, Barry."

Barry turned to Bronte, and before Jace could stop him,

he said, "You're mean. Why did you make Emily cry? Why did you come here if you were going to make her cry?"

He ripped free from Jace's grip, this time running through the kitchen and into the family room.

Bronte stood gripping the dish towel, her eyes sparkling with tears. But as the swinging door slapped into place, she knelt to wipe up the spilled cocoa.

"No, Bronte. I can get that." Jace moved to pull her up, but she shook her head, carefully mopping up every drop. Then, after gathering the broken pieces of the mug in her hand, she set the cloth in the sink with more care than it deserved and threw the crockery into the garbage.

"Thank you, Jace. For taking care of my children these past few nights."

Then, before he could say anything more, she shrugged out of his jacket and walked outside, intent on finding her girls.

BRONTE lay curled in a near fetal position in her grandmother's bed. Her head pounded and her eyes were swollen and sore from crying. But worst of all, her heart ached in tandem with her children's.

What a mess. What an absolute mess. In the past few hours, she'd tried to talk to her children about the divorce, about why they'd come to Utah. She'd tried to keep things as upbeat and general as possible.

Your father and I have grown apart.

This is a fresh start for all of us.

Her explanations sounded weak and halfhearted even to Bronte. But she couldn't force herself to shatter the last of their illusions by sharing the ugliness of the whole truth.

Your father is a drug addict. He's been an addict for years. I tried to help him, but he's become irrational and violent. When he threatened your safety, I couldn't—I wouldn't—*live through one more day of fear.*

From its spot on the bedside table, her cell phone chirped, signaling that she'd received a text.

Her eyes squeezed shut and she battled against the pressure building in her chest. Trust Phillip to continue his never-ending campaign to harass her. Since she'd insisted on a formal separation several years ago, his messages followed a familiar, sickening cycle: a request for money or time with the girls or a reconciliation, followed by flattery, sharp-edged cajoling, bitter complaints, then acid recrimination, and finally threats. At first she'd read them all, blaming herself for not being kind enough, patient enough, loving enough—until he'd torn down every shred of self-respect that she'd been able to scrape together.

Early on, she'd blamed herself for not seeing the signs, for not knowing that her husband had begun to depend on the painkillers prescribed by a colleague for a knee injury, that he'd then begun to "self-medicate" with samples from his clinic, then with forged prescriptions, then whatever street drugs he could score. By the time her suspicions were finally confirmed, his medical license was in jeopardy and their home life was in turmoil. So they'd agreed he would go to rehab.

Within a few months of his return, things began to slip again, expensive items in their home disappeared as he pawned them for cash. Soon, he was missing appointments at work, or she would find him passed out on the bathroom floor. Which led to another rehab . . . and another . . . and another. Before long, Phillip's relapses were occurring within days of his return from the treatment centers, then hours.

It was at that point that Bronte had insisted on the formal separation. She needed to get her children away from the toxic environment that Phillip's addiction created—and she'd thought that the threat of losing his family would finally shock him into sobriety.

But he'd loved the promise of euphoria more than he'd ever loved any of them.

Her phone chirped again and she growled, snatching it from the table. She'd divorced him, damnit—and she didn't need to worry how her children would react to the news because they'd already made their feelings clear. They hated her for not sticking things out, for not trying harder, for dragging them halfway across the country, for—

She was about to turn the phone off when she caught sight of the number. It wasn't one she recognized, and the area code was from Utah.

Bronte hesitated before touching the notice to see the entire text.

R U OK?

The previous message was the same.
Jace.

A sound that was half laugh, half sob escaped her lips. She was ready to send back a noncommittal reply when her thumbs seemed to move of their own accord.

No.

Only seconds passed before she received a response.

Meet @ swing in ur backyard. Ten minutes.

He was coming here. If her children saw them together . . .

But at that point, Bronte didn't care. After everything that had occurred—that last bitter argument with Phillip, her headlong escape to Bliss, her grandmother's accident, the blowup with her children—she would take comfort wherever it might be offered.

Dragging a pair of jeans on beneath the oversized T-shirt she'd worn to bed, she jammed her feet into a pair of flip-flops. She checked Lily first, finding her curled in an exhausted ball, the covers bunched beneath her chin, then Kari, who was sprawled across the bed, the earbuds to her iPod firmly in place. After kissing both children, adjusting the covers, and removing the earbuds entirely, Bronte padded down the stairs, mindful of each squeak and creak of the floorboards. She hadn't heard Jace's truck yet, but she slipped outside, wincing at the low whine of the screen door.

As she headed across grass that was already wet with dew, a tall shape detached itself from the tree and she immediately recognized Jace's silhouette. Behind him, a horse snuffled in greeting before returning to lazily crop a patch of grass with its teeth.

"You're a smart man," she murmured, gesturing to his mount.

"Apparently not smart enough. I'm sorry. I should have—"

"Shh."

The need to touch him, to draw comfort from the warmth of another human being, was so overwhelming that she placed her fingers over his lips to silence him. "It doesn't matter. It really, really doesn't matter. I don't want to be told I need to feel ashamed of something that I wanted to happen."

Wordlessly, Jace drew her into his arms, tucking her head beneath his chin. Unspoken between them was the fact that they had crossed an invisible line somewhere in the last few hours. They could no longer call themselves mere friends. But Bronte also knew that was all they could ever be. Life had already grown so complicated that she couldn't add another element to the mix. Her children needed to remain her chief priority. Even if it meant denying herself this tiny shred of happiness.

Her fingers curled into his shirt, digging into the taut strength of his back. She knew that she should step away. But she couldn't remember the last time she'd been held like this. She hadn't realized how starved she'd become for simple human contact until the heat of his body seeped into hers.

Jace wrapped his arms even more tightly around her, one broad hand cradling the back of her head. She could hear the thump of his heart and the steady sound lulled her into a semblance of peace.

"What can I do to help?" Jace asked, his voice a low velvet murmur.

She shook her head against his chest. "What happened tonight was inevitable. It's my fault for not telling them right away about the divorce. I figured that I had a little more time to broach the subject."

Knowing that if she stayed where she stood, she might never allow Jace to let her go, Bronte reluctantly took a step backward. But when she would have withdrawn completely, Jace snagged her hand, lacing their fingers together and drawing her toward the glider swing under the porch awning. Brushing stray leaves and dust off the seat, he sat down, then pulled her onto the cushion beside him. He draped an arm around her shoulders, pulling her into the crook of his arm.

"Weren't you and your husband already separated?"

She grimaced. "That's probably where I made my first mistake. We had a brownstone in Boston and there was a walk-down apartment in the basement. When Phillip became . . . erratic, I insisted that he move there. Looking back, I should have insisted that he move out altogether, but . . . I thought it would be better for the girls if he were nearby."

Jace nudged at the ground with his foot, causing the swing to sway. Silence pooled around them and Bronte appreciated the way that Jace didn't push for more details. He seemed content to let her feel her way through her own emotions.

"I tried to hold things together, Jace. But there came a point where I had to say, 'Enough.' I couldn't pretend that he was the same man I'd married anymore. I couldn't allow him to hurt my children."

The swing eased to a stop and she wondered if she'd said too much. She'd heard it all before: *Stand by your man, especially in the grips of his addiction. You're his lifeline. He needs you.*

She'd done her best. She'd supported him as long as she could. She'd tried to be his wife, his friend, his mother, his conscience. She'd tried babying and tough love. She'd kept an encouraging smile on her face as they'd drained their bank accounts sending him to rehab over and over again. Even their divorce proceedings had been started in an effort to scare him into seeing that he was throwing his life away.

Through it all, she'd watched him morph into a stranger—one that frightened her. She'd been sapped of every ounce of emotional and physical strength as she worked two jobs to keep food on their table and a roof over their heads while Phillip's practice had dwindled in neglect. Eventually, each day had become an exercise in survival. She went through the moves like a zombie, dead inside. Even then, she'd willed herself to "stand by her man."

Until he'd pulled a gun and threatened to hurt their children.

She jolted when a hand touched her face. Too late, she realized that she'd sunk back into a morass of memories. But it wasn't until Jace's thumb swiped her cheek that she felt the tear slipping down it.

"What can I do to help you, Bronte?"

His voice was warm and low in the darkness. The velvety timber seemed to seep into her bones and wrap around her heart.

"I'll stay away, if you want," he whispered. "Maybe you need this time alone with your kids—"

"No." She hadn't meant the word to interrupt so forcefully, but once it had been uttered, it couldn't be taken back. Her hand closed around his wrist and she absorbed the warmth of his skin and the hard masculinity of sinew and muscle. For some reason, that concrete anchor gave her the courage to say, "No. I don't have so many friends that I can afford to throw one away."

The word *friend* tasted strange as she uttered it—because the term didn't fit as well as it should. But she shied away from using anything else, knowing that she had to keep her focus on her girls and her grandmother.

Jace pulled her toward him, kissing her lightly on the forehead. A friend's kiss—as if he'd accepted the role she'd given him. Then, he tucked her beneath his chin, his arms surrounding her and warding off the spring chill. Touching his toe to the ground, he set the swing in motion.

Bronte closed her eyes, knowing that she wanted to hold on to this moment for as long as it lasted. The warmth of

Jace's body seeped into hers like a balm, easing the stiffness of muscles held too tightly in check for a cross-country journey, and longer. It was as if her body had been clenched in brittle readiness for flight long before her mind had been willing to acknowledge the need.

Beneath her ear, she heard the *thump, thump* of Jace's heart, the soft sough of his breath. He smelled subtly of soap and man and leather. With each nudge of his boot, she breathed out the remnants of her tension and breathed in Jace, until she couldn't determine where she ended and he began.

Don't do this. Don't allow yourself to feel anything too intimate. Don't do anything that could jeopardize what you already have.

But as her eyes began to drift and her limbs grew heavy . . .

Bronte knew it was already too late.

NINE

———✦———

JACE knew when Bronte surrendered to sleep. She burrowed closer to him, and then, in an instant, her body became boneless in his arms.

He supposed that he should wake her and urge her to go inside. It was getting cold and her arms and feet were bare. But he couldn't bring himself to disturb her yet.

She was so beautiful, especially in sleep. Her guard was dropped and her vulnerability was clear. Although she'd only hinted at the troubles that had driven her to Utah, he could see the evidence of her struggles in the dark circles beneath her eyes, the jut of her cheekbones. With only the porch light as illumination, she was a study in angles—and he'd bet it had been some time since she'd had regular meals. He could imagine that her circumstances had made eating anything at all a chore. But none of that detracted from the velvety softness of her skin, the fullness of her lips, and the incongruous splash of freckles across the bridge of her nose.

Jace threaded his fingers through her hair. It was longer than he'd first supposed. She usually wore it in a ponytail or twisted at the back of her head. But tonight, it hung in long wavy strands that twined around his fingers like a silk waterfall.

If she was this beautiful now, with worry and tension creasing her brow, how much more lovely would she be once she realized that she didn't have to look over her shoulder anymore?

A surge of possessiveness shot through him. More than anything, he wanted to see that metamorphosis. He wanted to see the haunted light fade from her gaze.

But even as his protective instincts raged through his body, he realized that he had no right to feel that way. Bronte had made it clear that she wanted nothing more than friendship from him.

Much as he might want to argue, he knew she was right. She had enough on her plate without adding a relationship to the mix. And her children had made their position on such a possibility crystal clear.

Hell, the last thing *he* needed was a woman in his life. He had a ranch to run, his brothers to oversee—and he wasn't on Barry's list of favorite people either. If Jace didn't get out of here soon, away from the pressures that had been piling on top of him for far too long, he was going to crack.

So he would have to keep things casual with Bronte.

Knowing that he couldn't keep Bronte out in the cold for much longer, Jace ran a finger over her cheek, her jaw, then very slowly across her bottom lip.

Friends.

He'd focus on what had to be done: planting, the mares about to give birth, doing the books, taking care of Barry.

Friends.

He could keep his eye on her by continuing to drop by for breakfasts or bringing his brother to play with Lily. He could invite them to the Big House for Sunday dinner or horseback riding. Surely, with the promise of Wi-Fi and the animals, he could get back on the good side of her girls. Especially if he kept things between himself and Bronte completely platonic.

Friends.

Good friends.

He bent to give her one last kiss on the top of her head. Then, knowing he was risking World War III, he maneuvered so that he could stand, then scooped Bronte up into his arms. Judging by the circles under her eyes, she hadn't been sleeping well—and he wasn't about to wake her. So he would have to carry her into the house and tuck her into bed—hopefully, without waking her daughters.

Really, really good friends.

Bronte seemed to burrow into him, wrapping her arms around his neck. He thought she was rousing, but mumbling something under her breath, she sank back into sleep.

Carefully, he crossed the yard, wincing at the squeak of the screen door. But then he was moving silently through the kitchen. Once on the staircase, he kept to the sides of the treads to avoid most of the creaks and groans of an old house, then he slowly made his way down the hall to Annie's room. Lifting one finger, he pushed the door open, clenching his jaw when it swung wide on noisy hinges.

He wasn't really sure where Bronte was sleeping, but a quick glance around the room let him know that there were no children present. The rumpled bed and yawning suitcases seemed to point to Bronte having made this her temporary resting spot.

Moving forward, he lay Bronte on the bed, then, much as he did with Barry each night, he made sure she was covered by the blankets. She probably wouldn't be too comfortable spending the night in her jeans, but he knew that he would definitely stray across the "buddy" line if he tried to take them off her.

Besides, the sight of those long legs bare and kissed by moonlight would probably be his undoing.

So he stood there for one last minute, risking exposure, but unable to move away. A rush of emotions thundered through him—tenderness, impatience, attraction, possessiveness—becoming muddied together with an insurmountable need to break free of the constant *sameness* of the ranch, his brother's care, and the shackles of his responsibilities.

Dear God, was this it? Was this how the rest of his life was supposed to be?

Or could there be more?

Ashamed and overwhelmed, Jace turned away. As quickly as he dared, he hurried from Annie's house, rushed through the dewy grass, and threw himself into his horse's saddle. Then, after guiding the horse a fair distance away, he spurred it into a gallop, needing the thunder of hooves and the wind tearing at his clothes to drive away the needs that could never be fulfilled.

ELAM stood leaning against the deck railing outside his bedroom, waiting for P.D. to finish with her shower. A warm cup of decaf was cradled between his palms, but it wasn't the night or the full planter's moon on the horizon that captured his attention. From his vantage point high on the hillside, he could see most of Bliss below him. Yet, it was the horse and rider streaking across the pasture that he tracked.

"Damn fool is going to break his neck," he muttered to himself.

But it wasn't the dangerous gallop in the darkness that concerned Elam most.

Until P.D. had stormed into his life, Elam had been so wrapped up in his own misery that he hadn't paid much attention to what was going on around him. But since meeting Prairie Dawn, he'd returned to the world of the living with a bang—and in doing so, he'd become uncomfortably aware of how many of the responsibilities had fallen onto Jace's shoulders.

"What's going on?"

P.D. slipped her arms around his waist and pressed tightly against him from behind. It wasn't lost on him that P.D. was wearing the silky robe that he'd proclaimed was his favorite . . . and nothing else.

He gestured to the valley below and the horse tearing into the main yard of the Big House.

"He's going to break his neck," P.D. remarked, echoing Elam's words. "Where's he been?"

Elam gestured toward the trees that obscured Annie Ellis's house.

P.D. laughed. A low velvety laugh that would have tightened Elam's body if it weren't already reacting from the pressure of her breasts against his back. "They might try to fight it, but there's . . . zing between them."

"P.D.," he drawled in warning. Since the two of them had linked up, P.D. had caught the "love bug" and seemed intent on matching up the rest of her friends two by two. "Leave him alone."

"Whatever do you mean?" she asked innocently.

Elam scowled, watching as Jace brought the mount to a skidding halt under the bright light over the barn. For several minutes, his brother seemed frozen in place, then he dismounted with a weariness that Elam wouldn't have thought possible from such a young man.

"Don't interfere."

P.D.'s fingers were straying toward the buttons of his shirt. "I don't know what you're talking about."

Her gentle foray down his chest was playing havoc with his thoughts, so he grabbed her hand and pulled her around into his arms.

"Don't push the two of them together."

She stood on tiptoe to press a kiss to his jaw. "Don't you think Jace needs someone in his life?"

Elam's heart was thudding into second gear, then third, but he forced himself to pull away. "Please. Leave him alone."

P.D.'s brows creased in confusion when she realized that Elam's warning held a more serious edge than he'd intended. "Elam?"

Elam's jaw clenched as he tried to put his gut feelings into words. There wasn't anything tangible that he could use as a defense. Outwardly, Jace was the same as he always was. He handled everything with methodical ease—the planting, Barry, the business end of Taggart Enterprises. He even kept Bodey in line, which was tantamount to a miracle.

But . . .

Elam sensed that something was going on underneath it all. There was a tension to Jace's voice, a brittleness to his posture.

Elam waited, absorbing the warmth of P.D.'s embrace until his brother emerged from the barn and strode toward the house, his head down, shoulders hunched, arms bent and held slightly away from his body as if he expected a fight. In that instant, Elam knew what it was about his brother's manner lately that was so concerning. Elam had seen Jace acting this way once before.

"He's about to go renegade again," Elam muttered, watching as Jace disappeared into the house.

"What?" Sensing Elam's concern, P.D. twisted to follow his line of sight. "What do you mean: 'He's about to go renegade'?"

Elam held his breath, watching a trail of lights turning on and off as Jace made his way through the house. Family room, staircase, upper hall. Elam waited for the lights to lead toward the attic, praying for the light in the attic. Heaven only knew that the time had come for Jace to reconcile himself with the past.

"Jace has always been different from the rest of us Taggart males. Sure, he's got his fair share of testosterone, but there's a sensitive side to him as well. While Bodey and I were kicking cans and breaking windows, Jace . . . well, Jace was tending to wounded animals or bringing home the new kid who had no friends. When we got older, Bodey and I both joined the high school's football and rodeo teams—as did Jace. But I don't think they were the live and die activities that they were to Bodey and me. I think, for Jace, they were just something to do. Instead, he liked to draw and sculpt. And he was pretty damned good.

"Looking back on it now, I think we all thought it was just a hobby. None of us really took it too seriously. When he insisted that he had no interest in going to college or working on the ranch because he wanted to be an artist, we thought he was kidding."

"Really?" P.D. was genuinely surprised. "Didn't you tell me that Jace has an advanced degree in business? I can't imagine him doing anything else." She burrowed closer. "He doesn't seem unhappy now."

Elam shook his head. "It's not something I can point to, it's . . ." He looked down at P.D., marveling again at how this woman, this incredible human being, had thrown him a lifeline when he was about to go under. If it weren't for her, he would still be stomping around mad at the world—or worse.

But Jace . . .

His was a different kind of pain.

"A few years before my parents' accident, he started acting . . . I don't know. Itchy, discontented. Like the world was pressing down on him with such force, that if he didn't break away from it all, he'd crack. Jace was about eighteen, nineteen, when he got this way before. My dad was bound and determined that—since I was in the military and away so much—he needed to train Jace to take over Taggart Enterprises. I know what Dad was thinking. This ranch has been in the family for generations and he didn't want another son to opt out of seeing to its success." Elam felt a flash of guilt, knowing that he was partially to blame for his father's worries.

He pulled P.D. even more tightly against him. "Anyway, Dad was openly antagonistic about Jace's own goals for the future. Crazy as it sounds, he thought Jace was . . . soft and needed toughening up. He was sure that a few years of hard work and added responsibilities on the ranch would show Jace how fulfilling the job could be. At first, it seemed like a good fit. Jace agreed to give it a try and he caught on quick—even Dad was impressed. He started taking classes in business and accounting at Utah State and handling more of the business aspects of Taggart Enterprises."

Elam held his breath, waiting—praying—for the attic light to turn on.

"So . . ."

The hall light had been blazing for some time, as if Jace stood there, undecided.

Elam looked down at P.D., seeing that he'd passed his concern to her.

"Then he started to get tense. Restless. Short-tempered. Until, one afternoon, when my father criticized something Jace had done. I don't even remember now what Bodey said it was—something nitpicky like the way he'd stacked bales in the yard. From what Bodey told me, Jace exploded. He and my dad got into a rip-roaring, raise-the-roof argument. Then Jace stormed out of my dad's office, strode up to his room in the attic, gathered some of his things in a backpack, and left—no word, no explanation, no contact."

"For how long?"

Elam took a breath and admitted, "Until we finally got ahold of him in Germany a week after our parents' and little sister's deaths—it took a private detective to find him. By that time, he'd been gone over two years. Since then . . . he hasn't said a word to anyone about where he was or what he was doing all that time. He won't talk about it."

Now it was P.D.'s turn to look concerned. "You think he's contemplating taking off again?"

Elam nodded. "Jace has always had a long fuse. But something's building up in him—like a powder keg stuffed beyond its capacity. If something doesn't happen soon to relieve the pressure . . ." Elam rested his chin on P.D.'s head, watching, waiting as the hall light continued to stay on for an awfully long time. Then, the entire house went dark.

Damn.

"Elam?"

He glanced down, realizing he hadn't finished his thought. P.D.'s eyes gleamed up at him with concern.

"If we can't help him find a way to release his stress, it's only a matter of time before he explodes. Either that, or he may disappear again. If so, this time, we'll never be able to find him."

JACE'S phone began ringing at seven the next morning, only a few hours after he'd finally been able to fall asleep.

By the fifth or sixth caller, it was clear that the town grapevine had been hard at work again, passing on updates about Annie's condition, the arrival of her relatives from back east, and the plan to ready Annie's house for her return. Judging by the messages he'd been fielding, the community felt that—even though Bronte had only been in Bliss a week—they'd waited long enough for her and her family to settle in. Now, they were gathering together to offer their help.

At first, Jace tried to head off the efforts at the pass, sensing that today, of all days, Bronte didn't need a herd of well-wishers arriving on her doorstep ready to help fix up her grandmother's house. But after a few dozen telephone exchanges, it became clear that God Himself wouldn't be able to stop the volunteer brigade gathering in the wings. Furthermore, as he answered his cell to discover that a cement truck would be at the Ellis residence at eleven sharp, he realized he didn't want to bring a halt to the wave of volunteers coming her way. Bronte needed to know she wasn't in this alone.

And he needed to see Bronte.

It didn't seem to matter that he'd spent the night convincing himself that they should put some distance between them. Nor was he particularly put off by the thought of encountering her kids again. She was becoming a drug to him, and he needed a fix. What better way to assure her children that they were merely friends than by surrounding them with as many chaperones as possible? He would play his role to the hilt and show Lily and Kari that he didn't have designs on their mother.

Yeah, right.

By the time he'd showered and dressed in his oldest work clothes, he'd convinced himself that things would be fine. He simply had to play it cool.

But as soon as he clattered down the stairs and went in search of Barry, he was confronted with the stark reality of the situation.

Barry sat at the kitchen table glowering at a bowl filled with more marshmallow surprises than Lucky Charms. Judging by the cereal scattered all over the wooden surface in front of him, Barry had upended the box to find all of his favorite treats.

"I thought we had a deal. No sugar cereal except on Saturdays."

Barry didn't even look at him. He stabbed at the milk-soaked bits of marshmallow as if he were planning to harpoon a whale beneath the surface.

"It *is* Saturday."

Shit.

"I thought we'd also agreed that I would do the pouring."

"I'm not a baby, Jace," Barry said, his voice deepening with resentment. "Sometimes, you treat me like a baby."

Damn. This wasn't how Jace wanted to start his day. But since there would be no peace until Barry had spoken his mind, Jace poured himself some coffee and sat down opposite his brother.

"I don't mean to treat you like a baby, Barry. I want you to be safe and happy."

Barry looked up, peering at Jace through his too-long hair. A part of Jace realized he needed to get his brother into the barber for a trim even as the rest of him registered the anger being thrown his way.

"That's a lie, Jace. If you wanted me to be happy, you wouldn't have chased away my bestest friend."

Aw, hell.

"Barry, I didn't chase Lily away. That's the last thing in the world I wanted to do."

"Then why did you make everybody mad? What did you do?"

Jace sighed, rubbing a hand on the muscles tightening at the back of his neck. How on earth was he going to explain the situation with Bronte and her family when he didn't understand all of the elements himself?

In the end, he decided that there was no other option than to tell the truth.

"Lily and Kari noticed that Bronte and I were holding hands."

"Is that bad?" Barry asked, his brow knotted in confusion.

"No, that's not bad. But Lily and Kari are used to seeing Bronte holding their daddy's hand, so it upset them. They didn't know yet that Bronte and their daddy were divorced." When Barry continued to blink at him wide eyed, Jace asked, "Do you know what divorced means?"

Barry nodded. "It's when your daddy doesn't live at your house anymore and you only see him during the summer, like Scott's daddy."

Scott's parents had divorced more than three years ago, but to Barry, the event was still fresh.

"That's right."

"Why didn't they know?"

Jace sighed. "I think Bronte wanted to tell them when they got to Bliss."

Thankfully, Barry seemed to accept that limited answer.

"So why is Lily mad at me? I didn't hold hands with Bronte."

Jace felt his heart twist at Barry's earnest expression.

"Aw, Barry. She's not mad at you. You know how things happen sometimes, grown-up stuff, and you feel left out and confused. That's what happened to Lily. As soon as you see her again, you'll find out that she still wants be your friend."

Barry pushed away his cereal. "I need to go to Lily's house," he announced, jumping to his feet. He was halfway to the door before Jace managed to bolt from his own chair and catch him.

But for the first time, Barry wrenched free—using such force that Jace wasn't able to hang on.

"Don't you stop me, Jace! I need to make sure she's not sad anymore."

Jace held his hands out in a calming gesture, realizing that his days of forcing Barry to do anything were swiftly coming to an end.

"I'm not going to stop you, Barry. There's a whole group of people heading to Annie's place to help clean out flowerbeds and fix up the house. I came down here to invite you to come along. If you want to go now, that's fine." He pointed to Barry's pajama-clad figure. Barry was well on his way to being over six feet tall, like his brothers. Yet, somehow, P.D. had managed to find Barry a pair of Spider-Man footsie pajamas with room to spare. "I thought you might want to put on some work clothes first."

He offered his brother the choice: Go now, or change. Jace knew there would be plenty of times when Barry wouldn't be allowed to make his own decisions, when someone else would have to step in and make them for him. But for now, in this instance, Barry needed the freedom of making up his own mind.

Barry seemed poised on the balls of his feet, ready to bolt. But at the last minute he turned and raced toward the swinging door.

"I'll be down in a minute, Jace. Wait for me."

Wait for me.

As his brother thundered upstairs, Jace felt as if a huge fist had reached in, grabbed his heart, and twisted.

Wait for me.

Wait for me to grow up.

Wait for me to become a man.

The hand in his chest squeezed tighter, nearly blocking off his windpipe. This was why Jace stayed, why he fought to stay sane as each day mirrored the next, and the next, and the one after that.

Because one day, Barry would be a man. Outwardly, he would be tall and strong and physically fit.

But he would always be a little boy.

And Jace needed to be there to help pick up the pieces whenever the two disparate realities crashed headlong into one another.

Which was why he couldn't even consider getting closer to Bronte—or any other woman like her. There wasn't a female alive who would want to tie herself to such a permanent responsibility. Unlike other children, Barry wouldn't be growing up, going to college, beginning his own family. Yes, there would be opportunities for him, of that Jace was sure. Barry had already conquered many of the obstacles that doctors had insisted he would never overcome. If he continued to progress, there might be chances for jobs or group homes in his future—if he didn't decide he wanted to stay and work on the ranch. But Jace and his brothers would always need to be there to serve as his safety net.

Judging by the past couple of women Jace had dated, that wasn't a commitment that most women were willing to make. They wanted a man who would make them the center of their universe. They wanted their own homes, their own children, their own responsibilities. When the time came, they wanted to boot those baby birds out of the nest and spend their golden years free of the burdens of a child with special needs.

Special needs. Sometimes Jace hated that term. Barry didn't have *special* needs. He had the same needs as anyone else. Love, security, and opportunities. Jace would see that he got them. Even if it meant sacrificing a few of his own goals.

So he should stay away from Bronte. She already had a boatload of her own responsibilities. There was no way in hell that she would want one more added stress. Jace would keep things cool, friendly. *Neighborly.*

And try his damnedest to forget how good she'd felt in his arms.

TEN

— • —

"WHY are you sleeping in your clothes?"
   The question seemed to come from far away. Bronte stirred, feeling as if she were being cradled by a thick cloud. She was warm here. Safe. Oh so relaxed.

"Mom!"

Bronte jumped, her well-being scattering. Blinking her eyes open, she faced the light streaming through the window of her grandmother's room. The softness that surrounded her was the thick featherbed and eiderdown duvet that she'd pulled under her chin.

"Why . . . are . . . you . . . sleeping . . . in . . . your . . . clothes?"

Kari was speaking to Bronte as if her mother were a two-year-old, but for the life of her, Bronte had no idea what she was talking about.

Glancing down, she saw her arms draped in a T-shirt, then became aware of the rough fabric of her jeans. At the end of the bed, one foot, still clad in a flip-flop, peeked from under the covers.

How on earth?

Then, in a rush, Bronte remembered slipping out of the house to meet Jace, sitting with him on the glider. Heat seeped up her neck and into her cheeks when she recalled being held so tenderly . . . and then nothing.

Great. She'd fallen asleep. Probably with her mouth hanging open.

Then what . . .

Too late, she realized that Jace must have carried her into the house, up the stairs, past the room the children were using, and set her on the bed.

Wondering how much Kari knew, Bronte pushed the hair out of her face and asked instead, "What time is it?"

Thankfully, Kari's attention was distracted by something on her iPod. She scowled at the screen and mumbled, "Ten thirty. Eleven."

"*What?*" Bronte threw back the covers and rolled to look at the bedside clock, sure that Kari was exaggerating, but the huge red numbers read 10:57. At about the same time, she became aware of voices and pounding from outside, the whine of an engine. "What's going on?"

She scrambled to the window, pulling aside the curtain.

"There are some people here," Kari answered vaguely.

Not just "some" people. When she looked below her, the yard was filled with vehicles of every description, piles of lumber and sacks of cement. There had to be fifty individuals swarming over the area like ants on an anthill, each of them bent on their own particular task—weeding, shoveling, hauling lumber.

"How long have they been here?"

"About an hour."

Bronte's mouth dropped. She couldn't help it. She could only stare at her daughter like some cartoon character whose chin rested on the floor.

"Who are they? Why didn't you come get me?"

Kari shrugged, still regarding her iPod.

Tested to the very limits of her endurance, Bronte snatched the device out of Kari's hand.

"Hey!" Kari protested.

"Why didn't you wake me up?"

Kari thrust her chin out. "Because most of them came at the same time as that Jace guy. Why don't you tell him to leave us alone? Why does he have to keep poking his nose in our business?"

Although Kari's tone was belligerent, a sheen of moisture warned Bronte that her rudeness was merely a shield to much more vulnerable emotions. So when Kari snatched her iPod from Bronte's hand and stomped out of the room, Bronte didn't bother to call her back. Coward that she was, she would avoid that battle for now.

The shrill *beep, beep, beep* of a utility vehicle being put into reverse sent her to the window again just in time to see a cement truck easing toward the house.

Now what?

She might have stood rooted to the floor in confusion for some time if a familiar, lanky figure hadn't moved toward the house. She instantly recognized the cowboy hat that had been jammed down over his brow, but this time, instead of a button-down shirt, he wore a T-shirt that was faded and spattered with several colors of paint. His jeans were similarly worn, with patches of denim that were beginning to wear out at his knees and along the hem. They had obviously been a favorite pair at one time because the fabric coated his legs and thighs like faded indigo ink. When he turned to gesture to the driver of the truck, Bronte couldn't help noticing that one of the rear pockets was coming loose at the corner—which drew her attention to the man's butt.

He really did have a fine butt.

As if he sensed her regard, Jace turned and looked up at the house. When he saw her, he waved a hand sheathed in a leather work glove.

Bronte offered him a weak salute in return, hoping that he hadn't known how intensely she'd been ogling him. Then, when he turned to the driver again, she reared back, her hands flying up to her head.

Crap! She'd forgotten that she'd spent most of the night burrowed under the covers. Her eyes flew to the mirror, confirming her worst fears. *Bedhead* didn't even begin to describe the riot of tangled waves.

Groaning to herself, she dodged into the bathroom and beat her own record for the shortest shower of all time. Armed with plenty of conditioner, she used a wide-tooth comb to coax the snarls out of her hair. Then, after a quick rinse, she twisted the long strands into a smooth braid.

After drying off with one of her grandmother's threadbare towels, she spent precious minutes putting on her makeup before racing back into the bedroom. A squeal of disappointment leaked free when she realized that she desperately needed to do some laundry. But after digging to the bottom of her bag, she was able to come up with a lacy embroidered shirt and a pair of sky blue linen pants. She'd be a tad overdressed for whatever was going on downstairs, but it would have to do. So far, she'd stopped at the local grocery store for the basics, but she hadn't topped off Annie's meager supply of laundry soap and softener.

That thought made Bronte groan again when she realized she had a yard full of people and—except for staples—her grandmother's cupboards were nearly bare. As she slid her feet into flats and hurried down the stairs, Bronte prayed that she had enough flour, sugar, and eggs to at least whip up a batch of cookies.

But as she rounded the corner into the kitchen, she saw P.D. unloading groceries from the mound of sacks piled on the table.

"I hope you don't mind that we made ourselves at home," P.D. said.

Bronte could only shake her head in confusion.

P.D. grimaced. "After last night . . . well, I figured you were running on fumes, so I wouldn't let anyone go into your bedroom. I insisted everyone tippy-toe around, especially if they came into the house. But then the damned cement truck showed up. I hope it didn't wake you."

"No. I was already up." Bronte didn't add that it was Kari's insistent questions that had dragged her to consciousness.

Bronte moved to the back door and peered through the window. "What's going on?"

P.D. grinned. "The grapevine has been hard at work."

Bronte's brows creased in confusion.

"Annie's been a part of this community as long as anyone can remember—she taught half the people out there," P.D. said, gesturing with a bunch of celery. "As soon as folks heard about her accident, they wanted to find some way to help. Thank heavens, someone managed to channel their energy into something productive."

Bronte felt her stomach twist into knots. When she'd shown Jace the list of improvements that she'd hoped to make, she hadn't planned on doing them all right away. She had less than two hundred dollars left in her wallet—and that would have to last until she could come up with a job. The trips to the hospital in Logan would probably eat most of it up in fuel.

Some of her unease must have shown because P.D. touched her arm. "Hey, you don't need to worry about any of this. Bliss has a habit of pulling together and volunteering their time and a few odd supplies when someone needs it. Last year, there was a fire in my restaurant and when I first saw all the damage, I was sure it would take months to re-build. But the next day, there were dozens of volunteers helping to remove the debris and scrub the place from top to bottom. They did in a day what would have taken weeks—and probably more than I could have afforded—to get things started." P.D. offered her an encouraging smile.

"But all of these supplies—"

"The lumber came from surplus piles in countless barns in the community. The shingles are left over from those used to replace the damaged roof at Vern's."

"But the cement—"

"Donated by Enid Wilkerson, matriarch of the Wilkerson family and CEO of Wilkerson Cement. She and Annie are part of a quilting group that meets at the Civic Center every Wednesday."

"So what can I do to help?"

"My friend Helen and her husband Syd have already got their famous Dutch ovens cooking outside, but I thought we could throw together a couple of salads." P.D. frowned. "A lot of boys showed up with the Scout groups, and I don't know if the bread I brought and Helen's cherry chocolate cake will spread far enough, so maybe I should send someone to the store for more rolls and some cookies."

"No!" Bronte said hurriedly. She rushed to the fridge, opening it to find cartons of eggs, milk, and orange juice had been pushed to one side on the top shelf. "Let me do that. How long before lunch is served?"

"Probably an hour, an hour and a half?"

"Perfect."

As she pulled ingredients from the cupboard and began arranging them on the counter, Bronte felt more in control of her circumstances than she had since arriving at Bliss. She might not be able to hammer nails or drive a backhoe, but she could supply bread and dessert—and she could do it with her eyes closed.

After uncovering her grandmother's mixer, she began measuring flour and sugar into a stoneware bowl. Bronte would be the first to admit that she was far from being the expert in the kitchen that P.D. was, but she'd always loved to bake—probably due to summers spent in this very kitchen learning how to make cookies, doughnuts, and cake. None of Annie's recipes were complicated. But they were down-home favorites that were as satisfying to the soul as to the taste buds.

Within twenty minutes, she had mixed up a sweet biscuit dough, rolled it out on the table, and spread butter and a thin glaze made of powdered sugar, orange juice, and grated orange zest in the middle. Then she rolled it into a log and cut slices, which she placed in several greased pans. After placing dish towels over the biscuits until it was time to bake them, she washed out the mixing bowl and paddle and began making oatmeal raisin cookies from another recipe she knew by heart.

P.D. had long ago finished unloading the groceries and

was making piles of chopped purple onions, olives, and marinated vegetables for a pasta salad. A huge pot on the back of the stove was bubbling away, churning multicolored rotini in a fragrant roiling tide while the timer marked the last few minutes of cooking time.

"You know your way around the kitchen," P.D. said.

Bronte shook her head. "Nothing even close to what you do. But I've mastered some of the baking that Annie taught me as a kid." She allowed herself a self-satisfied grin. "I paid for part of my first year of college by selling cookies in the student union building."

"What was your major?"

Bronte felt her smile falter. She'd wanted to teach English literature and write poetry. But after only a year of school, she'd married Phillip. He'd insisted there was no need for her to continue her education since he would support her for the rest of her life. For a while, she'd continued to fill journals with scrawled lines of blank verse—but even that had fallen by the wayside when life intruded.

"English and secondary education. But . . . I-I didn't finish."

P.D. nodded matter-of-factly. "So when are you going back?"

Bronte eyed her in surprise, a teaspoon filled with warm, fragrant cinnamon suspended over the mixing bowl.

"What do you mean?"

P.D. set down the knife and propped her hips against the counter. "It's obvious that you regret not having a chance to finish. Why don't you go back now? There are several excellent universities within commuting distance from here."

Excitement spilled into Bronte's veins, building up steam until it thundered through her body. But just as suddenly, reality doused it with an icy wave. Turning back to the mixer, she blindly dumped the cinnamon into the bowl, her mind frantically trying to remember if she'd added one teaspoon or two.

"There's no way I could go back right now."

The buzzer went off and P.D. punched it into silence, then

lifted the heavy pot from the stove and carefully dumped the water and pasta into a waiting colander.

"Why not? I bet you could qualify for a scholarship. You're a single mother looking to finish your education. There's got to be financial aid available."

Again, Bronte was tempted by a spurt of adrenaline, but she firmly pushed it away. "Maybe in a year or two." Why did the words taste more like *never* in her mouth. "Right now, things are too . . . unsettled. Too . . ."

She didn't even know how to finish the sentence. How could she plan something as definitive as an education when she didn't know how she was going to pay for the next round of groceries?

Turning the mixer on high—and hoping it masked the note of disappointment in her voice, she said, "Right now, I've got to get my kids in school, find a job . . ."

P.D. nodded. "About that. I might have an idea, if you're interested."

But before she could say anything more, the door to the kitchen opened and Kari stomped inside.

"That man sent me to get you," she said, her arms tightly crossed, her expression thunderous.

"What man?"

"Jace. He needs you outside."

Before Bronte could ask any more questions, she stormed through the door again.

Embarrassed by her daughter's behavior, she turned to offer an apology to P.D., but P.D. was laughing. "You've got your hands full," she murmured, then gestured to the pans. "The oven's hot. Do you want me to put these in while you see what Jace needs?"

"Yeah. Thanks."

"How long do they need to cook?"

"Twenty minutes."

Bronte hadn't realized how steamy the kitchen had grown until she stepped outside. A balmy breeze buffeted the grass and teased at the strands of the willow tree. The air was warm, hinting at the hot, dry summer that was around the corner.

Bronte paused on the stoop, automatically searching for her daughters. Kari—whose bad mood clearly extended only to Bronte—was standing next to several teenagers near the old barn. She was twisting and untwisting a lock of hair around her finger while she peered under her lashes at Tyson, Jace's hired man. Something he said made her laugh. The kid must have had superpowers, because when he held out a shovel, Kari took it. Then, still laughing, she began using it to pry hunks of weed-choked sod out of the flower bed.

Will wonders never cease?

It took a little longer to find Lily, but finally, Bronte saw her huddled in the corner of the tree house, her chin on her knees.

"Do you want to come down and help, Lily?" Bronte said, her hand shading her eyes.

Lily shook her head, her gaze darting over the crowd below.

More than anything, Bronte wanted to rush to her daughter's side and encourage her to mingle, but the rigid line of her back was a sure sign that now wasn't the time. Once again, Lily had shyly crawled back into her shell. Even Barry, dressed in his Scouting regalia, couldn't seem to tempt her to join him on the grass. So he scrambled up the ladder, sitting next to her.

Bronte's enthusiasm drained from her, leaving her limbs clumsy and heavy as she descended the rickety steps and circled the house. What must Lily be thinking? That Bronte had invited all these strangers to the house? Too late, Bronte realized that most of the workers were men. To be surrounded by a sea of people she didn't know—especially those of the opposite sex—must be overwhelming to her. But thankfully, Barry seemed to know what to say because Bronte saw her daughter's lips tip in a shy smile. Maybe she needed a friend right now, rather than a mother.

Sighing, Bronte rounded the house, then came to a standstill. She'd guessed that the cement truck had been brought in to replace the front steps, but what she hadn't foreseen was the complete overhaul that was being made.

The entire front porch had been removed, the roof above supported by a network of two-by-fours temporarily nailed to the wall and stakes pounded into the ground. Everything else had been dismantled to make way for a much wider staircase, a sitting area, and a wheelchair ramp. Even as she watched, a thick stream of concrete was being pumped into molds made of plywood and two-by-fours.

Jace was carefully overseeing the process while Elam and a younger, more mischievous version of Jace smoothed it into place with shovels. Was that Brodey . . . no, Bodey?

Jace must have sensed her regard because he turned, then grinned at her. And that smile—that damned, no-holds-barred smile—caused a stampede of butterflies to take wing in her stomach. Sinking his shovel into a pile of concrete, he walked toward her, sweeping the hat from his head and wiping at the moisture beading his brow before replacing it again.

"Hey, there."

Her knees grew weak at the warmth of his tone. There was something . . . intimate about his greeting. As if the two of them shared a secret that no one around them would ever know.

What had she done after she'd fallen asleep?

"Hi."

"Did you sleep well?"

She nervously folded her arms, one hand casually straying toward her hair to make sure that it hadn't escaped from the braid.

"Yeah. Yeah, I did. Thanks."

He was looking at her closely, his eyes rich with warmth and a spark of something more. Bronte braced herself, sure that he was about to let her know how much she'd embarrassed herself by falling asleep and then . . . what? Had she snored? Drooled?

Dear sweet heaven above, she hadn't grabbed him, had she?

"What do you think?"

It took her a second to realize he wasn't referring to last night at all, but to the new stoop.

"You really shouldn't have, Jace—"

"You don't like it?"

"No. Yes!" She gazed at the project and could already envision what it would look like finished. Not only would it be safer for Annie to negotiate, but there would be room for chairs and a table so that her grandmother could come outside and enjoy the sunshine. "I think it's . . . fantastic! I just . . ." She bit her lip and said truthfully, "I don't know how I'm ever going to repay everyone for all they've done."

Jace laughed. "You don't have to do a thing, Bronte. Folks have been wanting to help Annie for years, but she wouldn't hear of any of us stepping in to lend her a hand when, in her words: 'There were other folk needing it more.'" Little lines appeared at the corners of his eyes. "Everyone figured they could blame you if Annie got mad, so it wasn't hard for the folks in charge to get a few people to come help."

"A few? There's probably fifty people here."

Jace nodded, his own gaze sweeping over several groups of Scouts pulling weeds, giggling girls scraping and painting the wooden trim around the windows, and the clusters of men shouting and hammering on the roof as loose shingles were removed and replaced.

"We wouldn't have had nearly so many if it weren't for you."

Her brows rose. "Me?"

He nodded imperceptibly to a spot behind her and she twisted to find Kari glaring in their direction.

A wave of guilt washed through Bronte, dousing the warmth Jace had inspired. But that guilt was quickly submerged beneath a healthy dose of pique. Damnit, she was the adult in this situation, not Kari. She and Jace hadn't done anything but share a kiss.

So why was Bronte feeling so defensive?

"We probably would have had only a half dozen people here if it weren't for the rumors."

Bronte's head whipped away from Kari's inspection as she was filled with a rush of horror. "What rumors?" she demanded.

Damn, damn, damn. How was it possible that a single stolen kiss could spread through a community like wildfire?

Jace leaned toward her, close enough that his breath stirred the sensitive tendrils of hair near her ear, but not close enough for Kari to think that Jace was being anything but "friendly."

"That Annie's beautiful granddaughter from Boston has come to visit."

Bronte braced herself, waiting for the rest of the dire rumor. But when Jace backed away, it was clear that he had nothing more to add. Nothing but a wicked grin and an intimate sweep of her frame, head to toe, then up again.

Then he was turning back to the men directing the cement.

It took several minutes for her to realize that Jace was keeping to his promise. To anyone who watched them, he was nothing more than her friend.

She turned and hurried toward the side entrance so that she could finish the cookies. But she paused when her phone chirped in her pocket. Sighing, she retrieved it, seeing that she had a text.

Sit w/ me @ lunch?

A frisson of sensation caused gooseflesh to pebble her skin. Glancing behind her, she saw Jace striding toward his truck. He looked back at her for only a second. One hot, hot second. Then he bent over the toolbox built into the vehicle's bed.

Bronte glanced at Kari, who had finally gone back to her chores, then the wary curve of Lily's smile as Barry sat beside her and handed her a sticky dandelion.

She should concentrate on them. Only on them.

Even as the words popped into her head, Bronte knew it wasn't enough. For too long, she'd focused all her energies on Phillip and her kids. She'd starved herself of every scrap of joy, knowing that there was none to spare. But now that she'd been given a morsel of kindness—a tiny bit of hope—there were parts of her that were waking from her self-imposed stasis. As her mind and her soul returned to complete sentience, she was consumed with a raging hunger to feel.

To *feel*.

Happiness, joy, anger, and yes, even pain. She didn't want to numbly stumble through life any more. For the first time in years, she wanted to make her own decisions. She wanted a house that was a home, not a museum. She wanted kids who laughed out loud, argued at the top of their lungs without fear of reprisal, and tracked dirt in from the yard. Damnit, she didn't want a job. She wanted an education and a career.

Her fingers hovered over the glowing keypad of her phone.

Most of all, she wanted to be courageous enough to admit that *friend* was only a small part of the description she wanted applied to her relationship with Jace.

As soon as the thought appeared, the inner voice she'd grown to hate began its incessant nagging, telling her that she was making a mistake. It was too soon to even *think* about dating or even a close friendship with someone of the opposite sex. But as the familiar warnings began to flood her head, her fingers were already flying over the illuminated letters.

Is that good idea?

Seconds later, she had her response.

I'll B friendly.

Bronte laughed out loud.

CU there.

ELEVEN

————•—•————

B RONTE had no time to wonder if she were playing with
fire. As soon as she stepped into the kitchen, the buzzer
on the oven rang. She quickly checked on the biscuits, taking
the pans from the oven and replacing them with a sheet tray
of cookies.

"Those look wonderful," P.D. remarked as she leaned
close to inhale the heady combined scents.

"When they're cool, I'll put another layer of glaze on top.
If I'd had more than a single orange, I would have used
fresh-squeezed juice for the glaze. But these will do."

"Yum. And the cookies?"

"Oatmeal raisin. Normally, I'd freeze the dough in a log
and slice off pieces to bake." Bronte grinned. "When we
were kids and Annie made these, the dough would rarely
make it to the oven. We would sneak into the kitchen and
cut off hunks of frozen dough and eat it raw."

P.D.'s expression became thoughtful. "Do you suppose
you could leave out the egg and put the raw dough in ice
cream?"

The buzzer signaled that one batch of cookies was done.

With the ease of years of practice, Bronte removed the pans and replaced them with yet another batch.

"I don't see why not."

Since Annie didn't have a cooling rack, Bronte placed folded newspapers on the Formica, then covered them with brown paper grocery sacks that had been stacked in her grandmother's drawer for such a purpose.

"What are you doing now?" P.D. asked curiously.

Bronte laughed. "One of Annie's tricks from her own mother. If you place the hot cookies on the brown paper and newspapers, it draws the heat out and lets them breathe like a cooling rack. When I was a teenager, I thought it was part of the recipe and insisted on doing it at home. Even after Annie explained it was simply a makeshift tool, I put them on the brown paper if I had it handy. Somehow, it seemed to intensify the scent of the cooling cookies for me." She shrugged. "It's probably in my head, but I do it anyway."

"Mind if I try one?"

"Of course not. I'm about ready to finish the biscuits, so I'll get you one of those as well."

Using a large spoon, Bronte scooped up the glaze, then drizzled it over the biscuits in diagonal stripes. When she'd finished, she cut one from the corner and put it on a small plate then put the cookie to the side.

"Is that all you make? Cookies and biscuits?"

Bronte shook her head. "I'm one of those people who bakes to relieve stress. Bread, cake, cookies, pies." She grimaced. "The last few years, my neighbors have loved me. I've been baking more than my family could ever consume."

P.D. took a bite of the cookie and smiled, closing her eyes. "Mmm. This is what childhood should taste like."

Bronte wondered at her odd turn of phrase: *should* taste like.

Then P.D. pinched off a corner of the biscuit. She took a bite, then made a silly, happy face. "To borrow a phrase from Elam . . . *Wow!*"

Bronte laughed. "I bet he says that a lot, with your cooking."

P.D. put the plate on the counter and leaned back, peering at Bronte in a way that made it clear the wheels in her head were turning.

"You've done these from memory. Do you have other favorites?"

"Sure. I've got a whole recipe collection if you want to look at it. Jace said you were looking for new dishes for your restaurant."

P.D. nodded. "I'm always looking for those, but . . . what I'm really looking for is a baker. Mine is quitting to have a baby."

She waited expectantly, but Bronte wasn't sure what help she could give in that regard. She didn't know anyone in Bliss.

"How would you like the job, Bronte?"

For several long seconds, Bronte stared at her blankly.

"You'd have early hours, so you wouldn't be able to see your kids off to school, but you'd be home well before they returned in the afternoon. Your shift will start around four in the morning and you could leave as soon as everything is ready, hopefully before the busy lunch hour. You'd be in charge of the fresh bread for the day. Each table is given a variety of three small loaves on a cutting board when the diners sit down. The buns for our burgers and sandwiches are already handled by an artisan group in Logan, so you won't have to worry about those. But I'd like to do a rotation of desserts throughout the month: pies, tarts, cakes, homemade ice creams with unusual add-ins, cheesecakes, and cobblers. I'd need you to help with those. If you join us, I think we should add a selection of cookies as well. It would be a unique homey touch to the menu. I can't pay a whole lot, but it would be over minimum wage and benefits would be included. There's also some take-out and catering involved with Vern's—something I'd like to build even more. So if the demand on your products is high, you'll receive a portion of the sales as a bonus at the end of each project."

Bronte stared at P.D., sure that she'd blacked out and this whole scenario was a hallucination brought on by her worry. But when P.D. lifted her brows questioningly, Bronte realized that there was a more logical explanation for the offer.

"Did Jace put you up to this?"

P.D. shook her head.

"Then why?"

"Honestly?" P.D. asked.

Bronte nodded.

"I'm desperate. My baker is leaving in a couple of weeks. When Jace mentioned eating one of your cinnamon rolls, I thought I'd come by and talk to you about helping out temporarily." She grinned, grabbing her biscuit and biting off another piece. "But after seeing and tasting your work, I knew I had a permanent candidate for the job. And," she drawled temptingly, "come fall semester, you might even be able to squeeze in a class or two at Utah State after your shift."

A tingling began in the tips of Bronte's fingers, spreading out through her whole body, filling her with an effervescent joy—one that she hadn't felt in oh so long.

"You're sure about this?" she asked, just in case. The beeper on the stove began its insistent alarm, but she ignored it.

P.D. had closed her eyes to savor the rich, gooey center of the orange biscuit. But she opened them to say, "Oh, I'm sure. I know you need to get your kids settled in school and Annie will still need regular visits. I'll give you some time to settle in, but be at Vern's bright and early a week from Monday. That way, Marta can work with you for several days to make sure you're settled."

Bronte held out her hand. "It's a deal."

After the two of them sealed the arrangement, P.D. took a pan of biscuits in each hand and carried them outside.

Bronte waited until the screen slammed behind her. Then turning away, she uttered a squeal of delight and did a quick victory jig.

She had a job.

She had a job!

AS Jace had suspected, the lunch break became more of a party than a meal. He snagged a couple of lawn chairs for

Bronte and him, then scooped a cold Pepsi from a plastic tub that had been filled with ice and assorted sodas. Although he stood with a group of friends and their wives, he kept one eye on the house until Bronte walked outside carrying plates of cookies. She was immediately surrounded by the younger kids. Clearly, they weren't willing to wait with the adults, who were sidling down a long line of squat black pots filled with roasted chicken, Dutch oven potatoes, roasted vegetables, and Helen Henderson's killer cherry chocolate cake. Sawhorses covered with lengths of plywood served as makeshift tables, and as the minutes ticked by, more cars appeared—primarily women this time—carrying picnic salads and Crock-Pots filled with baked beans.

As Bronte laughed and set the cookies with the rest of the food, a van pulled up next to the barn. Jace recognized the band that played at Vern's on the weekend.

Bronte's expression was bemused as she took in the activity around her. In the space of a few hours, the flower beds had been weeded, raked, and edged. The flaking trim on the house had been scraped away and repainted, the roof was repaired, and the new stoop was well on its way to completion. There would still be work to do inside, but a week's worth of hard labor had been completed in a couple of hours.

"It's looking pretty good, isn't it?"

Bronte looked at him, wide-eyed, and for the first time he saw a spark of joy in her dark blue eyes.

"I can't believe it. I thought I'd be spending most of the summer just getting the yard in shape."

"Come on, let's get you something to eat."

Mindful of the way that Kari followed their every move with a none-too-subtle death glare, Jace made sure that he kept at least a foot of space between them as he began introducing Bronte to her neighbors. He figured the names would all run together after a while, but they'd all remember Bronte. Then, he led her down the line, introducing her to Helen and Syd. Helen immediately took Bronte under her wing. Before Bronte knew what had happened, Helen had organized a group of women to come help her deep-clean the house the following weekend, filled up her plate, poured her a cold drink, and ushered her to the waiting lawn chairs.

Jace slid into the chair next to her, and when Helen moved on to help P.D. set up extra tables, he chuckled softly. "You have now experienced the full power of P.D. Raines and Helen Henderson. When the two of them put their heads together, there's no stopping them."

Bronte regarded her heaping plate with bemusement, then looked up to say, "Did you know she offered me a job?"

Jace twisted the lid off his drink and gulped the soda down, then said, "Who? Helen?"

"No. P.D."

Jace's brows rose. "Really? Doing what?"

"She wants me to take over as her baker."

Jace laughed, realizing the source of her good mood. He was sure that having a job lined up was a huge relief.

"Are you going to take it?"

"I've already told her I will."

"You'll be great."

"You think so?"

"I know so."

Her smile spread over her face like sunshine, and Jace felt his breath catch. God, she was beautiful. More than ever, he wondered how difficult her life in Boston must have been the past few years, if the promise of a job and the help from a few neighbors could chase away the haunted expression in her eyes.

He gestured to her plate. "You'd better eat. You're going to need your strength."

THE rest of the afternoon passed quickly. Jace was pleased with the way that Bronte was welcomed into the crowd. He watched as she laughed and chatted. One of the women worked as a secretary at the high school and she told Bronte what she needed to do to get her kids enrolled. Another was an elementary teacher who reassured Bronte that the curriculum in

Boston was similar to that in Bliss, so Lily should be able to ease into one of the current third-grade classes.

With each assurance, some of the emotional weight seemed to lift from her shoulders until he had a glimpse of the woman she must have been before a dissolving marriage and the pressures of shielding her children from the fallout had begun to weigh on her.

Jace tried to remind himself that they were simply *friends*. But the term had never really fit—and it certainly didn't fit now. With each minute that he spent in her company, his attraction to her increased. More than anything, he longed to reach over and touch her. But Kari had taken a seat only a few yards away with some of the other teenagers. She watched him with the intensity of a nineteenth-century chaperone intent on guarding a virgin bride-to-be. Lily, who had been coaxed down by Barry to investigate the creek and the outbuildings, had alternately spent her time with Barry or clinging to her mother. But now, she was back up in the tree house again. Barry must have shoved some of his ranch toys into his pockets because the two of them had dragged a blanket up the ladder and were galloping plastic horses over the folds.

So he contented himself with watching Bronte, memorizing the brown and green flecks in her eyes and the slope of her cheek. He realized that she crossed her arms when she was nervous and unconsciously bit her lip when she was thinking.

When the crowd of people began to disperse, Jace knew that was his cue to leave as well. Kari's steely gaze had eased from outright anger to suspicion, and he wasn't about to push his luck. But as he scanned the area for his little brother, his gaze fell on the glider beneath the porch eaves.

Unable to resist the temptation, Jace took his phone from his pocket. As soon as he'd unlocked it, he tapped the texting icon and sent a message to Bronte.

What R U doing tonight 11:00?

He saw her straighten from where she was clearing the last of the food and utensils from one of the tables.

Why?

He turned away, afraid that the intensity of his need to be alone with her again would be telegraphed into the very air around them for everyone to see.

How about another ride on the glider?

There was no response. The urge to turn and look at her was nearly overpowering. Finally, her answer popped into view.

I'll B there.

Jace nearly cheered aloud. But tamping down his joy—as well as the flood of longing that swept through his body—he typed one last message.

Bring jacket.

He chanced a look at her then, sure that she could see the need that rocked him to the very core. But rather than looking alarmed, she merely gazed at him, her cheeks growing pink before she looked away.

Nevertheless, she responded with: OK.

Sure that his grin was far too telling, Jace quickly schooled his features and slipped his phone back into his pocket. Crossing to where Barry was still holed up with Lily in the tree house, Jace called up, "Time to go, bud."

But Barry didn't respond. Sighing, Jace used the ladder bolted to the side of the tree to climb up far enough to see inside. He grabbed Barry's empty paper plate and cup. But when he saw Lily's uneaten food, Jace felt a twinge of concern.

"Lily? Aren't you hungry?"

She shook her head, her eyes wide.

Barry frowned. "Maybe she's got a tummyache. I put lots of good stuff on her plate, but she won't even eat a cookie."

Jace felt a twinge of guilt, realizing that he was probably the source of her loss of appetite.

"Maybe she's tired, Barry."

Barry shook his head, offering in a stage whisper, "I think she's been crying. Her eyes are all red."

Damn, damn, damn. He might have taken a step forward with Kari, but Jace worried he'd taken three steps back with Lily.

"Maybe she needs some time alone with her mom. Once you've come home with me, then Bronte can talk to her."

Barry considered that idea. Clearly, he didn't want to leave a friend who was in distress, but somewhere, way back in his memory, perhaps he tapped into the image of their own mother scooping him up to comfort him.

"I'll be back tomorrow, Lily."

Barry stubbornly waited until Lily offered, " 'Kay."

"But you can call me if you need me before then. We have a phone, don't we, Jace?"

"Yes. We do. The number is pinned to the refrigerator with a magnet."

"Hear that, Lily? You can find the number if you need it. I can run right over. Or saddle a horse and ride. I can come if you need me."

Jace's gaze narrowed. His brother had used the little girl's real name.

So he wasn't mixing her up with his twin. Right?

Lily's smile was tremulous, not quite reaching her eyes.

"Okay," she whispered.

Barry reluctantly backed toward the ladder.

Jace dropped to the ground and waited until Barry did the same. But before Jace knew what Barry meant to do, he ran toward Bronte.

"Lily needs you to hug her," Barry said baldly.

Jace hurried to interpret, but Bronte glanced up at the tree house, then set down the stack of plates she'd been gathering.

"Thanks, Barry. I think you're right."

Knowing that they would only be in the way, Jace nodded to Bronte, then steered Barry toward the truck.

Once inside, Barry clicked his seat belt, then asked, "What if a hug isn't enough, Jace?"

Jace turned the key in the ignition. "Then we keep being her friend until we find out what we can do to help her feel happy again."

Barry nodded, his brow furrowing as the wheels began turning in his head.

Jace realized—now more than ever—the emotional land-mine he would have to walk in order to pursue a relationship with Bronte. As much as they might think that the feelings they shared were between the two of them, everything they did could have far-reaching consequences with the children under their care.

Putting the truck in gear, Jace forced himself to turn the wheel and head toward the ranch—even though it was the last place he wanted to go.

THE yard was inky and filled with shadows as Bronte eased outside, carefully closing the screen behind her. Despite the full moon that hung heavy on the horizon, the grass was thick with shadows. A cool breeze was blowing, but she left the door ajar so that she could hear if her children called out.

She'd spent most of the evening doting on Lily. She'd washed and plaited her hair, cuddled her on the couch, and colored pictures of princesses with crayons they'd found in one of Annie's cupboards. Through it all, Bronte had tried to gently draw her daughter into conversation. Lily had always been a daddy's girl, and Bronte tried to reassure her that she would still see her father for holidays and summer vacations.

But rather than talking, Lily kept changing the subject. What little interaction Bronte was able to inspire revolved around Barry and toy horses and whether princesses ever wore lemon-lime gowns instead of cotton-candy pink.

Padding toward the glider, Bronte was alerted halfway by the soft snuffle of a horse.

She glanced in the direction of the noise, then altered her course when she realized that, this time, Jace was still atop the animal.

With each step closer, her heart pounded more audibly in her ears. The tingling awareness that she'd felt each time in his presence even more pronounced—so much so, that she seemed to flash hot, then cold.

Sweet heaven above. What was it about a man on horseback that aroused a response in the average red-blooded woman? Was it a reaction encoded in her DNA after hundreds of years of survival? Was it that a male astride an animal represented the warrior that the female sex had gravitated toward for countless generations?

Or was it the sheer show of strength and dominance.

Whatever the reason, with each step she took, Bronte felt as if she were walking into her own private fantasy. A shadowed clearing. An enormous steed. A powerful man.

In the darkness, Jace's physique was even more pronounced. The moonlight that filtered through the trees silvered the shape of his hat and cast his eyes into darkness before limning the jutting shape of his jaw, the breadth of his shoulders, the strength of his arms. He sat effortlessly in the saddle, the reins held loosely in one hand.

When she was only a few feet away, his voice slipped through the night like liquid silver.

"Ever been on horseback?"

She nodded.

Jace kicked free of one of the stirrups and held out a hand. "I'll boost you up."

As soon as she'd found her foothold, he lifted her behind him in one smooth motion. Then, he looked over his shoulder, his eyes dark and fathomless. "Put your arms around my waist."

Her fingers trembled as she did as she'd been told. She experienced a wave of wonder as her palms registered the hard planes of his abdomen. Even through his shirt, she could feel the contours of a well-defined six-pack. But hard on the heels of that thought, came a burst of panic. She might have ridden before, but that had been years and years ago.

"I should stay close to the house . . ." she began—and she could have cursed herself for the tremor in her voice.

But Jace reached down to cover one of her hands with his own. The warmth of his palm, the slightly rough texture of calluses brought on by ranch work, caused a delicious frisson to dance up her arms.

"We're going to the ridge on the other side of the creek. I need to get you out of the trees and there's a good vantage point up there. You'll be able to see if any lights come on in the house."

She nodded, willing to do anything so that he continued to touch her.

Dear heaven, when had she become so needy? So desperate?

He clucked to the horse, reining him away from the house and the huge willow in the backyard, to the creek that slithered through the grass and headed toward the Taggart property. Beyond the creek was a steep hill covered in scrub and cedar.

Clasping her hands together over the cold metal of Jace's belt buckle, she pressed her cheek against the firm surface of his back, trying not to think about how far the ground was from her current position, how precarious her perch was behind the saddle, and how much it would hurt if she fell off.

But as the horse picked its way through the grass, then the cold, shallow creek, she grew calmer. Maybe, like maneuvering a bicycle, riding was a skill that wasn't really forgotten.

Unfortunately, as soon as the thought drifted through her mind, the horse began lunging up the steep slope.

A squeak of terror escaped her throat and Jace laughed. Again, he pressed his free hand over hers in reassurance.

"Relax. I won't let anything happen to you."

After a half-dozen more lunges, the horse's gait evened out. Seconds later, the animal came to a complete halt.

Reluctantly, Bronte peeked out of one eye. When she finally let out a long breath and straightened, she found Jace watching her with a smile.

"All done. The ride wasn't too bad, was it?"

She shook her head even though her pulse was still knocking at her throat in an uneven tattoo.

"Give me your hand again and I'll help you down."

Her fingers didn't seem inclined to release him. But this time, it wasn't because of her fear, but because she didn't want to abandon the warmth of his body seeping through his shirt.

Jace, thankfully, didn't seem to notice. He easily lowered her to the ground. Then, after she'd stepped away, he dismounted himself.

After tying the horse to the branch of a Russian olive tree, he untied the blanket that had been rolled up and attached to the saddle with leather straps.

"Hold this."

She took the blanket while he grabbed a set of saddlebags that he'd looped over the pommel. Then, to her infinite delight, he laced his fingers with hers and drew her toward the bluff.

Just as he had promised, they were still within a hundred feet of Annie's house. Farther on, she could see the twinkling lights of the Taggart's Big House, and farther on, their barn.

"Barry's in bed?" she asked.

"Barely. Bodey's latest relationship seems to have fizzled out, so he's home tonight. He'll herd Barry back to his room if he gets up."

Bronte turned in the opposite direction, expecting to see a view worthy of the trip up the hill, but a stand of trees in the distance prevented her from seeing much more than distant lights.

Her face must have registered her confusion because Jace laughed and said, "That's not the view we came here to see. If we'd been at my place, we could have relaxed on the porch, but there's too many trees around Annie's house."

He grabbed the blanket and shook it free, then arranged it on the ground. Sweeping the hat from his head, he set it carefully on one corner. Then, before she knew what he meant to do, he lay down, crossing one foot over the other ankle, and held out an arm in invitation saying, "Come here."

Bronte frowned, wondering if she'd given him the wrong impression. Yes, she was attracted to this man. Yes, she wanted to spend time with him . . . touch him . . . even kiss him. But . . .

"Relax. I'm not making the moves on you. Just lie down for a minute."

Deciding that after everything he'd done for her she could afford to humor him, she lay stiffly at his side.

TWELVE

———•═•———

AGAIN, Jace chuckled, a low, soft, *delicious* sound that seemed to come from the depths of his chest. Then he pulled her head onto his shoulder and, gesturing to the sky above them, said, "Look."

Bronte obediently followed the direction of his finger, seeing what she had expected to see—a sky black as pitch. But then, her eyes took in the glittering pinpoints of starlight—large and small, white hot, pale pink and icy blue, rounded orbs that were probably distant planets, and glittering dusty smudges that hinted at faraway realms that hadn't been explored by mere mortals yet.

Bronte shivered at the beauty pulsing above her, and Jace pulled her tighter against his body for warmth. Not even the latent power of his body could distract her from this incredible view. She'd forgotten how beautiful the sky could be when the glow of the city was removed. For some reason, the stars seemed closer against the blackness.

"It's fantastic," she breathed.

Bronte felt Jace's head turn and knew he was watching her. He'd pulled her more securely into his shoulder and she absorbed the rise and fall of his chest and the nearly imperceptible sound of each breath swelling his lungs. Making herself more comfortable, she rested one hand on his sternum, her fingers intuitively deciphering the rhythm of his heart.

She was about to tilt her face toward him when something streaked through the sky like an arrow of light. Then, it was gone, making her wonder if she'd imagined it.

A soft "*oh!*" of surprise burst from her lips. Then she frowned in disappointment, not really sure what she'd seen, but wishing she'd been forewarned so that she could have given it more of her attention. Then, to her delight, another thread of silver shot through the pinpoints of light, seeming to head for the mountaintops in the distance.

"Right on time," Jace murmured under her cheek.

"What are they? Shooting stars?"

He nodded. "Technically, the earth is passing through an asteroid belt. I think that's what they called it on the news. It happens every few years in the spring, but the weather doesn't always cooperate. Since there weren't many clouds today, I was hoping that our luck would hold."

Bronte waited, barely breathing. Several minutes later, another star seemed to plunge to earth, then another. Soon, she realized that the intervals between the phenomena were growing shorter and shorter, until the sky seemed streaked with lights that shot through the blackness like a spider's web. Then—as if weary of performing a private fireworks show—the night grew still again.

"It's over?" she whispered to Jace, barely breathing in case she should miss something by daring to speak.

"Mmm hmm. You might see a stray one, but the whole thing usually lasts only about twenty minutes."

"This happens every few years." It wasn't a question. Instead, it was a statement of wonder.

"Did you make a wish?"

She looked at him in alarm. "I didn't think about it."

"Do it now. I'm sure the statute of limitations isn't up yet."

His eyes twinkled as the arm around her waist nudged

her, encouraging her to suspend her cynical adult wisdom for a few minutes.

Closing her eyes, she searched for a wish that would equal the grandness of the occasion. But as the quiet settled around her, it wasn't a wish that came to mind. Instead, she grew intimately aware of the warmth of Jace's body, the strength of the arm that held her, the almost imperceptible knock of his heart against her fingertips. Suddenly, the future seemed inconsequential and oh so far away. Instead, her senses were flooded with thoughts of Jace and what she wanted—no, *needed*—from this man.

Her eyelashes flickered open and she was hooked by his gaze—one that seemed as intense and hungry as her own.

"Did you make a wish?"

His voice was low and raspy, echoing the awareness that raced through her body like a tidal wave, sweeping away everything but the need for his arms around her. And his kiss. Please, let him kiss her, right now, in this hushed clearing, in this magical moment.

"Yes." The word emerged as an almost imperceptible puff of sound.

Then, when she felt she couldn't bear one more second of loneliness, his fingers sifted through her hair, drawing her down toward him.

He let her control each move, his hand suggesting the movement rather than commanding it. But there was no hesitation as she bent toward him until their breaths tangled together. Then, he was lifting his head the last scant inch until he whispered a hairsbreadth away from her mouth, "You have no idea what you do to me."

Before she could react to the pronouncement, his lips were against hers, softly, sweetly, urging her to relax against him as his head returned to the ground. The hand that had been at the side of her face moved to cradle her nape, pulling her gently closer until her hair fell around them like a dark curtain, providing them with an illusion of privacy that they didn't really need. Except for her children in the house down below, there was no one around for miles. There were just the two of them, lost in exploration.

As Bronte leaned into him, Jace's tongue traced her lower lip, bidding entrance, and she immediately complied, knowing that there was nothing on earth that she wanted more. Immediately, he swept inside, tasting and exploring—and teasing Bronte into doing the same.

It seemed like a lifetime since she'd been in Jace's arms, since she'd felt his lips against hers, his breath hitching in time with her own erratic gulps for air. Almost immediately, her body was hit with a raging wave of sensation. She flashed cold, then hot again as desire and want and need rushed together, storming through her body and robbing her of all coherent thought. She could only *feel*—feel his strength, his masculinity, his adoration. As she pressed more hungrily against him, slanted her lips to give him better access, Bronte realized the enormity of her isolation and loneliness as her body, which had felt heavy and dull and weighted with ice, melted beneath the heat of Jace's simple caress. As the fire licked through her arms and legs and chest with the swiftness of a flashover, she found herself hungering for more and more and more.

Without conscious thought, it was Bronte who deepened the caress. Her tongue tangled intimately with his, seeking the very essence of his soul, while her body pressed tightly against his, absorbing each ridge, each valley, as if he had been tailor-made to give her pleasure.

One hand plunged into his hair, absorbing the silky softness, the way the short strands ran through her fingers like quicksilver, while the other fist gripped at his shirt.

Heeding her silent cues, Jace wrapped his arms tightly around her waist, rolling her onto her back. Their legs twined intimately together, even as her hands swept over the musculature of his arms, the strength of his back. Like a blind woman, she reveled in the bunch of muscles across his shoulder blades and the Braille-like bumps of his spine. Unable to stop herself, she gripped handfuls of his shirt, pulling it free from his waistband so that she could splay her palms over the heat of his bare flesh.

Jace gasped, pulling back, and they both struggled to breathe. She honestly couldn't remember if she'd ever seen Phillip breathless. Not even in passion. Not for her.

But Jace was searching her face, gauging her reaction. Then a slow smile spread over his lips while his eyes continued to burn in the darkness. The warmth of his expression spread through her body like hot molasses, thick and slow and filled with latent promise.

Thankfully, he didn't speak—he didn't have to. Bronte was sure that her need was broadcast as transparently as his. But when she tried to bring him closer, he lowered his lips for a quick kiss, then another, then another. Then he sighed against her lips.

"Shh. Relax and enjoy it. There's no rush."

But there was. Bronte nearly whimpered aloud with her need to glut herself on the sensations this man was inspiring. She couldn't remember the last time that she had been held or even touched in passion. It wasn't a matter of months, it was years—probably before Lily had been born. Phillip had craved his drugs and the high they gave him more than he'd ever longed for her. Day by day, she'd tamped down her own needs and desires until she'd convinced herself that she was too old to feel the headiness of sexual awareness any more. She'd even wondered if something had happened to her after Lily's birth. The pregnancy and the delivery had been hard on her, and she'd begun to believe that something inside her had been damaged.

But Jace easily dispelled all of those concerns. When his lips settled in for a long, slow kiss, she surrendered herself to his ministrations, especially when one broad hand slipped beneath the hem of her shirt and made a slow pass from the nipped-in spot at her waist, up to her rib cage, then higher, until the tips of his fingers brushed against the fullness of her breast.

A bolt of white-hot passion shot through her body and she gasped, her hips unwittingly bucking against him, her back arching so that his hand settled more firmly around the aching globe. As she fought to breathe, Jace's lips left hers, slipping lower and lower, dropping down the sensitive column of her neck to the notch in her collarbone. Then to her utter amazement, he licked the sensitive hollow, nearly causing her to come completely unglued.

"What are you doing to me?" she gasped, nearly incoherent.

She felt him smile against her. "Good things, I hope."

Her hands lifted to frame his face, her fingers plunging through his hair.

"Oh, yeah," she whispered.

He pushed up the hem of her blouse until her bra gleamed white in the darkness. Bared to him, there was no question that she was aroused. Her nipples were so tight, so sensitive. When he bent to take one of the aching nubs in his mouth, she arched into him again, crying out.

Dear sweet heaven above. What was he doing to her? Was it simply that it had been years since she'd been touched so intimately? And even longer since she'd made love? Or had some new power taken over her body and her mind, making her more susceptible to a man's caress?

But no, that wasn't possible, because what Jace was doing to her—with his tongue, his fingers, even the mere pressure of his breath was more arousing than anything that she could ever remember experiencing.

Sensing her wantonness, Jace allowed their legs to tangle, his body to press hers more firmly into the ground. She reveled in the pressure, in the strength of his thighs, the rasp of their jeans as she arched against him. But most powerful of all, she felt a blaze begin low in her belly at the evidence of his arousal as it rocked against her, mimicking the very act that she found herself craving most.

A delicious tension was building in her—one that she'd only experienced a few times before. But it was different this time, holding her in its grip, making every muscle in her body strain toward a single goal, even as her mind whispered, *"Not now. Not yet!"*

But there was no holding it back. Before she even knew

what was about to occur, she seemed to shatter so fiercely that she was sure bits of her soul streaked through the night sky like the shooting stars she'd recently witnessed. On and on, the powerful contractions shuddered through her body as she clutched Jace tightly against her, rocking against him in need.

Finally, as the last rippling sensations seeped from her body, she found herself gripping Jace around the neck as if she were drowning and he alone could save her. But then, as her wits slowly returned, and she became aware of the secluded clearing, the stars overhead, and the man above her . . . she was inundated with flashes of emotion—awe, embarrassment, joy, shame.

How could she have lost control so quickly—and obviously—with a man she hardly knew?

But when Jace lay her back down on the blanket and bracketed her face with his broad hands, she found herself looking at him—*really* looking at him. It wasn't a stranger she saw. Instead, she absorbed the broad brow and deep-set eyes, the blade of his nose, the slash of his cheekbones, and that square jaw with the faint cleft in the chin. In that instant, a part of her recognized much more than his face. It was as if she'd been searching for something all this time, and she'd finally found it in him. A part of her soul welcomed him into her heart even as her mind reared back from the idea.

As if sensing her inner turmoil, Jace rolled onto his back, pulling her with him so that she lay against his chest. She buried her face against him, afraid of what he must think of her. But the fingers that smoothed her hair were gentle.

"I take it that it's been a while," he murmured.

There was a teasing note to his tone that was meant to put her at ease, to convey to her that he wasn't put off by her reaction—and indeed, he was pleased with himself for inspiring it. It was that playful acceptance that gave her the courage to lift her head and meet his gaze again.

"I've never felt like that," she whispered, confessing the awful truth. Oh sure, she and Phillip had enjoyed a healthy physical relationship. At least at first. But her husband had found it necessary to remark that she was "slow to warm up." She'd never been the one to instigate lovemaking. With Phillip's late hours and the arrival of the girls, quite honestly, she'd been too tired most of the time to find such encounters with her husband worth the time and effort. It wasn't long after that when Phillip was injured in the automobile accident. Little had she known, but as his addiction to pain medication had increased, his sex drive had withered. For years, she'd blamed herself for the lack of physicality in their relationship. If she'd only tried harder to be the woman he wanted her to be. If she'd only reached out more, been creative, made the time. If she'd only been prettier, younger, more voluptuous.

But now, gazing at Jace, she was struck by an astounding epiphany. Perhaps, the lack of desire she'd felt and the rarity of her climaxes hadn't been entirely her fault.

A portion of her thoughts must have been reflected in her expression, because a crease appeared between Jace's brows.

"What's wrong?"

She opened her mouth to try to explain, but even as she tried to formulate the words, she realized it didn't really matter what had happened in the past. This was *now*. This was Jace.

A smile spread slowly across her features. "Nothing's wrong. Absolutely nothing." But quick on the heels of that thought came the blinding realization that *she* might have reached the pinnacle of pleasure, but Jace . . .

Jace laughed softly, clearly interpreting her thoughts. He stroked her cheek, her jaw, bringing her down for a butterfly-soft kiss. "Don't worry about it. I enjoyed myself immensely."

"But—"

"Next time," he promised. Then he pulled her back against the crook of his shoulder.

She lay there, her palm resting against his chest, absorbing the pounding of his heart as it eased back into a more normal rate. Her own body was following suit, tensions she hadn't even known she'd possessed draining from her muscles like heavy sand from an hourglass, until she felt weightless and lighter than air.

Jace traced idle circles on her back, each stroke still having the ability to raise gooseflesh. "How's Lily?"

Bronte sighed against him. "I don't know. For once, I can't reach her. Sometimes, she seems fine—like when she plays with Barry. Then at other times, she seems so . . . sad. Then, I feel like the worst mother in the world."

"She'll come around," Jace said. "Divorce isn't easy on kids—and maybe she's too young to understand anything more than her daddy isn't coming home to see her anytime soon."

"Logically, I know all that. Logically, I know that my kids need time to get used to the idea that their father won't be a daily part of their lives. I understand that it may be even longer before they'll accept that I might start seeing someone else." She shied away from admitting the entire truth. Bronte wished that he could be that man, that they could openly explore the attraction between them instead of relying on a few odd moments together.

"How about if I stay away for a few days—and make sure that everyone else in the community does the same? That would give you and your kids some alone time."

She lifted her head to protest, knowing that her encounters with Jace gave her much-needed strength. Somehow, whenever he was near, she was able to tap into her own inner resolve, she was able to focus on what she wanted most out of the future—and she was able to find the courage to begin working toward those goals.

But when she met his gaze, she saw in their depths a wealth of understanding, and knew that he was right.

Unable to speak, she merely nodded and sank against him again. "Not too long, okay?"

She felt him press a kiss to the top of her head.

"It's a deal."

THE house was dark and silent when Jace let himself into the kitchen. He kicked off his boots at the door, hung his jacket and hat on a hook, then opened the refrigerator. As he stared into the barren confines, he realized that no one had bothered to shop in over a week and the selection was becoming pretty sparse. There was a jar of pickles, a half-empty bottle of ketchup, a bag of carrots—which Barry wouldn't eat anymore, since he'd started on his bacon cycle—and a container of ranch sauce. The last remaining gallon of milk, which had been full when Jace had left, now had a few scant tablespoons left in the bottom—which usually pissed Jace off since he knew Bodey was responsible. His brother should either leave enough for someone else to get a drink, or finish the whole thing off and throw the jug away.

But somehow, that familiar pet peeve didn't have enough power to put a damper on his good mood. Not when Jace could still catch a whiff of Bronte's familiar floral perfume on his shirt or close his eyes and remember how she'd felt in his arms.

She'd surprised the hell out of him tonight. He'd known from their first embrace that she was warm and responsive. But tonight . . .

Hell, it was as if she'd caught fire in his arms. She'd met him kiss for kiss, touch for touch. He'd never been with a woman who was so responsive, so passionate. Her body had reacted to each caress as if she'd been waiting years for him. When she'd come against him . . .

He'd nearly lost control himself.

The soft beep of the refrigerator's alarm brought him back to awareness. Too late, he realized that he was still staring at the empty shelves. Closing the door, he ignored the hollow feeling in his stomach, realizing that it had little to do with the fact that he hadn't eaten since the Dutch oven feast at Annie's. He'd been more concerned with getting his work done and Barry in bed so that he could meet Bronte in time to see the shooting stars.

How had she managed to get under his skin so quickly and so completely? Every logical bone in his body warned him of the inadvisability of a relationship of any kind between them. She'd barely filed the last of her divorce papers, for hell's sake. While he . . .

He didn't know what he wanted anymore. He was torn between responsibilities that threatened to crush him and the secret need to flee. How could he offer a woman any sort of commitment or relationship when he couldn't even come to terms with who he was anymore? Most of the time, he felt like the world's biggest liar. Outwardly, he wore the façade of an organized and dedicated businessman. Inwardly, he was a seething mass of discontent.

Sighing, he pushed through the kitchen into the family room, carefully weaving his way through the miniature ranch toys scattered over the floor.

Even his plans to take a break once the snow returned were in question. He'd thought that if he took a vacation, revisited some of his old stomping grounds in Europe, that he could get rid of the itchy need for change. He could glut himself on the art and culture to be found there. Then, by spring, he could return with a better perspective.

But the thought of leaving for that long, knowing that Bronte would be here . . .

Hell. He didn't know how he was going to keep his promise and stay away for a few days, let alone—

"I don't want to live with you anymore, Jace."

Jace started, wrenched from his thoughts to find that Barry sat hunched at the top of the staircase. Even in the dark, Jace could feel his brother glaring at him.

Crap.

Jace flipped on the light. Noting his brother's expression of defiance, he took the steps one by one, using the same care he would display if he were approaching a ticking bomb.

"What's wrong, Barry?"

His brother was still dressed in his Spider-Man pajamas. But at some point since Jace had tucked him into bed, he'd donned his jacket, his cowboy hat, and a pair of boots. In his lap, he gripped a backpack stuffed so tightly that it wouldn't close at the top. Judging by the tip of a blanket and the toys poking out of the top, his preparations were probably light on underwear and heavy on entertainment.

"You went to see the dinosaur lady, didn't you?"

"Bronte?"

Barry nodded, his movements jerky.

Jace had learned a long time ago that it was a bad idea to lie to Barry. Inevitably, it would come back to bite Jace in the butt. So he sank onto the tread below his brother and said, "Yeah, Barry. I saw Bronte tonight."

Barry's eyes glittered with unshed tears. "Why, Jace? Why would you make Lily mad at me again?"

Jace sighed. "Lily was asleep, Barry. She didn't even know—"

"You told me it was bad to break a rule, even if no one knew you did it."

Shit.

Jace rubbed at the ache that was beginning to drill through his skull, right between his eyes. How the hell was he supposed to respond to that?

"Bronte is my friend, Barry. She needs someone to talk to—like Lily talks to you."

"But if you make her mad again, Lily might not talk to me," Barry said earnestly.

Jace tried to touch Barry's arm in reassurance, but Barry reared away from him, so he tried again. "She's not going to be mad at you, Barry."

"But she is! You're going to make things worse. So I don't want to live here anymore. I want to go live with P.D. and Elam cuz they won't sneak out at night to break their promises!"

He stood up, ready to lunge past, but Jace jumped to his feet and caught him around the waist.

"No, Barry, no!"

Barry fought to wriggle free and it took all of Jace's upper-body strength to keep them both from toppling down the stairs.

"Barry. Barry!" Jace's voice was tight and husky as he finally understood the extent of Barry's distress. He'd known that Barry had found a friend in Lily, but until tonight, he hadn't fully comprehended how much Barry had begun to rely on that friendship.

Too late, Jace realized that Barry had experienced his

own brand of loneliness. The kids his age were kind and accepting, but they were eager to leave adolescence behind. The younger children in the area found Barry's size intimidating. But Lily had accepted Barry for who he was, a boy with a heart of gold. She didn't care if he was older or taller or even that he was a boy.

Unable to help himself, Jace pulled his brother tightly into his arms. At first Barry resisted him, still visibly upset. But Jace held on until the fight drained out of him. Finally, Barry dropped the backpack to wind his arms around Jace's waist and grip him close. Huge sobs welled from his body, threatening to shake him asunder.

"I'm sorry, Barry. I'm so, so sorry," Jace murmured as his brother cried. "I didn't think far enough ahead. I didn't consider how Lily would feel if she found out I'd been talking with Bronte tonight."

"You have to, Jace. You have to think!"

Out of the mouths of babes.

Barry sobbed, then added sadly, "That's why I have to go to live at Elam's."

An ache settled in the center of Jace's chest. Even though he'd toyed with the idea of having Barry spend more time with Elam, the thought of such a thing becoming a reality hurt more than he'd anticipated.

Hugging Barry even tighter, Jace said slowly, "The decision is yours, Barry. This isn't a prison, it's our home. Yours, Bodey's, mine—and even Elam's. He might not sleep here, but it's still his home. If you want to live with Elam, you know he and P.D. would love to have you."

Jace drew back, the ache engulfing his chest so much that he found it hard to breathe, let alone speak.

"But I'd miss you, Barry. More than you'd ever know. If you'd be willing to wait until tomorrow morning, we can try to think of a way to help Lily feel better. Then, maybe when she's not so sad, she won't mind so much that Bronte is my friend, too."

Barry seemed to consider that for long, endless minutes. He finally nodded.

"Come on." Jace hooked the straps of the backpack with one hand and let the other rest on Barry's shoulder. "Let's get you back to bed."

Neither of them bothered to turn on the overhead lamp once they reached Barry's room. A nightlight glowed from one wall and the ceiling was dotted with plastic constellations and planets that glowed in the dark. For a fleeting instant, Jace thought of Bronte lying in his arms under the sky, watching shooting stars plummet to earth. But then, he turned his attention to helping Barry out of his boots and jacket. Barry bounced onto the mattress and set his hat on top of the stuffed panda that slept in the spot next to him in the larger double bed that had been installed in Barry's room at Christmas time.

Jace pulled the covers up to his brother's armpits, then ruffled his hair affectionately. "Sweet dreams, buddy. Tomorrow's Sunday, so you can sleep in to make up for staying up so late."

Barry's eyelids were already flagging. " 'Kay. Then can I go see Lily?"

"We'll call Bronte first thing."

His brother's head rolled in the pillow, seeking a more comfortable spot, and Jace took that as his cue to leave. He was poised at the door when Barry called sleepily from the bed.

"Jace?"

"Yeah, bud?"

"Do you think I'll ever find a friend who wants to hold my hand like Bronte likes to hold yours?"

Ah, shit. The question was so innocent, yet it had the ability to stab Jace through his heart with its poignancy.

"I don't know, Barry," Jace said, when he finally trusted himself enough to speak. "I guess we'll have to wait and see."

Jace waited for a response, but soon realized that Barry had fallen asleep.

Slipping into the hall, he eased the door closed, leaving a gap so that he could hear if Barry called out to him. Then, he padded down the hall, feeling very old and world-weary.

His goal was the bedroom, a hot shower, then sleep. But without consciously being aware of it, he found himself pausing in front of the stairs leading up to the attic.

It had been a little more than ten years ago when he'd thought that he had his life all figured out. He'd gathered up a couple of changes of clothing, what few belongings he thought were vital, and the wages that he'd saved up from working for his father. Then, retrieving the passport he'd obtained without his parents' knowledge, he'd slammed out of the house, swearing he wouldn't return until he'd shown his father what he could do on his own.

It had been the best thing he'd ever done.

And the worst.

Since coming home, Jace had tried to forget those few stolen years. He'd tried to conform and become the man his father had wanted him to be—and for the most part, he'd been successful. But he was discovering that by pretending that those years—those dreams, that person—no longer existed, he'd only made things worse in the long run.

He raked his fingers through his hair, then laced them together behind his head. For several minutes, he stared at the attic steps. Interestingly enough, for the first time in years, he didn't experience the old familiar tug of shame and regret. Instead, he felt the first stirrings of . . .

Anticipation.

Maybe it was time to put the old ghosts to rest and come to terms with the person he'd left behind when he'd returned home from Europe.

Even as the thought appeared, Jace knew that such a confrontation wouldn't come tonight. Not when he was bone tired and rattled from his conversation with Barry.

But soon.

THIRTEEN

A WEEK later, Bronte was already regretting the pact she'd made with Jace. After he'd called to explain the confrontation he'd had with Barry, they'd both agreed that they wouldn't see each other for a while.

Bronte had hoped that some "alone time" with her girls would help them adjust to all of the changes they'd experienced. She'd been under no illusions that Kari and Lily would wake up and accept the decision she'd made to divorce their father. But she'd thought that once they'd been enrolled in school and unpacked their bags, they would feel reassured by having a familiar routine, bedrooms of their own, and their belongings nearby.

So far, her predictions hadn't proven to be true. Kari seemed to have adapted to her new school without any problems. Maybe it was because she was a social animal, and being set adrift in a sea of strangers was preferable to being marooned at Annie's without any contact with kids her own age. Or maybe it was the fact that a few of the teenagers who now invited her to join them at lunch or after-school activities had been among the volunteers to help fix up Annie's house.

Even so, as soon as Kari returned home, it was as if a switch had been hit. Her smile would fade and her chin would adopt a defiant tilt. She went out of her way to stomp around the house, muttering under her breath. In typical teenage fashion, whatever Bronte said was W-R-O-N-G. If Bronte said it was a warm day, Kari insisted it was freezing. If Bronte complimented Kari's outfit, her daughter would change. She argued about the food they ate, the television they watched, the trips to the hospital, and the limitations of living in the country—until Bronte's nerves were raw from the constant negativity.

On the other hand, Bronte would have done anything if Lily had shown even a spark of anger. Instead, her daughter seemed to have shrunk inside herself. Unlike her older sister, being enrolled in the local elementary school hadn't helped matters. The classes were bursting at the seams while a newer, larger building was under construction—which meant that she was one of nearly forty kids in her room. Bronte was worried that, with Lily's innate shyness, her daughter was doing her best to fade into the background. Her teacher, Mr. Benson, had already called to ask if Lily had any "developmental or socializing challenges" since Lily refused to participate in class.

Even worse, Lily's depression seemed to be deepening—to a point where Lily would disappear into the tree house each day after school. She wouldn't come down unless absolutely compelled to do so. Her appetite had disappeared and she slept fitfully each night. Bronte tried fixing her favorite foods, playing with her, joining her in the tree house, even allowing Lily to sleep with her part of the night. But nothing she did seemed to ease Lily's sadness. Only Barry seemed to have the magic touch. Whenever he came to visit, she seemed diverted enough to smile.

All in all, Bronte was sure she was a shoe-in for World's Worst Mother. More than anything, she longed to talk to someone about Lily. Her grandmother improved more each day, but she was still on a ventilator. There was no one in

Boston that she could call. Although she and Jace continued to text one another at night, it was clear that Jace was trying to keep things "friendly." Besides, Bronte didn't want to scare the man off with her family's mounting tensions.

At the sound of hoof beats on the lane leading up to the house, Bronte's heart seemed to lurch in her chest. But it wasn't Jace who galloped into the yard. It was Barry.

Wiping her hands on a towel, she grabbed a paper sack that she'd filled with pouches of applesauce, small bags of carrots and celery, packets of animal crackers, and a pair of miniature bottles of milk.

Pushing through the screen door, Bronte called out, "Hello, Barry! How was school today?"

"We made piñatas out of balloons and newspapers," he reported enthusiastically. He swung out of the saddle and carefully tied the reins to the stoop railing.

"That sounds fun. I bet Lily wishes they'd done the same thing in her class." Bronte looked up at the spot where Lily had sunk cross-legged onto the floor of the tree house. There was no response. "Lily's been working hard on decorating her room. You'll have to have her show it to you."

"I have some extra tractors if she needs 'em."

Bronte laughed. "Why don't you ask? She picked one of Annie's pretty quilts to put on her bed. It's covered in flowers and butterflies. That should work with tractors, don't you think?"

Barry's brow creased in a frown. "No. She needs cowboys and cows if she's got butterflies."

His pronouncement was filled with conviction and punctuated with a decisive nod, so Bronte didn't bother to ask him to explain. Clearly, Barry knew what was best.

She handed him the sack and he started to move to the tree, but she stopped him with, "Hey, Barry?"

He turned, his brows disappearing beneath the shock of hair that hung over his forehead. "Yeah?"

"Do you suppose it would be okay for me to meet with Jace, just for a few minutes, as long as the girls know?"

Bronte didn't know what possessed her to even ask. She was already in Mom Purgatory for perceived indiscretions. She would be crazy to incite even more emotional outbursts.

But as she gazed up at her daughter, Bronte realized that right now, she needed some help. Judging by the kind young man that Barry had become, Jace was no amateur in the art of child rearing.

"Can I keep coming to see Lily after school?"

"Of course," she said with a smile. "We love having you. You're a really good friend to Lily. She would be disappointed if you didn't come play. Seems like the only time I see her smile anymore is when you come to visit."

"Don't make her mad, okay?"

Bronte prayed such a feat was possible. Kari would be angry—but lately, Kari wore her anger like a badge of honor. Lily, on the other hand . . .

Lily was sad. Incredibly sad. But Bronte couldn't get her to talk enough to determine what upset her the most—the divorce, the move, or the fact that Bronte had been seen holding Jace's hand. Whatever the cause, it was clear that Bronte needed some outside help. Maybe with his EMT training or his own experiences with Barry, Jace could give her the name of a good pediatrician or a counselor.

BARELY a week had passed since the night on the hill, and Jace found himself wishing that he hadn't agreed to stay away from Bronte. Now that he'd truly tasted her, caressed her, felt her come in his arms, he was like a starving man longing for a meal. There wasn't an hour that went by that he didn't find his thoughts wandering toward her and the passion she'd displayed in his arms.

His distraction was unfortunately evident in his work. His brothers were giving him hell about his absentmindedness—and even the hired men were eyeing him with amusement. Try as he might, Jace couldn't seem to rein in his thoughts and concentrate on preparing fields and drilling corn. As soon as he climbed into the cab of the tractor or his pickup, his thoughts headed down the road to Annie's house.

It wasn't as if they'd stopped all contact between them. At odd times throughout the day, when Jace couldn't stand it another second, he would send Bronte a text. She was always quick to respond. He knew that she'd managed to get the girls enrolled in the local schools and that she'd begun working with P.D.'s current baker to learn the ropes at Vern's. He heard about each visit to the hospital and Annie's progress and setbacks throughout the week, as well as all of the sorting and cleaning that had been going on in the house.

But those sporadic contacts made him long to touch her even more.

This morning, Jace's tension had ratcheted up since he'd known that Bronte would be doing all the baking on her own at Vern's. Knowing how nervous she'd been about going solo, he went through the morning growling at whoever dared to cross his path until Elam stomped away from him, jammed his hat on his head, and muttered, "For hell's sake, Jace, call the woman and put us out of our misery."

So, with an eye on the clock, Jace waited until he was sure that she would be done with her shift at Vern's but still had a good hour before the bus would appear with her kids.

She answered on the first ring. "Hi."

"How was your first day baking on your own?"

Her laughter skittered over his spine like the caress of her fingers.

"Great! At first I was worried I'd made a mistake and have to remake something—P.D. has equipment in her kitchen that looks like it's straight out of NASA control. But once I got going, I was fine. Marta did a good job of getting me used to everything."

"What did you make?"

"Easy stuff, since it was my first day in charge. A banana blueberry loaf, an artisan bread with spinach and feta cheese, and P.D.'s beer bread." Again, she laughed. "I opened more bottles of beer in one morning than I've opened in my life! Then I rounded out the day by making chocolate chip cookies the size of a saucer."

"And . . . do you like your new job?"

"Yeah." The word emerged in a sigh of pure pleasure. "The rest of the staff has been great." There was a pause, then, "Where are you?"

He felt a prickling of awareness at the mere question. "I'm loading the corn drill down by angle field."

"Translation, please."

This time it was his turn to laugh. "Why?"

"I want to meet you."

"I thought we weren't going to see each other for a while." He forced himself to remind her of their pact, even though a jolt of heat had gone straight to his groin.

"Yeah, but I talked it over with Barry, then mentioned to the kids that I needed to have a quick conversation with you today."

"How did they take it?"

"Kari rolled her eyes and made a rude noise. Lily . . ." She sighed. "Well, Lily is part of the reason why I want to talk to you." Jace heard the thread of concern in her voice. "Do you have a minute? The girls won't be home for more than an hour. And I have cookies," she added temptingly.

"Well, if you have cookies," he teased, wondering what it was about Bronte that lifted his mood simply with the sound of her voice. "Behind Annie's house, next to the creek, there's an old service road. Follow it about a mile until you come to the gate. I'll be there in five minutes."

"Okay, but make it ten. I'm still in town."

"Ten it is."

Jace finished filling the bins with seed, then glanced at his phone. He had enough time. Jogging to the end of the field where he'd parked his truck, he climbed inside, his tires spitting dirt and gravel as he raced to the far end of the canal road where the tilled earth butted up against one of the prime pastures used to hold the mares and their colts. Stopping at the water trough, he opened the spigot of a pump drilled deep into the earth and waited for the fresh, clean water to begin gurgling out. Quickly, he washed his hands, then splashed more water on his face and the back of his neck. Then he climbed in his truck again, and spun toward the track that led to the service road.

He arrived only minutes later, but Bronte's familiar van was already parked on the other side of the gate. As soon as he pulled to a stop, she stepped from the driver's side.

She was dressed simply—a pair of faded jeans and a pale blue shirt. But the sight of her was enough to cause his heart to knock against his chest and his blood to flow like slow, hot molasses through his veins. As he dropped from the truck, he surreptitiously adjusted himself, already hardening at the mere thought of being closer to her again. Holy hell, what she did to him. Just the memory of her exploding against him in hedonistic joy could get him going.

"Hey, there."

She sauntered toward him, her hips swaying in unconscious pronouncement of her femininity. As Jace climbed over the gate, she held a white paper sack aloft as well as a plastic bottle of milk.

"I brought you an after-school snack—or whatever it is you ranchers have at about this time of day."

As soon as she was close enough, Jace snagged her around the waist.

"How about we call it a 'quickie.'" The words burst from his lips without thinking and Jace could have kicked himself. Damn, damn, damn. He was trying to be cool about things. The last thing he wanted to do was rush Bronte or make her feel pressured. But even though her cheeks flamed, her smile was mischievous.

"Somehow, I don't think our first time will be all that quick."

Will be.

He wrapped his arms even more tightly around her back, letting her know the effect she had on him. He felt, rather than heard, the way her breath hitched. Then she draped her wrists around his neck, the bottle of milk resting coolly between his shoulder blades. But even the chilly plastic couldn't draw his attention away from the softness of her body or the beauty of her smile.

Then she was lifting on tiptoe for his kiss and he willingly met her halfway, his mouth crashing over hers, immediately bidding entrance.

She sighed, opening her lips, and he felt her moan against him.

Hungrily, he swept inside, tasting her natural sweetness as well as a faint hint of chocolate and vanilla. His hands swept over her hips, her rear, knowing that this was what he had been longing for all week. Her passion, her unfettered enthusiasm, her innate femininity.

Again and again, he plundered her mouth—and Bronte gave as good as she got. At some point, the milk jug and sack fell to the ground. She began stroking his spine, his shoulders, burrowing beneath his shirt with fingers that felt cool against his hot skin. Then, Lord help him, she tunneled beneath the stricture of his belt, cupping his bare buttocks with her palms.

Jace thought that he couldn't get any more aroused. But his blood was raging, all of it seeming to flow toward his groin. He turned to press Bronte against the sturdy railroad tie that supported the heavy gate. When he ground against her soft hips, she broke free to laugh softly.

"I missed you, too," she whispered.

He grinned against her. "Good."

Her eyes were bright and sparkling with humor and passion. Jace was struck dumb. He didn't think that he'd ever seen anything more beautiful than the radiance of her smile. Then he was kissing her again, more slowly this time, drinking deeply of her sweetness, reveling in the rush of possession and passion that swamped him as their tongues intimately tangled.

He forced himself to slow things down. Beneath his hands, she felt so small and delicate. She was still too thin— like a bird that had worn itself out after being blown off course. But there was a resiliency to her body, and an innate strength to the arms that still held him tight.

When she finally pulled away, she was breathing as hard as he was. Her cheeks were pink and her eyes sparkled.

"Maybe you should eat your cookies. They're going to get trampled."

"To hell with the cookies," he said against her lips, then his mouth wandered to the spot beneath her ear and he felt her shiver against him.

"I-I worked very hard on them."

Realizing that she might still have doubts about her ability to bake on the large scale that would be demanded at Vern's, he traced the line of her jaw with the tip of his tongue—knowing that no dessert could equal the taste and texture of her skin. Then, reluctantly, he drew back.

"Maybe a bite, then."

Desire flared in her gaze—and he knew that she'd interpreted him correctly. The cookies weren't all he wanted to nibble on.

As she reached for the sack, Jace leaned his back against the gate, pulling her with him, until their limbs were intimately entwined. When she broke off a piece of the chocolate chip cookie, he didn't release her. He merely opened his mouth.

She hesitated before slipping the bite inside. But before she could draw completely away, he caught her wrist and kept her there, sucking on the end of one finger and her thumb.

Her eyes flickered in delight and she moaned.

"You are a dangerous, dangerous man, Jace Taggart," she whispered.

His tongue roamed over her fingers, absorbing melted chocolate and the natural saltiness of her skin. Heaven itself couldn't have tasted any better. When she finally lowered her hand, he chewed absently on the cookie, absorbing a mixture of dark sugars, earthy walnuts, silken chocolate.

And Bronte.

How was it possible that a woman could wrap herself around his heart and mind so quickly? They'd known each other only a few weeks, but he couldn't imagine a day without some kind of contact with her.

When his eyes drifted open, he saw an echo of his own thoughts in her eyes. Passion, wonder, and a shadow of disbelief. As if something that had flared up this quickly would be as easily doused.

Jace leaned forward, kissing her softly, carefully, wanting to reassure her that what they were experiencing wasn't fleeting. That it could be more—even as his mind shied away from what *more* might mean. He only knew that he wanted—*needed*—to preserve this fragile beginning. He couldn't push too hard, too fast, or too far. Hell, Bronte had only come to terms with the dissolution of her marriage. And her kids . . .

Her kids probably hated his guts. Or they would, if they caught even a hint of what Jace wanted to do with Bronte.

Knowing that he had to throw on the brakes while he still had the ability to do so, Jace finally drew away—slowly, reluctantly. But unable to sever the link entirely, he continued to hold her, his forehead resting against Bronte's.

"Do you have any idea what you do to me?"

She wiggled her hips against him. "I have a fair idea."

A sound that was half laugh, half groan pushed through his throat.

"If you keep this up, there's no way you'll get to the bus on time."

She started, shoving the food into his arms. "Oh, heck."

Jace couldn't help laughing again. "Such colorful language."

She glanced at her watch, and he saw the panic of a harried mother. "I wanted to talk to you about something, but I've got to go."

She lifted on tiptoe to kiss him again. But what started as a quick farewell lingered and lingered until they were both breathless. Then, with a groan, Bronte broke free. Wriggling out of his arms, Bronte hurried backward toward her car. "Can I meet you again tomorrow? Maybe a little earlier so we have time to do more than"—she made a vague gesture with her hand—"you know."

"I'd love to . . . 'you know.'"

She grinned, nearly taking his breath away yet again. "Text me tonight?" she asked as she opened the van door. "I'd much rather have you call, but Kari has the hearing of a bat, and if she heard me talking to you, she'd have her ear pressed up against the keyhole."

That would be the stuff of nightmares considering the things Jace wanted to say to Bronte. If Kari caught wind of Jace's hunger for her mother, he was sure he'd be struck dead by the withering glances she would throw his way. Only that morning, he'd driven past the bus stop to casually make sure the girls were safe on the lane next to the main road, and Kari must have sensed the true nature of his errand. If he'd been any closer, his hair would have caught on fire.

"I'll get ahold of you around eleven. Or is that too late? I know you have to get up early."

She bit her lip in that endearing manner that he was beginning to recognize whenever she faced a dilemma. "Any earlier and Kari won't be fast asleep. I probably should be in bed by then, too, but . . ." Her expression radiated a warmth that had the ability to burrow into his chest and wrap around his heart. "I need to hear from you. Even if we can't talk for long." With a final wave, she climbed into her car and started the engine.

Although Jace knew he'd be cutting it close to finish his fields before the allotted time, he still found himself loath to move until she'd turned the van around and disappeared down the lane in a cloud of dust.

Finally, he scooped up the sack and the milk jug, climbed the fence, and jogged to his own vehicle. After revving the engine and executing a tight turn in the narrow lane, he hurried back to the fields.

Unfortunately, as soon as he rounded the bend, he could see that his "unauthorized break" had already been noticed. Elam's truck was parked on the lane beside the tractor, along with the smaller pickup used by the hired men. Bodey's rig was only a few yards behind.

"Damnit."

Jace rolled to a stop and killed the engine. Then, grabbing the sack and the milk, he strode through the field to where his brothers stood by the tractor and their hired hands waited impatiently in their vehicle.

As soon as he got close enough, Bodey began to grin in a way that left no doubts that he was itching to give Jace a hard time.

Elam, on the other hand, tipped back the brim of his hat and offered Jace an all-knowing gaze that could only be meted out by an older brother.

"It's about time you got back. We've been waiting for twenty minutes," Elam said drily. He gestured to the sack. "Did you decide to eat rather than work?"

Jace fought the urge to flip his brother off. "Bronte dropped by with a snack."

"Oh, ho! Bron-*tay!*" Bodey offered in a singsong voice, his smirk growing even wider.

Jace would have punched him if he were close enough.

Elam grinned with wicked enjoyment. Clearly, he wasn't finished giving Jace shit. "Did she bring us anything?"

Jace clenched his jaw to keep from swearing aloud before offering a short, "No. She didn't."

"Too bad. P.D. mentioned that she's really pleased with Bronte's work."

Jace mentally tucked the information away so that he could pass it on to Bronte later. Then he asked pointedly, "Why aren't all of you hard at work?"

He'd hoped his brothers would take the hint, but they didn't move. "You told the boys to meet you here when they needed seed."

"And?"

"It's in the back of your truck."

Hell. Jace had forgotten that the totes were stacked in the bed.

"Why didn't you take the tractor back to the shed and grab another one?" Jace grumbled.

Bodey's eyes twinkled. "Because you also took the keys to the 290," he said, indicating the tractor behind him. "You also forgot to bring me the checks I was supposed to deposit in the bank."

Shit, shit, shit.

Jace tunneled into his pocket, extracting the stud service

payments they'd received from a couple of local ranchers hoping to improve their own stables.

Bodey snatched them up, wisely staying safely out of swinging distance. But his sly laughter accompanied him all the way back to his truck.

Elam gestured to the boys waiting in the Toyota. Tyson hopped out of the passenger side and climbed into Jace's ranch truck. Then, with the haste of a pair of teenagers with a severe case of lead foot, the two vehicles barreled down the access road to where the ranch hands had been drilling corn into the acreage below Elam's cabin.

Elam strode toward Jace, his boots sinking into the rich loamy earth. To his credit, he didn't razz Jace about what had clearly been more than a meeting of the minds between Bronte and him. Instead, he gestured to the corner of Jace's mouth and murmured in a silky voice rife with amusement and innuendo, "You've got a little bit of chocolate smeared on your face right about here."

Jace couldn't help himself. His hand shot to his cheek, encountering a sticky streak.

Elam laughed and kept right on walking. Even so, Jace heard him mutter, "Maybe now we can get some work done."

AS Elam climbed into his truck, he automatically reached for his phone. Seeing Jace so . . . happy had Elam automatically thinking of P.D. He remembered those first heady days when he and P.D. had started dating. He doubted if an hour passed without his wondering when they could be together.

But even as he lifted his cell from the dash, he remembered that P.D. was in Salt Lake, picking up supplies for the restaurant. He knew from experience that the huge warehouse had horrible reception.

Pushing the text icon, he quickly typed: Call when U can. Miss U.

As he dropped his phone back into the pocket of his shirt, Elam marveled at how his feelings for P.D. grew stronger every day. He supposed that, because he'd been deployed a lot during his marriage to Annabel, and the way she'd died so suddenly, he was especially mindful of how precious love could be.

So what are you waiting for?

The thought raced through his brain. More than anything, he wanted to share his life with P.D.—all of it. Hell, they already lived like a married couple for the most part. If it weren't for the way they traded sleeping arrangements back and forth between their houses, no one would ever know the difference.

If Elam were solely in charge, he would have taken her to Vegas, a church, or a justice of the peace by now. But even though he had no doubts about P.D.'s feelings for him, he'd known that—because of her upbringing with a pair of free-spirited, neglectful parents—P.D. had needed to come to the realization that Elam wasn't going anywhere.

Now, it was time to nudge her into taking that last, final step.

A warmth flooded through his body at the mere thought. Hell, yeah. Let's face it, he was an old-fashioned man. Elam wanted his ring on her finger and her name linked to his. He wanted to wake with her head on the pillow next to him for the next fifty years—even longer, God willing. He yearned to introduce her as his wife to his business associates and hoped she would enjoy doing the same. Heaven help him, he ached to stop all this moving back and forth and make a permanent home—either in his cabin or her house, he really didn't care.

So go ahead and ask her.

In the past, the thought was enough to make him break out in a cold sweat. But right now . . . he felt nothing but peace.

It was time.

He just had to think of a romantic way to pop the question.

FOURTEEN

B RONTE was subdued as she left the elevator and headed down the hall to her grandmother's hospital room. On the way to Logan, Lily's teacher had called again. He'd tried to encourage Lily to participate in class and she'd burst into tears.

Bronte had reassured the man that her daughter was struggling with her father's absence. But the call had merely reaffirmed her decision to get Lily some help.

"Bronte?"

Yanked from her thoughts, she looked up to see Steff Sato striding toward her.

"You're going the wrong way," Steff said with a smile. "They removed the ventilator from your grandmother this morning. She's no longer in ICU. She's sitting up in bed, alert, and asking about food."

Relief shuddered through Bronte's frame. With everything that had been weighing on her, she needed some good news.

Steff gestured in the opposite direction. "She's in the south wing."

The petite nurse led her down the hall and through a pair of double doors. Here, the colors were slightly more vibrant. Walls of windows on either side allowed the sunlight to stream in.

Steff led her to a room at the end of the corridor. Since the door was closed, Bronte hesitated before going in and touched Steff's arm. It had suddenly occurred to her that Jace wasn't the only friend she'd made who could help her with Lily.

"Could I ask you a question?"

Steff slid her hands into the front pockets of her scrubs. "Sure."

"My daughter . . . Lily . . . I've been growing concerned about her lately. At first I thought that she was reacting to the move and the fact that her father and I have divorced. But now . . . I think she needs a pediatrician or even a counselor."

The thought was still daunting. Although her job at Vern's miraculously gave her some health insurance, it wouldn't take effect until all of the paperwork was filed. Bronte would have to wait until the end of May before receiving her first paycheck and she'd been pinching pennies like a miser. After school fees and filling her tank up with gas had dented her stash, she didn't have much left.

But she couldn't worry about that now. Not when Lily might need more help than Bronte could give her.

Steff must have sensed some of her disquiet because she squeezed her hand. "I know two really good pediatricians who work in Bliss—and a few more here in Logan. I'll make up a list. Any of them could recommend a counselor that will work with your insurance."

"Thanks, Steff."

"Come by the nurses' station in ICU when you're done and I'll have the names and numbers ready for you."

That sliver of hope increased when Bronte pushed through the door and Annie looked up, smiled widely, and held her arms out in a tremulous greeting.

Bronte willingly sank into her grandmother's familiar embrace. Soon, at Annie's gentle prodding, the events of the past week, past month, past year spilled out of her mouth in what she feared would be an incoherent jumble. But once she'd finished, Annie squeezed her hand, saying, "You all must stay here in Bliss with me."

Bronte offered her grandmother a sheepish glance. "I was hoping you would say that. We've been high-handed about getting things ready for your homecoming so the house will be easier for you to maneuver. The girls and I have commandeered your spare bedrooms. Once you're on your own feet, we'll find a place—"

"No," Annie inserted firmly. "You'll stay here with me. For as long as you like. Make yourself to home." Her eyes sparkled briefly with tears. "I can't tell you how wonderful it will be to have you all to myself for a while."

After that, Annie insisted on hearing more about the girls. Bronte soon had her laughing about Kari's latest attempts to get Tyson's attention. When she confessed that Lily had not taken the news of the divorce well, Annie reassured her with, "Give her time. No need to worry yet."

Less than an hour had passed before Bronte saw that Annie's energy was flagging. Leaning down to kiss her cheek, she promised to bring the children on the weekend and stay for a longer visit. Even so, by the time Bronte had gathered her things, Annie was asleep.

One last time, Bronte leaned down to squeeze her grandmother's hand and kiss her on the forehead. Then she was hurrying back to her car.

As she headed over the mountain pass into the valley again, she couldn't account for the way her pulse adopted an uneven bossa nova. A glance at the clock showed her that, because her visit to the hospital had been briefer than usual, she had several hours before the children's bus would arrive.

Impulsively, she turned into the parking lot at Vern's. She'd brought a loose-leaf with her favorite recipes so that P.D. would have a better idea of her current baking repertoire. If she hurried, she might have time to grab another treat to take to Jace.

But as soon as she stepped into the busy kitchen, P.D. waved to her from the far side of the room.

"I was thinking about you," she called. "Have you got a minute?"

"Sure."

"Go on through to my office. I'll be right there."

Bronte nervously headed through the large swinging doors to the corridor beyond, then walked through to P.D.'s office. Slightly nervous, she perched on the edge of a leather chair, taking in the antiques that filled the room—a battered partner's desk, wooden filing cabinets, and an old swooning couch. Somehow, P.D.'s deft hand made the pieces look elegant. Bronte wasn't sure she could have carried off the same effect. In Boston, the brownstone had been decorated with ultramodern furniture with sharp edges and clean lines. Bronte had been so young when she'd married that she'd allowed Phillip to take the lead, and he'd insisted that their home be a showplace—until he'd begun to pawn the pieces one by one to support his habit.

Bronte realized that if she were asked to furnish a house now, she wouldn't even know what she wanted.

No. That wasn't true. She'd lived too long in the museum-like atmosphere of the brownstone to do that again. Instead, she would decorate for comfort with soft couches and over-sized pillows—and thickly carpeted floors to encourage bare feet.

"Sorry about that," P.D. said, hurrying inside and taking her place behind the desk. "It's been crazy busy today"—she held up her hands—"not that I'm complaining!" Grinning, she reached into her desk drawer and took out an envelope, pushing it across the blotter. "I meant to give you this before you left, but I didn't catch you in time."

Curious, Bronte picked it up. "What is it?"

"Your check for the last two weeks. I know I told you that payroll is done the end of the month, but I decided to pay you twice in May. I'm sure you've got some expenses with the move and traveling to Logan every day. In June, I'll put you on the same schedule as everyone else."

Bronte glanced at the amount of the check and gasped. "But this is too much!"

P.D. shook her head. "Remember, I told you that there would be a bonus if your baked goods were sold in take-out orders or catering jobs. That's your share. In fact, that's what I wanted to talk to you about. We're running out of the cookies by midafternoon, so I'd like you to double the batches, if you can. Same with the banana blueberry loaf. I've also got a couple of catering jobs coming up next month for some school events and a Ladies' Civic Club tea. I was hoping you'd be able to help me there."

"Absolutely!"

"Great. I'll get the particulars written out for you so that you can let me know what supplies to order. If you need help with the catering jobs, we can probably spare someone from the line early in the afternoon. Let me know."

Since it was clear P.D. was finished, Bronte stood, still slightly dazed. She was at the door before she remembered the recipes.

"Do you still need the binder I brought? I, uh . . ." She paused, clearing her throat and trying to offer as casually as possible. "I'm meeting Jace and I thought I'd bring him some cookies or something."

P.D. grinned. "Atta girl," she said.

Bronte's cheeks flamed. "No, I, uh . . ."

"Relax, Bronte," P.D. said, still smiling. "I'm not implying anything. I'm simply glad someone is looking out for him." She gestured toward the kitchen. "I'd bet money the man hasn't eaten yet—and I doubt you have either. Why don't you get some to-go boxes. Grab a couple of specials and some of your cookies. That way, you can show off what you've been doing here."

Bronte couldn't prevent the smile that slid over her features. "Thanks, P.D. I'll do that." She lifted the envelope. "Thanks for this, too."

Twenty minutes later, she had gathered the food and cashed her check at the bank. Then, just as she'd done the past few days, she pulled over long enough to call Jace.

"Hi. Are you anywhere close?"

"Yeah. I'm heading down the canal road. I need to pick up a couple of seed totes at the yard and some checks from my office."

She was quickly beginning to learn some of the jargon used on the ranch. A "tote" was a huge two-thousand-pound bag of seed. The "yard" was the work area behind the Big House. The "barn" held the stables, paddocks, and smaller feed pens, but the "shed" was the enormous metal building used to house the larger equipment—tractors, swathers, balers—as well as a welding station for making repairs. Near the large rolling door was the "man cave"—an area that had been taken over by the hired men. There were several old couches and reclining chairs, a couple of pop machines they'd bought at a flea market and stocked with soda from the grocery store, and a pair of battle-scarred tables. Jace had told her that, during the summer months when watering turns required around-the-clock attention, the hired men used the shed as a place to catch a few hours of sleep or a quick bite to eat. She'd even learned that Tyson's hat with its FRIENDS DON'T LET FRIENDS DRIVE GREEN slogan was a tongue-in-cheek reference to the friendly rivalry that existed between those who used Case machinery, which was predominantly red, and those who used John Deere equipment, which was green.

"Are you in a hurry?" she asked, her heart stuttering in anticipation.

"No," he drawled. "Not really. What have you got in mind?"

His voice seemed to drop an octave, bringing all sorts of ideas to the forefront. She vainly tried to push them away.

"If I bring you some lunch from Vern's, could you spare me some time?" Against her will, the query was tinged with the same intimacy that had invaded his. Probably because she was wondering how long she should wait before launching herself into his arms.

"I'd be happy to give you whatever time you need, with or without the lunch."

A delicious shiver chased up her spine, and she had to clear her throat in order to speak coherently.

"Where should I meet you?"

"Have a seat on the back porch of the Big House. I'm almost there."

Bronte had just set the sack with the containers of food on a round picnic table under the Big House portico when she heard Jace's truck pull into the yard. He drove past her in a cloud of dust, parked, then jumped from the cab.

A frisson of excitement shot into her extremities when she realized he wasn't even going to bother with his errand. Instead, he strode toward her, his long legs eating up the distance, his hat pulled low. He tugged at a pair of leather work gloves, stuffing the tips into his back pocket, then smiled.

"Hello, beautiful," he murmured.

By this time, Bronte had already come down the steps to meet him. Without any more fanfare, he wrapped his arms around her waist. Since she stood on the last tread, their faces were about even, and he took advantage of that fact, swooping in for a kiss.

Bronte's body responded to him immediately—a fact that still had the power to astound her. He only had to touch her and she flashed hot and cold, every inch of her skin tingling to life.

Slipping her arms around his neck, she opened her mouth, allowing his tongue to sweep inside, closing her eyes so that she could hungrily absorb the heat of his body, the firmly muscled shoulders and strong back.

And his mouth . . . heavens, what he could do to her with little nips and sucks. He broke away from her lips to explore her temples, her cheekbones, her jaw. He softly nipped her earlobe, causing her to gasp, then moved lower to trail a string of kisses along her neck.

"Mmm. You smell good," he whispered. "Like chocolate. What were you baking today?"

"Cherry chocolate jumbles and mint brownies," she gasped, barely able to say the words. "I brought you some."

His lips moved against her in a smile. "I'd rather taste you right now."

Lordy, lordy, what this man did to her. With a few whispered words, he managed to make her feel like the most beautiful woman in the world.

"I brought sand . . . sandwiches," she gasped as he explored lower, moving to the hollow between her collarbones, then down, down.

"Uh, huh."

"And . . . and . . ."

But his tongue was slipping into the valley between her breasts, and she didn't give a damn what was in the sack—or if they even ate. This was what she had come for, and she wasn't fooling either one of them. She'd been counting the hours, the minutes, until she could be this close to him again.

Suddenly, she was scrambling to pull the cotton shirt from his belt so that her fingers could plunge beneath to explore the hair-roughened skin. She fumbled with the buttons until she managed to undo them. The minute her hands spread wide over the hard ridges of his abs, then higher to flatten over his pecs, to the taut buds of his nipples, Jace's arms snapped around her waist and he was carrying her toward the back door.

Without conscious thought, her legs wrapped around his waist, even as she began her own delicious tasting of his jaw, his neck, the curve of muscle leading into the breadth of his shoulders. She was barely aware of the way he carried her through the kitchen and beyond, somehow reaching a hall that led into a room with floor-to-ceiling bookshelves, a huge oak desk, filing cabinets, and a long leather couch.

He slammed the door behind them and she heard the click of a lock snapping home.

As if the sound released the last of her inhibitions, she lowered her feet to the ground, lifted the hat from his head, and tossed it in the general direction of the desk. Then, grasping the hem of her T-shirt, she quickly pulled it over her head and threw it to the side before smoothing his own shirt off his back.

Jace's chuckle was low and sweet as honey. His gaze burned a path over her bare shoulders and down to where a white satin bra cupped the fullness of her breasts. There was no disguising the hardened points of her nipples.

"Holy shit. What's come over you?"

She countered with, "Do you mind?"

"Hell, no." He smoothed his hands over her shoulders, then down her back. "I don't want you to rush into anything you're not ready—"

She touched a finger to his lips. "I've never felt this way before. Ever."

He couldn't hide the flare of passion and pleasure that appeared in his eyes at her words.

"So we'll take it slow."

She smoothed her palms over the warm flesh of his chest. "Why?"

"So we can enjoy it longer."

She couldn't argue with that.

"We've only got an hour before the school bus arrives," she reminded him, reaching to unhook her bra.

"I can work with that."

AS soon as Bronte's bra dropped to the floor, Jace had serious doubts about his most recent pronouncement.

She was so beautiful.

It wasn't merely the round globes of her breasts bared in front of him. It was everything. The dark hair tousled around her shoulders, her beautiful creamy skin. A wild light had entered her gray-green eyes and he still marveled at the fact that she looked at him that way.

At him.

Her expression alone was enough to bring him to a fever pitch. He'd never known a woman who was so responsive to his touch. Even now, as he trailed a single finger across her lips, down her jaw, the slender stalk of her neck, and down, down to the hollow between her breasts, he saw a trail of gooseflesh rising in his wake. When he strayed to circle her nipple, she shuddered, the tiny bud becoming rock-hard beneath his touch, her eyelids growing heavy with sensation. A rosy flush stained her cheeks, but not one of embarrassment. No, the color was due to arousal, pure, un-adulterated arousal.

Bending, he took the dusky pink nub in his mouth, licking, tasting, before sucking on it with a gentle pressure.

Bronte arched against him, her breath catching, her whole body seeming to hang suspended. She ground her hips against him even as her hands wrapped around the back of his head, pulling him even closer. Then, to his infinite delight and astonishment, she gasped, her body convulsing in a way that left no doubt that she was climaxing.

Jace held her tightly, letting her absorb the sensations, watching as the pleasure washed over her in a molten wave. Then, when she grew still in his arms, he kissed her, deeply, forcefully.

They parted only briefly enough for her to gasp against his lips, "How do you do that to me? How can you make me feel so . . ."

"Horny?"

"Wonderful."

He didn't even bother to check his words—couldn't have done so if he tried. "Maybe because we're meant to be together," he murmured, his lips straying down to the place where her neck swept into her shoulders. Again, she shivered, and he made a mental note to remember that spot.

"Jace?"

"Mmm."

"I don't think I want to go slow anymore. I know you said we should, but . . ."

He drew back to see that her eyes were feverish. She moved restlessly against him, and he realized that she was already so on fire that she could come apart. This time, she wanted them to be together.

He didn't bother to answer, just reached for the buttons to her jeans—and she was doing the same, wrestling with his belt and zipper.

"Hold on," he whispered when she reached beneath to sweep the fabric away.

As quickly as he could, he reached into his pocket and took out his wallet, fumbling clumsily with the worn leather until he felt a familiar packet. Placing the condom on the desk, he returned his attentions to Bronte, trying to tug down her jeans. But her pants were tight—a plus when he watched her moving from across the room, but a definite drawback when he wanted her out of them.

She laughed softly, kicking off her shoes, then wriggling out of the denim in a way that was far more titillating than any harem dancer's routine. Then she straightened . . .

Jace forgot to breathe. Never in his life had he seen anyone more perfect. She was lithe and slim, her hair spilling over her chest, her breasts arching into the air. He followed the gentle sweep of her waist to the fullness of her hips. Here, he could see the evidence of her motherhood in the faint remnants of stretch marks and a sliver scar left from what must have been a Caesarean.

Bronte flattened her hands over the area self-consciously, but he moved them away again, pulling her toward him, murmuring, "God, you're gorgeous. All of you."

He thought he saw a glimmer of tears in her eyes—and wondered at their cause. Had that prick, her ex-husband, made her feel that she was somehow "less-than" because she'd borne two children? What kind of man did that? Especially considering the two beautiful girls in question?

Jace felt a primal surge of possession, knowing that if he ever found himself in the company of Bronte's ex, Jace would willingly pound him into the ground for the sheer pleasure of it. But then, Bronte was reaching to stroke the length of him through his jeans and all coherent thought scrambled. He could only arch his head back and wallow in the sheer pleasure that galloped through his veins and seemed to center on that point of contact. He couldn't think of anything but her stroking his bare flesh.

He reached to push his pants down, but she held him at the wrists.

"Uh-uh," she breathed, lifting on tiptoe to press her lips against his. "I want to be in charge of the reveal."

What the hell? Did she have any idea what she was doing to him? She'd always come across as rather prim and proper, controlled, reserved. But as soon as they were alone, she morphed into a sex kitten with a mind of her own.

She eased his zipper down with the leisurely pace of a connoisseur, then reached to push his pants down around his hips. Before he could summon enough presence of mind to kick free, she grasped him in her hands.

This time, it was Jace who nearly came unglued. Her expression of rapt enjoyment was enough to push him over the edge, and the steady pressure of her fingers . . .

Growling, he quickly reached for the condom while he still had the presence of mind to do so.

Bronte released him only long enough for him to prepare himself. Then, she was reaching to pull him down for her kiss, even as the warmth of her body pressed tightly against him.

Suddenly, it was Jace who felt out of control. Her kisses, the sweeping arcs of her hands, the way she ground against him, were more than he could bear.

"Damnit," he rasped against her. "I can't hold on much longer."

"Then don't," she said with a temptress's smile. "Next time, we'll be slow."

Next time.

The words were his undoing. Lifting her against him, he strode toward the nearest wall. Clearly interpreting his intent, she wound her legs around his waist and . . .

In one thrust, he was sliding home. Bronte's head arched backward. Her lashes formed dark half-moons against her cheeks. Then a cry of utter abandon escaped her lips and—*damnit all to hell!* He could feel her coming around him.

The sensations pushed him over the edge and he felt his own release come hard and fast as he thrust into her again and again, his whole body seeming to explode in sheer passion. Never in his life had he felt like this with a woman. Sure, he'd enjoyed sex. But this . . .

This was an atomic bomb of pleasure that robbed him of reason. His entire being was swallowed up in sheer sensation. Even when it was over, when he stood trembling, holding her weight, pressing her into the paneling of the wall, he couldn't release her—didn't want to release her.

Distantly, he felt her fingers sift through his hair, but his eyes remained closed as he soaked in every last detail of her skin against his, her moistness surrounding him. She smiled against him and he felt her lips move to his ear.

"Wow."

This time, it was his turn to smile—an idiotic grin that he couldn't seem to control any more than he'd been able to control his passion.

"Yeah. Wow."

She laughed softly, an intimate sound that was husky and oh so enticing.

"I've never done that before."

He managed to crack open an eye, then became immediately contrite when he realized that he'd been pounding into her against the wall.

Damn. Had he hurt her?

"Sorry, I—"

She stopped him with a finger against his lips. "I wasn't complaining. I was . . . congratulating you." Her smile became even more wicked. "I'm looking forward to exploring your repertoire."

Instantly, he felt his body reacting to the challenge.

"How much time do we have left?"

"About fifteen minutes."

Against her lips, he murmured, "I think I can rise to the challenge."

FIFTEEN

——•——

LONG after Bronte had raced out the front door to hurry home, Jace strode through the back, intent on meeting Barry's school bus at the end of the lane. He had business in town, and he was pretty sure Barry would want to come. If he hurried, he could make it in time.

As he stepped outside, he realized that his chances of an easy getaway were gone. Elam and Bodey sat at the picnic table, the remains of the Vern's containers scattered in front of them.

Hell.

"Thanks for lunch, Jace," Bodey said with a grin.

Jace's eyes narrowed in warning, even as he wondered how much they knew. Damnit, he didn't think that Bronte and he had been loud enough to be heard outside, but . . .

"What the hell are you two doing here, anyway?" Jace ground out between clenched teeth.

Bodey stood, scooping his hat off the table and settling it over his brow with leisurely care. Beneath the brim, his eyes sparkled with obvious humor. "I came to see what was taking you so long with the seed totes. But when I saw lunch was provided . . ." He shrugged. "I couldn't let the goat get it."

As if giving credence to the statement, Bitsy bleated from her spot under the trees. It was obvious from the goat's hopeful expression and wagging tail that she was hoping to receive the leftovers.

Jace's hands curled into fists, waiting for Bodey to say more and be his usual asshole self. But miraculously, he refrained.

Elam was the next to stand. "I came to get something out of the safe and find out why Bodey was taking so long."

Jace felt a surge of panic. The safe was located in the office. Had Elam made it as far as the door?

But Elam didn't seem inclined to give him a hard time. Instead, he said, "Once I saw another whole lunch going to waste . . ." He patted his taut stomach. "I never could resist one of P.D.'s brisket sandwiches—especially when it's been left outside where the raccoons can find it."

Jace consciously relaxed his hands, not wanting to transmit his tension to his brothers. "Glad you both liked it. Now get the hell back to work."

Bodey laughed and sauntered to the edge of the porch, then jumped over the steps to the ground beneath. "Your wish is my command," he called as he headed toward the flatbed truck that was already loaded with the necessary seed totes.

Elam, however, didn't move. He waited until Bodey was out of earshot before he stood and squinted up at the clear blue sky.

"Seems you've been taking some awfully long breaks the last couple of days," Elam remarked in a tone that could have melted butter.

Jace instantly bristled, already taking a breath so that he could mount his defense. But before he could think of a crushing rejoinder, Elam slapped him on the back and said, "Good for you. It's about time you did something for yourself. Let me and P.D. know if you'd like Barry to spend some evenings with us. With Bodey heading out of town soon to compete on the cow-cutting circuit . . ." He paused, glancing back at Jace, his eyes warm and filled with something that looked like approval. ". . . you simply might want some privacy."

Then he grinned, touching his finger to the brim of his hat. "We'll see you later," he drawled as he headed into the house.

Jace wasn't sure, but there seemed to be extra emphasis placed on the word *later*.

AS she waited at the end of Annie's lane for the school bus, Bronte relaxed against the headrest, one hand draped loosely on the steering wheel. Her body still thrummed with the effects of Jace's lovemaking. She would probably have a few new aches and pains to contend with come tomorrow. But she truly didn't care. Her entire being seemed a study in contradictions. She felt exhilarated, yet peaceful. Vulnerable and oh so powerful. She only had to think about Jace—about the things they'd shared—for a warmth to pool deep inside her.

Is this what she'd been missing all these years? She'd married Phillip so young—too young. There had been passion between them, sure. But she could now see that her relationship with him had been borne more out of curiosity and an impatient need to be considered an adult. Having come from a broken home, she'd been so sure that she knew exactly what—and who—she wanted.

But now?

Now, she realized that she'd jumped at the first man she'd felt would propose. She'd been so focused on marrying and forming a solid family of her own, she hadn't noticed that she'd been building that pipe dream on shifting sand.

The signs of Phillip's addictive nature had been there from the beginning—first in his obsessive eating habits, then his nonstop exercising routine. Then, there had been the nightly whiskies, which had soon become two or three. At one point, when he'd been working to get a second branch of his clinic off the ground, she'd suspected that he might have been using more than caffeine to keep him alert during the long hours, but she'd never been able to find definitive proof.

Then he'd been in the accident, which had torn up his knee. Two surgeries later, he was popping pain meds like they were candy. From there, it had been a downhill slide from prescription drugs to street drugs, until she hadn't even recognized the man who staggered into their bedroom each night.

Her brow creased at the memories, at the flood of pain and anger that came rushing back. She remembered the bitter fights, the countless visits in rehab, the crushing defeat when she realized that he was using again.

Finally, there was the night when she'd awakened from a dead sleep to find Phillip had jimmied the lock connecting the basement apartment to the rest of the brownstone. He'd crept through the dark house to her bedroom and slapped his hand over her mouth. Clearly high, he'd snarled at her, blaming her for everything that had happened to turn his existence into a living hell. He'd claimed that she'd never loved him enough, never helped him enough, never given him enough—in bed or out—for him to be happy. Pulling a pistol from his waistband, he'd struck her across the cheek so hard that she'd felt herself losing consciousness, Phillip disappearing down a tunnel of darkness as his face seemed to rearrange itself like scrambled pixels.

The only thing that helped to keep her from disappearing into that void was the fact that he was armed and her children were in the next room. If he was willing to hurt her, what might he do to them?

For the first time, she fought back, striking him hard with one of the pretentious marble sculptures kept on the bedside table. He'd fallen to the floor, stunned. His eyes filled with childlike tears and he began sobbing, piteously asking, "Why, Bronte? Why?"

It had taken every shred of strength she possessed to wrench the gun from his hand and push it as far as she could under the bed. Then, she'd called Phillip's business partner and insisted that if he didn't come and take Phillip away, she would call the police.

When Jeremy Montero's taillights disappeared into the darkness, Bronte had known what she had to do. Feverishly, she'd begun to pack. By the time her children awakened, the van was loaded with the most necessary items, and all that remained was for them to gather their clothes.

Then, she'd left the brownstone, her husband, and the life that she'd known.

And she'd come to Bliss.

Her eyes blinked open, seeing the school bus moving like a lumbering bumble bee that slowly went from stop to stop.

Bliss.

How could she have known that she would find more than a haven here? The town had lived up to its namesake, because for the first time in years, Bronte felt . . . happy. Even more, she was beginning to feel comfortable in her own skin again. She was realizing that Phillip had been wrong. She wasn't the weak, incompetent, colder-than-ice woman that he'd claimed her to be.

She was strong. Resourceful.

And if the last few hours were anything to go by, she was far from frigid.

The bus had stopped in front of the mailboxes belonging to the Taggart brothers. Although she couldn't make out much detail from this distance, she recognized the white truck that came skidding to a stop at the end of the road, and the gangly frame that jumped from the steps of the bus. Her heart thudded against her ribs when she realized that *she* was the reason that Jace was late in picking up his brother.

Sliding out of the car, she stood with her arm shading her eyes, wondering if he could see her in the distance. As the flashing lights of the bus shifted from red to yellow, she heard the quick honk of his horn.

In that instant, as she offered a broad wave, she experienced a brief jolt of uncertainty.

What was she doing here? Was she leaping from the arms of one man into those of another? Hadn't she learned yet that you couldn't know a person's true character in the space of a few days or weeks?

Even as the thought appeared, she purposely shoved it away. Jace wasn't Phillip—and she wasn't looking for marriage. Maybe this . . . fling . . . would fizzle out as quickly as it had raged to life. It didn't matter. She would enjoy it while she could. But if there was one thing she'd learned from her marriage to Phillip, it was that she didn't ever want to live her life hiding the truth. If she and Jace were going to enjoy a relationship, they were going to do it in the open. She wasn't ashamed of the time they'd spent together and she refused to live as if she were. So that meant that she needed to have a heart-to-heart with her daughters. Since she had some money in her pocket and the prospect of more paychecks to come, she decided that for the first time in years, she and her daughters were going to splurge. She would take them out to dinner in Logan—nothing too expensive, pizza or burgers. Then . . .

She'd been thinking it was time to switch phone carriers. She and Phillip were divorced. According to their agreement, any arrangements he might want to make to see the children had to be made through her lawyer. So there was no reason to endure his constant efforts to force her to respond. Instead, she would change her phone, her number . . .

And she would add a second phone to her plan. She wanted Kari to have the ability to contact her, anytime, anyplace, so that her daughter would have the freedom to spend time with her new friends. Lily, on the other hand, needed new pants and shoes. The fresh air of Utah seemed to be agreeing with her, and she'd had a growth spurt. Maybe she would like a pair of boots like Barry's. As for Bronte . . . she was feeling the urge to write poetry again. All she needed was a notebook and her children's smiles.

Once their shopping was done, they could go see Annie and still get home at a reasonable time for a school night. Through it all, Bronte would talk to them, really talk to them. If there was a question they wanted answered, she would tell them the truth, no matter what. Hopefully, by the end of the evening, she could gently make it clear that they wouldn't be returning to Boston anytime soon. Even more important, Jace would become a regular visitor at their home.

The bus rumbled to a stop, its red lights flashing. Bronte's eyes skipped to the white truck that had rolled to a halt behind it. Her gaze tangled with Jace's through the windshield—and he must have interpreted the thoughts that raced through her brain. Because even as she experienced a flashing montage of memories—the way he touched her, tasted her, filled her with his heat—he offered her a slow smile filled with his own remembered pleasure.

Then, her girls stepped off the bus and her attention was diverted. But that didn't mean that she couldn't feel the brand of his gaze as he drove past and looked at her one last time.

IT was nearly eight o'clock that night when Jace was roused from mindlessly gazing at the television set. It was Barry's turn to pick the program, so they were watching *Star Trek: Into Darkness*. Again. Sometimes Jace felt like he could recite the script from memory. Normally, Jace would find something to do in another room. But Barry had been restless and out of sorts all evening, and Jace was trying to head off a meltdown before he could get his brother into bed.

The doorbell rang and Jace waited for a minute, since Barry usually insisted on racing to get it first. But clearly, he was in a sci-fi coma, so Jace pushed himself to his feet.

"What do you say I go get that?" he muttered to himself.

He wasn't exactly dressed for company. After returning from Logan, he and Barry had spent another couple of hours feeding cattle. So once they'd come inside, Jace had showered and dressed for comfort in sweats and a T-shirt. He grimaced when he caught his reflection in the entry. He quickly tried to comb his hair back into place with his fingers, without much success.

Hopefully, whoever it was wouldn't be staying for long.

But as he opened the door, Jace immediately regretted the thought when he found Bronte silhouetted against the headlights of her van.

Jace immediately flipped on the porch light.

"Bronte. Is something wrong?"

She stood with her hands shoved into her pockets for warmth against the nighttime chill.

"No. But I wondered if I could talk to you a minute."

He offered her a slow grin.

"Sure. Come on in." He held the screen for her and she ducked inside. "Where are the girls?"

"In the van, so I'll have to hurry."

She stepped farther into the entry and he followed, only partially closing the door. He didn't want her kids to freak out, but he also didn't want to waste the moment. As soon as they were shielded from view, he drew Bronte into his arms.

She must have shared his feelings, because she immediately melted into him, wrapping her arms tightly around his neck and lifting on tiptoe so that she could hold him close.

"You've got me worried," he murmured against her, his eyes closing as he absorbed the familiar scents of vanilla and chocolate that clung to her clothing as well as the faintly floral hint that must be the remnants of her shampoo.

"Everything's fine—great, in fact." She drew back enough to smile up at him. "They'll be releasing Annie from the hospital this weekend."

"That's fantastic!"

"Yeah, I think so, too. I talked it over with Annie, and she thought she'd be up to a gathering Saturday afternoon. I was worried she might be too tired, but she insisted that she wants to see everyone. So I thought we could have an open house, with sandwiches and cookies. You know, some finger food. People can stop in to visit and leave again depending on their schedules. She would especially like to see you and all of your brothers."

"I'm sure they'd love to come."

"Good." Bronte seemed to choose her words before offering him a crooked smile. "I also had a chat with my girls tonight and . . . we wondered—as a kind of thank-you for everything you've done for us—if you and Barry would . . . come for dinner Friday evening."

Jace wondered if the "we" she spoke of reflected the girls' true sentiments or merely Bronte's wishful thinking.

"Barry and I would love to come." Jace's eyes narrowed as he carefully searched her features. "But won't that cause more problems?"

She eased back in his arms. Her lip caught between her teeth in a way that was becoming completely endearing. It was her tell, conveying to Jace that she was feeling her way through a situation fraught with complications.

"That's just it. I don't want to sneak around, Jace. I don't want to have a relationship with anyone if it can't be open and aboveboard."

The words were so unlike what he'd been expecting, that Jace felt as if he'd been thrown into a runaway elevator. He couldn't think—couldn't breathe.

No. God, no. She couldn't be dumping him. Not yet.

"So you, uh . . ." He had to swallow hard when his voice emerged husky and inarticulate. "You don't want to see each other after Friday?"

Her shocked expression reassured him even more than words could have done. "What? No! Of course, I want to see you." She placed a hand on his chest, right over his still-thumping heart. "That's just it. I want to see more of you. I want us to be free to explore whatever is happening between us. But Barry's right. We have to go about it the proper way. My girls have to understand how much I've grown to care for you. Even more, they need to see what a loving, healthy relationship looks like. Maybe then, they'll understand why I had to divorce their father."

Jace stared down at Bronte, wondering if she knew what a good person she was—what a good mother. Even more, he wondered if she knew how much she'd revealed to him. Clearly, Bronte wasn't regarding their time together as a "casual fling." Until now, when he felt corners of his heart begin to unfurl and relax, he hadn't realized how much he'd dreaded that Bronte would be like the other women he'd dated in the past—willing to accept a little fun and some casual sex, but opposed to anything deeper.

Abruptly, Jace realized that he wanted more from Bronte—he wanted everything that she was willing to give him. As astonishing and as inconceivable as it seemed, Jace found his feelings for her growing exponentially each day. She was everything he'd ever dreamed of finding in a woman. She was beautiful, loving, and kind. She was accepting of his brother and understanding of Jace's work schedule. But his emotions went beyond that—beyond a good time and great sex. With her, he felt at peace. When she was gone, he counted every minute until he could see her again.

"So what's the plan?" he asked.

She sighed. "The girls and I had a long discussion tonight. Or rather, I talked, they listened, and then they sulked. But . . ." She smoothed away a lock of hair that hung over his brow, then ran the backs of her fingers over his temple and down to the line of his jaw.

"I'd like to date you, Jace Taggart. I'd like to have you drop by my house whenever you want, and I hope you'd be willing to have me do the same."

Spots of color had appeared in her cheeks—as if suggesting that they spend time together was something too forward. The thought made him smile. There was something so sweet and proper and a little bit old-fashioned about this woman. Yet, as soon as they were alone, she became thoroughly modern, wanton, and sexy as hell.

"So you're asking me to go steady with you?"

Her eyes rolled, and he laughed. So that was where Kari had learned the gesture.

Sensing his amusement, she sidled closer, one hand slipping between them to cup him through his sweats. "If that's what they're calling it these days."

He didn't even think of the fact that Barry was in the next room—or that her daughters waited in the car. Swooping down, he captured her lips, kissing her with the hunger that had been brewing all day. For the past hour, zoned out on the couch, with Captain Kirk and Spock yammering in the background, he'd relived every minute of their lovemaking from the kiss on the steps of the back porch, to pinning her against the wall, to christening the bearskin rug. But as arousing as the memories were, they were nothing compared to having the real woman in his arms.

All too soon, she broke free, whispering regretfully, "Sorry. It's a school night and . . ."

He kissed her softly, once, twice. "I know. I've got to get Barry in bed, too."

She groaned softly, moving backward toward the door, but pulling him with her as she went.

"Can we meet tomorrow afternoon then? I'll call as soon as I'm back from visiting Annie."

"Mmm," he affirmed against her lips as he kissed her again.

She swore and wrapped her arms around his neck, deepening the caress, then pulled back. "I gotta go."

" 'Kay."

He waited, knowing she was making up her mind about something.

"Maybe tonight . . . we could text?"

"Okay. I'd like that."

"Good." After one last kiss, she wrenched free and pushed open the screen. At the last minute, though, she poked her head back in and said, "Because I've never had text sex before."

Then she was gone, the screen slamming behind her.

Text sex? Did she mean *sexting?*

Jace stood stunned, her words seeming to ricochet in his skull like a fading echo. But then, as he heard the crunch of her tires on the gravel outside, he broke into a grin and shook his head in disbelief. Just when he thought that he had every aspect of Bronte's personality nailed down, she would throw out a curve ball in the way of a ribald comment—or she'd strip off her shirt or grip him by the balls.

And damned if it wasn't sexy as hell.

P.D. padded through the cabin, searching for Elam. She could have sworn that she'd heard him heading down to the kitchen. But when she flipped on the lights, it was empty.

"Elam?"

"Out here."

She retraced her steps through the house to the main living room where a wall of windows looked out over the valley and the twinkling distant lights of town. Sliding the door open, she stepped outside, rubbing her arms when the evening's chill raised gooseflesh.

"I'm beginning to believe you're a stalker," she said as she approached the deck railing where Elam leaned on his elbows, watching something below. "You've been out here almost every night. What is it you hope to see?"

Elam straightened, drawing her into his arms, her back against his chest. "I don't know."

She rubbed his forearms. "Still worried about Jace?"

"Mmm," he offered noncommittally.

P.D. glanced over her shoulder, then took another harder look at Elam. He was concerned, yes, but there was also a mischievous gleam in his eyes.

"What?" she asked suspiciously.

Rather than answering, he pointed toward the big house.

Squinting into the darkness, she frowned. "Is that Bronte's van?"

"Mmm hmm?"

"How long has she been there?"

"Now who's the stalker?"

P.D. elbowed him in the gut and Elam made a sound that was half laugh, half grunt. Relenting, he said, "Only a few minutes."

"Shoot. I've been hoping that the two of them would hit it off."

"Oh, I don't think there's any doubt they're . . . 'hitting it off.'"

His tone was so ripe with meaning that she peered at him again, her brows lifting. "Care to explain?"

"Can't. Bro code."

P.D. snorted.

"Let's say your lunch almost went to waste this afternoon. Until Bodey and I found it untouched and abandoned on the porch."

Interesting.

"How long do you suppose the lunch was . . . abandoned?"

"We found it around three."

"She left Vern's about one thirty."

Elam offered her a knowing grin. "Apparently, they had some business that necessitated the use of Jace's office for a while."

This time, it was P.D.'s lips that spread in a slow smile. Then she looked down at the disappearing lights. "Wonder why she didn't stay longer."

"She's got kids."

"He's got Barry."

"It'll require some creative juggling of schedules for them to find some time alone together, but I think they'll manage." His arms tightened around her waist. "Speaking of which . . ." Elam said slowly, ". . . any chance you can take a couple of hours off tomorrow afternoon?"

"Sure. What did you have in mind?"

"I'd like to take you to lunch."

"Mmm. That sounds great."

She turned, resting her head on his shoulder. "In the meantime . . . Is there any chance you could stop spying on Jace for a while and take me to bed?"

Elam scooped her into his arms, and she squeaked in surprise, her hands whipping around his neck. But she didn't complain. Every time he held her like this, she felt dainty and light as a feather. So she soaked up Elam's efforts to spoil her.

But as he turned toward the house, his attention strayed to the valley below.

"Would you look at that?" he mused.

"What?"

She looked down at the Big House, not seeing what had caused Elam's rapt attention or the flood of relief that softened his features.

He stood in silence for several minutes, staring down at his childhood home, then finally said, "The attic light is on."

Sixteen

———◆———

JACE flipped the switch and watched as a warm glow illuminated the bedroom he'd used as a boy. The garret took up nearly the entire length of the Big House. Although the sharp slope of the eaves made the spaces around the edges all but unusable, the center was long and broad and open. In the day, natural light spilled through the windows of the dormers and gleamed off the hardwood floors. It had been the perfect spot for a kid who didn't completely fit into the rough and tumble, bronco-busting, cow-roping Taggart mold. Not that Jace hadn't done his fair share of those things as well.

His gaze skipped to the rows of shelves built beneath the sloping walls. Besides the thrillers and tattered westerns, there were dozens of trophies for football and baseball, high school roping and cow cutting. But what set Jace apart from the rest of the Taggart males were the sketchbooks and port-folio cases, lumps of half-finished clay figures and welded animals he'd fashioned from bits of scrap iron, nuts, and bolts.

For long minutes, Jace stood where he was, absorbing who he used to be. There had been a time when he couldn't function unless he'd indulged in a few hours of art every day. The desire to create had been as strong as the need for food and water. He'd been driven to make something of himself. Big things. Murals and bronze statues and marble reliefs. He'd wanted to graduate from the School of the Art Institute of Chicago, study in Paris and Milan. He'd wanted gallery showings in New York, Miami, and L.A.

But his father hadn't understood the obsession that bloomed inside Jace. He was a practical man who couldn't fathom why Jace would throw away a "good education" in the basics—math, business, and science—for a dead-end career like art.

What are you going to do the rest of your life? Sell caricatures at the fair? You can't make a living doing that.

So Jace hadn't even applied to SAIC. He'd walked around with the application burning a hole in his pocket for a year, sure that his father wouldn't approve—and even if, by some miracle, he had agreed—knowing that he'd balk at the tuition.

But Jace had soon discovered that the regrets he suffered for not even broaching the subject were worse than any talk with his father might have been. So he'd set his sights on a prestigious art college back east. But when Jace approached his father about the possibility of helping him with the tuition, Boyd Taggart had clenched his jaw and proposed a deal. Two years. Jace would give him two years of work on the ranch and college at Utah State. During that time, Jace would do everything he could to learn the ranching business from the inside out. Then, if his father was happy with Jace's progress, he'd pay for two years of tuition to the art college and Jace could pay the rest.

Jace hadn't been happy about the agreement. He'd known what his father was hoping would happen. He would work Jace hard and train him well, thinking that two years would be enough to get the "drawing nonsense" out of his blood.

In part, his father had been right. Jace had thrived under the added responsibility. He'd discovered that he loved the business aspects of the ranch. Within a year, he'd been handling the land leases and a good share of the equipment loans and purchases. He'd converted their accounting process to a computer system and replaced his father's jammed filing cabinets with digital scans.

But unbeknownst to his father, the need to draw and paint and sculpt had merely been simmering below the surface, building up pressure until Jace could scarcely contain it. He grew irritable and itchy, feeling as if the ranch and the valley walls were hemming him in, keeping him from exploring the world he wanted to experience.

The day he'd met his two-year quota, he'd cornered his father. Looking back on it now, Jace realized that he probably hadn't picked the best time to broach the subject. Elam had been called overseas to Afghanistan and water shortages were stressing the crops. His father had lost a couple of hired men within a week, and fuel reports were due. So when Jace mentioned—no, demanded—that his father make good on his promise, Boyd hadn't been long on patience. He'd tried to bargain for more time, telling Jace that "next year" would be better. Or the year after that. By that time, Jace would have graduated from Utah State and Elam's enlistment would be up.

But Jace had been nineteen and filled with youthful hubris and dreams. What began as a "discussion" soon erupted into a full-fledged argument as Jace accused his father of reneging on the deal, and Boyd claimed that Jace was being self-centered and shortsighted.

Even now, Jace wasn't sure how things had escalated so quickly. He couldn't even remember everything that was said. All he knew was that his father became red-faced and angry and the shouting became bitter and personal and then Jace completely lost it. He'd accused his father of never supporting him, of being ashamed of the person he was, of trying to mold him into something he wasn't. Before he knew it—before his mother could calm things down between them as she usually did—he was up in his room, shoving a passport, his savings, and a couple of changes of clothing into a backpack. Then he was storming out of the house. An hour later, he was catching a flight to Chicago because it was the first plane to get him somewhere else.

Jace ran his fingers through his hair, then linked his fingers behind his head, not seeing the room anymore, merely remembering the desperation that had caused him to flee. He couldn't deny that his decision had been a good one. In the next two years, he'd backpacked across Europe, soaking up art, history, and architecture like parched earth waiting for a storm.

But it had also been a mistake. A huge mistake. Because he couldn't have known then that it would be the last time he would speak to his father. Their relationship ended in harsh words that he would have given anything to take back. Even worse, Jace had spent every day since knowing that his father had been ashamed of him and everything he'd tried to become.

Jace squeezed his eyes shut, trying not to think about it. Heaven only knew that he went to bed most nights wishing that he'd been less stubborn and pig-headed. If he'd been more understanding, more diplomatic, more patient . . .

But he'd been a hotheaded teenager who was sure he knew best. Once he'd flown off in a rage, his pride had kept him from being the first to try to repair the breach—even though, by the time the accident occurred, Jace already knew it was time to come home.

His eyes opened, and he blinked against the light and the unexpected moisture that gathered behind his eyes.

Damnit.

Hadn't he gone over all this a million times in his head? Hadn't he vowed that he wouldn't make the same mistakes again? That he would do everything in his power to be the man that his father had wanted him to be?

So why was he standing here, staring at the remnants of a life he'd abandoned, drowning in his need to return to those old goals? Why had he been secretly planning to take a "vacation" next winter, when, deep down, he'd known that what he really wanted to do was binge on the art to be found in Europe's finest museums, then return to his hotel room and purge himself of the need to sketch and paint. He'd told himself that his family would never have to know what he was doing. They wouldn't have to worry that he was about to abandon the ranch in favor of continuing this "drawing nonsense."

But things had become infinitely more complicated. If he continued to pursue a relationship with Bronte, he couldn't afford such self-indulgent behavior. It would be hard enough leaving Barry with Elam and P.D. for several months. But to add a girlfriend and her kids into the mix would be even more difficult.

By all rights, he should pack up the frantic obsession to paint and sculpt. He could chalk up his need to create as another youthful enterprise that a sane person shucks off as soon as he reaches adulthood, like playing tag and wrestling on the ground.

Jace dropped his hands again, willing himself to put away the desire that burned within him, growing stronger each day, until he thought he'd go crazy from it. Where other men might see the Taggart Ranch as a successful enterprise, Jace saw it as a movable picture show of shapes, colors, and textures that he longed to tame, rearrange, reexpress.

He rubbed at the spot in his chest that ached at the thought that he was once again faced with the choice of doing what was responsible or letting loose and allowing his passions to take him where they would.

But isn't your passion for Bronte growing just as strong?

"It's been a long while since you've been up here."

Jace started, glancing over his shoulder to see that Bodey was leaning a shoulder against the doorjamb.

"I always envied you for having this room," Bodey mused, his gaze wandering around the open space. "If I'd had my way, I would have moved into it the minute you left."

"Why didn't you?"

Bodey offered a bark of laughter. "As if I could. Mom and Dad would have killed me. They kept it the way you left it." His eyes, which were usually filled with a mocking humor, were clear and serious. "I think they hoped that if it remained untouched, you might come home sooner."

Jace grimaced. "Mom might have thought that. But Dad?" He shook his head.

"He felt bad that he lost his temper with you. He blamed himself."

"I doubt that," Jace said flatly. "His only regret was that I wouldn't conform to what he thought I should be."

Bodey straightened, shoving his hands into his pockets. "I know you believe that—and you have every right to think so. But I was here; I saw what happened after you left. At first, Dad was angry, sure. I don't think I've ever seen him so stomping mad as those first few days after you disappeared. But then, when it became clear that you didn't intend to come back anytime soon—and even worse, you weren't even going to let them know where you'd gone . . ." He met Jace's gaze with eyes that were dark and serious. "It got to him, Jace. Damn near broke him."

Jace clenched his jaw, sure that Bodey was exaggerating.

"I don't think he realized how serious you were about your art," Bodey continued. "Every now and then, I'd find him up here, sitting on the edge of your bed, staring off into space." He nodded toward the projects scattered around the room. "I'd wager he went through every one of your sketch books, every portfolio, every box of junk trying to figure you out—and I think it stunned him. He knew you could draw, but I don't think he absorbed how good you were until he really started studying your work. Especially the things that you'd tucked away to apply to art school."

Jace shifted in discomfort. He'd never told anyone about those pieces. Not even Bodey.

"He was proud of you, Jace. When you started sending boxes home? The ones labeled DO NOT OPEN?"

Jace tipped his head in acknowledgment. After a while, he'd had so many sketchbooks and project designs that he hadn't been able to carry them all. So every few months, he'd pack them up and send them home. Despite the labels, he'd secretly wished that his parents would look at the contents and acknowledge that he had some real talent.

"Yeah. I know them," Jace said shortly. He pointed to the parcels piled in the corner. "They're over there."

"Bet you didn't know Dad opened every single one."

Jace shot Bodey a disgusted look. "They haven't been touched since the mailman delivered them."

"Take a closer look. I was told that the minute one arrived, I was to put it on Dad's desk. He'd use his penknife to carefully slit open the flaps. Then he'd dump everything out and pore over it like clues to a treasure map. Eventually, he'd pack them up again, seal the opening he'd made, and bring them here."

"Now I know you're making this up."

Bodey offered him a cockeyed smile. "I can prove it to you." He walked to the far corner of the room, reaching behind the stack of postal boxes bearing stamps from France, Austria, and Italy, and pulled out a large frame.

He walked back to Jace, studying it as he neared. "I remember the day this came. Dad made no efforts to return this one to the box. He left a few minutes after it arrived. A week later, he brought it back into the house, all professionally framed and matted, and hung it on the wall opposite his desk." Bodey's voice dropped to a whisper. "God, he was so proud of you. He showed off this painting every time someone came to the house."

Bodey turned the picture around to show it to Jace.

Jace instantly remembered the piece. It was one of the few watercolor paintings he'd done during his sojourn in Europe. It was a herd of horses, writhing and twisting in the sun, the shapes suggested by broad strokes of a large flat brush, then overlaid with pen and ink.

In a rush, he found himself transported back to that ranch, that pasture, that day in Northern Italy. He'd topped the rise, seen the horses, and had been overcome with the smells of dust and heat, and the stink of sweaty horseflesh. In that instant, he'd been struck by such a wave of homesickness that he'd nearly fallen to his knees. Instead, he'd yanked out his sketch pad, a small set of paints, and his water bottle.

The whole piece had taken him less than twenty minutes to complete. But when he'd finished, he'd realized that he could scour Europe for another fifty years and he still wouldn't find the answers to what he wanted to do with his art. Those answers could only be found at home. Because everything he wanted to draw, paint, and sculpt were within a hundred miles of Taggart Valley.

And this same picture was the one that struck a chord with his father.

"Why didn't I ever know he saw this?" Jace asked, his voice husky and raw.

"Because one afternoon, I was playing baseball with some friends out back, and I hit a perfect fast pitch . . . right through the window of Dad's office." He pointed to a crack in the glass that ran from one corner to the next. A spiderweb of smaller cracks and portions of missing pieces testified to the strength of the speeding ball. "Dad nearly skinned me alive—not so much because of the window, but because the impact on your painting put a nick in the paper." Bodey pointed to the spot. "Dad was going to take it and get the glass repaired so he could hang it up again, but you know how things get in the summer and fall. Eighteen-hour days don't allow a whole lot of time for running into town." He cleared his throat. "By that time, the painting had taken second place to finding you."

Jace frowned. "What do you mean?"

"After that crack happened"—Bodey said, pointing to the piece—"Dad hired a private detective to track you down." He walked to the door, pausing only long enough to say, "How do you think we were able to contact you in Germany so quickly after the accident?"

Jace stood stunned, everything he thought he'd known about his father falling away much like the shattered glass in the frame he held.

His father had seen his work.

He'd been proud of him.

Tears sprang to his eyes and clogged his throat and he

impatiently scrubbed them away. Hell, he was thirty-one years old, nearly thirty-two . . .

But you were never too old for your father's approval.

Jace rested his back against the wall, still staring at the painting. Slowly he sank to the floor, resting the frame on his knees, tracing the crack, the frame, the last few pieces of remaining glass as if he could absorb his father's spirit.

"Jace?" Barry's voice floated to him from deep in the house. "Jace, where are you? Can I get out of bed and get a drink?"

"You don't need a drink, you little outlaw," Bodey interjected before Jace could compose himself enough to respond. "You want to check what's on television."

"Do not. I'm thirsty."

"All right, my man. We'll get you some water, then you can go right back to bed."

"I might need to go to the bathroom first."

"Naturally."

His brothers' voices faded as they disappeared downstairs and Jace tipped his head back, resting it against the wall.

The Taggart brothers were a team, he realized. All this time, he'd thought he was holding things together on his own. But his own misery had blinded him to the fact that his brothers had always been there, waiting in the wings, willing to help. Jace only needed to ask.

All at once, he realized that *he* was the only person responsible for the way he'd turned his back on his art. Maybe, unconsciously, he'd thought it was a form of penance for leaving home the way he had. Nevertheless, he suspected that if he announced tomorrow that he needed to go to Timbuktu to commune with nature and finger paint, they might not understand it, but they'd do everything they could to help him get there.

He touched the nick that Bodey had shown him, that tiny imperfection that had concerned his father the most. The regret was still there. Jace couldn't change the fact that the last words he'd shared with his father had been in anger. But at least he knew that his father had accepted him for who he was.

Maybe it was time for Jace to start doing the same.

BRONTE felt her pulse quicken when she rounded the bend leading up to Annie's house and saw a familiar ranch truck parked near the front stoop. Even from a distance, she could see that the new concrete ramp and porch had been finished and a stout railing had been fastened into place.

Immediately, her gaze skipped over the figures of Tyson and another of the teenage hired men. But when her search finally settled on the familiar frame of a Taggart, she felt a rush of disappointment when she realized it was Bodey who was overseeing the work, not Jace.

As soon as he heard the sound of her car, Bodey straightened and handed the socket wrench he'd been using to Tyson. After a couple of murmured words to the boys, he walked to intercept her.

Bronte braked the car and rolled down the window.

"Hi, Bodey."

He grinned, tipping his hat back so that she could see his eyes. "It's shaping up pretty quick, isn't it?"

She eyed all of the changes that had been made. The house looked nothing like the dilapidated building she'd been dismayed to find nearly a month ago. Now, the two-story dwelling sported a new coat of paint, bright trim, and a refurbished porch and stoop. The grass was freshly cut and the flower beds were weeded and ready for annuals as soon as the weather permitted.

"It's looking wonderful. I can't tell you how much I appreciate everything you've done."

"Our pleasure. We've been looking for a chance to help Annie for some time. We simply didn't want to dent her pride."

Bronte nodded. Her grandmother might still balk at the repairs that had been done, but Bronte had warned her about all of the changes, and she'd caught the hint of relief in Annie's eyes.

"I think she's going to love it all."

"Hope so." Bodey swept his hat from his head and raked his fingers through his hair. Unlike Jace, his was straight and a caramel brown. His eyes, rather than being lake blue, were flecked with green.

"Will you be coming to the party on Saturday?" Bronte asked.

"Wouldn't miss it." He gestured to the house. "I hope you don't mind, but I put some beef in your freezer—a few roasts, some hamburger, and a package of steaks. It's the least we can do for the way you've been feeding us off and on."

She opened her mouth to refute his statement, then realized he was speaking of the lunches she'd brought to Jace. Her cheeks flamed when she remembered that Jace had said they'd been eaten by Elam and Bodey.

"You probably should be thanking P.D. since my latest efforts came from Vern's."

"Even so." His smile was rife with mischief. "You'll be feeding Jace and Barry often enough, I suppose. So I thought I'd contribute to your efforts." He pointed in the direction of the Big House. "Speaking of which, Jace would have been here himself to finish this up, but he got . . . distracted. Why don't you go see if he's come up for air yet? He's in the shed."

Bronte felt her cheeks grow even warmer. It wasn't as if she and Jace were trying to keep their relationship a secret. It was . . . new and still felt private. But when Bodey offered her a wink and said, "Don't worry about the kids. I promised Barry I'd take everybody to the Corner for a drink and a burger. I'll bring them all back to the Big House around five. We've got a couple of new colts they might want to see."

Since Bronte wouldn't be going to visit Annie in Logan until later that evening, it offered Bronte and Jace several hours alone.

Bodey settled his hat on his head and touched the brim. "Try to sneak up on Jace if you can. You won't want to startle him," he said cryptically. Then he returned to the finishing touches on the stoop.

Bronte drove along the service roads to Taggart Hollow.

Following Bodey's advice, she parked near the Big House, then made her way to the shed on foot.

Even before she reached the huge building, she could hear the hiss and staccato stutter of someone using the acetylene torch. As she grew even closer, amber sparks spit through the opening. Then they disappeared to be replaced by the clang of metal on metal.

Mindful of Bodey's advice, she silently moved into the huge, arching doorway—one built to allow the larger equipment to be driven directly into the welding bay. But it wasn't a tractor or a swather that was being repaired. Instead, she could see the skeletal beginnings of iron beasts that already seemed to fight for dominance. They curved in on one another, some on two legs, some on four. There, at one end, she could see the outline of a horse in the scraps of iron that were being welded onto the armature. Its head was arched, twisting toward the shape of another animal behind it. Its mouth was open, its nostrils flared. The eyes were wild and lifelike, the ears flattened in warning, and the mane flew wildly about its neck, giving the illusion of wind and movement.

Even with so little of the massive sculpture completed, Bronte could already see the raw power of the piece. The thought of what it would look like when it was finished was mind-boggling.

In a rush, Bronte was reminded of several sculptures she'd seen in Rome on her honeymoon. Phillip had timed their trip to coincide with a multinational conference being held in Italy, so while he'd attended his meetings, she'd spent her time sightseeing. There was something about the forcefulness of Jace's animals that reminded her of the vibrant ocean horses of the Trevi Fountain.

Why hadn't he ever said anything about being an artist? Judging by what she was seeing, the man had an incredible amount of talent. He had to be a professional. Yet, he'd never mentioned anything about needing time to work or preparing for a show.

Not wishing to disturb his work, Bronte moved to the shade inside the doorway and perched on a folding chair.

But soon, it wasn't the art piece that captured her attention. It was the man who made it.

Jace's head was covered by a welding helmet, but the rest of him was on display. A tight, faded T-shirt clung to his skin. Damp patches had begun to form at his neck and between his shoulder blades, attesting to the heat of the torch and the red-hot metal, as well as the exertion of positioning the heavy iron slabs that were starting to form the front breast of the animal.

As Jace moved, she found herself privy to an anatomy lesson unlike any she'd ever had before—the bunching of muscles along his shoulders and arms, the pull of tendons, the strength of bone, the supple play of his spine.

Unbidden, Bronte's body began to prickle with awareness. She'd seen those planes and angles without the benefit of clothing only days earlier, but there was something primal, almost . . . warrior-like about a man pounding hot metal and fashioning it into another form. It would be easy to picture Jace as a blacksmith or a knight of old.

Heavens. She was starting to sound like the historical novels that P.D. had loaned her—and she had to admit that she'd grown as addicted to them as her friend. But she liked the way that the novels—and the scene before her—played on fantasies that she hadn't known she'd even harbored until now.

Something about her intense regard must have pierced Jace's concentration, because he straightened, glanced over his shoulder, then apparently did a double take. He shut off the torch and set it on a nearby bench. One by one, he tugged off a pair of heavy leather gloves, then finally lifted the welder's hood and tossed it beside the rest of his protective gear.

"Don't stop on my account," Bronte murmured.

Jace cast a self-conscious glance at the sculpture, then tipped his head to ease the strain of tired muscles.

"I was due for a break anyhow," he said with a self-conscious smile.

"I meant the striptease," she said tongue-in-cheek.

He chuckled, his head dipping and his finger rubbing his

nose—and she realized that she'd managed to catch him off guard with her bluntness.

"Come here," he murmured.

He held out a hand, but even as she rose, he met her halfway. As she wrapped her arms around his neck, he grimaced.

"I should probably take a shower before you get anywhere near me. I've been at this awhi—"

Bronte kissed him—and just as before, when their lips met, the reaction was instantaneous. She stood on tiptoe, trying to lessen the space between them as his arms wrapped around her body and pulled her up.

Jace's mouth slanted over hers, his tongue plundering inside, and she met each thrust eagerly, reveling in the way that his mere touch could send her over the edge.

Finally, he drew back, resting his forehead against hers.

"Why didn't you tell me you're an artist?" She glanced over his shoulder at the sculpture. "Your work is . . . It's amazing!"

He hugged her even tighter, then turned so that they could both survey the piece.

"Actually, I haven't done any art in . . . a dozen years or more."

"What?" she breathed in disbelief.

"It's a long story. One I'll tell you over lunch, if you have time."

Bronte wrapped her arms around his neck, finding it hard to pull her mind back to anything as mundane as lunch. It was hard to reconcile the fact that this tough, hardworking cowboy had a creative side as well. Not just that, he was literally wrestling such a work of beauty into being through the use of sheer fire and strength.

She touched his cheek. "You are so amazing," she whispered.

A touch of color tinged his cheeks. The man was blushing at the compliment. She'd never seen a grown man blush before.

"I've got to be honest with you," she said, lifting on tiptoes so that her lips were close to his ear. "This whole scenario—the horses, the welding, the pounding . . . It's turning me on."

A low, rumbling chuckle melted from his chest. If anything, the color in his cheeks deepened.

"It is, huh?"

"Mmm hmm. And Bodey announced he was taking the kids for sodas and burgers at the Corner. He won't bring them back until five."

A spark ignited in Jace's eyes. "Really," he drawled.

"That gives us about an hour and a half? Maybe two."

"That long, huh?" Jace grabbed her hand. "Come on. I'll take a shower and change. Then I'm taking you out to lunch."

"But"—she gestured to the sculpture—"I don't want to interrupt you if . . ."

He gently touched her cheek. "It'll wait. It's already waited this long"—he glanced at the piece, which nearly filled the bay—"and I've discovered I can come back whenever the mood strikes me." He stroked the line of her jaw with his thumb. "Right now, I'd rather spend time with my muse."

"Your muse?" she echoed, sure that he was teasing her.

But he continued to eye her with something akin to wonder.

"Mmm. My muse." He leaned forward to whisper close to her ear. "Maybe next time, I'll have to consider doing nudes."

Bronte felt the fiery heat surge into her own cheeks. "Don't you dare."

"Oh, I dare," he murmured.

Then he kissed her once again.

SEVENTEEN

———•◆•———

ELAM was unaccountably antsy as he waited in the parking lot of Vern's. Not for the first time, he checked his hair, his button-down shirt, and the crease he'd ironed into his jeans.

Hell. If P.D. didn't hurry up, he'd find something else to polish. And he'd already put a sheen on his going-to-town boots and his belt buckle.

He knew that it was nervousness that had kicked up his grooming habits a notch, but he wanted everything to be perfect. He remembered his late wife, Annabel, saying once that the most important part about a proposal was the story the woman would retell for the rest of her life. Elam was hoping he'd come up with enough romantic pomp and circumstance to do P.D. proud.

Because he was tired of waiting. Last year, during the Wild West Games, he and P.D. had assumed the roles of "pioneer bride and groom." Elam wanted to make that role a reality.

The back door to the restaurant finally opened and P.D. hurried out. As she climbed into the truck and slid over to sit next to Elam, she breathlessly said, "Hurry and get out of here. With the lunch shift as crazy as it's been, I don't want anyone to stop me."

Elam didn't need to be told twice. He set the gearshift into drive and punched the accelerator. Then, once they were on the road, he draped his arm over her shoulder.

"Where are we going?" P.D. asked, her hand curving around his thigh.

"Someplace special."

Her brows rose with patent curiosity. "I don't know if I've got a whole lot of time to go to Logan—"

"We aren't going to Logan," Elam interrupted with a smile.

P.D. was clearly mystified. Here in Bliss, dining options were limited. Other than a McDonald's near the freeway, the lunch counter at the Corner, the Cake Dump, and Vern's there weren't any other options.

Elam smiled down at her, his heart doing a crazy bossa nova in his chest. "Trust me."

Her eyes grew warm at that and she melted against him again. "I always trust you."

Her statement had the power to turn his insides to jelly, and Elam wondered if she knew how much it meant to him that she'd given him that trust. She'd had a crappy childhood—one that had stripped her of the belief that relationships could last for a lifetime. He was hoping that he'd managed to change her mind.

Slowing down, Elam turned from the old highway onto a gravel service road that dissected fields planted with winter wheat. Since the ground was leased by Taggart Enterprises, P.D. didn't react until she saw that the gate at the end of the lane—one clearly marked with a NO TRESPASSING sign—was open.

"We're going to Henry Grover's cabin?" she breathed.

"Mmm hmm."

He felt the way she leaned forward in anticipation. It had been over a year since they'd been here last. The secluded valley with its towering willow trees, quaint cabin, and sheltered pond had been one of the stops during the Wild West Games. When they'd found themselves with a few hours of unexpected privacy, it had been the first place where he and P.D. had made love.

There was no hiding the joy on P.D.'s features as they followed the lane down, down, into a hidden dell. Elam followed the same track they'd once taken in a buggy, circling behind the cabin, around the pond, and coming to a stop near a trough that was kept full by a dribble of chilly artesian water.

"Oh," P.D. breathed when she caught sight of the thick grass under the willows. Elam had been here earlier to spread a blanket under the trees and leave a picnic basket in the center. On top of the basket was a huge bouquet of pink roses, sweet peas, and daisies.

"Helen helped me come up with the menu, so it ought to be good."

P.D. was eyeing him with something akin to wonder. He could tell she was searching her brain, trying to come up with a logical reason for the romantic gesture.

Birthday?

No.

Anniversary?

No.

He opened his door and slid out, reaching for her hand. "Come on."

Elam had it all planned. They would have a leisurely lunch, laugh, talk, maybe make love. Afterward, he would hand her the bouquet, drop to his knees, and ask her to marry him. Only then would he draw her attention to the ring that had been tied into the ribbon wrapped around the stems and looped into a bow.

But as they neared the blanket, Elam's heart began to pound so hard, he wondered if P.D. could hear it. His mouth grew dry as a desert—and, good hell almighty, his knees began to shake.

When he hesitated at the edge of the blanket, P.D. looked at him curiously.

"What's wrong?"

Damn. He must look like a rabbit about to bolt.

As he tried to summon up enough spit to talk, Elam realized that there was no way that he could get through the meal without looking and acting as skittish as an unbroken colt. So he reached for the bouquet, then turned to P.D., taking one of her hands.

"I . . . uh . . ."

Hell.

He looked at P.D., and as quickly as his nerves had appeared, they seeped away. This was the woman he loved, the woman with whom he wanted to spend the rest of his life. And he knew she loved him, too. Every time she looked at him, touched him, talked to him, she conveyed her feelings in a hundred different ways.

Slowly, he sank to his knees in front of her.

"Prairie Dawn Raines, I know I'm supposed to come up with some kind of flowery speech, but . . ." He squeezed her hand, searching her features and absorbing her look of confusion. "But suddenly, I can't remember anything I planned to say except . . . I love you, body and soul. I love you more today than I did yesterday, and tomorrow I'll love you even more than today. It's time to ask you . . . Will you marry me?"

He'd prepared himself for her reaction. He was sure that she would hesitate, that she would be pummeled with indecision. She might even ask if he was sure or tell him she wasn't quite ready.

What he hadn't expected was that she would burst into tears.

Immediately he stood, hauling her into his arms, his stomach sinking as he wondered if he'd rushed her. But then, she began peppering him with kisses, whispering, "Yes . . . yes . . . *yes!*"

He laughed—in joy and relief—crushing her against him. "I thought for a minute you were going to tell me no."

She drew back long enough to regard him quizzically. "Why would you ever think that?"

Then she was kissing him again and the air was redolent

with the bouquet that was being crushed between them. Wrestling the blooms free, Elam tossed them to the ground, next to the forgotten picnic basket. There would be time for all that later—the food, the flowers, and his great-grandmother's heirloom ring, which he'd retrieved from the safe in the Big House.

Right now, he planned to make love to his fiancée, his wife-to-be, in the same spot where their relationship had once begun.

WHEN Bodey's pickup appeared, Jace and Bronte were sitting casually on the porch. But appearances could be deceiving, Bronte thought with an inner *yippie-ki-yay.* The two of them had never left the property long enough for lunch. Instead, they'd made love in the shower, then his bed, and then—*great googly-moogly*—on the kitchen table. She was beginning to realize her ex-husband had sported a very limited repertoire where lovemaking was concerned, because Bronte was keen to experiment—and Jace was more than willing to comply.

So when the truck pulled to a stop by the back porch, Jace and Bronte were sitting a good distance apart. But Bronte was pretty sure that Jace's body must be thrumming with the same sensual exhaustion that made her loathe to move.

"Did you have fun?" Bronte asked as the kids clambered out of Bodey's stretch cab.

She was surprised when Kari volunteered a quick, "Yeah, they have pretty good burgers. I saw Brinnley there."

Brinnley Atencio was one of Kari's new friends from school. Bronte had met her several times and she was secretly pleased that Kari had bonded with the down-to-earth teen.

"She wants to know if I can meet her and some other friends at the bowling alley. Her mom will stay with us, then bring us home. Since it's a school night, Mrs. Atencio said she'd have us back by nine."

Bronte didn't know which part of Kari's statement surprised her most—that Kari actually wanted to go to a *bowl-*

ing alley, that she had volunteered the fact that a parent would be present, or that said parent was willing to provide the transportation *and* get them all home at a reasonable hour. But then, Bronte supposed that such arrangements were probably the norm in Bliss. With school friends scattered for miles throughout the county, after-school activities necessitated some planning.

Before she answered, Bronte made a mental note to offer her driving services for future activities. "I think that sounds like fun."

"Can I text her back?"

"Sure."

As Kari's thumbs began forming her reply, Jace leaned over to comment lowly, "You got her a phone?"

Bronte smiled. "Yup. I realized that it's important to have access to a friend, especially when things are new and scary."

Jace must have caught the double meaning behind her words—that Bronte considered him her own valuable friend as well—because he reached over to stroke the back of her hand with his finger.

"I think that's a wise decision. But I'll miss her willingness to come here for the Wi-Fi."

Bronte grinned. "Don't worry. She'll probably be hitting you up for a chance to use your horses so she and her friends can go riding."

Jace smiled. "I'd like that. You're welcome to drop by anytime," he said to Kari. "Bring your friends. If there's one thing we have in abundance, it's horses."

Kari glanced up from texting to offer him a startled smile. "Thanks, Jace."

"You can come riding, too, Lily."

Lily blinked at him, clearly surprised that she'd been included in the invitation. But Barry brushed over any awkwardness by grabbing the little girl's hand.

"Come inside with me, Emily, and I'll show you my room." He turned to include Kari. "If you wanna come upstairs with us, there's a really good view of the pasture with all the baby horses. You could put it on your Facebook."

Surprisingly, when Barry and Lily hurried to the door, Kari followed.

"Ten minutes," Bronte called after them. "We don't want to keep Mrs. Atencio waiting!"

Bronte wasn't sure if the girls heard her or not. The door slammed and they disappeared inside.

"Are you still worried about Lily?" Jace asked, taking Bronte's hand.

Bronte grimaced. "She's had some good days, thank goodness. But I've made an appointment with a pediatrician next week, and I'm hoping she can arrange a counselor." She sighed. "I finally came to the conclusion that Lily needs an expert's help. Luckily, my health insurance will be in effect by then. Honestly, I don't know what I would have done if Barry hadn't come by after school every day. I think she's been mulling things over with him, but I'm still clueless about what's going on in her head. When I talk to her, she just changes the subject."

Jace squeezed her hand. "She's lucky to have such a loving mom."

Jace's comment caused her throat to tighten with emotion. Uncaring of the fact that her children could emerge, Bronte leaned forward to kiss him. When their lips touched, a familiar warmth flooded into her extremities.

"Are you still coming to dinner tomorrow?" she asked when they parted.

He smiled. "Absolutely."

"Burgers, steaks, or roast beef? Your brother said he left some meat in our freezer."

"The kids would probably rather have burgers."

She nodded. "I'll pick up some buns, make a couple of salads, and slice up some potatoes for french fries."

"They'll love that."

He remained close, so close that she was able to brush her thumb over his lips.

"I might not be able to stop by earlier in the afternoon. I've got some things to get done for Annie's open house."

"Do you need any help?"

Did she need any help? That wasn't the response that she would have received from Phillip. For the first time, Bronte realized how comforting it was to have someone willing to share some of her burdens.

"If I do, I'll let you know."

JACE wasn't the sort to spend a whole lot of time in front of the mirror. Most days, if his clothes were clean and he could find his hat, he didn't bother with much more. But the next night, he couldn't help checking and rechecking. He'd shaved carefully, splashed on cologne, donned his church-going Justin boots and a crisp white button-down shirt—he'd even ironed his jeans, for hell's sake. Yet, as he slid into a jacket, he found himself looking at his reflection again.

Tugging the sleeves over his cuffs, Jace realized that his nerves were as jangly as if he were about to go on a first date. He'd probably spent more time primping tonight than he had the whole rest of the year.

But even as he grimaced at his efforts, he knew the preparations had been necessary. It might not be his first meeting with Bronte, but he did want to make the right impression on her girls. The few stolen meetings they'd been able to have weren't nearly enough. Jace wanted the opportunity to court her openly.

Court.

Was that what this was? A courting?

For some reason, the antiquated term stuck in his brain like a burr. He'd dated many women—not as many as Bodey's wild record—but he'd had his fair share. But "court-ing" implied something different. There was a gentleness to the word and a more long-lasting intent. It was what a man did when he was toying with the idea of a commitment.

Commitment.

In the past, Jace had shied away from the word like a yearling colt. But somehow, when he thought of Bronte, the idea didn't seem so terrifying and restrictive. It seemed . . . reassuring.

"Whatsa matter? You got to go to the bathroom or some-thin'?"

Jace started, turning to find Barry eyeing him inquisi-tively.

"No, I do not need to go to the bathroom," he insisted firmly, heading Barry off at the pass. "I was just thinking."

"You sure think a lot lately."

Wasn't that the truth. Jace found himself ruminating far too much about Bronte, about how she tasted, how she came undone in his arms.

"Whatcha thinking about, Jace? You got that funny look again."

Jace opened his mouth to offer a harmless reply, then stopped when he realized that Bronte's children weren't the only ones who would need to be prepared for a possible "courting."

"I was thinking about Bronte, Barry."

"Why?" Barry looked alarmed. "She's not going to change her mind about us coming to dinner, is she?"

"No. I'm sure she's getting everything ready right now."

"Then why are you thinking about Emily's mom?"

Jace sighed, momentarily diverted. He grasped his broth-er's shoulders, forcing his little brother to meet his gaze.

"Her name is Lily, Barry. I know you want to give her a nickname so she knows you're her friend, but maybe you should think of another one."

"Why?"

"People might think that you're confusing Lily with our sister, Emily." He paused before adding gently, "You know. Your twin. The one who died in the crash."

Barry's face scrunched up. "That's stupid. I know she's not my twin, Emily. My twin, Emily, is in Heaven and you already told me that I'll see her again someday after I'm really old. Lily is . . . Lily Emily."

Jace opened his mouth to insist again that Barry think of a new nickname. But he huffed instead, deciding tonight wasn't the time for a confrontation. As long as Barry wasn't confusing Lily with his late twin, was there any harm to the use of the name? A far more pressing problem was what Barry thought about Jace spending more time with Bronte.

Jace slid his hands into his pockets, choosing his words carefully. "Before we leave, I want to talk to you about something, Barry."

Barry's expression became suspicious. "What? You're not changing your mind about going to Bronte's house tonight, are you?"

"No. I've been thinking about Bronte herself. About the way I might want to be more than Bronte's talking friend."

Barry's eyes narrowed slightly as he thought that over. "So's you want to be a holding-hands friend?"

Jace nodded. "What would you think about that?"

"You made everybody mad last time you did that."

Jace couldn't help a grimace of regret. "Yes, that's true. That's why I'm going to ask you ahead of time if it's okay."

Barry opened his mouth, then whirled and stormed down the hall. Seconds later, Jace heard his bedroom door slam shut.

Well, that *went well.*

Sighing, Jace followed in his brother's footsteps, fearing that he might have ruined the night at Bronte's before it had ever begun. Pausing at the door, he tapped lightly.

No answer.

"Barry? Come on, buddy. I need you to talk to me and tell me what you're feeling."

Still no answer.

Jace tried the knob, and thankfully, it was unlocked. Slowly opening the door, he found his brother sitting on the bed, his arms wound so tightly around the stuffed panda that the animal was nearly beheaded. Barry had his back to Jace, but his shoulders trembled and a sob burst from his throat.

"Barry? What's wrong? I didn't mean to upset you." Jace rounded the bed. A huge fist seemed to squeeze his heart when he saw his brother's face, contorted with tears.

Crouching in front of him, Jace reached to touch his knee, moving slowly as if Barry were a skittish foal. Thankfully,

Barry allowed the contact and didn't rear back, so Jace squeezed slightly in reassurance.

"I would never want to do anything to hurt you, Barry. That's why I'm asking you first."

Heaven help him if Jace couldn't get his brother's blessing to pursue Bronte, because Jace didn't know what he was going to do if he didn't. The thought of *not* being near Bronte was as untenable as causing his brother pain.

"Please. Tell me what's wrong."

Barry's lower lip trembled, but he finally took a deep, shuddering breath and swiped at his cheeks with his fist.

"If you an' Bronte s-start being holding-hands friends"—his breath caught in a hiccoughing sob—"then next, you'll be k-kissing friends."

That horse has long since left the barn, little brother.

Jace was surprised at Barry's astuteness. But even though he knew he might be walking into his own execution, he said, "Yes, that's possible."

Barry's eyes welled with tears again. "Th-then you'll be like Elam and P.D. and you'll build a house somewheres else and you won't want to live with me anymore!"

EIGHTEEN

BARRY'S pronouncement slid through Jace like a spear. Suddenly, everything slipped into place. Ever since Elam and P.D. had become a couple, Barry had attached himself to Jace like a cocklebur. He'd become clingy, unwilling to play with friends or enjoy the activities with his Boy Scout group. And Jace, Big Brother Extraordinaire, had chafed beneath the unaccustomed neediness, not knowing its source.

Moving to the bed, Jace hauled Barry into his arms, holding him tightly. Barry resisted him, then threw the panda on the floor and clung to Jace as if his older brother were a life raft in a stormy sea.

"I'm not going anywhere, Barry."

In those words, Jace knew his decision was made. There would be no extended vacation in Europe, no escape from the routine, no revisiting of his year of freedom.

In an instant, Jace was plunged back to that horrible day when he'd hurried from Salt Lake City International Airport to Primary Children's Medical Center. He'd been traveling for more than a day. Bad weather had forced layovers and cancellations until he felt as if he'd never get home. But when he'd entered the trauma wing of the hospital, he'd heard Barry's screams as soon as he'd stepped off the elevator. Rushing toward the sound, he'd burst into his brother's room in time to see a pair of nurses and a physician trying to control Barry enough so that he could be sedated.

In that instant, Barry had looked up. His gaze had latched onto Jace, and his screams had faded to a plaintive cry.

"Wait for me, Jace! Don't leave me here!"

Jace had been trying ever since to be there for Barry.

His throat grew so tight that Jace could barely speak, but he forced himself to say, "Elam's situation is different, Barry. He always wanted a house up on the hill. I remember when we were kids, he would ride up to that spot whenever he needed to think. And Bodey . . . well, I'm not sure if Bodey knows what he wants, or if and when he'll eventually settle down." The words feathered his brother's hair with each breath, and Jace hoped that Barry was detecting the strength of conviction behind them.

"But you and me, Barry . . . We belong in the Big House, and that's where we're going to stay. This is where we're most happy. I'm not going anywhere, and neither are you. This house has seen four generations of Taggarts, and it will see a lot more."

His brother's posture eased ever so slightly.

"You know you're always welcome to stay with Elam and P.D.—especially now they're getting married. When you're all grown up, you might even decide you want to live somewhere else. But this bedroom will be yours until you're a little old man, anytime you want it. I'll be here, too, waiting for you."

"W-what about Bronte?"

Jace paused, but knew that he couldn't lie, even to reassure his brother.

"I don't know, Barry. It might be too soon to tell. But would you mind if, one day, Bronte and her girls lived here, too?"

Jace hadn't allowed himself to think that far ahead until

now. But as soon as the words left his mouth, he knew he couldn't retract them—he didn't want to retract them. Somehow they seemed . . . right.

"So Lily would stay here?"

Jace didn't miss the fact that, this time, his brother had used the little girl's real name. It dawned on him that, when emotions were high, Barry called the little girl Lily, not Emily.

"Sure. We've got plenty of space and lots of empty bedrooms."

"And Bodey?"

"Well, you never know what Bodey is going to do. But he'll always have a spot here, too."

Barry drew back. For an instant, Jace was confronted with the image of his brother's tear-streaked face, too-long hair, and man-boy earnestness. But it was the hope that shone from his brilliant blue eyes that nearly brought Jace to his knees. Then Barry swiped at his cheeks with his sleeve and his expression changed in an instant to eagerness.

"When can they come, Jace? Emily can have the bedroom next to mine."

His brother's leap from despair to joy had Jace reeling, but fighting his own emotional whiplash, Jace did his best to head Barry off at the pass. The last thing he needed was for Barry to propose before Jace had a chance to do so.

Propose?

Was that really what he was thinking? Hell, he'd only known Bronte for a few short weeks. Let's face it, dating her would be complicated enough with her children, Barry, and their crazy work schedules to contend with.

But once again, the idea didn't scare him nearly as much as he'd thought it would.

He jumped up to catch Barry by the arm. "Don't be saying anything to Lily yet, Barry. These things take time— months and months, sometimes years. I think Lily needs a chance to get used to Bronte and I becoming holding-hands friends first, don't you?"

Barry considered the idea, then nodded.

"So this is a secret between you and me, okay?"

"I thought it was bad to keep secrets."

Hell.

"It's not so much a secret as a surprise. We have to wait until the right time to tell them."

Barry grinned widely. "I love surprises!"

"I bet Lily does, too. So we'll wait until it's time, okay?"

"When will it be time?"

"I don't know yet. But I'll let you know as soon as I do."

"Yes!" Barry clapped his hands and did a victory jig.

A glance at his watch made Jace realize that they were running late. "Get in the bathroom and wash your face and hands, Barry. We've got to get going. I need to stop in town before we go to Bronte's and we're already behind schedule."

"Why are we going to town, Jace?"

"I need to get some flowers."

"We got flowers in the lawn, Jace."

Jace grimaced, realizing Barry was referring to the crop of dandelions that had sprouted in the yard. Not for the first time, Jace wondered why other ranchers had found success in having goats tame the weeds, while Barry's pygmy goat, Bitsy, would only eat chips and candy corn.

"That's true, but I need some special flowers. Pretty ones."

"Why do you need flowers, Jace?"

He clapped his brother on the shoulder, leading him out in the hall and steering him toward the bathroom. "Because when a lady invites you to dinner, you bring her a gift. It's the gentlemanly thing to do."

Barry nodded, then ran ahead of him. "Okay!"

Ten minutes later, Jace waited in the truck, impatiently tapping his fingers on the steering wheel. He honked the horn twice, then shouted out the window, "Barry! Let's go!"

To his surprise, instead of bursting out of the back door, Barry ran around the side of the house, clutching a mason jar in one hand and a fistful of dandelions in the other.

Jace leaned across the seat to open the door for him and Barry quickly scrambled inside.

"What's that?" Jace asked, gesturing to the items Barry held.

"You said we have to bring a present when we get invited to a girl's house for dinner, but you forgot that there's three girls that live there. So we need three presents."

Looking more closely, Jace saw that the mason jar held one of Barry's most prized possessions. Inside was a portion of a milkweed branch. Last fall, Barry had spent a whole day watching a caterpillar fashion a chrysalis to the slender stalk. Since then, he'd kept it warm and safe, checking it every day to see if there were signs of the butterfly that would emerge. Jace knew that jar was more precious than gold to his brother.

"Are you sure you want to give your caterpillar away? You've been taking care of it for a long time."

Barry nodded. "Lily has a new room and Bronte said she has a quilt with flowers and butterflies on it. I'm thinking she'd like a real butterfly, too. Maybe it will cheer her up so's she's not sad anymore."

Jace had to swallow hard against the lump of emotion that his brother's selflessness inspired.

"Has she said anything to you? About why she's sad?"

Barry offered him an odd look, one that made it clear that he wondered how much he could say to Jace without betraying a friend's confidence.

"Is she sad that her mom and dad got a divorce?"

Barry shrugged noncommittally.

"It's okay if you tell me, Barry. Bronte's trying to find a way to help Lily, but she can't do that unless she knows what's worrying Lily. She'd really appreciate it if you'd let her know what's on Lily's mind."

Barry considered that idea, then slowly offered, "She's sad about the divorce. But mostly, she's worried about the summer."

"She doesn't want school to get out?"

"Oh, she wants school to get out. I don't think she likes her class very much. She says they don't color very often."

"Then why is she worried about summer?"

Barry shrugged again. "I don't know. She wouldn't tell me."

Jace made a mental note to pass the information on to Bronte. Maybe she would understand.

"So the dandelions . . ."

"They're for Kari. I know you said that we needed pretty flowers, but I don't think she wants the same ones as Bronte. So I picked these. I figured she wouldn't mind they were dandelions because she's kinda ornery." He lifted them to his nose and sniffed. When he lowered them again, there was a dusting of yellow from the pollen. "But they don't smell so good."

Jace laughed and reached to brush the golden powder from the tip of his brother's nose. "How about you leave those here and we'll find something else in town to bring her."

Barry beamed. "Good idea!" He tossed them out the window, then reached to pull his seat belt into place. "She probably wouldn't like dandelions anyway. She doesn't seem to like much of anything 'cept her phone and Tyson."

Jace chuckled again and started the engine. Clearly, nothing escaped his little brother's attention. "True enough, Barry. True enough."

WHEN Bronte heard the truck, she stepped onto the rear porch, her heart seeming to stumble over itself in excitement and nervousness.

Good grief. She was a grown-up, a mother.

But even as the thoughts flew through her head, her brain quickly countered with: *You're a woman, too.*

Inviting the Taggarts to the open house hadn't been a problem. But asking Jace to come for a more intimate meal had required diplomacy worthy of a Middle Eastern peace delegation. Surprisingly, Lily hadn't seemed to care much one way or the other. But then, it was hard to tell when she wasn't talking a whole lot. Kari, on the other hand, had sighed and grumbled until Bronte had finally been forced to pull the mom card. Which meant that Jace was included, but one child had threatened to spend most of the night in her room while the other was up in the tree house. Again.

What was she doing wrong?

But when the truck doors opened and Jace stepped out, her discouragement was diluted with a wave of anticipation. What was it about this man, that his mere presence gave her strength . . . and more? As he walked toward her wearing his "going to town" hat, crisp white shirt, jacket, jeans, and shiny tooled boots, she felt a purely feminine shot of desire plundering through her veins.

Her knees were slightly weak as she went down the steps to meet him halfway. When he produced a bunch of white daisies and baby's breath, she could have melted into a big puddle of girlish pleasure that would have put Kari's raging crush for Tyson to shame.

"Thank you," she breathed, so delighted by the offering that her eyes pricked with unexpected tears. She buried her face in the blooms to hide the reaction, not wanting to appear like a silly fool. But when she looked up to find Jace watching her, she was struck by the mix of sheepish pleasure and boyishness that peeked out from the mature, Western Male persona.

"These are for Kari," Barry announced loudly as he came up behind Jace and held out a box in Bronte's direction. Beneath the very large bow was a pair of neon yellow earbuds with plastic grips shaped like corn cobs. "I picked 'em out. Jace said when you come to a lady's house for dinner, you bring a present."

"Your brother is a very wise man, Barry. Women love flowers. I'm sure Kari will love her new earbuds as well."

"Emily has a present, too, but it's my present. Jace didn't help me."

"Oh. Then it must be really special."

He held up a jar with holes punched in the top and what looked like dried twigs inside. "See? It will match her room."

Bronte looked at Jace in confusion, but kept a smile on her face. "I'm sure she'll love it because it came from you, Barry."

He nodded. "Where's Emily?"

"In the tree house," Bronte said, pointing. When he ran out of earshot, she murmured under her breath, "She's always in the tree house. Sometimes I wonder if she goes there to keep her distance from me."

Jace moved closer, his hand surreptitiously settling in the small of her back. That touch alone had the power to unleash a host of tantalizing memories.

"I don't think so. Barry said she's not that upset about the divorce. She's worried about summer coming."

"Summer?" Bronte was more confused than ever. "What does that mean?"

Jace shrugged. "I don't know, but if you give him long enough, he'll figure out what's going on. He seems to be pretty good at that."

Bronte felt a prickling of unease. "Oh, no," she breathed, shooting a glance at Jace, then back at Barry who was tucking the jar into his shirt so that his hands would be free when he negotiated the ladder. "He didn't find out about us in the shower—"

"No, thank heavens. But he admitted why he's been mad at the prospect of our seeing one another. He was afraid that if we went from 'friends' to 'holding-hands friends' to 'kissing friends,' I would move away to a new house like Elam."

Bronte's mouth opened in a silent "oh." She couldn't help whispering, "Poor thing."

Jace pulled her more tightly against him. "I reassured him that I wouldn't be going anywhere."

He paused, causing her to look away from Barry's climb. Instantly, her gaze tangled with the warmth of his.

"I let him know that I wouldn't be going anywhere. Not without him."

There was a flash of uncertainty in his eyes—and it struck her like a bolt of lightning. He wasn't telling her. He was asking her. He wanted to know if having Barry around would be a deal-breaker.

She felt a flash of anger for all of the women who had ever made Jace believe that having Barry as part of the bargain was a drawback rather than a blessing.

Knowing that she couldn't keep from touching him another minute, even if her children were watching, she slid her arm around his waist. "Look at that," she whispered, gesturing to the boy who pulled himself onto the wide planks of the tree house. "Who wouldn't want a kid like that around every day?"

Message received.

Jace's arm tightened around her waist and she felt the kiss that he placed on the top of her head.

"I hope Lily doesn't hurt his feelings when he presents her with a jar of sticks," Bronte said.

"It's not a jar of sticks. It's a butterfly."

"What?"

"There's a chrysalis hanging from one of those branches. He's been watching it like a mama hen since he found it last fall."

"He's giving it away?"

"He said Lily needed it more. To match her room."

Bronte's hand flew to her mouth, but she couldn't speak. Not now that Barry had removed the jar from his shirt again. He sank onto the planks next to Lily who sat with her arms wrapped around her knees.

"Here, Emily. This is for you."

Bronte held her breath, waiting to see what happened. Lily looked up, but other than that, she didn't move.

He set the jar down and pointed to it. "See here? That's what Jace calls a chrisamus. But I call it a caterpillar house. See, before Halloween, I found a caterpillar. It was kinda creepy looking and all wriggly like a worm. But it was hanging off this branch and he was making a little sleeping bag for the winter. So's Jace helped me bring it home and put it in the jar."

Obviously entranced, Lily relaxed her grip on her knees and leaned closer to look.

"One of these days real soon, it's gonna break open the chrisamus—an' you know what? It's not going to be a caterpillar anymore. Some kinda magic happens in that chrisamus thing. When it comes out, it's a butterfly!"

Bronte watched as Lily looked up, her eyes wide. "We can see it happen?"

"We can't watch it turn to a butterfly 'cause that goes on inside. But we can see it get loose and then it will try to fly."

Barry squinted, studying the chrysalis. "But Jace says it wouldn't be happy in the jar. When it comes out, we gotta set it free and let it fly away."

Lily seemed slightly disappointed, but Barry hurried to reassure her.

"It's okay, 'cause I know the perfect place to let it loose. Up in the mountains where we keep some of our cows, there's a place where there's lots of grass and these red flowers. I think Jace said they were puppies—like they have in *The Wizard of Oz* show that comes on TV. But these puppies don't make you fall asleep and the butterflies really like 'em. I like to ride up there on my horse with Jace, an' when I do, I lie down really still in the grass until they land on me. Then they rub their magic on me an' I feel all brand-new, like the butterflies."

Bronte released her breath when, wonder of wonders, Lily spoke.

"Really? Can I go?"

"Yup. I bet I can get Jace to take us there when it's time." Both of them were now bent down, their faces close to the glass. "We got to be careful with it 'til then. We don't want to stop the magic inside."

"Maybe we'd better take the chrisamus inside," Lily whispered.

"I think that would be a good idea. 'Sides, it needs to see its new room."

Barry stood and tucked the jar back into his shirt, carefully fastening the buttons again so that the precious cargo wouldn't slip free.

"You go first. Then, I'll come down."

Lily scrambled to her feet, scampering down the ladder with lightning speed. Barry quickly followed. Once on the ground, he unfastened his shirt and handed the jar to Lily. Then, with Lily asking him a million questions at once—"Where should I put the jar? Do I have to feed it?"— they hurried past Bronte and Jace into the house.

Just like that, Lily's dark mood seemed to dissipate as the sound of her laughter echoed from deep in the house.

Bronte unconsciously gripped Jace's hand. How? How

was Barry able to break through her daughter's misery when everyone else failed?

Jace lifted their laced fingers to his lips, kissing her softly on the knuckles.

"He's like that. He can drive you crazy sometimes when he peppers you with questions or stubbornly refuses to do something that you really need him to do. But when you're sure you're going to lose your cool . . . he does something wonderful."

Bronte turned to him then, wrapping her arms around his neck. "Just like every other kid."

"Yeah. Just like every other kid."

Then, unable to stand another minute of waiting, Bronte lifted on tiptoes, pressing her lips against Jace's.

"Where are we going with this?" she whispered when they parted again.

Jace rested his forehead against hers. "I don't know. But I don't want to go it alone anymore," he answered.

"Me either."

As soon as the words were said, a weight seemed to lift from her chest. Nothing had been solved—her life wasn't miraculously made less complicated. But by putting her nebulous feelings into words, it did make everything . . . *easier*, somehow. Because *this*—this man and the storm of emotions he inspired in her—felt right. For once in her life, she wasn't going to analyze it. She wasn't going to weigh her options and study every angle, every possibility. She was going to rely on her heart to guide her.

So maybe, just maybe, the magic from Barry's butterfly was already beginning to take effect.

AS Bronte turned the van into the lane that led to her grandmother's house, she heard a visible gasp from the backseat, where Annie sat with her cast-covered leg extended into the center aisle and her wrist propped on a pillow.

"Oh, Bronte," she whispered, her voice tremulous with surprise and emotion.

Bronte smiled. In the month since Bronte had first driven

up this lane, weary from her cross-country flight, the lilac bushes had exploded with blooms and the heady fragrance poured through the open windows. One of Jace's ranch hands had maneuvered a swather down the lane, mowing down the weeds, while another had filled the potholes with fresh gravel. Then, as a finishing touch, P.D. and the girls had fastened yellow helium balloons to each of the fence posts.

"Welcome home, Grandma."

Bronte kept one eye on the rearview mirror as she rounded the bend and the house came into view. In the bright May sun, it gleamed with its fresh coat of paint, and the flowerbeds were dotted with starts of perennials and pansies. The new porch held chairs and a small table that P.D. and Bronte had found at a local hardware store, and the railings were festooned with more yellow balloons.

As soon as the car appeared, the small gathering of people surged forward in greeting. Besides Bronte's children, the entire Taggart family was there, as well as their hired men. There were several neighbors, Helen and Syd Henderson, and a group of women who were members of Annie's quilting club. In the shade beneath the trees, tables and chairs borrowed from the local church had been decorated with bright tablecloths and more yellow balloons, with a larger buffet table located in the middle.

"Bronte, you've gone to so much trouble," Annie scolded. But there was no censure to the remark, merely a sense of wonder.

"Everyone pitched in, Grandma. I think the whole town was really worried about you. Helping to get things ready for your return gave us something to do other than worry."

Annie's eyes sparkled with tears, but her smile was one of pure joy.

She was saved from making a response when Bronte stopped the car. Almost immediately, Bodey Taggart was there, sliding open the door.

"There's my girl!" he said with a grin.

To Bronte's surprise, Annie giggled like a teenager and spots of color appeared on her cheeks.

"You're a scamp, Bodey Taggart."

He climbed into the van and effortlessly scooped Annie into his arms. By the time he'd made it to the door, Jace was waiting with the wheelchair that he'd retrieved from the trunk. Annie was quickly transferred to Jace's arms and from there to the chair. Then, as Bronte hurried to circle the van, he pushed Annie toward the waiting crowd.

Within minutes, the gathering took on the air of a party. Annie was quickly surrounded by well-wishers who offered her small gifts, filled her plate with tempting bites of food, and replenished her cup of punch.

Bronte kept a careful eye on her grandmother, not wanting to tire Annie on her first day home. But she needn't have worried. Annie's friends were equally concerned. When Annie seemed to flag, they helped her inside, settled her into the overstuffed recliner, and covered her with a lap quilt. For a time, the festive mood shifted as neighbors took the opportunity to congratulate Elam and P.D. on their engagement. But then, one by one, the visitors began to leave.

Soon, all that remained were P.D., the Taggart men, and Syd and Helen. As Bronte and P.D. collected serving dishes and utensils to be washed, Helen and Syd gathered up the Dutch ovens, and the Taggarts started to disassemble the borrowed tables and chairs and load them onto the back of Bodey's truck.

As they all worked together, chatting and laughing softly, Bronte realized that in coming to Bliss, she hadn't simply found a haven in her grandmother's home, she'd added the support of good friends as well. These people cared about her family. They'd not only rallied around Annie when she'd needed help, but they made it clear that they truly cared about her and her girls.

In many ways, that acceptance made her feel as if she were emerging from a long, isolated winter into the warmth of spring.

Her eyes skipped to Jace. She still marveled at how quickly she'd grown to care for this man. Even now, with as many times—and ways—that they'd made love, she couldn't get enough of him. It wasn't only the sex. It was the way he made her feel—strong and beautiful and valued. She loved the way he followed her with his eyes, or his lips twitched into a smile whenever he caught sight of her. For the first time she could remember, she was completely comfortable being herself around another person. He inspired a sense of safety, physically and emotionally. Deep down, she knew there was nothing she could do or say that would change the way he cared for her.

She wasn't so foolish to think that either of them were perfect, that if they continued on with this relationship that there wouldn't be tiffs and quarrels. But even then, she felt secure, sensing that the two of them could have a rip-roaring argument, but nothing would shatter the foundation of mutual respect that they'd already begun to build between them.

That was something she'd never had with Phillip. From the beginning, she'd known she could never push her own views in a disagreement. She'd learned early on to bite her tongue and feign appeasement in order to avoid the repercussions that would surely follow.

She looked up from the balloons she'd been gathering to find Jace watching her and she shot him a quick smile. After last night's dinner, her children seemed to have decided that ignoring any intimacy between Jace and their mother was the best tack, and she was glad for that. She felt more relaxed having everything out in the open. Even better, Jace had been able to subtly announce their relationship to the rest of the gathering with an arm around her back or by lacing their fingers together at the dinner table.

The crunch of gravel and a low rumble signaled that a late arrival was heading up the lane. P.D. straightened from where she was sweeping cups into a garbage bag to shade her eyes.

"Looks like someone's come late to the party," she murmured.

Bronte turned to look. "Oh, dear. I wonder if we should head them off and have them come back tomorrow. I think Annie's hit the end of her endurance for the day."

P.D. scowled. "I don't recognize the car right off. Elam? Do you know who that could be?"

Elam walked up to slide his arms around her waist. "No. Sorry."

The car drew to a stop a few yards away from the scattered Taggart vehicles, but the angle of the sun hitting the windshield made it impossible to see the driver until he opened the door and stepped out.

At first, Bronte didn't recognize the man. But even before her eyes were able to send the information to her brain, a frisson of warning ran up her arms, over her shoulders, and lifted the tiny hairs at the nape of her neck. Then came the recognition that had her instantly alert, every muscle in her body poised for action as she scrambled to remember the last whereabouts of her children.

Kari . . . where . . . *where?*

Kitchen.

Lily . . . dear heaven . . .

Tree house.

Close enough that she would probably hear everything.

Inwardly, she prayed that the girls would remain where they were, hidden, out of reach during the confrontation that was about to come.

Bronte felt rather than saw Jace ease toward her. Without a word of explanation, he apparently sensed the threat.

"Is that Phillip?" he asked lowly, moving into place behind her shoulder.

NINETEEN

———◆———

B RONTE nodded—or at least she thought she did. Her body seemed frozen and unable to respond.

Behind her, she sensed the Taggart males moving closer as well—first Bodey, crossing over from his truck, then Elam, stepping firmly in front of his fiancée—forming a none-too-subtle ring of support behind her.

Phillip must have sensed the rise in testosterone, because he lifted his hands and adopted a charming smile. "Easy, boys! I haven't come to make trouble. I've come to visit my wife and kids, that's all."

"*Ex*-wife, Phillip."

His eyes flashed with something akin to malice, but he paused, rested his hands on his hips, and regarded the dusty toes of his shoes for a second before echoing, "Ex-wife."

"What are you doing here, Phillip?" Bronte demanded, hoping he didn't hear the slight tremor in her voice.

"Can't a man come see his daughters?"

Bronte folded her arms tightly under her breasts, ignoring the way her pounding heart seemed to vibrate through her whole torso.

"Actually, no. According to our divorce agreement, your visits need to be arranged in advance so that supervision can be provided."

His cheeks flushed, but he didn't back down. "I figured we could take care of all those details here." He shrugged disarmingly, flashing another hearty smile.

There had been a time when that grin had been warm and genuine. Now there was an oily, used-car-salesman insincerity about it. Even more important, Bronte discovered that she was no longer swayed by his attempt at levity. Weeks ago, she would have felt obligated to smooth things over. Now, she merely wanted him to leave.

"That's not the way it works, Phillip."

"I suppose sneaking off in the middle of the night without even letting me know where you were going was by-the-book, eh, Bronte?" he snapped in return. But when Elam and Bodey took another step forward, he quickly altered his tone. "The least you could have done is let me know where you were headed so that I wouldn't worry about my girls."

Bronte bit her lip to keep herself from pointing out that he hadn't shown any concern for their safety when he'd been high most of their childhoods or that night he'd broken into the brownstone with a loaded weapon. If there was one thing she'd learned, it was that, in Phillip's mind, he was a victim of circumstance and there was nothing she could do or say that would make him admit he held any responsibility in the current state of affairs.

"Damnit, Bronte, I called, I texted, I even emailed," Phillip continued in an angry rush. "Then I get this message that your cell number is . . . *discontinued*." He sneered to show what he thought of that, apparently unaware of the way Elam, Bodey, and Jace had begun to form a phalanx of angry Western males around her.

"You can't do that, Bronte! I've got to be able to reach you!"

Although her body was shaking with a combination of anger and fear that had been building in her for years now, Bronte drew upon the strength that surrounded her.

"Any contact you think you might need to have should be arranged through my lawyer from now on, Phillip."

"Bullshit! You're my wife! Kari and Lily are *my* kids!" he shouted.

In that instant, her control snapped. "I'm not your wife, Phillip! I haven't been your wife in years. Instead, I've been your mother, your counselor, your warden, your nurse, and your housekeeper!" Her voice rose with each word. "I don't have to answer to you anymore. Even more important, I don't have to answer your phone calls, your texts, your emails, or any other form of communication you might decide to use. As per the agreement in our divorce, I don't even have to see you to drop the kids off for your scheduled visitations. All of those arrangements are to be made through my lawyer. So I would appreciate it if you would get back into your car and leave." She took a deep breath in order to calm herself. "My grandmother has been ill and this is a family celebration. One to which you were not invited."

She could see the anger building behind his eyes. But for the first time in as long as she could remember, she didn't back down. She knew without a doubt that Jace and his brothers had her back—that they would have been there for her even if she wasn't Jace's girlfriend. But since she was, Phillip was going to have to go through them to get to her.

"You're making a mistake, Bronte." In an instant, his tone changed from anger to a cajoling murmur. "You need me. You've always needed me. You've never had to do things on your own." He offered her a tilted smile, one which she was sure that he thought was disarming. But it only served to underscore the shocking changes he'd undergone in the scant weeks since she'd seen him last. His skin was gray, his eyes bloodshot. She could see that his hands were beginning to tremble. He was only forty-five years old, but he looked sixty.

A bitter laugh slipped from her throat. "What do you think I've been doing for years now, Phillip? I've raised our children, paid our bills, managed our household, our finances and our taxes. I've handled medical crises, school

projects, and your countless counseling and rehab appointments. Frankly, I don't think there's anything single life can
throw at me that I haven't already done."

A muscle in Phillip's jaw jumped. "You'll come to regret
it. You love me, Bronte."

She sighed, shaking her head. "It's time for you to leave,
Phillip."

His face seemed to crumple in contrition, but Bronte
found herself curiously unmoved.

"Come on, Bronte," he wheedled. "I've come all this way.
At the very least, you should let me see the kids."

"Not until you arrange it through my lawyer."

"But it's only a couple of weeks until summer vacation.
Even you can't deny the fact that I've got the right to a full
month of visitation."

"Supervised—"

"I could take them back to Massachusetts with me now.
They don't really need to attend the last couple of weeks of
school, do they?"

"No! No, no, *no*!" Kari burst out of the side door, her face
contorted in horror. "You can't make me go back now! I've
got friends here and we've made plans! I'm not missing the
last few weeks of school when all the fun stuff is going to
happen. There's a dance and a carnival and . . . and a
dance, Mom!"

As if summoned by her sister's distress, Lily eased down
the ladder from the tree house, seeming small and uncertain.
Within seconds, Barry took his place by her side. In the past,
she would have raced into Phillip's arms, but that had
changed over the past few weeks as well. Now she clung to
Barry's hand, studying her father, clearly trying to gauge
his mood and his sobriety.

To his credit, Phillip's face immediately brightened.
"Kari. Baby," he crooned. "And Lily. My Lilliput. Look how
you've grown."

Bronte felt a twinge at the evident love shining from Phillip's eyes and realized that this honest fatherly affection was
the reason why she'd stayed with him for so long. She hadn't

wanted to deny her children the love of their father. She'd thought she could "fix" him. That she could hang on long enough for him to get his act together. But judging by the tic under his eye, the sallowness of his skin and the gauntness of his mottled face, Phillip was still in the grips of his addiction. She wasn't going to subject them to their father's dependency any more than the custody agreement forced her to do.

Before she could speak, Phillip plunged on. "You'll see, we're going to have a great time. I've already arranged it with my partner, Jeremy. He and his wife have invited us to stay with them at their place in the country. You can swim in the ocean and—"

Without warning, Lily began to scream and scream and scream. A high-pitched cry filled with anger and torment, anguish and grief. The sound lifted the hair away from Bronte's skull and severed the last of the regrets that had rooted her in place. As she ran to her younger daughter, sure that Lily had been stung or bitten or worse, Lily raced to meet her halfway, arms clawing, feet kicking, so that she seemed to scale Bronte's form in her terror.

Lily clamped her arms around Bronte's neck so tightly that Bronte could scarcely breathe. Immediately, she held Lily, absorbing the shudders that wracked through the little girl's body as huge sobs threatened to tear her apart.

"Shh, Lily, shh. What's wrong? What's wrong?"

Lily was crying so hard, she didn't seem to hear Bronte's voice. Bronte turned to Kari, wondering if she'd seen what had happened. But Kari was regarding her sister with wide, worried eyes.

"I didn't do anything. Honest!"

Seeking help, Bronte turned back toward Jace, knowing he had medical training, but in doing so, she caught such a look of guilt and fear on Phillip's features that she immediately zeroed in on him.

A montage of images raced through her head like old-fashioned popping flashbulbs. Lily's change in behavior, her lack of appetite, her reticence, her timidity, her somber mood, the depression.

Her fear of men.

An icy sliver pierced through Bronte's heart.

"What have you done, Phillip?" she rasped, barely able to form the words. When he didn't speak, she repeated more sharply, "What have you done!"

He offered a weak laugh. "I haven't done anything. How could I? I was over here when she started screaming."

Lily grabbed Bronte's cheeks, forcing her to meet her daughter's wild gaze. "Don't make me go, Mommy," she sobbed, the words barely distinguishable in her pain. "Don't make me see that man again."

"What man, Lily? Tell mommy who hurt you."

When Lily hesitated, Bronte soothed her hair, knowing that the next few minutes could be crucial to her daughter's well-being.

"Mommy won't be mad. Not at you, sweetie. I could never be mad at you. If someone hurt you, Mommy needs to help you so you don't have to be sad anymore."

Lily's eyes brimmed with tears.

"That's what Barry told me."

"He's right, Lily. He wants to help you, too. We've all been so worried about you. Let us help you, sweetie."

Lily's chin trembled, but then she finally whispered, "D-daddy's man."

Bronte's brow creased as she scrambled to make sense of it. "Which man, sweetie?"

"Th-the one at his . . . office."

"You mean Jeremy? Mr. Montero?"

There had been a time when Jeremy and his wife had been in and out of their home so much that the kids had called them Uncle Jeremy and Aunt Noreen, so Bronte took note of the way her daughter refused to use his name.

"Wh-when Daddy took me to him to check my hurt arm . . . H-he made me come into his office . . ."

Bronte barely dared to breathe, needing to know the truth, but fearing the words nonetheless.

"It's okay, Lily. Tell Mommy what happened so I can help to make it better."

"He made me . . ." She stopped, then continued in a mere whisper, "He made me pull my pants down."

Oh, sweet heaven, no.

"What else, Lily?" Bronte prompted through a voice thick with her own tears.

"He . . . he took pictures of me. Then he took his pants down, too."

The bile rose in Bronte's throat, but she forced herself to ask, "Did he touch you, Lily?"

Lily shook her head. "I-I wouldn't let him. He got mad at me, but I wouldn't let him."

Bronte nodded, her own tears falling. "You did the right thing, baby doll." Bronte swallowed hard, forcing herself to ask. "D-did he make you touch him?"

Lily began crying again. "I ran away from him, Mommy. I ran away."

She whipped her arms around Bronte's neck again and Bronte held her as tightly as she dared. "You did the right thing, Lily. You were a brave, brave girl. I'm so proud of you. I'm so, so proud."

Still clutching Lily, Bronte turned toward Phillip, but before she could even think of a way to put her whirling thoughts into words, he threw out a hand, offering a nervous laugh.

"Now, Bronte," he said in a tone far too light for Lily's revelation. "I didn't know anything about this. Honest, I—"

Lily reared, her face becoming mottled as she screamed, "I told you, Daddy! I told you and you laughed! You said it was something girls did to help their daddies make points."

Bronte watched as the blood drained from Phillip's face, and she didn't need Lily to clarify her remarks.

Phillip had bartered his daughter's innocence in order to *score* drugs.

Apparently, Jace must have reached the same conclusion because he leaped toward Phillip, throwing him to the ground. Before his brothers could react, his arm came back and his fist connected with the center of Phillip's face. There was a sharp crack, then blood began to flow from his nose.

But even as he drew back to hit him again, Elam and Bodey were there, pulling him backward.

"No, Jace! Not in front of the girls!" Elam shouted while Bodey added, "Wait 'til we've got him alone."

Phillip's eyes widened in terror and he scrambled backward, hurrying toward his car.

"This isn't over, Bronte."

"Yes. Yes, it is, Phillip. And my first call won't be to my lawyer, but to law enforcement."

The threat was enough to cause him to dodge into the car. The engine had barely turned over before he stomped on the accelerator and veered violently to the side. The car fishtailed, then rocketed down the lane.

"Bodey?" Jace called out as he ran toward his truck.

"Already on it, Jace!"

Before Elam could catch him, Jace was in his vehicle and speeding after Phillip.

Bodey began punching numbers into his phone and running toward his pickup. "This is Bodey Taggart. I need to report that a man named Phillip Cupacek is heading toward the old highway in a green late-model sedan, license plate . . ."

The rest of his words were drowned by the roar of his engine.

Elam was already jogging backward to join Bodey. "P.D., I've got to—"

"Go, go!"

Soon, Bodey's truck disappeared into a cloud of dust as well, leaving a trembling, unsettled silence fractured only by Lily's sobbing. Bronte buried her face in her daughter's hair, crooning to her in the same way that she'd done when her daughter had skinned her knees. But this was worse, so much worse.

How? How could this have happened?

And why hadn't she known? What kind of mother was she that she hadn't pieced together the clues before now?

She started when a pair of arms slid around her.

"Don't blame yourself, Bronte. You couldn't have guessed. Not without more information," P.D. murmured.

"But . . ."

"It's what happens now that matters."

Stricken, Bronte met P.D.'s gaze, drawing strength from the mix of emotions she saw there.

"I-I don't know what to do. I need to . . . to . . ."

P.D. squeezed her shoulders. "You simply need to hold her, love her. Helen is contacting the crisis center to find out who can help you and Lily, and I'll take care of Kari and Barry. You're not alone in this. We're here for you."

Bronte nodded, hugging Lily even tighter.

"Jace—"

"Elam and Bodey will catch up with him."

"I don't want him to get hurt chasing Phillip."

P.D.'s lips twitched. "Trust me. If he manages to force Phillip to pull over, it won't be Jace that you need to worry about."

TWENTY

J ACE wasn't sure what had prompted him to jump into his truck and follow the bastard. He only knew that after what he'd heard—after what Lily must have experienced— he had to do something. Since Lily needed her mother and the soothing influences of the female members of her family, he figured it was his job to make sure that the worthless piece of shit who dared to call himself a father didn't get away scot-free.

He drove without conscious thought, catching sight of the sedan as it headed south and away from town, thank goodness. Phillip Cupacek had to be going sixty on a road with a limit of forty. Punching his own accelerator, Jace eased closer. He'd love nothing more than to ram straight into the car's back bumper and force the prick off the road before he left another innocent bystander in his wake. But Jace was pretty sure that his brothers would have called the authorities, and Jace wasn't about to do anything that could cause Bronte any more distress.

He was washed with another wave of fury when he realized what Bronte must have been dealing with for years—the lies, the selfishness, and the hurt. He could see now why she'd seemed so small and fragile when she'd first come to Bliss. Escaping the wild manipulations of an addict must have been like abandoning a war zone. Jace was proud of her—so damned proud of the way she'd become so independent and strong. It humbled him to think that after everything Bronte had experienced, she was willing to trust Jace at all.

But he wondered if her girls would ever be able to do the same. Especially Lily. She'd been betrayed by her own father and his business partner. A man considered to be a trusted family friend. Jace prayed that, somehow, she could learn to understand that she didn't need to fear Jace or his brothers.

Shit.

He forced his attention back to the car ahead. Phillip was weaving erratically over the center line. There was a sharp curve ahead as the road followed the bend of the creek. Beyond it was a narrow bridge. If another car came from the opposite direction, Phillip could hit someone head-on.

Too late, Jace saw a semi with a cattle trailer turning onto the highway from a side road. There was no way that the Peterbilt and Phillip would be able to make it across the bridge at the same time. Rather than slowing down, Phillip moved even faster into the turn, clearly wanting to outrun the larger vehicle, but he wasn't going to make it. The semi was already crawling onto the bridge, beginning to gain speed as the driver worked his way through the gears. With a trailer filled with livestock, the unknown driver wasn't going to make any sudden stops.

Too late, Phillip must have realized the same thing. He slammed on the brakes, swerving to avoid the bridge supports and the blocked lane. His tires caught the gravel on the side of the road and he was skidding out of control, flipping once, twice, before heading down the embankment into the creek.

"Aw, hell," Jace muttered, bringing his own truck to a more controlled stop next to the spot where the skid marks disappeared off the side of the road. Behind him, he heard the semi's air brakes whining as the driver attempted to stop on the opposite shoulder. Grabbing his phone, Jace called the county dispatcher to report the accident and request an ambulance, then jumped out of the truck, grabbing his medical kit from the back.

His boots sent a shower of gravel down the embankment as he scrambled toward the spot where the sedan had landed, inexplicably, right side up. The hood was dented and askew, the driver's-side door was a mangled heap of metal in the middle of the creek, and Phillip was nowhere to be seen.

"Damnit," Jace muttered to himself. How had the bastard managed to escape a rollover and still have the strength to run?

But then, Jace heard a low moan. Veering toward the sound, he saw a pair of battered trainers poking out of the matted underbrush.

Altering his path, Jace waded through the weeds to the spot where Phillip lay, stunned but conscious. Dried blood caked his face from where Jace had punched him, but there were newer streaks and smears from a gash on his forehead and a dozen smaller cuts and abrasions all over his face.

Phillip looked up, a flare of relief touching his eyes, then a hint of panic when he recognized Jace.

"I should leave you here to the buzzards," Jace growled. But he moved forward, crouching in the grass and opening his kit.

Phillip tried to rear back, but hissed and became still again, his eyes squeezing shut. He panted softly and Jace figured the man had broken ribs to add to his other injuries.

"Jace!"

He recognized Bodey's voice and quickly shouted in return, "Down here!"

From above, he heard his brother skidding down the slope, so Jace leaned down toward Phillip.

"You're a lucky man, Cupacek. If you weren't injured and bleeding, I'd probably beat the shit out of you myself." Knowing his time was limited, Jace leaned closer, his voice adopting an ominous, steely thread. "But if you ever do anything—anything at all—to hurt Bronte or her girls again . . . I will kill you. Then I'll put your body somewhere even the buzzards won't be able to find you."

Again, Phillip's eyes widened and he began to tremble violently. But this time it wasn't just from his injuries and the need for a fix.

BRONTE added a notation to the margins on the latest poem she'd written, then looked up, her gaze scanning the yard and the lane again. It was growing late and Kari hadn't arrived home from school yet. Since getting her phone, she'd been so good about telling Bronte if she was going somewhere, but today, there'd been no word.

Sighing, Bronte shoved her notebook back into her bag, knowing that she wouldn't be writing any more today. Not when her nerves were jangling and an aura of dread seemed to hang over everything she did.

The days since Phillip's appearance had begun to run together for Bronte. At P.D.'s insistence, she hadn't gone to work but spent her time at home, tending to her grandmother and Lily, and trying to patch up the recent damage that Phillip had flung their way.

There were interviews with the police, calls with her lawyers, appointments with a pediatrician, counselor, and other crisis professionals. Through it all, Bronte was never alone. Either P.D. or Helen or one of Annie's friends would arrive to offer whatever support she needed. Her freezer mysteriously filled with casseroles, and if she arrived home late, there would be one waiting in the oven.

With only two weeks of school left, Bronte spoke to Lily's principal and teacher and arranged for her daughter to receive her lessons through a "homebound" instructor, who visited Lily every other day. Bronte didn't know if the lessons were of much use since Lily had sunk back into the same silent depression that had plagued her for weeks. The only difference was that Bronte knew the cause.

No, that wasn't the only difference.

Lily was also refusing to see Barry.

Bronte knew that Lily's self-imposed silence was devastating to Barry. P.D. had told her that Jace had tried to explain the situation to him. But each time the boy rode to the house after school and Bronte was forced to turn him away, it was clear that he didn't understand. He only wanted to help. He promised that he wouldn't even talk to Lily; he'd merely hold her hand.

More than anything, Bronte wished her daughter would talk to Barry. Maybe he could do something for Lily to ease her pain.

But then, Bronte supposed she wasn't being much better than Lily. Several times, Jace had tried to call or text, but Bronte hadn't answered. Not when, in one awful day, her husband had completely shaken the foundations of her new life. She was no longer confident about her ability to make proper decisions. Where mere days ago, she'd been sure that coming to Bliss, beginning a new life, and becoming involved with Jace had all been positive events, now she wondered if she'd tried to do too much, experience too much, when she should have been focusing on her daughters.

Even more unsettling was the fact that Jace had been witness to the very worst that her life had to offer. And even though she hadn't planned on keeping anything a secret from him, she had thought she could make those revelations on her own time and in her own way.

Which left her feeling emotionally naked and unsure of herself. She wasn't sure she was ready to discover Jace's reaction to everything he'd learned about her. She didn't think that she could bear it if he thought less of her. Even though there was a part of her that whispered she should call things off with Jace—or at least cool things down—she couldn't bring herself to do it. She didn't know how she would carry on if he wasn't out there, waiting in the wings.

IT was getting dark when Jace pulled the empty feed wagon to a halt next to the shed and jumped from the cab of the Case 290 tractor. As he strode toward the house, he noted that there weren't any lights on in the Big House—not that he'd expected any. Bodey had gone on the road early that morning, beginning his season of competitive cow cutting. When Barry had come home dejected after another failed attempt to see Lily after school, Elam had invited him to stay overnight at his cabin.

Which left Jace alone.

He ruefully shook his head. Two months ago, he'd bemoaned the fact that he never had any time to himself. He'd thought that some solitude and self-indulgence would solve all of his problems.

Now he was beginning to realize that his analysis of the problem had been fairly shallow. Instead of looking to the roots of his discontent, he had erroneously decided that, in order to be happy, he needed to return to one of the happiest periods of his life.

Despite his reasons for leaving home and escaping to Europe, it truly had been an adventure. Not only because he'd traveled to exotic locations, eaten new foods, and saturated himself with art and culture, but it had also been a time of self-discovery. He'd learned the length and breadth of his endurance, emotionally and physically. He'd tested his abilities to solve problems and organize creative solutions. He'd been hyperaware of every moment because he didn't want to waste a single experience.

In the process, he'd discovered that there was a season to every exploit in life. By the end of the two years, he'd known that it was time to come home. Time to begin a new adventure: returning to his birthplace to perfect his role as a rancher and a son.

But even as that decision had been made, Fate had other ideas. His parents and little sister had been killed, his youngest brother injured, and Elam . . .

Well, Elam had been flung into his own brand of hell.

Somehow, they'd all managed to fight their way back to a form of happiness again. For a time, the ranch responsibilities had been enough for Jace. He'd been content. He'd been challenged. Only in the last year or two had the dissatisfaction begun to grow.

Looking back on it now, Jace realized that part of his problem had come from ignoring the fact that work would never be enough.

His brother Elam was a physical man. He loved running, shooting, and working out. After joining P.D. for last year's Wild West Games, it was clear that he'd like to try his hand at winning again.

Bodey lived to compete—cow cutting, Single Action Shooting Society, even women.

Jace . . .

Well, Jace needed to create—whether it was the perfect field of corn, or an iron sculpture. Now that he'd allowed his artistic nature free rein again, he was discovering that it gave him a new way of viewing his surroundings, infusing everything he did with a measure of joy.

But even that wouldn't have been enough if Bronte hadn't walked into his life.

It wasn't until he'd met her that he'd realized that his unhappiness had begun when Elam and P.D. had become a couple. Subconsciously, he'd begun to long for that same kind of connection, that sharing of minds and emotions and bodies. He didn't want to play the field, didn't want to be lined up, didn't want to do the bar scene.

He wanted to belong.

He'd had a taste of that with Bronte. He still longed for that with Bronte.

But he was out of his depth here. He didn't want to push her—and he certainly didn't want to scare off her children. He just needed her to know that he was here for her.

"Mr. Taggart?"

As if summoned from his own imagination, Jace thought he heard a familiar voice. But when he glanced up, it wasn't Bronte who sat on the shadowy porch swing. It was Kari.

"Kari," he said softly, stopping when he saw the way she gripped her arms in front of her. "Is something wrong?"

She shook her head, then bit her lip. In that unconscious gesture, she looked so much like a younger version of Bronte that his heart twisted in his chest.

"How's Lily?"

She lifted her shoulder in a shrug.

"Is Annie doing okay?"

She nodded. "Yeah. They've got a physical therapist coming to help her learn how to get around."

Jace stopped, not wanting to crowd Kari by getting too close. Her tension was palpable even from several feet away.

"How about your mom?"

"She's . . ." Kari rolled her eyes, but for once, the gesture wasn't one of teenage pique, but more a quick self-reflection. "I don't know."

"Can I help you with something?"

Kari rubbed her hands on her jeans, then stood. "Actually, I came for a couple of reasons."

When she didn't immediately continue, Jace said, "Okay."

"First, I wanted to thank you."

"Thank me?" Jace couldn't think of anything he'd done to deserve Kari's approval. When he remembered the way he'd lost his temper and nearly broken Phillip's nose—right there in front of Kari and Lily—he winced.

Kari's chin tilted and she forcefully stated, "I want to thank you for punching my dad."

Jace couldn't help a burst of ironic laughter. Whatever he'd expected her to say, *that* wasn't it. "I shouldn't have done that."

"Maybe," Kari said. "But I'm glad you did. It's what I wanted to do."

She looked down at her toes, seeming to mull something over in her mind. "Are you busy?" Before he could answer, she hurriedly added, "I mean, I know you're probably busy, but . . . could I talk to you for a second?"

"Sure." Jace gestured to the house. "But it's getting chilly out here. Why don't you come in where it's warm."

Her relief was apparent, making Jace wonder how long

she'd been waiting. With a storm front moving in, the temperatures had dropped about twenty degrees in the last couple of hours.

"Are you hungry?" he asked as he opened the door.

Kari stepped into the hall, glancing suspiciously over her shoulder. "That depends on what you're offering. I don't think I could face another casserole."

Jace chuckled. "How about a hamburger?"

She looked like he'd proposed a filet mignon after a weeklong fast.

"I'd love a hamburger."

Jace led her through to the kitchen.

"Does your mom know you're here?"

Kari shrugged, not quite meeting his eyes.

"Mind if I let her know?"

"I guess not."

Removing his phone from his pocket, Jace quickly texted Bronte—realizing that it was the first time he'd done so in several days. When Bronte hadn't responded to his overtures earlier in the week, he'd told himself that he wouldn't bug her until she reached out to him. Now, he was relieved to have an excuse.

Kari my place. Wants 2 talk. I'll make her burger then bring home.

The response was almost immediate.

Thank you! Been worried.

There was no personal addition to her text, but Jace refused to worry about that now. At least the silence between them had been broken.

Shrugging out of his jacket, he hung it and his hat on the hook by the back door. Then he checked the refrigerator.

As usual, there weren't a lot of choices there, but a package of beef patties had been left on a plate to defrost. He had buns and condiments galore, lettuce, and most of a tomato. After placing the burgers in a frying pan, he rounded up a bag of chips and grabbed some corn from the freezer.

Sensing that Kari didn't want to talk about anything serious until the cooking was done, Jace asked her about school and her friends. Since he knew so many people in the valley, he was subtly trying to determine if she was hanging out with a fairly responsible crowd. So far, he could tell that she'd collected a pretty good group.

"If you or your friends would ever like to go riding, let me know. There's a path heading into the mountains above Elam's cabin. It's a fairly easy ride. There's a clearing toward the top with an artesian spring where you can get an icy-cold drink of pure water and have a picnic lunch. Then, on the way back, there's a watering hole in the creek where you could cool off. It's not too deep, but it's still fun."

"Really?" Kari's burger hung in midair. "I know you said I could do that before, but . . . You'd really let us do that?"

"Sure. Why not? We might not have Starbucks and a subway, but there are some great things to do, especially in the summer."

She set her nearly finished burger down on the plate. "Did my mom tell you that?"

Jace frowned. "Tell me what?"

"About the Starbucks and the subway?"

He shook his head. "I'm not following. I don't remember your mother saying anything about that."

Kari pushed her plate away. "My mom wanted to bring us here ever since we were little. But every time she brought up the subject, my dad would say that any place without a Starbucks and a subway wasn't worth seeing."

"No. She didn't tell me that."

Kari twisted her glass, watching the milk make cloudy designs against the sides. "When we came here, I gave her a hard time. I kept thinking that if Dad didn't like it . . . why should I?"

Jace knew better than to comment. He merely nodded to show he'd heard.

"I was pretty wrong, huh?"

"I wouldn't go that far. Everyone gets nervous when they experience something new. I can't imagine that it was easy to pack up everything and come to Utah. Especially so close to the end of the school year."

"Yeah. I was pissed." When she looked up, it was easy for Jace to see the remorse in her eyes. "Why would my dad let that creep do that to my sister?"

Her change of subject was so abrupt that Jace nearly missed its significance. But he took the time to think about his answer carefully. "Your father . . . has a serious drug problem," he countered instead.

Kari scowled. "It's pretty obvious, huh? I think my mom tried to shield us as much as she could, but it's not hard to see what's going on when you walk in on your dad and he's stoned. Even the other day, I could see he was starting to tweak. He wouldn't have made it another twenty minutes without a fix. But that's not an excuse for what he let happen to Lily. It's not like he's stupid. Geez, the minute Lily told him what was going on, he should have done what you did to him. He should have run up to Jeremy and hit him in the face."

Clearly, Jace wasn't going to live that event down anytime soon.

"You're right. He should have done something. Right then. Right there." Jace proceeded as carefully as he could. "Your father loves you both—"

"He loves his drugs more!" Kari interrupted forcefully.

Jace dipped his head, conceding to her point. "But that doesn't mean he can't change."

"Get clean, you mean."

"That would be a start." He sighed. "I'm not an expert on any of this. I know that addiction is incredibly complicated—and there are no easy answers on how to overcome it. I wouldn't presume to tell you how you should think or feel about the way your dad has . . . let you down."

Kari's eyes grew bright with unshed tears.

Jace leaned forward to rest his weight on his forearms.

"But there is something that maybe I can speak about with some certainty. And that's what it means to be a man."

She blinked up at him and somewhere, deep inside of her, he could see the scared girl hidden behind her teenage bravado.

"A man takes care of his loved ones. He doesn't hurt women and he doesn't hurt children. He fights like hell to keep them safe and if something or someone threatens their well-being, he does everything he can to protect them. If he somehow screws up, a real man admits his mistake and makes things right."

As much as he hated to even speak of the prick, Jace forced himself to say, "Maybe one day, your dad will find a way to get clean and get better."

"And man up?"

"Yeah," Jace said softly. "I think you deserve that much, don't you?"

She nodded, a tear plunging down her cheek.

"Just don't judge every male you meet too harshly, okay? Some of us are trying our best to be among the good guys. If you've got a boy that needs vetting, my brothers and I would be happy to stand in as your welcoming committee."

She offered him a laugh that was half sob.

"Thanks, Jace."

He gestured to her plate. "Still hungry?"

"No. I think I'd like to go home now, if that's okay."

"Sure. I'll take you back in the truck. It's getting too cold out there for a walk."

He started to stand, but she stopped him with, "Before we go, there was one other thing I wanted to talk to you about."

He relaxed into his chair again. "Okay, shoot."

"I kinda gave you a hard time when you and my mom . . . when . . ." She took a deep gulp of air, then hurried on, "I want you to know I don't mind anymore." She briefly met his gaze. "I figure anyone who would stand up for my sister like that can't be that bad of a guy to have around the house."

Jace felt his cheeks flush. "Well, I . . . uh . . ." He cleared his throat. "I appreciate that."

"Anyway, I think you should start coming by," she said softly. So softly, that Jace nearly missed the words. "I think my mom needs you right now. P.D. and Helen have been great, and my grandma is so cool, but . . ." Kari lifted her shoulders and released them again. "I think she needs you. Maybe when you drop me off, you could . . . talk to her?"

"I don't know if—"

"Lily won't know. She's in bed by eight and she sleeps like a log. Annie goes to sleep about the same time. Promise me you'll think about it?"

Sighing, Jace reluctantly offered, "I'll think about it."

But he couldn't deny the way his heart started beating harder in his chest.

BRONTE gently closed the door to Lily's room, sighing softly. Following the advice of Lily's doctors and therapists, Bronte hadn't tried to force her daughter to talk about the incident in Jeremy Montero's office. Instead, she'd concentrated on giving Lily love and acceptance and comfort. But she knew her daughter was hurting, knew she was confused. More than anything, Bronte wished that there was a way to help her daughter. If there were a magical incantation she could offer, Bronte would willingly bear Lily's pain herself.

Unfortunately, there were no easy fixes to what had occurred. Bronte could only weather her own guilt at not realizing earlier why her daughter's personality had taken such a sudden shift—then at the way she'd reassured her over and over again that Lily would still be able to see her father on a regular basis.

Sweet heaven, if she'd only known. If she'd left Phillip years ago, if she'd recognized the depth of Lily's depression faster, if she'd contacted a doctor earlier . . .

If . . . if . . . *if* . . .

She found it a sad irony that her daughter's first real deep breath had come after Bronte had carefully relayed the news that Phillip was in custody and would be doing some jail time over the next few years. Besides the reckless driving charge he'd received from the local authorities, it hadn't taken long for them to discover that he also had an outstanding bench warrant for his arrest from Boston. Her ex-husband's lifestyle was catching up to him, with charges of fraud, embezzlement, and theft. Although Bronte had witnessed his downhill slide for years, she still had a hard time reconciling the vibrant, successful man she'd married with the gaunt mug shot she found buried in one of the rear pages of a Salt Lake City newspaper.

Jeremy Montero had fared even worse. The investigation was still in its early stage, but it was clear that Lily wasn't his only victim. Police had raided the clinic, uncovering evidence of a child pornography ring . . . and worse.

The thought of what could have happened gave Bronte nightmares. But she did her best to paint a positive smile on her face, knowing that this was one challenge she could not fail. She would find a way to help her daughter—both of her daughters—get past Phillip's betrayal.

The phone in her pocket chirped, causing her to jump. Glancing at the screen, she saw a text from Jace.

Jace.

The sight of his name on a text filled her with more longing than it should, but she forced herself to push the sensation aside. She already had more than she could handle on her plate. She couldn't afford to indulge in romance.

Nevertheless, she punched the icon for the text.

On our way back.

She stared at the words for a long time, wondering what had possessed Kari to even go to the Taggarts' ranch.

Unable to help herself, Bronte typed a response.

Thanks.

But he wasn't finished.

Could we talk tonight?

Talk. She didn't want to talk. She didn't want to think. She wanted . . .

Sighing, Bronte realized that she wasn't sure anymore *what* she wanted. She only knew that she couldn't handle one more thing.

Her thumb hovered over the *N*, but then, as if unable to control her own digits, she typed instead:

Give me an hour.

Only a few minutes passed before she heard the rumble of Jace's pickup. Bronte stood at the top of the steps, wondering if he would try to see her now—hoping he would, fearing he would. But when the door opened, only Kari walked through.

When she saw Bronte on the steps, she offered her a quick, shy smile—one that Bronte hadn't seen in years.

"Hi, Mom."

"Hi, there."

"Sorry I didn't text to let you know where I was."

Bronte was beginning to wonder if she'd stepped into the *Twilight Zone*. "That's okay. Jace sent me a message."

"Yeah, I know. He made me a burger, too. It was really good." Kari bounced up the stairs as if she didn't have a care in the world. When she would have passed Bronte, she paused, then leaned forward to kiss her mother on the cheek.

"He's a good guy, you know. I told him he needed to come to the house more."

Huh?

"Everybody else in bed?" Kari asked, continuing her climb.

"Yes. Your . . . uh . . ." Bronte was having a hard time thinking coherently. "Your grandmother turned in early and Lily fell asleep watching television."

"I'll be quiet so I don't wake her up. I'm going to go to bed, too. I have a history test tomorrow." Kari paused at the door to her room. "You should call Jace and have him keep you company. I told him to come over, but he said he'd leave it up to you."

"I, uh . . ."

"Night, Mom."

With that, Kari disappeared into her bedroom, leaving Bronte completely rattled.

What on earth had Jace said to Kari to bring about *this* transformation?

Weary, she crossed into her own room. If Jace were coming, she needed to shower, change her clothes . . .

Sinking onto the bed, she pressed the heel of her hand to her forehead. Her brain seemed to whirl with a million thoughts, but was curiously numb at the same time.

Unfortunately, by sitting down, by trying to corral the emotions roiling in her brain, she zoned out and the next thing she knew, the rumble of Jace's truck neared the house again.

TWENTY-ONE

———◆———

S UDDENLY panicked, Bronte rushed to the window,
already reaching for her phone. But even as her fingers
stood poised to text him and tell him she'd changed her
mind, it rang. Then it rang two more times before she
snatched it up and answered.

"Hi."

"Hi."

How did the sound of his voice manage to slide through
her veins like a liquid tonic?

"Are you still up to having me stop by?"

His concern was palpable, drawing her toward the
window as if she were attached to him by a string.

She pushed the curtain aside, causing a patch of light to
spill onto the ground. Jace immediately looked up and
smiled.

Bronte probably could have resisted the man except for
that smile. She could have made an excuse and sent him on
his way. But the gesture was filled with such love and concern that her face crumpled and tears pushed at the back of
her throat, making it impossible to talk, to breathe.

She heard a soft curse on the line. Before she could fathom what he meant to do, he pocketed his phone, climbed the intricate wrought-iron porch support, hoisted himself onto the newly repaired roof, and gingerly made his way to the window.

By that time, she'd gathered her wits enough to lift up the sash. Then, he was stepping inside to fold her into his arms.

Instantly, the emotions that she'd tried to tamp down since Phillip had appeared came rushing to the surface. Clinging to Jace, she surrendered to the storm of emotion, sobbing into his chest.

To his credit, he didn't seem put off by the display. Instead, he held her even more tightly, rocking her from side to side, stroking her hair and whispering, "Let it out. You don't have to carry it all alone anymore. Let it all out."

Never in her life had another person given her permission to cry. Not dainty feminine tears, but huge, air-gulping, chest-rending sobs that threatened to tear her apart. Yet Jace seemed completely undaunted, allowing her tears to soak into his shirt. There was no need for words. His actions conveyed everything she needed to know—that he loved her, cared for her, ached with her. As if the sobs loosened the dam she'd built around her emotions, the words also spilled free, rushing through her lips in a barely intelligible flood as she spoke of Lily, of what had been lost.

But when she began to blame herself, he held her even tighter. "No, Bronte, no," he whispered. He lay her on the bed, then stretched out beside her, cradling Bronte against him and drawing a blanket over her shoulders. "You're a great mom. Your daughters love you. Never doubt that. Ever."

In time, the storm of weeping eased, then passed, leaving her weak and trembling in his arms.

"You must think—"

"Shh. I think you're exhausted and worried. But you're not alone, okay?"

Her chin trembled and the tears threatened to fall again. It had been so long since someone had offered to share her burdens. No, her problems hadn't been magically solved, but she felt the soft sweet beginnings of hope unfurling in her breast.

When she tried to move, sure that Jace would be ready to sit up or even leave, he tenderly tucked her back against his chest.

"Shh. Lie still. I'll stay here until you fall asleep."

The release of emotion had left her so tired that she didn't resist. Instead, she allowed her heavy eyelids to close.

"You're a miracle worker, Jace. Do you know that?"

"Hardly."

She smiled against him. "You seem to have tamed the savage teenage beast that has been living in this house for the last few weeks."

"She'll probably make a reappearance in a while."

"What on earth did you say to her?"

"Not much. She was worried about her sister and upset with her father. I think she'd already come to a lot of her own conclusions concerning his behavior. I reassured her that she had some men in her life she could come to if she needed help."

Bronte damned the way her throat became tight again.

"Thank you, Jace."

"My pleasure." His voice rumbled pleasantly beneath her ear. "She gave me permission to come over tonight."

She smiled against him. "I know." She roused. "What about Barry? Do you need to—"

"Shhh." Jace drew her back down again. "He's with Elam."

"He's such a sweet boy, Jace. You've got to be proud of him."

"I am. Lily has been the best thing to happen to him in a long time. He misses her."

"Send him over tomorrow. I think it's time they talked."

"He'll probably bring a bag full of ranch toys."

"I'll buy him a whole new set if he can get Lily to smile again."

"Don't tell *him* that."

Jace's fingers began to trace long slow strokes up and down her back. Soon her breathing began to sync with the motion. Bronte felt her tight muscles release, one by one, until she felt boneless and adrift.

"Jace?" she murmured with the last shred of coherence that remained.

"Hmm."

"Love . . . you."

There was a slight hitch to the rhythm of his fingertips, then, from very far away, she heard, "Love you, too, Bronte."

THE next afternoon, Jace scowled up at the clouds gathering in the distance. Just as the radio had predicted, a storm was blowing in. He would have to hurry to get his work done so that he could meet Barry at the bus stop. He didn't want him to have to walk in the rain.

He hurried into the Big House, intent on grabbing something quick for lunch. But as soon as he walked through the door, his phone rang. Distracted, knowing that he only had a few minutes before he had to meet the hay broker in the yard, he yanked open the refrigerator door as he hit the call button.

"Yeah."

"Mr. Taggart?"

Jace had been expecting the low, melodious tones of Esteban Peña, so when a woman's voice greeted him, he straightened.

"This is Jace."

"This is Natalie Noorda from the high school. Barry's teacher asked me to get in touch with you and see if you'd like her to send his project home with one of the neighbors. They had the judging today and he won a prize."

"That's great. I know he was excited about the contest." Jace's brow creased. "Can't Barry bring it home himself? I could probably swing by at the end of the day to pick him up if it's too big to carry on the bus."

There was a heavy silence, then, "Isn't Barry home with you?"

Jace straightened, bumping the fridge door shut with his hip.

"Ms. . . . Noorda, was it?"

"Yes."

"I dropped Barry off at the bus stop this morning."

"Oh, dear." The woman was clearly upset. "Mr. Taggart, I'm one of the paraprofessionals that meets the buses each morning to gather the kids for the life skills class. Barry didn't get off this morning."

Shit.

Lunch forgotten, Jace headed for the door. "Is there any way you could talk to the driver and make sure he didn't see him at the bus stop?"

"Absolutely. I'll also talk to Jake Eddington. He gets on at the stop right before Barry's. As soon as I know something, I'll call back."

"Thanks."

As soon as the woman hung up, Jace was speed-dialing Elam.

"This is Elam."

"Elam, have you seen Barry?"

"Not since he headed down the hill this morning. Why?"

Jace was already climbing into his truck. "He came in, gathered his school stuff, and I dropped him off at the end of the lane like I always do. But the school called to say he never got there."

"Hell. Where could he have gone?"

"I don't know. They were having a special day today. His seed project was being judged, so I can't understand why he didn't get on the bus."

"I'm headed down the highway now. I should be there in a few minutes. I'll check my cabin first and then backtrack toward the house. In the meantime, I'll call P.D. and ask if she's seen or heard from him."

"Thanks."

"What about Bodey?"

"He left yesterday morning."

"All right. I'll call him, too. Not that there's anything he can do to help. He's probably in Cheyenne by now. But maybe he's heard from him."

Within minutes, Jace was in his pickup again, driving at a snail's pace as he wound down the lane toward the highway. Had Barry forgotten something, started home, and then fallen? It wasn't like him to wander off. Even when he was younger and still struggling with the limits of his disability, he'd remained emotionally tethered to familiar surroundings. He didn't like dealing with unaccustomed situations or places.

A quick sweep of the area left Jace with no more information than he'd had when he'd started, so he swung his truck in the other direction so that he could scour the lane again.

When his phone went off, he answered it mid-ring.

"This is Jace."

"Mr. Taggart. Natalie Noorda. I spoke with the bus driver and he confirmed that Barry wasn't waiting at the stop in front of your house when he drove by this morning. But Jake said that he thought he saw Barry before the bus appeared, but that he ran back toward home again with . . . 'that new girl.' Does that make sense to you?"

"Yeah. It does. Thank you."

Jace changed direction again, taking the access road that would take him to Annie's house. Even though he'd been given a better idea where Barry had gone, he kept a sharp eye on the fields and ditches on either side of the road.

When he pulled next to the house, he saw Bronte unloading groceries from the back of her van. As soon as she saw him, she set the bags back into the car and waved.

Skidding to a halt, Jace rolled down his window. "Have you seen Barry today?"

"No. Lily insisted on going to school, so I went to work this morning. Annie made sure she headed to the bus stop on time."

Jace sighed. "I don't know if she made it there. I got a call saying Barry didn't show up. One of the boys down the highway said he thought he saw Barry and Lily heading back toward the ranch."

"What?"

Before Jace could react, she ran into the house. He heard her speak briefly to Annie, then the sound of her footsteps disappearing upstairs. By the time Jace followed her inside, Annie had rolled her chair into the doorway of the living room.

"I saw her go off to school this morning," she said, her eyes wide and worried. "She seemed excited. It's the happiest I've seen her in days."

Bronte appeared at the top of the stairs. "They aren't here."

Jace bit back a curse. "I'll go check the tree house. Look through Lily's room one more time. See if there's anything missing—clothes, a suitcase—that could tell us if they decided to run away."

He hated the way Bronte's cheeks lost their color at the suggestion, but she quickly went to do as he'd asked.

Jace strode through the kitchen and out the side door in long loping strides. But after climbing the ladder, it was easy to see that the children hadn't been there. The wind had deposited a fine layer of dust and leaves on the plank floors. If they'd been up here, the debris would have been disturbed.

"Jace!" Bronte burst through the screen door and he dropped back to the ground. He caught her by the arms as she stumbled over the uneven ground.

"The jar," she gasped. "The butterfly jar is gone. And her quilt."

At the same time, the phone in his pocket emitted a shrill ring. Jace grabbed it from one hand.

"Yeah."

"When there was no sign of Barry at my place, I went back to the Big House to check his room. There was a note taped to his door. Heck if I can figure out what it says. See what you can make of it." There was the rustling of paper, then, "Gone to sit Goldie free. Be back super."

Bronte tugged on Jace's sleeve. "Lily named her butterfly Goldie. It must have come out of its cocoon overnight."

"That means that he's heading for the summer pasture."

On the other end of the phone, Elam said, "I'll head for

the barn and see if Snuffles is gone. The hired men have the ATVs."

"Bronte and I will head back that way. If Barry's horse is missing, saddle up Greystoke and put him in the trailer." Jace squinted up at the sky and the heavy clouds that seemed to be piling up against the mountaintops. "I'll see if I can head the kids off before the road runs out. If not, I'll ride toward the camp and intercept them."

"You want me to go with you?"

"No. I need someone to coordinate things here in case they head back and I miss them along the way."

Bronte tugged on his sleeve again. "Tell him to saddle two horses."

Jace opened his mouth to refuse, knowing he could make better time on his own. But when he caught the shadow of fear in her eyes, he knew that nothing on earth could have prevented him from going after Barry, and she probably felt the same.

"You'll need to saddle up a mount for Bronte as well. She's coming with me."

"How experienced is she?"

He saw Bronte stiffen as if she thought she would have to fight to be included, so he said, "She's a beginner. Snow-flake should work fine."

"Consider it done."

When he hung up, Bronte threw her arms around his neck. "Thank you, Jace. I couldn't stand to wait here. Not with a storm on the way."

"I know, sweetheart."

He absorbed the sensation of her pressed against him, to inhale the sweet floral scent of her perfume. Then he released her.

"Get your coat, some slick-soled shoes, a hat, and some gloves if you have them."

"Okay."

"Let Annie know what's going on and text Kari so she doesn't walk into this mess unaware when she comes home. I'll hook the trailer onto my truck and be back for you."

She hugged him one more time, then ran toward the house.

It took nearly thirty minutes for Jace to return to the ranch and load everything up. The whole time he kept an eye on the sky, which was growing more ominous. Since he was afraid he and Bronte might get caught in the weather, he packed more heavily than he would have if he were heading into the mountains on his own, adding extra food and water to the items Elam had already gathered. By the time he'd taken his place behind the wheel, he was anxious to be underway.

Jace heard the latch hit home on the trailer, then Elam rounded the back to approach his window.

"You're going to be out of cell service halfway up the canyon," Elam said. "After that, coverage is intermittent."

Jace nodded. "I know. I'll get word to you as soon as I can."

"Despite his disability, he's a smart kid, Jace. You've taught him well. If a storm breaks, he knows how to get out of the weather."

"I hope so. If he or Lily gets hurt . . ."

"Don't borrow trouble before it comes on its own. You know how much he loves that little girl. He'd never do anything to intentionally harm her. Remember that and trust him to do the right thing."

"If I could trust him to do the right thing, he wouldn't have run off like this in the first place."

Elam touched his shoulder through the window. "Look at it from his point of view. His friend has been in pain and he made a promise to take her up to the poppy grove when her butterfly emerged. He's not thinking about us."

"Obviously."

"He's thinking about her."

Jace knew Elam was right, but he still couldn't help thinking that if he'd stayed to watch Barry get on the bus, if he'd waited a few more minutes before beginning his own hectic day, he would have seen Lily approach.

But with the hay broker arriving and his own tight schedule, would he have canceled everything and helped

Barry? Probably not. He would have made him wait until the weekend. Or longer.

Maybe that was the reason Barry had decided to take Lily to the summer pastures on his own. Not because he was flouting authority, but because he didn't want to bother Jace when he was busy. After all, he'd followed the same procedure he would have used if he'd saddled his horse and gone for a ride to Elam's cabin or to Annie's. He'd left a note, clearly explaining where he was going and when he would be back. He simply hadn't realized how far away the poppy grove really was.

Elam slapped him on the shoulder.

"He'll be all right, Jace. They both will."

Jace nodded. He had to think that. Otherwise he'd go crazy.

His phone rang, and after seeing it was Bronte, he answered with, "I'm on my way to your place now."

"Good. Because someone at the school took it upon themselves to call the sheriff's department. I didn't pick up my phone in time and they left a message that they'd be stopping by as soon as they could to investigate the situation."

"Oh, hell." Jace reached to start his engine. Then, lifting the phone away from his mouth, Jace said, "Someone called the police."

Elam scowled.

Bronte's voice rose in panic. "Jace, I don't want to wait that long. Not with the weather closing in."

"Tell Bronte to send them to the Big House," Elam said. "I'll answer their questions so the two of you can get going. In the meantime, I'll keep my eye out for Peña."

"Bronte?"

"I heard."

Shifting the truck into gear, Jace shot his brother a look of gratitude, then slowly eased away from the yard.

"Hang on, Bronte. I'll be there in less than five minutes."

AS soon as Jace rolled to a stop in front of Annie's house, Bronte dodged out of the door. Thankfully, Kari had returned from school in time for Bronte to explain that she and Jace were going to try to intercept the children. Kari had wanted to come as well, but Bronte had taken her to the side and explained that, because Annie tired quickly, Bronte needed Kari to man the phones and help her grandmother until Bronte could return.

The truck hadn't even come to a complete stop before she was hopping into the passenger seat. Then Jace was putting the truck in gear and heading for the dirt service road.

Immediately Bronte became aware of the addition of the trailer. The truck handled differently, especially as they climbed up the road leading to Elam's cabin. When the horses shifted, Bronte felt the truck shudder slightly.

"Are you sure we can pull the trailer up such a steep slope?"

Jace smiled reassuringly. "This is nothing compared to what we usually pull." He lifted the center console and motioned for her to take the center spot. "Come on over here. We'll take this track up into the hills as far as we can, then we'll have to make the rest of the trip on horseback."

"How long will it take?"

"We'll have to take the switchbacks up the canyon at about twenty miles per hour, so . . . twenty or thirty minutes? Then about an hour on horseback, maybe a little more." He leaned forward to peer out the window at the clouds that piled one on top of each other. While Jace had been talking, they'd changed from gray to an ominous black.

Bronte felt as if a hand had begun to squeeze the breath from her body. Ninety minutes? Maybe more?

"Are the kids going to get caught in the storm?" she asked worriedly, trying to remember what Lily had worn to school that morning. Was she dressed in long sleeves or short, trousers or leggings, a jacket or a sweater? But her mind was whirling with so many thoughts and fears, she couldn't remember one day from the last.

Jace draped his arm around her shoulders and pulled her close. "I know it's not much comfort, but Barry has been trained to take a jacket and a bedroll if he goes out of sight of the ranch. It was a rule that was established early on, and one he's been good to follow. Judging by the fact that Lily's quilt is gone, it sounds to me like he insisted that Lily do the same."

Bronte nodded, but with the storm looming overhead, she knew that such precautions would provide minimal protection in bad weather.

"What if it rains?"

Jace squeezed her arm. "Hopefully, that doesn't happen until we find them. But if they left this morning, they've got a massive head start on us. The ideal scenario would be for them to have already reached the summer pastures—which is entirely feasible. If they've made it to the poppy grove, there's an old sheepherder's cabin we use when we move the cows. It's a sturdy building with a good roof and solid walls. Inside, they have everything they need—matches, some dry wood, a kerosene lantern, and even some basic food supplies."

Bronte touched his thigh, needing the solid strength to be found there to ground her.

"They'll be okay, Bronte," Jace said.

She had no choice but to believe him.

JUST as Jace had surmised, they reached the end of the service road just shy of the half-hour mark. A large metal gate with a padlock signaled the unofficial end of "civilization," as Bodey was fond of saying. The land beyond was a mixture of privately owned parcels and those governed by the Forestry Service. A dozen yards away, television and telecommunication towers added a slightly alien quality to a sharp, steep cliff. Beyond that were a series of jagged peaks and shallow valleys thick with pine and aspen.

This high up, the foliage was lusher, greener than it was in the valley below. Stepping from the truck, Bronte was able to look far, far down to where Bliss appeared like a scattering of children's blocks against a brown and green crazy quilt of farm fields and pastures.

She zipped her jacket up to her chin. A chilly, gusting wind had begun to drive the clouds to the east. The air was heavy with moisture and now and again, Bronte felt a stray drop hit her cheek.

"Do you have a hat?"

She shook her head.

Jace reached into the back of his truck, lifting the bench seat to reveal a storage space beneath. He grabbed a baseball-style cap with TAGGART QUARTER HORSES embroidered on the front. He tightened the strap at the back to make it smaller, then closed and locked the door, moving toward her.

"Here."

"I don't need a—"

"Wearing something on your head helps to conserve body warmth." He settled the hat over her hair and pulled it low over her brow. Then, for several long seconds, he studied her with a strange light in his eyes. One that made her feel warm and pretty despite the fact that she shivered in front of him, gripped with an almost overwhelming fear.

"Besides, you look cute with it on." His voice dropped, "I like having my name on you. It subtly claims that you're mine—even if that makes me sound like a caveman."

Bronte knew that as a modern woman, she should object to such a statement, but instead, she loved the idea of being claimed by Jace Taggart.

"How long has it been since you've ridden?" Jace asked as he took her hand and led her toward the docile mare that he'd tied to the side of the trailer. Bronte could tell by her sleepy eyes and placid disposition that the animal had been chosen for her calm manner.

"Too long for me to admit," Bronte grumbled under her breath.

Jace checked the fit of her saddle one more time, shortening the stirrups, then tightening the girth. "If that's the case, I'm going to give you control of the reins, but I'm going to tie the lead to the halter around my pommel. That way, you won't have to worry about anything but staying on your mount. Snowflake will follow my horse no matter the terrain."

"That sounds good."

"Up you go."

Holding on to the pommel, Bronte hopped slightly as she tried to get her foot into the stirrup. Then she attempted to haul herself into the saddle.

She'd made it only halfway when Jace planted his hands under her butt, causing her to squeak in surprise. But his boost was enough to help Bronte swing her leg over the broad back of the animal.

Jace made sure her feet were settled securely into the stirrups and the saddle was perfectly positioned.

"How's it feel?"

"O-okay."

"Good girl." Jace cupped her knee with his broad hand. "I'm going to push us as fast as I think you can handle. But if you feel yourself falling, or something doesn't seem right, you tell me right away."

Bronte nodded, then pushed her nervousness aside. She refused to slow them down.

"I'm ready."

He squeezed her knee one last time in encouragement, then walked around the back of her mount and tied her lead rope firmly to his pommel. "Don't be afraid to hold on to the horn until you get used to the rhythm of the horse. The only thing that persuades Snowflake to move with any real intensity is a barn and a waiting scoop of oats. If anything, you might need to encourage her to pick up the pace."

"Okay."

He took the reins of both animals and led them to the gate. It was only then that Bronte noticed that the padlock was for show. The chain had only been looped around the gate rather than firmly fastened.

Once they were on the other side, Jace closed the gate again and replaced the chain in the same manner. Then he swung onto the horse that he called Greystoke.

"Ready?"

She nodded.

He spurred his own animal into motion. For a split

instant, Snowflake refused to move. But then, when the lead rope grew taut, she finally deigned to follow.

At first, Jace kept the pace to a quick walk, allowing Bronte to get used to riding again. She was secretly grateful. Although she'd briefly ridden behind Jace the night of the meteor shower, she'd forgotten that, alone in the saddle, the ground seemed even farther away.

A wave of panic shot through her as she had visions of falling, falling. But Bronte forced herself to keep her gaze directly between Snowflake's ears. In time, she had no real choice but to adapt. Soon, her body began to adjust to the rocking motion of the animal's gate and her grip on the pommel eased.

"I'm going to quicken the pace, okay?"

She nodded, then nearly regretted agreeing with Jace when the horses moved into a jouncing trot. But when she was able to keep her seat, he eased the animals into a lope. The added speed offered her a moment of terror and she reached for the pommel again. But soon, she was able to hold on with only one hand, allowing the other to loosely hold the reins as she'd once been taught.

Unfortunately, as her fears about staying on the horse eased away, her worry about the children resurfaced. The wind was growing worse, cutting through the padded layers of her jacket. With the heavy clouds, light was fading, and she worried that if the storm hit in earnest, they might be forced to slow their pace.

It was clear that Jace knew the way. He rode confidently. While she concentrated on the terrain, he was more mindful of the brush, scouring the bushes and trees for any sign of the children. About twenty minutes after they'd begun, Jace drew back on the reins, allowing the horses to rest as he took a pair of binoculars from the pack that held some of their supplies.

"Any sign of them?"

"Maybe." He lowered the glasses. "There's some trampled underbrush up ahead. Let's go take a closer look."

TWENTY-TWO

———◆◆◆———

B RONTE'S heart knocked against her ribs.
Please, please let it be a sign of the children.

As he neared the spot, Jace slowed, then dismounted from his horse altogether. Keeping his reins in one hand, he neared a copse of trees, where he found a long strand of coarse hair that had been snagged by a tree branch.

Bronte's heart sank. Lily's hair was baby fine.

But when Jace turned to show her, he was grinning. "It's from a horse's mane. A quarter horse."

"That's a good sign?"

"That's a great sign. With the wind like this, it can't have been here for long."

He was about to get back into the saddle when he paused.

"What's wrong?" she whispered.

"Do you hear that?"

"What?" she breathed.

A bear? Moose?

Bronte couldn't hear anything but the wind and rustling grass.

He moved back into the copse of trees, his head cocking

slightly as he caught whatever noise had alerted him. Then he bent low, pulling aside the tall grass and laughing softly. When he straightened again, he held up a pair of foil wrappers with colorful cartoons of apples and bananas and strawberries on the front. Bronte instantly recognized it as the same brand of squeeze pouches filled with applesauce that she often gave Lily and Barry to snack on after school. Jace had caught the almost imperceptible sound of them rattling together in the wind.

"It's them," Bronte said eagerly. "That's got to be from them."

Jace grinned. "I'd bet money on it. Ever since you started feeding them to Barry at your house, we've been going through an applesauce cycle." He turned the packet over. "It's not weathered and . . ." He unscrewed the lid and squeezed and was rewarded with a small squirt of pink puree. "It's fresh."

A gust of wind threatened to tear the evidence from Jace's hand, but he jammed the garbage into his pocket.

"Let's go."

"How much farther?" Bronte asked as he swung back onto his horse.

He squinted against the gathering gloom. "About ten miles. Maybe more."

"Can we make it?"

"We're sure as hell going to try," he said grimly.

Now that they had a good idea that the children had come the same way, Jace kept to the faint trail that Bronte was beginning to see had been trampled into the grass. But as the slope increased, growing rocky and slippery, they were forced to ease their pace. Even worse, what had been only a few isolated drops soon became a drizzle.

Bronte pulled her hat as low as she could over her brow and hunched down into the collar of her coat. But she wasn't about to complain. Now, more than ever, she needed to know that both of the children were warm and safe.

Unfortunately, Mother Nature seemed to have other ideas. Overhead, an ominous roll of thunder began to rumble, grumble. Flashes of lightning made the gathering darkness even more pronounced.

Frantically, Bronte tried to remember. She knew she was supposed to count to determine how near the storm might be, but was she supposed to count from the lightning to the thunder, or the thunder to the lightning?

But as the weather roared in, harder and faster, it soon became apparent that there was no need to count at all. The flashes of lightning increased. At first it snaked down from the sky with jagged fingers. Then the streaks became less distinct and the slope was illuminated entirely. Worse yet, Bronte was sure that she could feel the very air begin to sizzle.

The horses must have sensed the same thing because they danced nervously, balking at Jace's control on the reins. Finally, he was forced to turn and shout over the force of the wind.

"We're going to have to find shelter! The cabin is located about five miles beyond that next rise, but we're bound to get electrocuted if we try to get over it now. We'll hunker down, then begin again once the worst of the rain has passed over."

Bronte nodded. Much as she would like to move on, she knew such efforts would be foolish. Even if they weren't struck by lightning, the horses were growing increasingly anxious and likely to bolt.

She saw Jace squinting as he studied the nearby landmarks. Rain dripped from the brim of his cowboy hat to darken the fabric of his jacket. He pushed himself up in the stirrups, then twisted, raising an arm to point.

"There. We'll backtrack about forty yards. There's a depression in the rock face over there. That, combined with some fallen boulders has created a nook. It will be a tight squeeze, but we should be out of the rain."

Another crack of thunder was followed almost simultaneously by a snake of lightning that had the hair on Bronte's body standing on end.

Jace spurred his mount and backtracked along the trail they had taken. Then he headed up a slope so steep that

Bronte had to grab the pommel with both hands. As the wet ground gave way beneath the horses' hooves, she feared that they wouldn't be able to reach the scant shelter that was being offered. But then, Jace's gelding lunged upward and Snowflake was forced to follow.

As soon as they'd reached the cliff face, Jace jumped down and reached for Bronte.

"Get in there! Far as you can!" he shouted against the noise of the wind.

Bending low, Bronte wriggled past the largest of the boulders where she could see a niche that sank a few yards into the side of the mountain. As Jace had predicted, there wouldn't be much room—barely enough for the two of them to sit with their backs against the wall. But even in the dim light, Bronte could see that the ground was dry and littered with a cushion of leaves. Using the side of her boot, she swept away the scattered rocks, sticks, and other debris until she had made the space as comfortable as possible.

Jace crowded in behind her, holding the pack and bedroll that had been attached to his saddle.

"I've tied up the horses for now. With luck, the storm will blow over in a few minutes. Then we can finish our ride."

Now that they had stopped, Bronte was becoming more and more aware of the icy rain that had seeped down her collar and soaked her jeans.

Jace handed her the woolen bedroll.

"Set this on the ground."

Shivering, Bronte did as she was told.

"Sit down and wrap yourself in this."

He handed her a silver space blanket and carefully tucked it around her shoulders.

"We've got enough of a natural vent near the opening to start a small fire if you're cold."

She shook her head. As much as she might crave the warmth, she didn't want to do anything that would delay them once the weather passed.

"I . . . I'm okay," she said, even as a shiver wracked through her body.

It was clear from Jace's expression that he didn't believe her.

Bronte sank onto the ground, gripping the tinfoil-thin blanket around her shoulders, sure that it wouldn't offer much warmth, but needing whatever comfort it might give. Now that she was still, the cold seemed to seep into her bones. She was hardly aware of Jace's movements as he gathered stray sticks from their hideaway and placed them over a pile of the leaves she'd brushed to the side.

"A little blaze isn't going to slow us down. It will help to dry your clothes off." He gestured outside. "I'm going to get a larger piece of wood, but I'll be right back."

Bronte nodded, pulling the blanket even tighter around her shoulders.

She wasn't sure how long Jace was gone, but she soon became aware of the snap and hiss of a lighter, then the tang of burning wood. Looking up from her perch, she saw Jace crouched near the opening of their shelter. A flickering flame was licking at the pile of kindling, and as it caught and grew, Jace added a small log.

The wet wood had a tendency to smoke, but Bronte didn't care. Even from a distance, she could feel some warmth wafting her way.

Shrugging out of his jacket, Jace placed it near the fire to dry out, then took another lighter jacket out of his pack.

"Come on. Out of your coat."

Bronte wasn't sure if she wanted to surrender its scant protection, but she did as she was told. Jace quickly wrapped her in the windbreaker and zipped it up to her chin.

"It won't take long for things to heat up. You'll see."

He settled onto the ground beside her, propping his back against the granite at their backs. Then he dug into the pack again and withdrew a thermos.

"Please tell me that's coffee."

He grinned. "Cocoa. I brought it in case we found the kids along the way."

Jace unscrewed the top and poured the dark liquid into the cup-shaped lid, then handed it to her. "Here. Drink."

She didn't need a second urging. Her first sip was taken gingerly, but finding that it was comfortably warm, she then drank deeply and handed the cup back to him.

Jace reached into his pack and withdrew a power bar. "Eat this."

While she tore the wrapper open, Jace poured another cup of the warm cocoa, drinking half, then handing the rest to her.

"Shouldn't we save some for the kids?"

He shook his head. "Judging by where we found the wrapper, they had plenty of time to get to the cabin. Like I said, there are supplies there for them to use. As soon as we can, we'll head that way and make sure the two of them are okay."

Bronte nodded, draining the rest of the cup. Not only was the liquid warm, but it was sweet and comforting, stilling her jitters and her shivers.

"You'd better drink the rest," she said, when she handed the cup back. Judging by the size of the flask, there wouldn't be much left. Turning her attention to her power bar, she took tiny bites, more to calm herself than anything.

By the time she ate the last piece, she was feeling much calmer as well as warmer. The fire had stopped smoking, and the heat was seeping into their shelter.

Jace cocked his head, listening to the storm, but even to Bronte's inexperienced ears, it hadn't abated.

He reached into his magical pack again and handed her a bottle of water, then grabbed one for himself as well. "You need to keep hydrated, so drink up."

She nodded, but took small sips.

As soon as Jace had finished his own power bar, he slid his arm around her shoulders and pulled her tightly against him. With each minute that passed, Bronte's worry increased.

"What if the rain doesn't pass before it gets completely dark?"

"Sunset isn't for another"—he glanced at his watch—"three hours. It seems later because of the cloud cover. Hopefully, this is a typical spring storm. It will bluster like hell for a little while, then the wind will blow the clouds away and we'll have sunny skies again."

Bronte scowled. "You don't have to paint a best-case scenario, Jace. I can take the truth."

IN an instant, Jace was undone. Bronte looked up at him with such fire in her eyes that he couldn't tear his own gaze away. Yet, beneath that blaze of independence, there was still a trace of vulnerability. One he would do anything to protect.

They'd known each other now for what . . . a little over a month? But he couldn't imagine going a day or more without some form of contact. She had become as necessary to him as breathing.

The thought should have surprised him. No. It should have terrified him. Jace had always been a loner. Even growing up, while Elam and Bodey had gravitated toward their friends, Jace had preferred to spend his time alone. His idea of fun had been grabbing a fishing pole and heading to the creek, or taking his horse up into the mountains. Once he'd begun to concentrate on his artistic pursuits . . . well, he could lose himself for hours in sketching or painting. Maybe that was how he'd managed to spend two years backpacking Europe. He'd been more than content to establish his own itinerary and his own pace.

When he'd returned home to Bliss, his biggest worry had been that he wouldn't be able to fold himself back into the family unit. He was sure that once he'd assumed responsibility for Barry, he'd go stark, raving mad if he had no time of his own. So when he'd become itchy and anxious for a change, he'd assumed that he needed to disappear for a few months, go away, leave everyone behind.

But he knew now that he'd been wrong. Even if he'd managed to leave the ranch for the most exotic of vacations, he would have found himself just as unhappy. Bronte had shown him that he wasn't searching for solitude. What he'd really needed was an intimate connection with another human being—one that went beyond mere physical desire.

Since meeting Bronte, he'd felt a peace in his soul that he'd never experienced before. The restlessness, the discontent, the longing for something new had disappeared.

But she was right in her assertion that she could handle more than half-truths. She was strong enough to make decisions for herself.

"Okay . . . here's the worst-case scenario. Barry is a good horseman. He's been riding since he was a baby—and the horses have been a big part of his recovery. But, there's always a chance that he could have wandered off the track. Or, the horse could have been startled and thrown them off."

Bronte bit her lip, but didn't interrupt.

"But I'm pinning my hopes on the fact that they made it to the cabin. Although the lightning seems to have eased, the storm still hasn't blown over." A glance at his watch told him that they'd been hunkered down in their makeshift shelter for more than twenty minutes. "I don't know. Maybe we could go ahead and push our way through. But this high up—and with lightning still a very real threat—the idea is foolhardy. We can't go anywhere on horseback until we have a little more light. I could never endanger a mount by making it travel blind over wet, unfamiliar ground that way. One misstep could cause a horse to break a leg or worse. We could proceed on foot—not an impossible hike—but if the storm decides to quit in the next ten or fifteen minutes, we'll be stuck hiking when, if we'd been patient, we could have ridden and made it there faster."

He glanced at his watch. "Why don't we give it another . . . fifteen minutes?"

She nodded, her gaze inexplicably flooding with relief that her waiting finally had a deadline.

"After that, we hike," she reaffirmed.

"Yeah."

He drew her back into his arms, holding her close, absorbing the way she clung to him as if he were the only anchor in a tempestuous sea. And he realized that she wasn't the only person needing the reassurance of another person's arms. Bronte soothed his raw nerves, her hope giving him hope. Her strength giving him the will to be stronger. He needed this in his life. He needed *her*.

Jace knew that some people might argue that he was merely in the throes of a new romance and the excitement would soon pass. But Jace had never felt this way with any other woman. Sure, he desired her—and he couldn't wait to see what new sexual experience would come out of her infinite curiosity. But it was more than that. He was content holding her in his arms, or talking to her on the phone, or receiving one of her texts. He found himself longing to experience even more—a date at a fancy restaurant, their first dance together, waking to her head next to his on the pillow. He wanted long, lazy nights in front of the television, and having her sit next to him on the tractor's jump seat while he worked. He wanted . . .

Her.

Passionately.

Permanently.

Jace remembered when Elam had returned from four days spent in P.D.'s company during the Wild West Games last year. Somehow, in a little more than a week, P.D. had transformed his brother from a grieving widower to a man with his eyes on the future. Jace had worried that his brother was rushing into a commitment without really exploring his options. But when Jace had suggested that Elam should "play the field," Elam had laughed and slapped him on the back, saying, "Sometimes a person doesn't need a whole lot of choices to know he's already found the best one."

At the time, Jace had thought his brother was ignoring the fact that, after falling so quickly under P.D.'s spell, he could fall out of love just as quickly.

But Elam had proven to be right. He and P.D. were as passionate and devoted to each other now as they'd been in those first heady days of their romance. Jace wasn't surprised that they'd decided to make their engagement a short one and marry in October. He was only surprised it had taken so long for Elam to pop the question.

For the first time in his own life, Jace felt a longing for that kind of permanence, that ultimate sense of belonging. He felt a tug in his heart at the mere thought, and he held Bronte even tighter. True, he wasn't quite ready to pull the trigger on marriage. He didn't think there was a man alive who jumped headlong into something like that without a few qualms. But he did find himself thinking about someday. Maybe even someday soon.

He smiled at the thought. If someone had told him mere months ago that he might be thinking of hooking up with a single mother with two children, he would have laughed. He had enough on his plate with Barry.

But even though he knew it would be a challenge adding two more kids to the mix, Jace couldn't deny that he'd grown fond of the girls. Lily was sweet and sensitive and loyal. And after his talk with Kari, Jace was beginning to believe her teenage bluster was more show than actual sentiment. He sensed that the two of them missed their father more than they would ever want to admit to Bronte. But they wanted the man they'd known when he was clean and sober, not the bastard Phillip was now. Maybe they wouldn't mind having someone around the house who would give them some attention, support, and a healthy dose of protective testosterone. Just like he and Barry could use a feminine perspective every now and then.

But first . . .

His phone rang in his pocket and Jace hurried to answer it. "Yeah."

There was a crackle on the other line, then a stuttering voice.

"Who is it?" Bronte whispered.

Grimacing, Jace shrugged and pushed himself to his feet. "Hold it, you're breaking up."

As he moved closer toward the entrance, he was surprised anyone had been able to call. Phone service up here was spotty at best.

"Okay, try again."

"Jace?"

He was barely able to make out Elam's voice.

"Yeah. Did the kids show up at home?"

"No . . ." Jace lost several words and shifted in an attempt to improve the sound quality. ". . . finished with the police . . . bad news . . ."

No. God, no.

"Did the police find them?"

"No." Jace heard Elam swear, then he began again, pronouncing each word slowly and distinctly. "New sheriff . . . prick."

Jace grimaced. Bliss's longtime sheriff had recently retired and Jace had to agree that his replacement was overly concerned with throwing his weight around. He was a by-the-book cop from back east who seemed determined to write up as many tickets as he could to prove that his services were invaluable. That thought alone was enough to cause Jace's stomach to twist in foreboding.

". . . claims Barry . . . abduction . . ."

"What the hell?"

". . . tried to reason . . . without . . . success . . ." The phone crackled ominously. ". . . you . . . get . . . cabin first . . ."

Jace didn't need all the words to understand the warning. The new sheriff was hot on their trail and Jace needed to be the first to find the children.

"Jace?"

"I heard you, Elam."

"I—"

Jace waited, shifting slightly to see if he could improve the signal. But he'd lost the call altogether.

Shit, shit, shit.

Jace didn't even bother to check the weather outside. He reached for his water bottle, poured what remained over the fire, then started kicking dirt over the embers.

"That was Elam. We've got to go now."

Bronte didn't need to be told twice. But as soon as she tried to stand, she hissed in pain.

"Sore, huh?" Jace asked ruefully as he kicked the remains of their fire apart, looking for any stray embers, then doused the last of the sparks with dirt.

"I'll be fine," Bronte said as airily as she could.

Jace pulled her into his arms and placed a quick kiss on the top of her head. "I know you will. I never doubted it. So you don't have to act all tough with me. I'm not going to leave you behind."

"Then my butt hurts like hell," she grumbled. "But let's go find our kids."

Our kids.

Jace liked the way the phrase slipped off her tongue.

THEY both shrugged into their jackets and hurried outside. Bronte noticed that it was still raining, but not as hard as it had been before. Jace gestured to the horizon. Beyond the wall of storm clouds, just as he'd predicted, Bronte could see a patch of blue sky.

By the time both of them had mounted their horses and headed back down the slope, the rain had eased and the sky was beginning to lighten, the heavy clouds scudding quickly away beneath a brisk breeze.

Their pace was slow at first, allowing the animals to pick their way over the uneven ground. Bronte concentrated on keeping her seat and searching the trail ahead of them. But soon she noticed that Jace seemed to be checking over his shoulder every few minutes.

"What's wrong?"

She could see the lines of worry etched on his face.

"That call I got from Elam has me worried." He grimaced. "More like half a call. The reception was so bad that he kept cutting out. But he managed to let me know that the new sheriff in town . . ."

He paused, and she felt her stomach tighten.

"He's bound and determined to find the children himself. When he does, it sounds like he wants to charge Barry with abduction."

"What?" Bronte stared at him, sure that she'd misheard. "Can he do that?"

"Hell if I know." The words were bitter. "The man's been in charge for only a few months—ever since George Hamblin retired. I've heard folks around the valley muttering that he's heavy-handed in his enforcement techniques. Frankly, I think he's young and trying to prove he's up to the job."

"But . . . kidnapping? How could he even think such a thing? At the most, he could call both of them runaways."

Jace shrugged. "I don't know what the hell is going on. I don't know how much Elam was able to convey to the man about Barry's disability—or if he was willing to believe anything that he was told. I'm sure that he's only considering the facts—that a sixteen-year-old boy has taken off with an eight-year-old girl—and he's jumping to a worst-case scenario. The whole thing can probably be settled as soon as he has a chance to talk to the kids. But we've got to get to them first. Can you imagine how frightening it will be for both of them if a policeman appears and slaps cuffs on Barry?"

Bronte's stomach roiled at the thought.

"If we can push a little faster—" He broke off, bringing his mount to a halt. Snowflake obediently followed suit.

Bronte opened her mouth to ask what was wrong, but then she caught a hint of the same sound that must have captured his attention.

"What is that?"

But before Jace could even open his mouth, the familiar *thwup, thwup, thwup* of a helicopter's rotors beat against her ears.

"Hell," Jace muttered. "Hold on, Bronte. We're only a few miles away and we've got to get there fast."

Bronte nodded, automatically clutching the pommel as Jace spurred the horses into a gallop. She didn't allow herself to wonder what would happen if she fell—or if, God forbid, the children weren't at the cabin as they'd hoped. Instead, she huddled low over the saddle, her eyes trained on Jace as he leaned into the wind.

The sight would have been awe-inspiring if it weren't so

terrifying. Jace represented the quintessential cowboy, at one with the horse he rode. His hat was pulled low, his Carhartt jacket adding bulk to his shoulders and arms, his leanly muscled legs gripping the saddle. The entire picture radiated power and confidence—and Bronte clung to that thought, knowing that the next few moments were critical.

Suddenly, they crested a rise, and there, less than a hundred yards away, Bronte could see a large meadow dotted with wild poppies. On the far side, a squat structure made of logs and split timber had been built in the midst of towering pine trees. The building was so weathered, so crude, that it seemed to be rooted to the ground rather than constructed by human hands.

The sight was enough to send a jolt of hope through her system. The sunlight was growing now, and somehow, in the last few minutes, the last of the rain had blown away and the wind was whipping the clouds apart. Overhead, the sky became a robin's-egg blue.

Like some futuristic bird of prey, a helicopter swooped into view. Looking back and forth from the cabin to the aircraft, Bronte tried to determine who would reach the structure first. She began silently praying, "Oh please, oh please, oh please." Then, as the helicopter began its decent, Bronte caught sight of movement from under the trees.

"Over there! It's Barry's horse, Snuffles!"

Unbelievably, Jace was able to coax more speed out of their mounts. As the helicopter landed in the clearing below, Jace rode pell-mell through the field of scarlet wildflowers. Around them, clouds of butterflies that had been attracted by the moist blossoms swirled and whirled, then settled back down again to bask in the growing light.

Jace brought the horses to a skidding halt next to the front door. He didn't even bother to tie them up as he jumped from the saddle, then rounded to help Bronte down.

Glancing behind them, she saw two men stepping from the aircraft. "They're coming," she gasped as Jace took her hand.

"I know."

Jace pulled her toward the door, grabbed the old knob and gently pushed his way inside, drawing Bronte with him.

It took a few seconds for Bronte's eyes to adjust, but when they did, a cry lodged in her throat. On an old bedstead that was only slightly larger than a cot, Lily lay napping, her butterfly quilt pulled tightly under her chin. On the opposite side of the room, Barry slept in a battered rocking chair, his *Star Wars* blanket draped over his lap. In the fireplace, red coals still glowed from a fire, and the air inside was warm, despite the draft seeping in from the open door. On the table were empty tin cans with labels proclaiming that they'd once held peaches and fruit cocktail. There were also more applesauce pouches and even a half-eaten box of granola bars.

Jace began to chuckle softly—a sound that was part relief, part pent-up fear, and part disbelief.

"They're fine," he said, his voice shaky. "They're—"

They were pushed aside as two men burst in behind them. Before Bronte could react, she and Jace were shoved aside and figures dressed in sheriff's parkas and uniforms stormed past them.

"Hands in the air!"

In an instant, all hell broke loose. Barry jolted awake, automatically standing, his eyes still bleary with sleep. On the other end of the room, Lily woke, took one look at the two unfamiliar men, and began to scream.

When one of the men pushed Barry toward the wall and pulled a pair of handcuffs from his utility belt, Jace was immediately on him, trying to yank the officer away from his brother, while the second lawman pulled his gun and shouted, "Freeze! Now!"

Jace was slammed back against the wall. He immediately lifted his hands to show he wasn't a threat, but the deputy still kept him in the sights of his pistol. The sheriff, freed from Jace's grip, stepped toward Barry and began to put the terrified boy in handcuffs.

"No! Leave him alone!"

Tearing across the room, Lily inserted herself between the lawman and Barry. Frightened for her daughter's safety,

Bronte tried to pull her out of harm's way, but Lily became hysterical, screaming unintelligible words while she kicked at the lawman with her bare feet and clawed at Barry's hands in an effort to free them from the metal constraints.

Wrenching free from the deputies' grip, Bronte grabbed Lily and hauled her into her arms. Her daughter was trembling uncontrollably, tears streaking her face. Bronte tried to comfort her, offering cooing sounds, wrapping the girl tightly in her arms to absorb the tremors. But Lily continued to weep, until finally, Bronte began to understand what her daughter was saying.

"Th-they h-have to let him g-go! The m-magic won't work without B-Barry!"

TWENTY-THREE

———•◆•———

*T*HE *magic.*

Bronte was flooded with details she'd forgotten in their efforts to find the children.

The missing mason jar.

The cocoon that Lily had watched for weeks.

When Barry had first brought Lily the container, he'd described what was occurring inside the chrysalis. Bronte clearly remembered her daughter's reaction when Barry told her how the butterfly would emerge, having become something completely different, beautiful. Even more, Barry had spoken of the way he liked to lie in the field of poppies until the butterflies touched him and thereby imparted their magic, making him feel "new."

Bronte realized why her daughter had been so fascinated by the cocoon, why she'd been willing to run off with Barry. Bronte was willing to bet that her daughter had begged Barry to bring her here, that she'd overruled any objection that he'd made—that she'd probably threatened to try to find the place on her own if he hadn't brought her here himself.

All because of Lily's desire to feel "new."

"Stop it. Stop!" Bronte shouted.

Amazingly enough, the other occupants of the cabin grew quiet and turned to face her.

Bronte carried Lily to Jace, transferring her into his arms. As Lily gripped him tightly around the neck, Bronte turned to the sheriff. "You need to take those cuffs off."

He opened his mouth to argue, but she hurriedly continued, "This has been a misunderstanding. A mistake. These kids might have been reckless in leaving home without permission, but that's all."

She stepped closer to the sheriff, lowering her voice so the children couldn't hear what she was saying. "Please, Sheriff. You know what my daughter has been through. What was . . . done to her. Please. She needs this to heal."

When the sheriff didn't respond, she continued. "I'm Lily's mother and I refuse to press any charges. In fact, I'm sure that Jace here would be more than willing to lodge a complaint for your treatment of a disabled minor."

When the lawman remained immovable, she tried one more time. "Please. For my girl."

The sheriff was still clearly suspicious, but he unlocked the handcuffs.

As soon as Barry was free, Lily wriggled out of Jace's arms and ran to the far side of the room where the familiar jar sat on a chair. Inside, Bronte could see the shattered remains of the cocoon and a beautiful yellow butterfly.

Taking Barry's hand, Lily whispered, "Show me."

Barry grabbed his blanket from the ground and gently led Lily outside into the tall grass and wildflowers. In the past few minutes, even more sunlight had begun to spill into the clearing. When he shook out the blanket, hundreds of butterflies fluttered into the air around them, as if the flowers had taken wing.

Barry drew Lily down on the blanket.

"Open the lid. Then we have to let the butterfly come out all by itself. We don't want to scare it."

He set the jar in the middle of the wet grass.

"Lie down," he whispered. "We probably look scary to the butterfly 'cause we're so big."

Lily did as she was told and Barry stretched out next to her. Then the two children waited, hardly breathing, as the meadow grew quiet again.

Gradually, many of the butterflies returned—drawn to the vibrant petals and the warm fingers of sunlight that were beginning to stretch down the slope. Bronte was too far away to see what was happening in the jar, but she supposed that the butterfly was testing its freedom because Lily's face lit up in anticipation. Then, a fluttering wisp of yellow rose from the jar, hovered in the air, then hurried to disappear among the other butterflies.

A soft "oh!" escaped Lily's lips before Barry took her hand, reminding her that she needed to be quiet.

For several long minutes, she and Barry lay still, so still, until the butterflies began to move from poppy to poppy again. At long last, a single delicate butterfly hovered over Lily's head, then settled onto her cheek. An expression of such bliss settled onto her daughter's face that Bronte sobbed, knowing this was what Lily had wanted—*needed*—to begin to truly heal.

In an instant, all of the anger and fear that had roiled within Bronte's consciousness since Phillip's arrival melted away, reminding her that she couldn't change the past or any of its events. But she could focus on the future, on making her children feel valued and loved.

Safe.

Silently, she reached for Jace's hand, squeezing it tightly, realizing that, like Lily, she was being offered a new beginning, a new life, a new chance at happiness. But as she turned to look at Jace, she knew all of those victories would be hollow without him.

As if sensing her thoughts, Jace tugged her closer, tucking her beneath his chin.

"I know this probably isn't the time or the place," he murmured. "But I love you, Bronte Cupacek. And I love your kids."

"Same here," she whispered.

He hugged her even closer. "I know that we've only

known each other a short while—and we're going to need to take some time to make this work. But . . ."

When he paused, she smiled and looked up. "But you want to go steady?"

He chuckled softly. "What's one step up from going steady?"

She lifted on tiptoes, saying against his lips, "Kissing friends?"

"Yeah. I'd like to be your kissing friend."

She wrapped her arms around his neck and said, "I think you already are." Then she pressed her lips to his.

The embrace was soft and sweet, filled with promise. But before either of them could deepen the caress, the meadow was suddenly filled with shrieks of laughter as Barry and Lily jumped to their feet and began to run willy-nilly through the poppies.

As she watched their innocent exuberance, Bronte laughed herself—even as her throat grew tight with joy and sorrow, hope and love. She wasn't naïve enough to think that all of the challenges her little family had endured were completely over. She knew it would take time for Lily to come to terms with the way she'd been wounded so deeply—and Kari's sudden sweetness could evaporate in a heartbeat.

But she also acknowledged that the Cupacek women had turned a corner. By coming to Bliss they'd found more than a refuge in her grandmother's home. They'd found good friends, a supportive community, and . . .

Love.

Grabbing Jace's hand, Bronte pulled him after her. "Come on!" she called out.

They ran toward the children, wanting to be included in their elaborate, nonsensical game. When Barry caught Bronte's hand and Lily launched herself into Jace's arms shouting, "Swing me! Swing me!" Bronte realized she'd also found the missing pieces to a new family.

Time would take care of the rest.

EPILOGUE

———————————

VERN'S was absolutely rocking with the sounds of blue-
    grass, boisterous shouts, and conversation, and that
made Bronte smile.

Elam and Prairie Dawn's marriage had started in elegant
reverence, with a beautiful autumn ceremony at Henry's
pond. The willows had been festooned with lengths of pale
pink and ivory ribbons that had fluttered in the breeze, blue
and pink potted hydrangeas had been scattered around the
yard, and an old ribbon-bedecked buckboard rescued from
the Taggart barn had become the perfect spot for gathering
wedding presents—as well as serving as the couple's "getaway" vehicle.

Since Bronte had been asked to be maid of honor, she'd
had the perfect vantage point to the proceedings. First, Lily,
in a sleeveless pink silk dress and ruffled skirt, scattered rose
petals down an aisle formed by dozens of antique chairs gathered from the community—carved dining room sets, cane
backs, ornate wicker pieces, and stately gentlemen's seats.
There were even a couple of wingbacks and settees for people
like Annie who needed a softer perch. Bronte wouldn't have

thought the idea would work, but as Barry went next, carefully holding a pillow with the rings attached, she'd realized that the variety had given the grove the look of an outdoor sitting room—warm and cozy and intimate.

Next, it had been Bronte's turn. She'd been intensely aware of the way that Jace, who served as one of Elam's best men, stepped forward so that he could watch her more clearly. Even now, Bronte grew hot inside at the memory of his gaze—one that was tender and passionate at the same time, his attention so keen that she'd nearly blushed.

After that, the bride had appeared in the doorway of the cabin. Helen had done herself proud by designing a gown that was the perfect combination of pioneer bride and modern romantic. The dress clung to her figure in all the right places. With an ivory satin corset and Nottingham lace chemise, it gave the appearance of being a piece of exotic Victorian lingerie before flaring out at the skirt with a flourish of silk and lace.

There was no denying the absolute joy that radiated from Elam and P.D. as they exchanged their vows. But even their first passionate kiss as man and wife hadn't affected Bronte as much as Jace's regard. The mixture of desire and anticipation in his silver-gray eyes had caused her heart to stutter-step in her chest.

Once their ceremony had finished, Elam and P.D. had made their way to Vern's—with a line of cars and trucks forming a procession behind them. The restaurant had been closed for the day and the tables had been transformed with rich linens and a variety of antique bottles and containers that held more bunches of hydrangeas. By the time the guests began to appear, the band was set up and ready to go.

Now, it was clearly time to party.

As Bronte stepped into the kitchen, she was greeted with a host of amazing smells—smoked meats, baking bread, and the heavenly aroma of sugar cookies.

"Here's the tray you needed."

Bronte smiled at Marci, one of the new managers at Vern's, as she accepted the heavy platter. "Thanks."

Returning to the dining room, she wound her way through the dancers and well-wishers to the buffet table. The guests could choose from a variety of P.D.'s most popular recipes: bison burger sliders with prickly pear compote; platters of smoked turkey, ham, and salmon; miniature barbecue brisket sandwiches. There were baked beans, roasted baby potatoes, and steamed asparagus stalks in a lemon glaze. In huge baskets, Bronte had arranged mini loaves of her banana blueberry and beer breads, as well as her new specialties, citrus cranberry and blackberry cardamom muffins.

Another table had been devoted to the sweets. A delicate multilayer wedding cake—another of Helen's creations—featured a bride lassoing the groom with a lariat and delicate hydrangea blossoms formed with gum paste. The flowers looked so real that they could have been plucked from P.D.'s bouquet. Surrounding the cake were plates of cookies—oatmeal raisin, chocolate crackle, bonbons, and sugar cookies, which had been cut and iced to reflect the Wild West Games, where Elam and P.D. had begun their romance. The kids in attendance were especially fond of the tasty horses, cowboy hats, boots, and revolvers.

"You've outdone yourself," a low voice said behind her. It was followed by a strong arm around her waist. After setting the tray in an empty spot, Bronte leaned back into Jace's embrace.

"Thanks, I was excited to help."

"I know. Come on."

Jace took her hand and led her to the dance floor. The band had begun to play a slow country-western ballad and Jace maneuvered them near the edge, away from the crush of people headed for the buffet table and the other swaying couples. He settled one hand in the small of her back and took hers with the other.

"Have I told you how beautiful you look?"

He had, but Bronte didn't mind if he was repeating himself. Country living hadn't given her many opportunities to dress to the nines, but today she *felt* beautiful, too. Not just because of the pale blue sheath and her upswept hair, but because of the light shining from Jace's eyes. She never grew tired of that look—a mixture of tenderness, wonder, and passion.

"You're creating quite the stir yourself."

It was true. She'd caught more than one woman offering him a lingering glance, but Jace seemed oblivious to the attention.

Which made Bronte feel even more loved.

Jace leaned down, murmuring next to her ear. "This is a fulfillment of one of my fantasies."

Bronte looked at him with raised brows. Over the past five months, the two of them had explored plenty of Bronte's requests.

"Really? How?"

"I've always wanted to dance with you. But with the summer rush, we never managed to get to Vern's when the band was playing."

She smiled. "Then I'm glad you finally got your wish."

They rocked together, moving only enough for their embrace to be considered dancing.

"I've got one more fantasy to fulfill today, if you're agreeable."

"Mmm. Name it."

His lips moved to her ear, his breath teasing the tendrils next to her temple.

"I meant to do this later, after all the fuss with Elam and P.D. is over—and I don't want to horn in on their day—but maybe we can keep this between us until the newlyweds make their getaway . . ."

He loosened his hold to pull away ever so slightly and reached into his pocket, withdrawing a ring. Bronte gasped when she saw that it had been fashioned of gold. A ruby lay in the center of what looked like a poppy, and hovering on either side were stylized butterflies.

"Did you design this?" she asked, stunned at the delicate beauty.

He nodded.

"But my birthday isn't for another month."

Jace's smile was slow and sweet. "It's not a birthday present."

Her brow puckered in confusion.

"Will you marry me, Bronte? Will you be my forever kissing friend and wife? Will you let me share a lifetime loving your girls, and will you enjoy a lifetime loving Barry?"

Tears sprang to her eyes, but she refused to spoil the moment, so she smiled instead. Even so, her voice was husky when she said, "Yes. I would love to be your forever kissing friend and wife, and I would absolutely love to blend our families into one."

She held out her left hand. His fingers shook slightly as he slid the ring in place.

Bronte laughed. "Were you worried I'd say no?"

"A little."

"Why?"

"I wasn't sure that you were ready to even think about . . . I don't know . . . dealing with the whole marriage thing yet."

Bronte lifted on tiptoe, hugging him tightly around the neck. "With you, I'm ready to take on anything the world might throw our way."

"Just so you know . . . I'm not rushing you into anything. You can set the date as far away as you want. Months. Years."

He looked so anxious that Bronte laughed, pressing her lips to his yet again. "Maybe months, definitely not years. So shut up and dance with me, Jace."

FROM a table on the opposite end of the room, Lily watched Bronte and Jace melt into one another's arms.

"They're kissin' again," Barry said matter-of-factly.

"They do that a lot," Lily agreed.

"Yeah, but this time it's a special kiss."

Lily squinted, studying her mother and Jace more carefully. "Looks like the same kinda kiss they always have."

"Uh-uh. Look. She's wearin' the butterfly ring."

From this far away, Lily couldn't see it too well, but every now and then, she caught a flash of red on her mother's hand.

"What's a butterfly ring?"

"Jace showed it to me when it was a bunch of swirly lines on a piece of paper. Then, he took it to this guy in Logan, who made it into a ring. Jace said the ring meant that he and Bronte were going to be forever kissing friends but I had to keep it a secret."

"What does that mean? Forever kissing friends?"

"It means you get to come live in my house and have the room next door to mine. You'll be my sister, even though Jace says you're really gonna be my . . . meece? An' I get t' be your uncle."

"You can't be my uncle. You aren't old."

"That's what I said!" Barry agreed emphatically. "So's Jace told me I could call you my sister." He snorted. "That's kinda dumb, cuz I've already been calling you my sister."

"When?"

"That's what the word Emily means. Everybody thought I was mixin' you up with my twin, Emily." He rolled his eyes. "They shoulda known that when I call you Emily, I'm calling you my sister. I've known forever that you were my sister."

"Oh." Lily digested that thought, wondering why it gave her a warm feeling in her chest. But then, she always felt warm and safe around Barry. "So what do I call you if you're my brother?"

Barry laughed as if she'd asked the silliest question in the world. Taking another bite of his sandwich, he chewed, then simply proclaimed, "You keep callin' me Barry."

KEEP READING FOR AN EXCERPT FROM

MAVERICK

COMING SOON FROM BERKLEY SENSATION!

B ODEY Taggart loved to win.
   He craved the surge of adrenaline that came with a
wager, the fire that settled into his chest at a challenge, the
pounding of his heart that accompanied the competition.
As a kid, he'd joined every team, run every race, and fought
to the bloody end for every point. He'd started with little
league, worked his way through junior varsity and varsity
sports. Once in high school, he'd added rodeo to the list with
bronco busting and bull riding—and he'd given it his all,
returning home at night with bruised ribs, bloody lips, and
black eyes. He'd been driven to be the best—to the point
where his mother had despaired of his reaching adulthood
in one piece. Time and time again, she'd warned him that
if he only set his sights on winning, he'd never be satisfied
with anything in life.

   "That glittering prize is short-lived," she'd cautioned. "If
you spend your whole life looking for shiny things, you're
bound to end up with a room full of tarnish."

   Bodey still didn't know what the hell he was supposed to
make of that statement. Maureen Taggart had died before

he'd turned twenty. If she hadn't, he was sure that he would have argued the point. He would have insisted to his mother that it wasn't the trophies filling the boxes in the garage that motivated him. It wasn't as simple as that. He competed because there was something deep inside of him, some restless, itchy portion of his spirit that demanded that he push himself to the limits, physically and mentally. He craved that oblivion of spirit as much as an alcoholic obsessed over booze.

Granted, things were getting a little out of hand. Where once he'd been content to use sport and athleticism as his sole means of getting his "fix," lately everything he did became a contest: cow cutting competitions, quarter horse races, fantasy sports, and poker. Hell, if someone was willing to play along, he'd make a bet on which side of the hill a heifer would leave a cow pie—and he'd do his best to make sure the animal cooperated.

Sad to say, even women had become a game to him. Bodey relished the thrill of the hunt, the excitement of the chase, the tender intricacies of wooing. He reveled in the first headiness of attraction, the anticipation of that first kiss, first caress, first connection. Hell, he loved women plain and simple, and he continued to love them, in his own fashion, after the romance died, considering them all his friends. And his efforts weren't nearly as cold-blooded as they might sound to an outsider. He never meant to "love 'em and leave 'em." Each time he set his sights on a new conquest, he was sure that *this was the one. This* was the woman who would ease the battling hubris within him and give him the sense of peace his brothers had found. Maybe then, he could settle down, abandon the never-ending need to prove himself, and consider a long-term commitment without feeling like a noose was wrapping around his neck.

But as he squinted against the blazing hot July sun and packed his long guns into his cart, Bodey realized that this time, *this time,* his need to win just might kill him.

Good hell, almighty. He'd made a huge mistake. *Huge.*

In lingering with the practice posse for the regional SASS Hell on Wheels Competition, he'd stayed outside too long in the hundred-plus temperatures of a Wyoming summer. Too late, he realized that he should have bowed out thirty minutes ago when he'd begun to feel the familiar throb of a headache blooming behind his left eye. But, no. He'd insisted to himself that he could finish one more stage, one more round of marksmanship. He'd been showing off in front of his buddies and the newest female recruit to their group, and he'd been driven to finish . . .

Ontop.

Yup. That was the crux of his error. A new member to the Single Action Shooting Society—or at least to Bodey's circle of friends—who went by the moniker of Ima Ontop.

As SASS nicknames went, it wasn't terribly subtle.

But it *was* effective.

From the moment she'd appeared on the range, testosterone levels had soared within the prominently male group. Men who usually spent the practice rounds laughing, joking, and slinging bullshit . . . well, let's just say they snapped to attention. What would have been a relaxed afternoon of marksmanship became a life and death struggle for the best score.

And Bodey hadn't been immune. He'd been immediately attracted to the tall, scantily clad brunette—and, *duh*, who wouldn't be? The woman had come to the practice match wearing nothing but calf-high Victorian boots, striped hose, tight ruffled shorty-shorts, and a frilly corset. The getup hovered somewhere between saloon girl and Miss July. Bodey would have been dead if he hadn't noticed her.

But as the heat of the day wormed its way through his head and the remnant side-effects of a recent concussion made each movement an exercise in torture, Bodey's interest waned. Especially when it became clear that she was a talker. For the past twenty minutes, she'd gone on and on and *on* about loading her shells with shot and glitter for a little extra "sparkle" on the range.

What the frickin' hell?

Normally, Bodey would have been more than happy to pick up on her "let's have some fun while we're in Cheyenne" signals. There wasn't a red-blooded male within a hundred miles who wouldn't have been interested. She was tall and voluptuous with legs up to her armpits and boobs that threatened a costuming malfunction at any moment.

But as the dull ache over his eye began creeping toward his nape and he broke out in a clammy sweat, the woman's chatter soon dissolved into a drone akin to adults in the Charlie Brown cartoons.

Wah-wah-wahwah-wah-wah.

Then it got worse.

The white-hot drill bit which had been screwing into his eye socket plunged straight through to his brain. The pain ricocheted through his skull, radiating, spreading like wildfire. Sweat popped out on his forehead and upper lip, and his stomach lurched ominously, reminding him that he hadn't eaten yet today, but he'd drunk lots and lots of water in an effort to stay cool. The liquid sloshed in his stomach, threatening to make a reappearance.

Which meant he was going to have to bow out.

Leave the competition midstream.

Lose.

Damnit, he had to get out of here. Now.

Grasping the handle of his gun cart, he turned away from the group without explanation, forcing one foot in front of the other as his head began to pound in tandem with the jarring thud of his footfalls. Tugging his hat low, he ignored the curious calls from his friends, knowing that if he tried to talk, the sound would reverberate through his cranium. Then, he'd lose his tenuous control on his stomach and begin yakking up all that water.

Squinting, Bodey tried to gauge the distance to his truck, but the glint of sunshine radiating off the trucks and RVs stationed in the distant parking lot seared through his retinas.

Damnit. If he could get to his trailer, he could pull all the curtains, turn on the AC, crash on the bunk, and pray he'd caught the migraine in time so that it only lasted an hour or two rather than days.

But he'd taken fewer than a dozen steps when he realized that he wasn't going to make it. His knees felt as if they were made of wet spaghetti. And even if he got to his "home on wheels," he'd have to take the time to unload his ammo and weapons from the gun cart and stow them away. Right now, he wasn't sure if he'd be able to go another few feet, let alone traverse several hundred yards to his truck.

Shit, shit, shit.

He quickly scanned his surroundings, his gaze settling on the tent city which had sprouted up overnight opposite the length of the range. Vendors from all over the country had set up shop, selling everything from hand-tooled holsters to wigs, artisan knives to Victorian hats. The cool shade beneath their awnings beckoned to him, but he could imagine the reaction if he stumbled inside and crawled beneath one of their tables.

But sweet heaven above, he was sorely tempted.

He forced himself to keep moving as more cold, clammy sweat began pooling beneath his shirt and his head felt as if it were being slowly squeezed in a vice. He was close to moaning aloud when a series of befuddled thoughts eased through the pain.

Tents.

Shade.

Syd and Helen.

Bodey altered his trajectory midstride. Syd and Helen Henderson—friends from Bodey's hometown of Bliss, Utah—had rolled into camp the night before. Most of the summer, they traveled from one SASS competition to the next, selling handmade Victorian garments that Helen designed and sewed. Bodey hadn't arrived in time to help them erect the enormous canvas tent from which they sold their wares, but he'd heard his brother Elam talking about it. If Bodey could find Helen, he was sure she'd have a stash of headache medicine in that massive carpetbag of hers. If not, he could at least sit in the shade for a minute until he felt steadier on his feet.

Scanning the line of tents, Bodey found the right one easily enough. Positioned squarely in front of its entrance was Virgil, a metal sculpture of a bow-legged gunslinger welded together from old farm machinery and mounted to an industrial-sized spring. The piece had been made by Jace, Bodey's older brother. Even now, gusts of hot wind caused it to sway back and forth, inviting customers into the yawning opening.

Normally, Bodey would have steered clear of the canvas structure with its racks of female frippery and chattering customers. Syd usually parked their motor home somewhere to the rear where Helen used a generator to run her sewing machine so that she could make onsite alterations. Unless he was on the range, Syd took refuge there. But Bodey was afraid the additional twenty yards would make his head pound with even more ferocity. So he stepped beneath the awning, braving the racks of calico and silk, ruffles and lace, making a beeline for a folding chair next to the cash register.

He didn't know how long he'd sat there, head bowed, eyes squeezed shut, hands wrapped around the back of his neck, when a voice asked, "May I help you?"

The question speared through him like a bolt of lightning, even though the question had been uttered softly enough. Without even opening his eyes, he rasped, "Is Helen here?"

"No. She and Syd went into town to get some supplies."

Damn.

Bodey dared to open one eye, just a crack.

Again, he was confronted with a WTF moment. Where his companion on the posse had been intent on "showing off her assets," this woman had gone to the opposite extreme. She was petite, probably only an inch or two over five feet, with a girlish figure that had been entirely obscured by a gathered chintz skirt, a schoolmarm blouse buttoned up to her chin, and a battered straw hat topped with flowers which had clearly seen better days. Where Ima Ontop had displayed her wares for all to see, this woman was openly declaring hers off limits.

Bodey clenched his jaw tight, his stomach pitching as he realized he was going to have to make it all the way to his trailer after all.

The woman's eyes narrowed suspiciously. "You're going to be sick, aren't you?"

Before he could even answer, she dodged around the counter and grabbed a wastepaper basket, which she thrust into his hands. Bodey considered the invitation to purge his stomach, but the trash can was made of wicker and unlined. Not the most effective of containers.

She seemed to realize the same thing at about the same time. Muttering an unladylike, non-Victorian curse under her breath, she grabbed a shopping bag from the pile next to the register, snatched the basket away, and handed him the sack.

Clutching the plastic, Bodey debated whether or not to use it as his stomach roiled dangerously. But one look at the woman peering down at him changed his mind. He didn't want her seeing him so completely . . . unmanned. Which he would be if he let loose the Technicolor rainbow.

Hell. Why couldn't he have found Syd manning the counter?

The woman's head tipped slightly to the side, and Bodey had the fleeting impression of a bird sizing up the situation, mentally calculating the threat before making a decision to fight or fly.

She must have decided to "fight" because she stepped slightly to the side—out of his field of range should his stomach start its heaving again—and asked, "What's wrong? Flu?"

Bodey shook his head, then wished he hadn't. "Migraine."

She folded her arms under her breasts—revealing that she did have a figure under that awful shirt she wore.

"Do you have something for it?"

"Not . . . on me." He waited a moment before finishing, "It's in my trailer."

He closed his eyes again, but not before he saw the way her lips pressed together and her brows furrowed in silent deliberation. Once again, she reminded him of the baby swallows which had hatched in a nest they'd built against his bedroom window. In the past few weeks, they'd been learning to fly. He'd seen that same expression of quick intelligence as they'd judged the distance to the nearest branch against their ability to get there safely.

Abruptly, she said, "Wait here."

Bodey couldn't summon the wherewithal to inform her that he didn't plan on going anywhere, so he grunted, only dimly aware of the rustle of her skirt as she strode from the tent. Seconds later, he heard her approach. Then, to his utter amazement, he felt her remove his hat and replace it with an icy cold pack against his scalp.

Daring to open his eye again, he saw her watching him with something that approximated concern. But somehow, he knew the sentiment had more to do with the danger of his woofing his biscuits on the merchandise rather than anything personal.

"I filled a shopping bag with ice from one of the water stations on the range," she said, referring to the large plastic totes that were regularly stocked with crushed ice and bottles of water to encourage the participants to stay hydrated in the scorching summer heat.

"Drink this." She held out a bottle of Pepsi that was wet with condensation and bits of melting ice. "Helen keeps a cooler in the back loaded with her secret stockpile. I don't think she'd mind if you had one."

Knowing that the caffeine would help, he gratefully took it, twisting off the top.

She dug into the voluminous pocket of her skirt and pulled out a pill bottle. "It's just over-the-counter stuff from the RV. Do you need something else?"

"This will work." Bodey had a prescription painkiller, but the thought of waiting even a moment longer for relief held no appeal. He grappled with the lid and shook four pills into his palm, then swallowed them with a swig of soda and leaned back, closing his eyes again. "Thanks."

There was a beat of silence. No, not silence, exactly. In the background, Bodey could hear the sharp *bang-ping* of bullets striking the metal targets. Laughter and good-natured jeering rode softly on the breeze.

"So you know Syd and Helen?"

He opened his eyes again when the woman spoke, and the caffeine must have hit his system because he didn't feel the need to wince. Even so, he was struck by the intent expression of the woman who had helped him. There was something . . . strikingly odd about her. She had delicate, gamine features and huge blue-black eyes. Rather than donning the Victorian wigs worn by most of the women at the matches, she'd kept hers short and spiky, but the wind and the heat had caused it to curl around her face. Even so, there was no hiding that the blunt, avant-garde haircut had been highlighted with a subtle shade of blue. But where the effect of the offbeat hair, her slight build, and her too-large clothing should have made her look like an orphan, she was clearly a grown-up woman. It was there in the "I've been knocked down by life but I've come back swinging" shadows in her eyes and the way she seemed comfortable in her own skin, if not the costume she'd been forced to wear.

Her brows lifted in silent query, but this time, there was a mocking hint to the deadpan set of her features. As if she'd heard his thoughts out loud.

Too late, he realized that she'd asked him a question.

Syd and Helen. Did he know them?

"Yeah. Syd and Helen are neighbors of mine in Utah."

"Ah."

He held out his hand, grimaced when he realized it was wet from the ice pack and the soda bottle, and swiped it down his thigh. Then he held it out again. "Bodey Taggart."

Her eyes narrowed, just for a moment.

Damnit. What stories had Helen been telling?

But she finally slipped her hand into his. Bodey liked the way that it felt there, small and warm, but with a firm grip. "Beth."

She didn't offer her last name and there was no further explanation of her relationship to Helen—friend, relative, acquaintance—which left Bodey curious. Beth wasn't from Bliss. He would have seen her around. So how did she end up working with Helen?

"That's it? Just plain 'Beth'? No last name? Or are you

one of those people who only needs one name, like Cher or Usher?"

It was a weak attempt at humor—mainly because he already felt like an idiot. He'd stumbled into the tent like one of the Walking Dead and nearly upchucked all over her shoes. He didn't like anyone seeing him that way, not even his brothers. He'd lived too long under a single motto: never let them see you sweat; never let them see you weak.

"I try to keep things simple."

Simple?

Oh, yeah. One name.

For some reason, he'd forgotten that he'd even asked a question. Instead, he'd grown conscious of the way her hand nestled in his, small and delicate, but strong. Even as he debated prolonging the contact, she tugged free—not quickly, not self-consciously. No, she did it . . . dismissively. As if she would be more than happy for him to remain a stranger. Then, very subtly, she slid both hands into the pockets of her skirt.

Well, hell. If that wasn't a subtle "keep your distance" move, he didn't know what was.

Nevertheless, even with his head pounding and his stomach tied in knots, Bodey found himself responding to the challenge—though, for the life of him, he didn't understand why her attitude rankled. He was a nice guy— charming as hell, if his sisters-in-law were to be believed. She didn't have to assume he was Jack the Ripper. Or worse.

Weak.

She'd seen him at his worst. He didn't want her to think this was all he was.

At the very least, she could smile.

"Thanks for your help." He held her gaze, searching her expression, her eyes, for any hint of emotion. "I'm pretty sure I would have face-planted it if I'd tried to get back to my trailer."

Dipping into his arsenal, he offered her a crooked grin, one that was guaranteed to get even the frostiest woman to lighten up.

But her features remained absolutely deadpan. "Mmm."
Mmm? That's all the response he got?

He sat back in his chair, still holding the makeshift ice
bag to his head, and regarded her curiously. He usually
didn't go for females like her. No, he gravitated toward
women who fell into certain molds: "girl-next-door," or
"Rodeo Queen," or "Miss Boobs and Legs." He liked women
who were tall and stacked and willing to indulge in a little
harmless fun. Like Miss Ima Ontop. But this one . . .

There was something brooding and intense about her.
And she was tiny. Hell, he could tuck her under his arm with
room to spare. But that didn't make her delicate. The way
she looked at him warned that she had a will of iron.

He must have been staring because she looked away,
offered a slightly annoyed sigh, then asked with a little more
conversational warmth, "Do you get them often? The
migraines?"

He shook his head, and this time, rather than feeling like
his brain was crashing against his skull, the movement
merely inspired a dull throb. "I had two concussions within
a month of each other. The migraines are a side effect. Hopefully, not a lingering one."

Especially since his brothers had "grounded him" for the
summer. No cow cutting, no bronco busting, no sky diving,
no ATVs. He was lucky that they hadn't forbidden him to
ride altogether—although he wouldn't be surprised if they
threatened to restrict him to the corrals back home and his
little brother's aging pony if they caught wind of this latest
headache.

In truth, Bodey couldn't blame them. The first injury had
occurred on the ranch when they'd taken a load of cattle up
to the summer pastures. A rabbit had darted from beneath
a bush, startling his mount. The horse had zigged and Bodey
had zagged. Next thing he knew, he'd been flying through
the air. When he'd landed, his head had struck a rock and
he'd been out like a light. The second concussion had been
more serious. On his way home from a competition in
Jackson, he'd been T-boned by a drunk driver and had spent

two days unconscious in the hospital. When he'd finally been allowed to return home, he'd been plagued by double vision, vertigo, bouts of nausea—and headaches that made the one he had now seem like a cakewalk. But, over time, most of his symptoms had disappeared.

Until today.

He should have known better and worn dark glasses rather than the lighter protective lenses he used for shooting.

A pair of women entered the tent and Beth backed away, murmuring, "Excuse me."

Bodey appreciated the way she kept her voice soft and soothing, unconsciously encouraging the other women to do the same. Soon, their conversation washed over him like lake water, allowing him to close his eyes again and sip his Pepsi. By the time the women disappeared with one of Helen's hand-sewn ensembles in a shopping bag, the pain in his head had eased to a dull ache. When Beth approached him again, he smiled ruefully.

"Feeling better?" she asked.

"Yeah. Thanks to you."

Nothing. She gave him the same inscrutable look Spock would give Captain Kirk if he announced he was beaming down to the inhospitable planet below where it was guaranteed he would be attacked by life-sucking aliens.

Shit. He'd spent too much time watching television with Barry during his recuperation.

"I'm serious. I doubt I would have made it back to my trailer."

He flashed her another broad grin.

Nothing.

Damn. Was he losing his touch? He'd expected a ghost of a smile at least. But her eyes grew shadowed with emotions that he couldn't translate, and her face remained neutral.

And damned if that didn't egg him on even more.

"So you're staying with Helen?" he probed, hoping for a little more information.

"Not exactly."

He stood and was pleased to find that he was steady on

his feet. Rather than lurching, his stomach responded with a twinge of hunger.

Good sign.

The makeshift ice pack had completely melted by now and the water was growing tepid, so Bodey grimaced, tossing it and the empty soda bottle into the wastepaper basket.

"I owe you a Pepsi at least."

"It's Helen you owe."

Again, although she gave no hint of emotion, Bodey sensed that she knew exactly what he was up to, that he was bound and determined to make her react. But she remained outwardly unimpressed. So much so, that he sensed she was toying with him, like a cat with its paw on a mouse's tail, taking great delight in watching it squirm.

But Bodey wasn't so easily cowed. "Then tell *Helen* I owe her a drink."

"If you insist."

He couldn't prevent a soft laugh. "I do." Moving toward her, he watched the way she subtly drew herself up to full height. Even so, she wasn't any bigger than a mite.

As he closed the distance between them, he saw the first chink in her armor when her hands clenched in her pockets and she rocked back on her heels—and once again, he was struck by the innocent high-necked blouse and voluminous skirt. The old granny charm of her outfit was completely at odds with her rocker hairstyle and the dark liner around her eyes. He'd bet money that the costume had been supplied at the last minute.

"Are you shooting on one of the posses?" He gestured to the range.

This time, he saw tiny lines appear at the corners of her eyes and he knew she was amused. "Me? Uh . . . no. I'm just helping Helen in the tent."

"Are you staying with them in their motor home?"

She shook her head again, and this time her lips actually twitched. Clearly, she knew he was fishing. "No."

He waited, but she didn't add anything more, so he was finally forced to say something to ease the silence. "I see."

Nothing.

Bodey knew that was his cue to leave, but he found himself curiously loath to do so. He couldn't remember the last time a woman had seemed so . . . unaffected by his easy charm. Normally, he could coax a self-conscious giggle out of even the most hard-hearted female, whether she was ninety or nine. But Beth . . . she was proving hard to fathom.

"I'd love a chance to properly thank you." Bodey lobbed her a softball flirt, figuring it was worth a try.

"Consider me properly thanked."

Strike one.

Clearly she wasn't willing to play. At least not with him. But he couldn't resist trying again. "Maybe I can follow up that vote of thanks with lunch."

Her head tipped back, a lock of blue hair falling over her brow. Normally, he didn't like that kind of thing on a woman. God had given women perfectly good hair. Why would they adopt a hue not found in nature? But with the rest of her tresses so dark, the color was subtle—reminding him of the blue-black tones of the crows that gathered around the silos during harvest time.

"Thanks, but no. I have to stay in the tent while Helen is gone."

Strike two.

"What about later?"

She didn't immediately answer.

"You've gotta eat sometime," he said, purposely dropping his voice. But his attempt at tempting her backfired.

"Maybe. But not necessarily with you."

You're out!

He lifted a hand to his chest as if wounded, but to his surprise, rather than feeling rejected, her comment made him laugh.

"You don't like me much, do you?"

She crossed her arms, eyeing him from tip to toe. "I don't know you enough to like or dislike you. But . . . Helen's told me about you."

Ouch. He was going to have to get with Helen and find

out what horror stories she'd been recounting. For the life of him, he couldn't think of anything so awful that this girl would shoot him down right out of the gate.

"And what has she been saying?"

He anticipated a recital of the women he'd loved and lost, but her response took him by surprise.

"That you're an adrenaline junky. A risk jockey."

Risk jockey?

He laughed, supposing he couldn't argue too much with that label. "And that makes me non-lunch-companion material?"

She regarded him with those dark, dark eyes, and again, he wondered if she could read his thoughts.

"I don't know. But I'm only helping Helen until the shoot is over, so there's not much point in finding out, is there?"

Bam! You're not only out for the inning; you're ejected from the game.

But again, rather than being put off by her frankness, he said, "You really don't pull your punches, do you?"

"I didn't think I was throwing any. Merely telling it like I see it."

And damned if he didn't feel a stupid-ass grin threatening to slide all over his face. How the hell could this woman shoot him down in flames and make herself seem even more intriguing?

He closed what little space remained between them. To her credit, she held her ground.

"Tell you what. If you're not opposed, I'll check back a little later. Maybe if Helen returns, and you decide you're hungry—*and* you can bring yourself to endure my company—I'll take you down the row for a brisket sandwich. That shouldn't be too . . . risky . . . for either of us."

She didn't jump for joy, but she didn't make a pithy comment. Bodey decided to count that as progress.

"What if I'm a vegetarian?"

"Then I'm sure we can scare up some lettuce and rabbit food somewhere."

Bodey wasn't sure, but he thought her eyes grew softer,

the tiny lines in the corners appearing once more, so he decided to press his luck. "After that . . . if you're up for it, I'll take you to the practice lane they've got set up for the scholarship fund. You can't leave Hell on Wheels without shooting at something."

"You're sure of that, are you?"

Again, the thread of mockery, so Bodey pushed things even farther, leaning down so that his lips were a mere hairs-breadth away from her ear.

"Oh, yeah, darlin'. I'm sure."

Then, knowing that he'd better get the hell outta Dodge before she could think up a snarky refusal, he snagged the handle to his gun cart and scooped his hat off the counter. He touched a finger to the brim.

"Later."

Then, he braved the glaring sunshine.